Star of the Sea

Star of the Sea

La Concepción

A Short Story

Charlotte Elizabeth Courtenay

Star of the Sea

Copyright © 2023 by Charlotte Elizabeth Courtenay

All rights reserved

No part of this publication may be reproduced, stored in a retrieval system, or transmitted, in any form or by any means, electronic, mechanical, photocopying, recording or otherwise, without the express written permission of the author.

Dedications

This first volume in the short story series Star of the Sea, titled La Concepción, is dedicated to my parents, Mary & James, my siblings, Bernard & Samantha, and the Sisters of St. Joseph De Cluny Nuns, world headquarters in Paris, France.

In the memory of my late husband Raymond Jr. Genius IQ 185 to 205 range. He encouraged me to write this book. Raymond suffered a traumatic brain injury in a traffic accident. He died of Covid 19 in 2021 during the worldwide pandemic.

In the memory of late world leaders:

His Holiness Pope John Paul II

Her Majesty Queen Elizabeth II

US President Ronald Reagan

US President George H.W. Bush

British Prime Minister Baroness Dame Margaret Thatcher

Governor General Sir Paul Scoon

Prime Minister Dame Mary Eugenia Charles

Acknowledgments

My sincerest appreciation and gratitude to my dearest beloved father-in-law, Professor of Medicine Dr. G.A. Howard for his encouragement and unwavering support in all my endeavors.

This book was written during my time researching various types of Boarding Schools in the United Kingdom such as the 'Seven Original Public Schools' and in the United States of America namely the 'The Ten Schools,' among other elite prestigious schools which collectively – historically are the 'Feeder Schools' to Oxbridge and Ivy League and Military Service Academies.

The conceptual framework for this book was written while a Graduate Student at the University of Oxford England UK. Then updated while working as a Deputy Warden in the largest Hall of Residence at the University of St. Andrews Scotland UK.

The first draft was written at Randolph Macon Academy, in Front Royal Virginia, where I served as Head of Middle School Boarding. The draft was updated while at Springdale Preparatory School in New Windsor Maryland, where I served as Head of Girls Boarding. Edited while researching summer enrichment boarding program offerings at schools and colleges in the USA & UK & the school for Princes in Switzerland. Then completed at Tanglewood Summer Instituite in Massachusetts, where I served as Head of Residential Life.

I also researched Public Magnet and International Baccalaureate Schools while serving as a High School English and Humanities and Social Science Educator at Celebration School in the Disney Town of Clebration Florida and at Broughton IB World School in the Research Triangle in Raleigh North Carolina, Feeder Schools to Public Ivy League and other prestigious private colleges and universities.

Many thanks to Project Manager Mr. James D., Account Manager Mr. Ryan H., Mr. James H., and the Editorial Team, the Book Cover Design Team, and the entire Team at Amazon Book Publications.

Foreword

This short historical ethnography is recollections of a pre-teen then young teen girl, Charlotte Louis, on La Concepción Island from the formation of the People's Revolutionary Government, March 1979, to the US invasion, October 1983, to the democratic elections 1984. Based on a true story, through the lens of Charotte Louis, gives insight into the History, Geography, Stratification and the Social Organization of the Matrifocal Culture, Religion, Education, Gender, Kinship Proximity erasing land boundaries and expanding empire through joining bloodlines, Urban and Rural Divide, and Community on La Concepción Island in particular, the Anglophone Commonwealth Caribbean in general.

Charlotte Louis full name, and the last names of her family are comprise this Poem.

My dearly beloved,

Star of the Sea, La Concepcion.

Beautiful sunray.

In fame and in war

My small home.

My guardian blessed mother,

Royal exotic queen,

Energy helper and stimulator.

The Court has given you leave.

Thou hath liberty!

Table of Contents

Part One 1

Part Two 45

Part Three 83

About the Author 103

Star of the Sea

La Concepción

A Short Story

Part One

"Charli, Greg, Carli!"

The voice of our Grand Duchess Commander in Chief, leader of our world, dearest beloved Mommy Meghan. The end of our day is near, and our playtime is over. Mommy Meggie is incredibly beautiful, with high cheekbones, the straightest nose I've seen on a lady in her image, huge brown eyes, and a rich sapodilla complexion. A perfect first-born blend of her mother and father. Mommy Meggie is widely admired for her beauty and charming charisma.

The routine of supper on Thursday evenings have become predictable and a ritual that continue to serve as a celebration of our family. Our weekend cottage, a miniature scale replica of the main house with its colonial Cape Cod-like shingle siding, reminiscent of magazines featuring homes in New England – Hyannis Port, Kennebunkport, Martha's Vineyard, and Nantucket. Ranch style, with a stone and concrete lower ground floor, windows on three sides, and a leveled walkout on Mommy Meggie's father, Grandpa Ralph's, historic country estate.

The property sits upon a knoll presiding over Windsor Farm. The garden comprises hibiscus, bougainvillea, and buttercup flowering shrubs with caterpillars that become beautiful, colorful butterflies. We children often attempt to observe the stages via putting caterpillars into mason jars with holes in the lids. Somehow, we only achieve pupa. Through the grounds of the acreage, beyond the lawn and the flower garden, are fruit-bearing trees of star apples, golden apples, sapodillas, cherries, plums, cashews, bananas, mangoes, and coconuts. There's a thick, well-manicured, chest-high hedge along the entire edges of the half-moon, pie-shaped acreage, with the road curving around the plat and creek ravine, a tributary of the nearby river flowing along the straight boundary. We were on an island to ourselves within an island, perfectly appropriate in keeping with the status of our proud, aloof, very straight nose, tall, caramel-tan-complexion Grandpa Ralph, of British and French paternal ancestry, and African maternal ancestry. The way he likes the order of things, to stand apart and separate from his plantation labors.

Our maternal grandma, Lucia, is strikingly tall and a presence when she enters a room. She's very attractive with high cheekbones, a very straight nose, and rich chocolate completion. Grandma Lucia lives a stone's throw away on her farm, next door to the larger home and farm of her husband, Grandpa Johnathan, and their children. Mommy Meggie's younger middle siblings, Uncle Anthony, has his own apartment on the ground floor, and Aunt Jenah has her own home next door on land given to her by Grandma Lucia. The youngest, Aunt Johana, lives at home with Grandma Lucia. Aunt Jen, and primarily Aunt Jo, is our live-in nanny whenever we are visiting Grandma Lucia, aside from our other non-live-in nannies at the cottage on Grandpa Ralph's estate.

Grandma Lucia's and Grandpa Johnathan's two other daughters had migrated to live on the Land of the Hummingbird, as that island is also known, with Grandma Lucia's childless sister, Grandaunt Rosie. Grandma Lucia's second daughter, Aunt Raquel, upon graduation from school and chose to remain, and their youngest daughter, Aunt Michelle, since she was seven is practically the adopted daughter and heir of Aunt Rosie. Upon graduation Aunt Jenah had also migrated to live with Grandaunt Rosie in the land of the Hummingbird; after completion of her three years of higher studies, she returned home. Grandma Lucia's youngest sister, Grandaunt Teri, also live in the Land of the Hummingbird, a very large island south of La Concepción Island. Grandaunt Teri has only one child, Kate, who's one year older than Aunt Michelle and the two grew up together like sisters. Aunt Michelle is currently studying at the University of the West Indies in the land of the Hummingbird.

Grandma Lucia inherited the farm from her parents, Great-grandpa Albert Louis and his wife, Great-grandma Clarissa Charles-Louis, who are both buried in the flower garden, as well as Grandma Lucia's and Grandpa Johnathan's fraternal twins that died during childbirth. They would've had another daughter and son. Great-grandpa Louis was of African ancestry. Great-grandma Clara, who was very light-skinned and could pass for white, was of Irish indentured servants' ancestry. Their two sons Alexander and Charlemagne are light completion, especially their eldest son, Granduncle Alex, is high yellow and almost as light as her. Granduncle Alexander was a widower with five sons. His three eldest, Julius and Winston and Daniel, are good friends with Mommy Meggie. His wife died during childbirth with the twins Kenron and Kevon. He married his second wife Judy who was also a widow with one daughter. Together he and Grandaunt Judy have two children, Andy and Amanda, who are Greg and Carli's age respectively. Their second son Granduncle Charlie and his wife Barbara has three sons, Kennedy and Robert and John are good friends with Mommy Meggie, and several younger daughters who are good friends with me and Carli. Grandaunts in-law Judy and Barbara are my favorites.

Great Grandpa Albert Louis was a widower prior to his marriage to Great Grandma Clara. He has two sons Willshaw and Brookshaw from that marriage. Granduncle Will whose daughter Whitney is a friend of Mommy Meggie, and Granduncle Brooks whose son Cory and daughter Louise are friends of Mommy Meggie.

During the potato famine in Ireland, the Irish migrated in large numbers to the US and worked on plantations in the American South. Following the abolition of slavery in 1834, thousands migrated to this region to work on plantations as indentured servants, to the aristocracy – the plantocracy upper social class of British and French Creoles.

Grandma Lucia's eldest sister, my favorite Grandaunt, Amy, lives nearby here in Windsor Farm with her husband Fredrick, who's from the Parish of St. Andrew's. They have, slightly larger farm than Grandma Lucia's, that grandaunt Amy inherited from her mom, Great-grandma Clara. Grandaunt Amy has three daughters, her youngest is Aunt Camilla, the best friend of Mommy Meggie. Aunt Camilla's two daughters Beatrice and Astrid are my favorite cousins. Her second daughter Aunt Katherine lives next door on land given to her by Grandaunt Amy, with her husband Smith and their children including their eldest daughters Sandy, Dorothy, and Doris. Grandaunt Amy's eldest daughter, Aunt Gloria, lives in the land of the Hummingbird with her husband and two children Stedman, and Yoland, the best friend of Aunt Michelle.

Grandma Lucia's younger sister Grandaunt Christine lives in Perdmontemps, which is west of Windsor Farm, the location of St. Dominics Church and School, the central midway point to Windsor Farm and Laurel Farm, with her son Calvin and her daughter Jasmine, good friends of Mommy Meggie. Grandaunt Christine is a regular visitor to Windsor Farm; like Grandma Lucia's other siblings, all have land in boundary with her and each other, that were left to them by their parents, Great-grandpa Albert Louis and Great-grandma Clara Louis.

Our Grand Duke First Man, Daddy Henry, is a tall, ebony, good-looking man like Nelson Mandela. Daddy Harry's middle, his father's name sake, by which is more commonly known. His first name is the name of the island that lies directly north of La Concepción. His late father was a later direct descendant of a Scottish Anglican Priest; his father's maternal ancestry was African. Daddy Harry is Grandma Violet's fourth child and her third son. His sweet mommy, Violet, is a widow, a biracial petite lady who could pass for white. She also lives in the Parish of St. David's, in Vincennes, a neighboring community to the east of Windsor Farm, with her three youngest children, Aunt Catherine, Aunt Anne and her little girl Vanessa, who's one year Carli's junior, and Uncle Edward, her youngest.

Her older children are eldest son, Uncle Harold and his La Concepción wife Eunice are naturalized Canadian citizens. They reside in Canada with their two children Joseph and Rose who are Canadian born. Grandma Violet's pride, her second child and eldest daughter, Aunt Sophie, is tied for my favorite of Daddy Harry's sisters. Aunt Sophie and her husband, a judge, have four children, Tatiana attended my St. Joseph's Convent Girls High School in the Capital city St. George's. Everyone considers her a future judge. She's currently attending Law School at the University of the West Indies in the Land of the Flying Fish. Aunt Sophie and her huband, fled with Tatiana, Gabriella, Harrison Archibald, and Davidson Henry, our favorite paternal cousins, to self-imposed exile to Flying Fish Island northeast of La Concepción Island, almost immediately after the first political coup d'état on La Concepción Island in March 1979.

Uncle Michael is Grandma Violet's third child and second son. He's a naturalized American citizen and he lives in New York with his white American wife, Robin, and their biracial son Barry. Uncle Michael's eldest child, his daughter Geneva lives in Windsor Farm with her mother and biracial maternal grandparents. Grandma Violet's fifth child and second eldest daughter Aunt Ellen, is very light complection. Aunt Ellen reside in Canada with her Anglo Canadian husband Gary. Aunt Ellen is tied for first place for my favorite of Daddy Harry's sisters.

Mommy Meggie often reinforce that we children need to have balance. Living in the guest cottage, which is essentially ours, when we come home to Grandpa Ralph's estate in the country on weekends, rather than taking up accommodation in the main house. Mommy Meggie gives us awesome, lighthearted, good times, and the best weekend holidays filled with laughter to our hearts' content.

The main house is furnished with antiques collected over time by Grandpa Ralph's parents, grandparents, and great-grandparents. In the living and dining areas and bedroom chambers are items well over a century old. We children would mind our Ps and Qs, when in the vicinity of Grandpa Ralph's most prized possessions inherited from our ancestors. While in the house, he would spend time naming and pointing to the living room walls adorned with their portraits and old black and white framed photographs in their proper frills as European Creoles in the new world of a bygone era.

Mommy Meggie would much rather have us play and explore the homestead acreage than sit about brooding in the main house with aristocratic-natured Grandpa Ralph, a descendant of the elite plantocracy. Grandpa Ralph's primary teaching to us is being segregated from others outside his social standing. Alternatively, Mommy Meggie cultivates values of inclusion, although tempered to some degree with conscious and unconscious innate values of power distance. The lawn and gardens of Grandpa Ralph historic estate is the largest manicured acreage grounds in all of Windsor Farm, which Greg, Carli, and I, have all to ourselves. The children in the Village were not allowed to have community our family and were forbidden by Grandpa Ralph to come to the great lawns of our garden. Although our cousins are allowed. Our two cousins who live with Grandma Lucia, grandsons Melvin and Ivan, the sons of Aunt Raquel and her husband Jacob. Melvin is two years younger than Greg, and Ivan one year younger than Carli respectively, would join us. Also occasionally Daddy Harry's niece Geneva, the daughter of his brother Michael who lives in New York. And whenever other cousins, and our God siblings come to visit, like Keith who's Greg's age and Preston and Sara who are younger than Carli, the children of high yellow bi-racial Aunt Vickie, a dear friend and co-worker of Mommy Meggie.

In the main house with Grandpa Ralph, when our 'debates' on topical national and international issues ventured outside the scope his world view, on which there are varying perspectives among us, Grandpa would ask that we keep to a quiet tone. Mommy Meggie likes us children to speak intelligently. She does not encourage passionate speech, only literate conversations. We children usually oblige her. Grandpa Ralph would much rather refrain from engaging with us at all about politics. Grandpa Ralph thinks politics is not a topic of discussion to have with women and children. Grandpa Ralph is in the image of a multi-racial landowner exemplified in the lasting colonial legacies of his era. His proud mannerisms are much like his paternal European ancestors; the only evidence of his African ancestry is skin deep. He does, however, converse regarding economies of scale, the current price of various exports of his mainstay interests like clove, cocoa, cinnamon, and nutmeg spice also known as black gold, for which La Concepción is renowned as our world's second-largest producer. However, since none of us keep score on these matters, such topics of conversation with Grandpa Ralph is not common. Although, he delights with animation in his enthusiasm at harvest.

The varying perspectives between the philosophies of Grandpa Ralph and Mommy Meggie diverge tremendously. Grandpa is very conservative and seems destine to carry on in the agrarian ways of the colonial past, which is important for the Agricultural Economy. Mommy Meggie embraces Tourism and modernity. They do have common ground in their keen passion for our Education. Grandpa Ralph has come to recognize that girls should receive the Higher Education privilege to study in the capital city as is afforded to boys. Mommy Meggie like most women of her era were restrained from that opportunity with parents choosing to educate girls closer to home. She vowed to educate all her children equally with an education in the capital city of St. George's. Greg, Carli, and I are among the only children in

Windsor Farm attending the best schools in La Concepción, along with Grandpa Ralph's youngest daughter who's several years my senior attends SJC. Along with Daddy Harry's niece – our cousin Geneva who lives in boundary with my first best friend since Pre-school – Nancy Richmond; as well as our chauffeur's daughter Halle who several years my senior, attends Anglican School and later Happy Hill Secondary School.

Mommy Meggie sponsored our mobility, engendering her two daughters and her son. Her strength mothered and fathered her three children, as is the matrifocal dynamics of former colonial island nation states in this hemisphere. All other children on Windsor Farm attended schools here in the Parish of St. David's.

Thursday is our favorite day of the week because we get to come to our home, the guest cottage on Grandpa Ralph's estate, in the rural countryside of Windsor Farm, after having seen our daddy, Henry, whom we fondly refer to as Daddy Harry. He's also nicknamed "Raven" by his friends, his best friend in particular, Mr. Paul Jones. Mr. Jones's mother, Head Nurse Wynona at the clinic in Vincennes, delivered Carli when Mommy Meggie went into labor and could not be transported soon enough to the general hospital in St. George's where Greg and I were born. We children call our dad, Daddy Harry, or Daddy Raven. He works onboard the cruise ship Victoria and comes into port in the capital every Thursday morning.

All three of us children heard Mommy Meggie call out to us. I ran inside the cottage via the kitchen, leaving Greg and Carli to catch up. Mommy Meggie needs me to carry the dinner she prepared in our English walkout ground-floor kitchen and dining room, up the stairs, and onto the second-floor open terrace. The lower floor, containing the kitchen with open-plan dining room and cozy sitting lounge area, also has the only bathroom in the cottage. The kitchen ground floor is about half the size of the main floor. On the main floor are the living room, Mommy Meggie, and Daddy Harry's bedroom chamber, and one other long bedroom chamber, the combined scale of the other two rooms, the full length of the main floor, intended as a four-square floor plan. There are two entrances from the hallway to that long bedroom chamber, which Mommy Meggie divided into two-bedroom zones with creative furniture arrangement. Among the pieces is her large Singer sewing machine, which she uses only a couple times a year around springtime when she makes two or three outfits for Carli and me to attend the Harvest Fairs. The larger divided section for us children with a double bed for Carli and me and a twin bed for Greg, dresser with mirror and a bureau. The other section for our live-in nanny whenever we are at Windsor Farm, our dearest Aunt Jo.

Here at the cottage, we have a breathtaking view facing the valley of lush green vegetation, sugar cane fields, nutmeg trees, cloves, cinnamon, breadfruit trees, and silk cotton trees along a meandering river, leading to the views that stretch beyond to the wide-open ocean of the Southeast Coast.

We children love eating on the outdoor terrace to get a glimpse of Daddy Harry's cruise ship. We take turns with Mommy Meggie looking through the binoculars that Daddy Harry purchased at one of his ports of call for this purpose, to allow us to have close-up views of the ship on the horizon. We also like this ritual for another reason. When dining indoors, Mommy Meggie is usually all about our table manners and the appropriate use of the correct utensils for various entrees.

"Please, try not to spill or make a mess,"

she would say, looking at Greg and Carli, knowing the domestic help were already gone for the evening.

The servants arrive at Grandpa Ralph's estate early in the mornings. They make breakfast for us in the cottage and then for Grandpa Ralph when he arrives in his Land Rover at the main house of his estate, which is his personal business office headquarters for the operations of his plantation estate, as well as his weekend retreat, especially whenever we are in residence in the guest cottage. Grandpa Ralph lives about a mile away in his mid-century modern home.

Our good housekeepers and nannies, my Sylvia, Greg's Elsa, and Carli's Francesca, will assist Mommy Meggie in getting us children dressed in our Friday Scouts attire. Me in my Girl Guides Scout uniform working towards becoming President of Girl Scout Rangers in my junior and senior year at SJC. Greg in his Cub Scouts uniform working hard towards the Duke of Edinburgh Award Scheme to eventually become an Eagle Scout. Carli in her little Girl

Scout Brownies uniform working on becoming a Girl Guide Scout.

Mr. Martin Thomas the eldest nephew of Grandpa Johnathan is our chauffeur will take to tooting the car horn whenever we're running late on pain of Mommy Meggie's routine of giving each of us children our all important cod liver oil and honey every morning. Mr. Martin lives with his wife, Margo, their daughter Halle whom he drives along with us to our schools in the capital city, St. George's. His younger sister Cicéle serves as Nanny to Halle. Cicéle is a cousin and good friends with Aunt Jenah and Aunt Johana. Cicéle taught Halle and I, and later Carli, to crochet, embroidery, and knit.

The home of Mr. Martin Thomas is next door to Grandma Violet's sister, our supportive grandaunt who shares her first name with the female prime minister of England, her husband, has the same first name as the current president of our United States of America. They do not have any children. Daddy Harry, her favorite nephew, spent a good deal of his childhood at their residence and is one of their heirs to inherit land, along with Eve, the only niece of granduncle, who will inherit the homestead. Their house is a stone's throw away from Grandpa Ralph's mid-century modern home.

St. George's Harbor: At Upper Church Street are the National Catholic Cathedral and St. Joseph's Convent Girls High School and the home of the Sisters of St. Joseph's De Cluny and Presentation Boys College High School. At Lower Church Street is the National Anglican Church. On the Carenage Wharf to the left are the Cruise Ship Port and The Nutmeg Restaurant and Sea Change Book Store and Food Fair, to the right are the historic Fire Station and the Port Louis Marina.

On Thursday mornings, Mommy Meggie is always in good spirits. Daddy Harry would arrive on the carenage in the harbor port of the capital St. George's. Mommy Meggie would meet him when he disembarked the cruise ship Victoria. Together, they would visit each of us children at our schools. Me at the Sisters of St. Joseph's De Cluny, St. Louis

Primary Girls School, Pre-K to Grade 6, up the connecting steps from the driveway of SJC. Later, when I started at the Sisters of St. Joseph De Cluny Convent Girls High School (SJC) Grade 7 to 12 in the USA context or Forms 1 to Sixth in the UK context, circa 1875 is the oldest school on La Concepcion Island. Located across from the House of Parliament known as York House, and adjacent to the National Cathedral where our dearly beloved Catholic Bishop of La Concepcion Monsignor Sidney Clarles officiate at our graduations, and where I was Christened by our longest serving and most senior Priest on La Concepion his adopted homeland – son of a neighbouring island the only state in our world named after a human woman – my dearest beloved Monsignor Father Lamontagne with whom I also received the blessing of my First Communion, and who performed the sacrament of marriage to Mommy Meggie and Daddy Harry.

I am in Blessed Anne Marie Javouhey House which is Red House also known as Adams House – named for the Oxonian Adams Prime Ministers of Flying Fish Island. The other three Houses, are Cipriani House which is Green House named for a late Politician in the Land of the Hummingbird. Manley House which is Blue House named for the Oxonian Prime Ministers of the Land of Reggae Music, and T.A. Marryshow House which is Yellow House named for an illustrious late citizen of La Concepción Island known as the Father and Elder Stateman of the Regional Federation.

I hope to be elected Captain of Adams House in September of my senior year at St. Joseph's Convent. Carli hope the same when she's in senior year at SJC. I hope to also become the one of four House Captains elected Head Girl also known as President of the Student Council. Carli hope to be the House Captain that will be elected Public Relations Officer of the Student Council in her senior year.

Getting elected Head Girl in my senior year will not be an easy feat. I had looked over the courtyard at St. Louis Girls School for years into the courtyard of SJC anticipating my normal progression to SJC. However, during the years of the Revolutionary Government, students like me, who were members of the Pioneers including the children of Members of Parliament, were initially assigned to public secondary schools with high government control such as La Concepción Boys Secondary School – the oldest boys school where the two daughters of Deputy Prime Minister Bear Cord were assigned and are currently attending, and some private secondary schools where the government have strong influence. This practice was phased out after the restoration of democratic election. Hence La Concepción Boys Secondary School became all boys once again.

I had to seek a transfer to St. Joseph's Convent St. George's which I am successful in achieving one of the three annual transfer admission places via written examination. Since the founding of SJC over a century ago no transfer student had ever been elected Head Girl. I hold out hope in becoming the first. I also hope that I can become the first person on La Concepción Island to gain admission to study at the University of Oxford in the United Kingdom, like the Adams and Manley Prime Ministers, and Prime Minister Williams in the Land of the Hummingbird.

Carli was transferred from St. Louis Girls School to St. Mary's Co-educational Primary School, Pre-K to Grade 6, downstairs the Cathedral, directly across the street like SJC from the House of Parliament. Mommy Meggie and Daddy Harry would visit Greg at the Anglican Primary School Pre-

K to Grade 6 next to the Anglican Church on Church Street. Then later at Presentation Boys Catholic High School the second oldest all boys school, Grade 7 to 12 in the USA context or Forms 1 to Sixth in the UK context, at Old Fort in Upper Church Street, next to St. Louise Girls Primary School.

Greg, Carli, and I, usually waited in great anticipation to seeing Daddy Harry. We would each watch his cruise ship Victoria come into port at St. George's Harbor from the large picture windows of our classrooms and through the arches along the colonnade at our elite schools at Upper Church Street earlier in the morning. The three of us take particular care with our studies and mind our behaviors. Daddy Harry would inquire impromptu of our teachers regarding how we are getting on. He would beam with pride, seeming to stand taller with each of their affirmative, desirable responses. On some occasions, when Mommy Meggie and Daddy Harry arrive, they would have to wait for the morning assembly to commence. I could see them through the queues in the quadrangle courtyard, their hands over their hearts as my peers and I sing the national anthem.

Hail! Grenada, land of ours,
We pledge ourselves to thee,
Heads, hearts, and hands in unity
To reach our destiny.
Ever conscious of God,
Being proud of our heritage,
May we with faith and courage
Aspire, build, advance
As one people, one family.
God bless our nation.

After visiting with us, Mommy Meggie and Daddy Harry would often visit Grandma Violet and Grandma Lucia, or make their way to the home in Tempe near the capital city that we share when school is in session, with Mommy Meggie's elder first cousin, Aunt Camilla, our godmother. She's the daughter of Grandaunt Amy, the eldest sister of Grandma Lucia. Aunt Camilla's two daughters, are our favorite older maternal cousins, Beatrice and Astrid. Beatrice completed her studies at St. Joseph's Convent then at the T.A. Marryshow College in St. George's and now works in St. George's. Astrid is in her senior year at SJC.

Aunt Camilla's rental home is within walking distance of the governor general's mansion on Upper Lucas Street. It is the residence of the Head of State, the Representative of Her Majesty, Queen Elizabeth II of Great Britain, Sir Paul Scoon. Walking home from school, I would hold the hands of Greg and Carli on my left and right, respectively. We would take in the majestic colonial home with its breathtaking panoramic views overlooking the picturesque St. George's Harbor, the same view we have from our prestigious schools at Upper Church Street.

I would say to Greg and Carli, "I, Charlotte Louis, someday shall serve as Governor General on La Concepción." Dame Hilda Louise Bynoe, alumna of my St. Joseph's Convent St. George's, is our first and only female Governor General on La Concepción and in our Americas. "In that role, I will serve as Her Majesty's Inspectorate, visit all the schools, and speak with the headmasters, headmistresses, teachers, and pupils. I will give speeches regarding what is best for Education and how to sustain our advancement and development in Education."

My younger siblings adore me. They would squeeze my hands and giggle, their eyes dancing with delight, hanging on every word I say, like it's the gospel, according to Charlotte. Sometimes, though, Greg would say,

"I think you should become Prime Minister if you want to work more for Education."

Carli would chime in, too, "I think you ought to stick to your other idea and become a Cluny Nun."

I like everything about Cluny Mission, 'The Holy Will of God.' Our Foundress, Blessed Anne Marie Javouhey, is the Patron Saint for People of Color. She received her vocation to become a nun, to free enslaved people, and to educate children of all demography. At school, each of our Cluny Nuns, all my teachers, and my peers across grade levels gave me a piece of their hearts.

I admire our Cluny Nuns, especially my favorite teacher, our brilliantly gifted and talented Music Directress, Sr. Bernard Ng Fan. Sr. Ng Fan is fluent in six languages. She's of Chinese and Portuguese ancestry, a graduate of the first circa 1836 our Sisters of St. Joseph De Cluny Convent Girls High School in this region in the capital city Port of Spain in the Land of the Hummingbird. I confide in Sr. Ng Fan, all my hopes and dreams. Our steadfast leadership in our Headmistress, Mother Superior General of Cluny Nuns in the Anglophone Islands of this geographic region Sr. Gabrielle Mason. Sr. Mason is a graduate of St. Joseph's Convent here on La Concepción, a brilliant gifted writer and the author of the book of poetry '*Blooming in the Dry Season.*' Sr. Masn is our first native in her image to lead St. Joseph's Convent St. George's, and she's an inspiration to all our citizens. Our gentle Religion teacher, Sr. Lecabel - her elder sister Petra is the Diocese Secretary and her office next to St. Mary's Primary School is a very good friend of Mommy Meggie. The Headmistress at St. Louise Primary Girls School, Sr. Keene Duncan, like Sr. Gabrielle Mason, and Sr. Lacebel Gabriel, are citizens of La Concepción Island. All our Cluny Nuns from St. Joseph's Convent in Port of Spain and other locations in the Land of Hummingbird. All our

Irish Cluny Nuns teaching in various capacities at Cluny Convents in this region.

Our Primary teachers at our Sisters of Cluny, St. Louise Girls Primary School, like Greg's paternal aunt Mrs. McMillian, is mine and Carli's favorite. Ms. McCall, Ms. Jerimiah, Ms. Mignon, Mrs. Wilkenson, Mrs. Tomlinson, Mrs. Philmore, Mrs. Scribes, and others.

At our Sisters of Cluny, St. Joseph's Convent Girls High School (SJC), I admire our Lay Catholic Teachers like Mrs. Dubois our English Teacher. Mrs. Christian our 11th & 12th grade English Literature and History and Theatre Teacher for her ability to get the greatest performances from each of us drama club students, and our Awesome Adams House Mistress. Mrs. La Torch for my early love of English Literature and Mrs. Jamison for my early love of History. Ms. Plymouth for getting our student athletes to victory. Ms. McLean the first person to announce to our Spanish class the birth of Prince Harry of our United Kingdom. Mrs. Nightingale, Mrs. Ballston, Ms. Kettle, Ms. Purcell, Canadian Ms. Raleigh, British Ms. Higgins, Mr. Sea Castle, Mr. Cadre who attended Barry University in Miami Shores

Florida, Mr. Springs, Guyanese Mr. Singh, American Mr. Hines, Catholic Bishop Monsignor Sidney Charles Scholar in Residence for a term intersession from Barry University in Miami Shores Florida, Mr. Peter-Greenidge our relative, and others. Also, our favorite campus cook, Ms. Vera, makes the best dhal and roti, perhaps tied only with The Nutmeg Restaurant in St. George's.

I have lots of friends at SJC, like Helen, Caroline, Cheryl, Maureen, Nancy, Andrea, Erin, Rachael, and Carol. Leann whose youngest brother is my first godson Cameron. We attend St. Dominic's Church together. Her father is the Headmaster of St. Dominics School. Carli and I have many friends in common, like my friends from St. Louis Primary Girls School and Carli's older friends from St. Mary's Co-Educational Primary School at St. Joseph's Convent Girls High School. Among my long list of friends Gaylynn, who has the same last name as the second wife of King Henry VIII, Nancy, Courtney, Shirley, Allison, Nicola, Holly, Germaine, Sheri, Ava, Claudine, Noelle, Yolanda, Tara, Ashley, Sandra, Sonia, Melinda, Jennifer, Jacintha, Yvonne, Tamara, Denine, Nadia, Charmaine, Shelley, Stephanie,

Melissa, Pamela, Crista, Amalie, Sophia, Linnea, Michaela, Susan, Devionne, Chantal, Adriana, Lisa, Agnes, Monica, Natasha, Lindsay, Alexandra, Jessica, Tonya, Deborahann, Jullianne, Pollyanna, Kimberly, Kayla, Mckenzie, and my favorite much older friend at school my namesake Charlotte Bethesda. All five daughters and only granddaughter of Granduncle Charlamagne – Larissa second fastest runner and heading to law school in one year, Gwendolynn, Breanna, Melinda, Emmalynn, Kerry, are among our favorite maternal cousins and good friends of Carli and I, at St. Dominics Church and St. Louise Girls School and at SJC. Also, my older friend Diana McClean and her sisters Sharon and her best friend and namesake Sharon and the youngest McLean sister, whose first name is the last name of the current president of our United States of America, are the daughters of the brother of Aunt Charlotte Spencer our adopted aunt and immediate neighbor in our seaside community on the Southeast coast. Rosalinda, the niece of Mrs. Nightingale and of our new neighbors on the Southeast coast the Mickelsons, who regularly visits her little cousin, Melia. My Indian friends, Loshni and Sherlini. Greg's cousins, the daughters of his aunt Mrs. McMillian, Donita, Denise, and Caren. The daughters of Mrs. Wilkenson, Sherline, Cherline, and Jenine. The daughters of Mrs. Tomlinson, Harriet, Sharline, and Carline. The daughter of Mrs. Scribes, who has the same first and last name as a Democratic Presidential nominee of our USA, who selected the first female vice-presidential nominee as his running mate. Two of my favorite best friends Chelsea and Taylor. Also my British and Swiss friends.

Carli's friends, Helen, Cheryl, Maureen, Geneva, Vanessa, Sara, Sandra, Sonia, Amanda, Anesha, Charlene, Reann, Macy, Josslynn, Agnes, Gracie, Melanie, Olivia, Julia and her younger sister Isabella, with whom Greg fell in love. Her friend Geni who lives on Fort Jeudy with whom our cousin Davidson fell in love. Astria, Shundra, Ariel, and more of our friends in common: Arabella – the niece of Sr. Keen Duncan, the nieces – sisters Tracy and Zara, sisters Rochelle and Yara, of Sr. Fleming who was Headmistress of SJC prior Sr. Gabrielle Mason.

Greg's best friend is his cousin, Dillon, the son of his biological paternal aunt, Mrs. McMillion. Dillon resembles his uncle, Mr. Mitchel – the biological father of Greg. Mr. Mitchell is a naturalized citizen and resides in Canada. Greg is Mr. Mitchell's only son. Greg has two older paternal sisters. Mr. Mitchell grew up in northern St. David's closer to the St. Andrew's border. Greg's long list of close friends – Vincent, James whom we nicked named Jimmy, David, George, Andrew, Alleyne, Patrick, John, Mark, Juan, Ashley, Christopher, Devon, Morris, Daniel, Terry, Steven, Warren, Jeff, Larry, Tom, Wayne, Gifford, Perry, Jason, our cousins Alvin and Kevin, Elven, Milton, at Presentation Boys College, including his favorite childhood friend since St. Dominic's Church, a white boy Kim, Noel who wants to become a Priest, and also Isaiah who wants to become a Priest, whose older sister, Hazel, is one of my friends at St. Dominic's Church and at St. Joseph's Convent, and his younger sister, Mariah, is a friend of Carli at St. Dominic's Church and SJC, and our many other good friends.

I must admit to my innermost self, I've often been conflicted regarding all the pillars of my life; Family, British Education System, French Catholic Religion, and British Westminster Style Constitutional Monarchy Political

System, with our beloved, Her Majesty Elizabeth II as our Greatest Queen of La Concepción. There's only one thing I know for certain: I want to make a difference to La Concepción Island and to our world. Greg and Carli often draw me out of my metacognition. Occasionally, Carli asks the rhetorical,

"Can we all live here together when you become Governor General?"

I would respond,

"Yes, dear, we can all live here together when I'm Governor General."

Carli is brilliant with her communication, verbal and written, to all audiences. She seems destine and determine to live in the Governor General's mansion. Perhaps in the many decades ahead, Her Majesty Queen Elizabeth, on recommendation of t Prime Minister will appoint Carli to serve as Head of State on La Concepción Island.

The governor general's residence is also a short walk from Westmorland Co-Educational School. At that vantage point, we can see Conception Boys Secondary School and the Anglican Girls High School looking towards the Tanteen Playing Fields of St. George's where some interscholastic literary and intercollegiate events take place aside from The Queen's Park then renamed The National Stadium where some of our events take place. St. Joseph's Convent reigns supreme in the girls' categories and Presentation College in the boys' categories; with good competition from Conception Boys Secondary School and the Anglican Girls High School, as well as Westmoreland private Co-Educational Senior High School, St. Joseph's Convent Co-Educational Senior High School operated by our dearly beloved Sisters of Cluny located in the town of Grenville in the Parish of St. Andrews, Wesley College Co-Educational Senior High School, St. Andrews Senior Secondary, Mt. Rose Secondary School, Happy Hill Secondary School, Boca Secondary School, among other secondary high schools on La Concepción. The pupils that are the best in all the inter-House competitions in each school are the students who participate among the schools in these national competitions. Mommy Meggie was the fastest female Track Athlete on La Concepción during her years at school, hence she's nicknamed Carlos, after the fastest racehorse during those years. She also left all male competitors in the dust.

The governor's mansion is a short walk to the rental home in Tempe that we share with Aunt Camilla and our cousins, Beatrice, almost eight years my senior, and Astrid, four years my senior. We are all mitochondrially Great-grandma Clara: Grandaunt Amy, Grandma Lucia, Aunt Camilla, Mommy Meggie, me, Carli, Greg, Melvin, and Ivan. Although males cannot pass on Mitochondria DNA, they certainly pass on the chromosomes of Nuclear DNA to their daughters and to their sons. We girls with our two XX chromosomes are our mothers' mothers and our father's mothers. Boys with XY chromosomes are their mother's mothers and their father's fathers. Learning about genetics, I'm intrigued how we are connected to our parents and ancestors, and to other human beings.

Mommy Meggie would head back into St. George's town with us children, sometimes also accompanied by Aunt Camilla and Beatrice and Astrid, to watch Daddy Harry board the cruise ship, to bid and wave our goodbyes to our

Daddy Raven until next Thursday as the ship disembark from the port of St. George's.

In the kitchen of our cottage, there is usually the scent of spice in the air. The aroma fills the entire cottage from the nearby spice-drying house in the shared garden with Grandpa Ralph's main house and mostly from the large storage room in the crawl space under the living room floor and under the floor of our bedroom section of the cottage. There is a huge tray the length and width of the crawl space that is pulled out on wheels onto two rows of side-by-side elevated concrete pillars to dry during the daytime by Grandpa Ralph's farm workers. There seem to be tons of nutmeg, cinnamon, cloves, and cocoa beans that are gathered and harvested by the farm workers on Grandpa Ralph's nearby working plantation, across the road south boundary of Grandma Lucia's homestead and Farm. Hence, the modern history term for our island is also commonly known as the Island of Spice. La Concepción Island is the late 15th century name Columbus gave our island upon sighting her on his third voyage on Conception Day, December 1st, 1498.

Daddy Harry also has a farm in nearby beautiful Laurel Farm with the landmark over one hundred tall palm tree line road on each side through the entire Laurel area leading to the historic antebellum plantation house. One of Carli's Godmother's Ms. Maryanne lives in the estate house with her parents Mr. and Mrs. Evans. They save the best mangoes and other fruits for us children.

We also keep over one hundred chickens in a large oversize coop within our garden at the cottage on Grandpa Ralph's historic estate. Grandpa Ralph would often say that all his net worth is the sum of all that is stored in the downstairs crawl space of the cottage for export, all his monies in the bank, and all his combined real estate holdings, which includes a much larger home at another location about a mile from the antebellum estate. It is a mid-century, modern, elegant 20th century home, which he shares with his wife and their four children.

Mommy Meggie as usual have everything for our dinner on Thursday evening ready for easy warming in the kitchen of our cottage, having already cooked some of the dinner meal earlier in the day at the home, which we share in Tempe with Aunt Camilla.

Mommy Meggie takes Thursday as her day off from her job as a Hostess at The Nutmeg Restaurant overlooking the carenage where cruise ships come into port in St. George's Harbor. Above the open porte-cochere with a wide panoramic view of the carenage and the inlet waters of the harbor leads to The Nutmeg, the largest restaurant in St. George's where Mommy Meggie and Aunt Jo worn the shared motor courtyard quadrangle attached to The Nutmeg is The Food Fair, the largest grocery store where Aunt Jen works.

The Nutmeg is always filled with tourists from all around our world. We children would wait on Mommy Meggie at a banquet table specifically for us kids, where we would do our homework looking onto the carenage and where the tourists and natives walking by often smile and wave to us. Years ago, there were the elegant late evening Easter Water Parade on the Carenage prior to the coup of 1979, and I can remember sitting and falling asleep on Aunt Camilla's lap.

Mommy Meggie would give us some of her gratuity tips to purchase story books from Sea Change Book Store located at the bottom of the stairs in a tiny nook on the ground floor of The Nutmeg. A magical enchanting world filled with treasures, much like the rabbit hole in Oxonian Lewis Carroll's *'Alice in Wonderland.'* The first treasure I purchased at the Sea Change Book Store, is *'A Child's Thought of God'* by Helen Drummond. We eventually purchased all of Enid Blyton's series of *'The Famous Five'* and *'The Secret Seven.'* Also the entire series of *'Nancy Drew'* by Carolyn Keen, and *'The Hardy Boys'* by by Franklin Dixon, and lots of magazines to clip the center double pages to post on my bedroom wall of the 1980s heartthrobs like Ron Howard, Rob Lowe, and others.

Mommy Meggie also opened individual bank accounts for each of us children at the bank branch downstairs The Nutmeg. She also has me doing the weekly payroll to remit payment on Friday evenings to the Builder and all the construction workers building our new home on the Southeast Coast. I simply multiply the number of days each person works by the day wage rate for each specific job type, by the number of days each person works weekly, then add all together. Mommy Meggie and I would go to the bank on Friday evenings to withdraw the total sum. Then we would distribute the pay to each of the workers. They all tip their hats and bow, thanking Mommy Meggie and me. "Thank you, Mrs. Meghan, thank you Mrs. G, thank you Miss Charlotte, thank you Miss Louis."

Mommy Meggie's entire monthly salary went directly to the bank to cover the mortgage payment of our new house for over 20 years. Mommy Meggie speaks words of Prudence, when she says a woman should make that decision for the security of all her children. Daddy Harry takes care of most other obligations and responsibilities, which are perhaps equal to the monthly house payment.

Upon entering the kitchen, we are delighted with the smell of recently warmed, delicious-smelling brown chicken stew with diced Irish potatoes, chicken curry, and baked macaroni and cheese, our favorites. Our nannies, my Sylvie, Greg's Elsa, Carli's Francesca, made freshly fried, still warm plain biscuits in place of dinner rolls to soak up the gravy of the stew and curry. In another casserole dish, Mommy

Meggie had some cooked breadfruit for herself, also known as 'Oil Down,' the native meal of La Concepción Island, that Aunt Jen and Aunt Jo had made and brought to her upon our arrival at Windsor Farm earlier that evening. We children did not fancy too much the native dishes, only on special occasions. We preferred imported foods from the United States, Canada, and the United Kingdom.

I ran up the stairs to the living room to retrieve the red and white gingham vinyl tablecloth and the outdoor green and yellow and red king-size quilt, the Scottish tartan patch and stripe design created in the image of our La Concepción Island Flag. Mommy Meggie keeps these in the lower base of the large China cabinet, which is nearly a third the width of the living room, together with most of her wedding gifts of wares and tapestries. She plans to display the items proudly in our newly built multi-story seaside villa, awaiting Daddy Harry to permanently return home to La Concepción Island whenever the communist regime comes to an end.

Our new home is a stunning multi-story Mediterranean with Victorian bay windows, neoclassical center portico, large floor-to-ceiling windows, French doors to private covered porches from the bedroom chambers, the wide wrap-around entertaining veranda on the main floor with decorative stone walls in the verandas and porches with retaining walls and balusters. Most important to Mommy Meggie are the magnificent closeup vistas of the beach and ocean. The horizon seems within reach, like the edge of an infinity pool rather than something away in the distance. At our seaside home and community on the Southeast Coast, our home is built directly overlooking Fort Jeudy Point and Westerhall Point Chemin Bay. And views of Egmont Point and Bay, where there's a soldiers training camp with Russians and Cubans since the first coup on March 13th, 1979, by the Marxists' Leninist New Jewel Movement.

Star of the Sea

La Concepción

A Short Story

Part Two

La Concepción Island is preparing for an impending United States intervention, which did not come soon enough for some to taste a new model of democracy. Freedom did not come until after the second coup of October 19th, 1983, following the internal political struggles of the more hardline faction within the New Jewel Movement Party. The United States and Allied Forces intervention came on the dawn of October 25th, 1983, which is celebrated henceforth on La Concepción Island as Thanksgiving Day.

Like many families, our family also had several members affected by the respective coups, including my eldest and tied for first place favorite paternal biracial Anglo and East Indian ancestry aunt, Laura. She lives in one of the largest historic country estate homes on La Concepción, about the scale of the governor general mansion, with unobstructed wide-open panoramic ocean views from the elevated position in the Parish of St. Andrews. Her younger half-brother, my father, also lived in St. Andrews when he resided on La Concepción Island. His mother was youngest of the four sisters of the late shaman, and the only one of the shaman's sisters to have children. The shaman about whom the illustrious late Anthropologist, Professor at UCLA, later Yale, then Head of Department at University College London, Dr. Michael Garfield Smith wrote the entire book '*The Dark Puritan*' wherein the Shaman discussed being a descendant of Nigerian Slaves on La Concepcion.

Aunt Laura's father, my musically gifted paternal grandfather, is a virtuoso on the guitar. He is of British ancestry and prefers his English and East Indian mixed-race children and grandchildren to his English and African mixed-race children and grandchildren, save for those of very light complexion.

My father, a very light-skinned man, migrated to the UK, before I was born. He married a UK Citizen, then migrated to the US, where he became a naturalized Citizen in the early mid 1970s. He accepted a position as the Director of Circulation of a newspaper. My biological father is currently residing for a number of years on the second largest of the US Virgin Islands where he owns and operates several businesses. He meets my Daddy Harry at the cruise ship port one day each week and would drive him to the port to disembark the island in the evening.

My father promises to sponsor my Green Card upon my graduation from high school. He said within four years in the USA than I can apply for full citizenship. I told him that while I will visit many more grand homes, I intend to remain a citizen of the modest tiny home of my birth, my beloved dearest La Concepción. The Green Card Permanent Residence however give me leave to remain in the United States of America as well as sponsor my higher education mobility enabling me to study in the United States at Barry University where my kin and a number of my teachers have gone before me. I shall endeavor to progress with my dream to proceed with my post graduate studies at the University of Oxford in the United Kingdom, although I may very well in the process become the first Barry alumni to gain admission to the oldest university in our English-Speaking World. I vow to give Carli a blessing to cover the full cost of her higher education. I promise myself to also give a special blessing to Greg, with a gift of one hundred percent of my stake in land that we have shared ownership. I also vowed to help Greg with his future children's higher education.

Aunt Laura's husband who was educated as a lawyer in England, is a judge on Concepcion Island, who was imprisoned after the coup of 1979. They have two children: a daughter, Elizabeth and a son William. We fondly refer to Elizabeth as Lili or Bess or Bet or Beth or Libby. Elizabeth married a physician also from St. Andrews. They reside in New Jersey in the United States where he's doing his Medical Residency. Their only child Caroline is my goddaughter. Everyone holds William in the highest esteem, and regard him as Master William, and as a future Judge. Bill attended Barry University in Miami Shores Florida for his first Bachelor's Degree and is currently attending the University of the West Indies in the Land of the Hummingbird for his Law Degree. Aunt Laura along with my father's elder sister Jean are tied for first place favorite my paternal Aunts. These two cousins Elizabeth and William, along with Aunt Jean's, eldest daughter, Colleen – one of my godmothers, who reside in Kentucky in the United States with her husband – African British-Educated physician and their three American born children, Aiden who's a gifted musician aiming to become a Grammy Award Winner,

Cadence and Hayden – my godchildren; are my three favorite paternal cousins from the parish of St. Andrews. Aunt Laura's best friend, Mrs. Gemma, of East Indian ancestry whose father was a pharmacist, is also like an adopted aunt to me, and her eldest daughter, Landel, is the same age as Mommy Meggie, two decades my senior, is like an older sister to me.

Our family is fortunate that Daddy Harry, like the smart "Raven" that he is, accepted employment on board a cruise ship in 1980, earning his salary in US Dollars, which has La Concepción Island among its ports of call in the Anglophone Commonwealth islands, the United States Virgin Islands, the British Virgin Islands, as well as the Netherlands Antilles, enabling his marriage with Mommy Meggie and his parental relationship with us his three children; myself, Greg, and Carli, to continue blossoming and growing.

I'm doing my part, too, to keep our family protected by masquerading as a young Pioneer. My skullduggery decision to appease the government that they would remain on good terms with my family. In early 1980, I had repeatedly requested Grandpa Ralph to give me leave to hold weekly community meetings – after school tutoring, in the large vacant hall with three pairs of double Dutch-style barn doors, on the lower ground floor of the main house on the antebellum estate, which opens onto the shared large common great lawn and gardens with our guest cottage. Grandpa Ralph eventually agreed as his way to pacify the government. So, as it were, I came to start a volunteer rural after-school tutoring program for the children in the village of Windsor Farm, many of whose parents, grandparents, and great-grandparents work on the estate plantation of Grandpa Ralph and their parents and grandparents worked for his colonial ancestors in the century past that time has forgotten. On the once monthly occasions that a Government Official visits, at the end of tutoring, after saying the usual evening prayers with the village children, I would also chant the motto and slogan of the Revolution.

'Forward ever! Backward never! Long live the Revolution!'

The children will echo the sentiment in repetition encore to the smiling official, whose facial expression of our expected behavior seems obviously very pleasing, with the thinking we must do this routinely.

Grandpa Ralph is the second largest landowner in the area. The largest landowner is a cousin of my paternal grandfather, whose daughter, Nancy Richmond, is my best friend in Windsor Farm, and one of my best friends at St. Joseph's Convent. Located to the South boundary of Grandpa Ralph's plantation, is the Richmond's working plantation. The homestead estate of the Richmond family, is to the north of Grandpa Ralph's mid-century modern home, with the homes of our relatives the Honorae's and Hertford's in between. Nancy and I with Carli and Greg along with our cousins, walk to church together on Sunday mornings after our parents 6am Mass has ended. We attend the 8am Children's Sunday School and then the 9am Children's Mass, along with Nancy's two young nephews Carson and Jayden – the sons of her elder sister Greta who lives in New York in the USA, and eldest niece Reann – the daughter of her eldest brother who is also the niece of Daddy Harry's maternal cousin who reside in boundary with the Richmond Family and became a Cabinet Minister and later Prime

Minister. The Richmond Family also reside in boundary with our cousin Geneva – whose maternal grandfather's mother is white. Geneva is Carli's younger twin cousin – born one week apart. We also have our cousins Melvin and Ivan with us on the walk to and from church, the sons of Aunt Raquel who lives in the Land of the Hummingbird.

The government of the New Jewel Movement, took notice of my community organizing, diligence, and dedication to the advancement and development of human resources on La Concepción Island in general, Windsor Farm in particular. I was named the most outstanding Pioneer for the Parish of St. David's in December of 1982. The most outstanding Pioneers, one from each of all six parishes, as well as one from each of the two dependency islands of La Concepción that we nicknamed Carrie and Marti respectively, were invited to attend the pre-Christmas Eve party at the residence of Prime Minister Marquis Cardinal Jr. The island of Marti is settled by desecendants of our Irish. My best friend who wants to becomd a Cluny Nun, my name sake Charlotte, Bethesda, is from the island of Marti.

In late July during summer vacation, mainland La Concepción residents occasionally spend time on the larger Carrie island – of the two dependency islands. We enjoy the boat racing Regatta, which occurs prior to the annual early August Carnival on the main island of La Concepción. The story of the Most Outstanding Young Pioneer Winner for each parish with our names were printed in all the newspapers on Christmas Eve, December 24th, 1982, and broadcast on television.

My Christmas wish communicated to Prime Minister Cardinal is that La Concepción Island must hold fair Democratic Elections. I reminded him of his solemn promise to our nation after the coup of March 1979, wherein he stated that elections would be held within five years. I told the prime minister that I am speaking for myself, the children, and the people of La Concepción Island, not on behalf of any members of my family. I told him he could start on the path to the restoration of a new democracy by traveling to the United States of America to talk with President Ronald Reagan and Vice President George Bush.

Cardinal's response to me:

"Comrade Charlotte, you will be the Minister of Education someday."

My response to Prime Minister Cardinal:

"Comrade Cardinal, Sir, I may serve as Governor General someday, or I may become the first female Prime Minister."

He smiled and took a couple of steps behind me. In that instant, I knew that the eloquence and wisdom in the voice of Almighty God had echoed through me to speak truth to power at that moment in time and point in La Concepción and world history. In his term as Prime Minister Cardinal is widely regarded and is indeed an advocate for the advancement of girls and women, as he's praised for implementing popular education policies such as free public secondary school education for all on La Concepción Island and her two dependency islands within less than one year of the political coup. His frame was putting a ceiling on what I could hope to achieve and accomplish under the current political climate of his regime.

My only opportunity of ever achieving these lofty goals and my initial goal in the first instance is becoming the first

La Concepción Island citizen to gain admission to attend the University of Oxford England, in the United Kingdom. Prior to serving in any of these leadership roles, I had to work hard to earn a spot at the table to speak with Prime Minister Cardinal to accomplish the goals of freedom and democracy for myself and my dearest dearly beloved family, and for my beloved fellow citizens of La Concepción.

When I was named, 'The Most Outstanding Pioneer for the Parish of St. David's,' Grandpa Ralph said to me,

"Charlotte, you are no ordinary girl, and certainly, if you were a boy, you would grow up to be an extraordinary man."

"My dearest Charli," my Grandma Lucia would say, "you will become a great lady. If you were a boy, you would become an even greater man."

One exemplary demonstration of Grandma Lucia's regard for my equal treatment among her grandchildren, although being her eldest I felt like her favorite; one Christmas, she bought me an airplane, the same for Greg, Carli, and our two cousins Melvin and Ivan. Greg inquired of Grandma Lucia because she'd not bought dolls for Carli and me. Grandma responded that she purchased the airplane in the first instance for my Christmas present, then decided to gift each of her grandchildren an airplane as well. Greg insisted that she needed to purchase dolls for Carli and me, to which Grandma responded,

"Charli will travel to all the places that her mind will take her, and that is more important to her than playing with dolls, although admittedly, she liked playing with dolls when she was younger."

When I was only seven years old, while awake getting comfortable arranging my blanket, I saw my Great-grandma Clara looking at me. We smiled at each other through the second-story bedroom window where we grandkids sleep after praying this prayer with Grandma Lucia when having overnight stays at our maternal home.

Now I lay me down to sleep,
I pray the Lord my soul to keep;
Angels watch me through the night,
And wake me with the morning light.
Amen

I recognized Great-grandma Claris from the framed photos hanging in the living room. In our familiar smiles, she certainly knew me, and I must acknowledge that I somehow felt like I knew her exceedingly well. Great-grandma Claris passed away a year prior to my birth. The next morning I told Grandma Lucia, and she said to me, I have the gift. I knew she meant she has also seen our late ancestors in the realm of the dimension of our Spiritual World. Grandma Lucia mentioned that gravity does not apply to those in the Spiritual World. Grandma Lucia regard me as having knowledge and understanding of life and the afterlife well beyond my tender age. I had the realization that although we live only one life, all time is one time, past, present, and future. When I was three years old, I was very ill and had to be hospitalized. I believe during that time I was with our Heavenly Father Almighty God, with our Heavenly Mother Blessed Virgin Mary, our Guardian Angels in Heaven like Great-grandpa Albert and Great-grandma Clara.

In some respects, my grandparents still view being a girl as having limitations in a way that my dearly beloved Mommy Meggie does not consider.

"There's no such word as 'can't.' Please take that word out of your vocabulary," our Mommy Meggie would often say to us.

We believe in Mommy Meggie. Whatever she says, her sentiments are meaningful and powerful. She's our Commander in Chief, and she would say in all of our the Americas and our entire World. We view Mommy Meggie as our Star of the Sea, our Iron Lady, with the combined mental strength and courage of Helen of Troy and Joan of Arc.

Mommy Meggie singlehandedly saved the tape of the most distinguished and notable journalist, Allen Hugh, during the terrible events that took place on La Concepción Island on January 21st, 1974, when Marquis Cardinal Sr., the first namesake of Grandpa Ralph, the late father of the current Prime Minister Marquis Cardinal Jr., was assassinated by police brutality during the Government era of Sir Gairy.

As the police were approaching the location of Allen Hugh, quick-thinking Mommy Meggie gave the symbolic interaction signal to Mr. Hugh to pass the tape to her. He obliged hurriedly, and she very discreetly saved his news coverage of the events by slipping the tape into her bosom. The police took the journalism equipment from Allen Hugh, including recording machines, and threw all the items into the sea to the dismay of onlookers. Mommy Meggie, then nonchalantly walked among the masses who were taking part in the peaceful demonstration along the Carenage harbor in the capital city of St. George's prior to the assassination of Marquis Cardinal Sr.

Mommy Meggie, with the help of Almighty God, made her way safely to Scott Street on the opposite side of The Nutmeg Restaurant. She then took the shortcut up the long steps connecting Scott Street with Church Street to deliver the tape to Allen Hugh. He was waiting to receive the journalistic treasure that she held for him, La Concepción, and our world, safeguarding with her body, physic, and soul. Allen Hugh regarded Mommy Meggie as a great, brave woman of courage, a patriot deserving of a Medal of

Freedom bestowed on persons by Presidents of our United States of America. The other La Concepción Island writer aware of this daring achievement of Mommy Meggie's delivery of the tape to Allen Hugh is an author with the last name as the first name of an American founding father on the US one-hundred-dollar bill and our world-famous clock in London, England.

I climbed out the window onto the flat roof without guardrails or balusters over the English kitchen of our country cottage. The south-facing back rooftop terrace has beautiful views. I spread the king-size quilt to attain a soft warm surface and opened the vinyl vintage tablecloth on top, covering a third of the quilt. Although there's only a light breeze, as usual, I placed the river stones painted primary colors, at all four corners, to ready the space for our feast. Mommy Meggie, with three trips to the kitchen aided by me, brought all the food up the stairs with the final trip, her three little Ravens in tow. Mommy carried her glass, a third filled with island brew punch to which she would add native golden apple nectar in the pitcher that I carried. Greg carried the three non breakable glasses for us children, and Carli did her part, minding her stride up the somewhat steep stairs. Then, as usual, I held out my right hand to Greg as I got out the window onto the roof top terrace. Mommy Meggie held out both her hands to Carli as she climbed daintily and carefully out onto the roof terrace.

Getting onto the rooftop terrace and staying on it with no rails is always precarious. However, we kept to the center and away from the risk of the periphery. We were only a quarter way through our supper when I started pointing to the ship in the distance.

"There, Mommy Meggie, look, Daddy Harry's ship has sailed all the way around already!"

"Oh yes indeed," Mommy Meggie, all smiles and cheerful.

"Oh look, yes, it is Daddy Harry's ship," Carli concurring looking through the binoculars.

"My turn," shouted Greg, reaching for the binoculars held tightly by Carli.

"Take your time, have patience, be careful, children. We can see Daddy Harry's ship; let's all have a turn with the binoculars. Carli, please pass to Charli."

I looked at Daddy Harry's ship, then passed the binoculars again to impatient little Carli. She then gives to our eagerly awaiting Mommy Meggie. Mommy looks intently as if anticipating Daddy Harry to see her from that far a distance and wave to us. She then passes the binoculars to Greg. We would all each do this ritual repeatedly until Daddy Harry's ship was out of sight beyond the horizon.

Daddy Harry would telephone us as always, once a week on Sundays between 1-3 pm after church at Windsor Farm when we have returned at home in Tempe. We would all delightedly take turns talking with him including Aunt Camilla and Beatrice and Astrid. Sunday is our second favorite day of the week.

Mommy Meggie keep us children home from school only for illness. Otherwise, we all have a near-perfect school attendance record. The very day Prime Minister Marquis Cardinal Jr. was assassinated, October 19th, 1983, the year of my 13th birthday, Mommy Meggie kept us children home from school. She packed several clothing changes for Greg, Carli, and me, and the four of us headed to Grandma Violet's home. Her statement to us that her Louis cousins, Members of Parliament, one a lawyer is named after the capital city of La Concepción, the other bears the name of the scholar who developed the Theory of Relativity, had recommended that she keep us at home. The reason and caution given is that students at the high schools in St. George's, are planning to demonstrate in the capital city in protest of the house arrest of Prime Minister Marquis Cardinal, which they are concerned could result in conflict violence clash between the students and the military forces.

In the evening, very alarming news reached our family, and I could tell that Mommy Meggie was gravely distressed learning of the second coup. She remained calm to avert the creation of any anxiety for us children. The students at the high schools in St. George's had gotten through the gates at the home of Prime Minister Marquis Cardinal Jr. The Cardinal was frail from the month-long house arrest. The students carried him out of the house all the way to Fort Cardinal Sr., which Prime Minister Cardinal had renamed in honor of his assassinated father, from the British name Fort George. There at Fort Cardinal Sr., Prime Minister Cardinal was assassinated along with seven other Members of his Cabinet. Among them, my biological father lost three close relatives: a paternal brother, a paternal male cousin, and the only woman in the group – a maternal female cousin who at the time was with child; her second for Prime Minister Marquis Cardinal Jr. Their first, a male, has a famous Russian name that begins with the letter V.

"The time has finally come,"

I overheard Mommy Meggie saying to her mother-in-law, Grandma Violet. After all the international attention of the first coup in March 1979, which was considered peaceful with only one self-defense death, with a much talked about in the international media, a near impending US intervention, the present situation of this second bloody coup today is already garnering widespread international rebuke. The US intervention is now imminent. Mommy Meggie turned to look at us children and announce she's certain that cruise ships would not be allowed to port in St. George's harbor on Thursday. We children were disappointed that we will not get to see Daddy Harry. However, there was not a single word of complaint or whining from any of us. We were all silent and seemed to have each matured at least a dozen years in 60 seconds. There will be a war. Mommy Meggie said she's convinced that American troops will arrive soon.

Prime Minister Cardinal had been placed under house arrest in mid-September upon his return to La Concepción Island after a supposed meeting with US President Ronald Reagan to discuss democratic elections, until his assassination today. Mommy Meggie thinks the American military is already offshore in submarines. The supposed meeting of Prime Minister Cardinal with US President Reagan and Vice President Bush; is thought of have made Deputy Prime Minister Bear Cord and Military General Chairman Hudd Augustine, both of La Concepción Island, and their more hardline alliance among some Members within the Central Committee of the New Jewel Movement Government, uneasy. Those members desired full communism, while Prime Minister Marquis Cardinal, a socialist, espoused mixed economy policy. These contrasting diverging ideologies of irreconcilable paradigms are believed to have contributed significantly to the extent to which at that point Prime Minister Cardinal's fate was sealed.

I was overcome with grief that Prime Minister Cardinal and seven others were assassinated. My Christmas wish communicated to him at the pre-Christmas Eve party at his home on December 23rd, 1982, may have prompted his decision to visit President Reagan and Vice President Bush. Upon his return to La Concepción Island, he was placed under house arrest. We still do not yet have elections, rather a much bigger mess now with this second coup. Even worse, we do not know when Daddy Harry will be able to come home again. I prayed for the American troops to arrive to save us all. Thank God we did not have long to wait.

We returned home to Windsor Farm that Wednesday evening, on October 19th, 1983. A curfew was put into effect with a radio announcement. In the rural countryside, we did have some limited movements with close neighbors. Mommy Meggie desired to remain near Grandma Lucia and her siblings during this uncertain time for whatever is to come in the aftermath of the assassination of Prime Minister Cardinal and his alliance members within his Cabinet. Aunt Camilla and our cousins Beatrice and Astrid decided to remain in suburban Tempe, St. George's. La Concepción Island residents have become accustomed to the all too familiar curfews during the government social psychology renormalization period of the first year of the revolution, which started on March 13th, 1979. The government-imposed curfews had been accepted as customary among a sizable segment of the population.

Curfews went into effect for various military exercises, including moving ammunition arriving on La Concepción Island from the Soviet Union, Cuba, and perhaps East Germany. La Concepción Island is part of the Cold War that US President Reagan and Vice President Bush and UK Prime Minister Baroness Dame Margaret Thatcher want to end. On this occasion, however, the curfew announcement statement is until further notice. We're entering an elevated period of indefinite conflict intuition and uncertainty. The mandatory house arrest for all residents of La Concepción Island, had become all too familiar and has achieved an unbelievably alarming level of normalization among the masses. On this occasion of the curfew announcement there's no telling when the beginning of what we think could be the final annihilation in hell will come to an end.

Have faith of a mustard seed, our parish priest would say during Sunday Mass. I believe in God the Almighty, Maker of Heaven and Earth, in all that is seen and unseen. I put all my confidence, faith, hopes, and dreams for my dearly beloved La Concepción Island in the hands of God and lay my hurting, broken heart at his feet, awaiting mending. Thinking aloud, I prayed,

"Glory to God in the Highest and Peace to all His Children here on Earth."

On Thursday evening, October 20th, we climbed onto the rooftop despite knowing that Daddy Harry's ship would not be seen sailing on the horizon. Looking to the setting sun, then later to the moon and stars, Greg, Carli, and I held hands with Mommy Meggie and trusted that God was watching over our family and his beloved magnificent creation, our La Concepción Island, Star of the Sea.

The Gipper and Poppy, as President Reagan and Vice President Bush are fondly known, came through with liberation for La Concepción Island. The US troops arrived on the seashore of La Concepción on the dawn of Tuesday, October 25th, 1983. Caribbean Iron Lady, our first female Prime Minister of Nature Island and first female elected Head of Government in the Americas, Dame Mary Eugenia Charles, visited with President Ronald Reagan and Vice President George H.W. Bush to request international intervention into La Concepción Island. Dame Charles is an alumna of my St. Joseph's Convent Girls High School in St. George's. She attended SJC as a boarding student together with another great dame, our first female Governor General of La Concepción, Dame Hilda Louise Bynoe. Dame Charles loves the Cluny Sisters and La Concepción Island.

Mommy Meggie and I, and whenever Aunt Jen and Aunt Jo could, leading up to the US and Allied Forces invasion of La Concepción Island, kept Greg and Carli involved in all the usual activities on Grandpa Ralph's estate that week, except church attendance due to curfew. I engaged them in getting on with our studies like I do every summer, teaching all the academic subject lessons so that they do not fall behind while school is out for long periods, such as at present during the war being out of school for most of Michaelmas Term. I rang the dinner bell between class periods and for recess and the end of the school day. In the evening we also spent time watching the adventures of Winnie the Pooh on the View Master that Daddy Harry had given to us for Christmas. I also included Melvin and Ivan in the study lessons as I do during summer. Since all of us are at in varying grade levels, I had to teach each their subject lesson, as well as complete my assignments in all my subjects.

Greg is a dashingly handsome and intelligent young lad. He's the most adorable good looking baby boy I had ever seen when Mommy Meggie came home with him from the hospital a couple days after he was born. He resembles Mommy Meggie around the forehead and eyes, and he always aims to please her. He has a blend of her skin tone in a darker much deeper and richer sapodilla complexion like his father. Greg looks like the mini me of actor Eddie Murphy. He's the typical middle child with the gentle temperament of a diplomat. Greg is a gifted and talented artist conceptualizing in 3-D, especially the architectural elevation of houses and brilliant design of floor plans. He's often referred to as Master George Louis.

Carli is incredibly beautiful and a bright 7-year-old girl, tall for her age, with structural facial features in the image of Daddy Harry and Mommy Meggie. She's the prettiest light sapodilla color baby girl I had ever seen when I came home from school the day she was born, and Mommy Meggie was holding her. On the day that Mommy Meggie and Daddy Harry got married, three-year-old Carli was looking adorable like a pink carnation. Carli loves reading aloud, annunciating with animation like she's acting out a skit. She's smart and has been reading passages from the Holy Bible on Sundays at church since she was a little girl at the tender age of 4. Projecting her voice such that the entire congregation can hear her without the assistance of a microphone is a sight to behold. Carli is greatly admired in the community. I, the proud eldest sibling, Daddy Harry's yellow jacket, have my head up high like a peacock.

Greg and Carli mind me almost like a third parent. Every adult and every child look upon me with respect and treat me with high regard and reverence. The men tipped their hats, nodding, addressing me,

"Howdy, Miss Louis," and ladies gave me a gentle bow while addressing me, "Howdy, Miss Charlotte."

They address me like I am the most important young lady in the community and on the entire La Concepción Island. The realism is that at least one person in every household in Windsor Farm or a relative from a neighboring community, works for Grandpa Ralph in one capacity or another.

I've been told on many occasions that I am very pretty, like Mommy Meggie, and our Carli, too, is a very pretty and attractive girl in my image of a richer silk medium chocolate. All three of us resemble Mommy Meggie and have her grit and tenacity. Whenever Mommy Meggie compliments me, which she does at the most pivotal moments, she would say,

"Charlotte, you're a very pretty girl; God took his own hands to make you so good-looking."

Mommy Meggie says the same to each of us whenever alone in her company, she makes each of us feel like her favorite child. She would say to me, Charli, you are special because you're my first-born child, Greg is special because he's her only son, and Carli is special because she's her youngest child and the baby of our family. I am slender and tall, light caramel yellow reddish complexion, chestnut below shoulder length thick curly hair, oval face with high cheekbones, almost straight nose like Mommy Meggie's although slightly rounded like my father's, an aristocratic appearance with a long neck, and huge brown eyes like Mommy Meggie's that appear hazel at times like my father's. Though quite kind and warm-natured, my appearance to some unacquainted with me might seem like one of aloofness with air about me, although I am not at all pretentious. I have a very intelligent, studious-looking appearance, wearing eyeglasses since age 7.

On Tuesday morning, October 25th, Mommy Meggie turned on the radio as she does every morning when we're at our cottage in Windsor Farm. On this occasion, however, a frantic and panic-stricken unfamiliar announcer, perhaps a cooperating regime member, shouting,

"block all roads, block all roads, the American soldiers are here, block all roads."

We were all elated that President Reagan and Vice President George Bush sent troops to liberate us! The radio announcer's attempt to persuade the masses were falling on deaf ears. The Cardinal and half his Cabinet have been assinated and our citizens are weary with zero confidence with those in charge. Mommy Meggie put her hands up and said,

"Praise God! Praise the Lord! God is good, and he's good all the time! Thank God! All praise and glory are yours, Almighty Father! God Bless Reagan and Bush for sending the troops to save us!"

She started sounding like an Evangelical Preacher. Her voice started to break, overcome, and overwhelmed with tears of happiness as she opened her arms, and each of us, me, Greg, and Carli, entered her wide, warm, protective embrace, as she held us lovingly and tenderly and reassuringly, combing lines from popular Bob Marley songs,

"everything is going to be alright, my three little birds."

Mommy Meggie roasted corn on the cob on the grill outside the kitchen patio. She and I make daily trips to quickly collect eggs, and to get a chicken a couple times each week, to the very large-scale deluxe chicken coop where we housed over one hundred chickens, in the shared garden near our cottage on Grandpa Ralph's estate, which Daddy Harry started this subsistence backyard farming, in anticipation for such purpose as our present situation. About twice weekly, one of our farmworkers, mostly Lennard, brought us vegetable provisions. The overseer farm manager, Harlan, would hurriedly deliver a butchered pig from the hundreds that we mainly prior to the war sold to neighbors and the Cubans who love roast compoyo, or a goat, from Daddy Harry's Laurel Farm, given away at no cost to those in need during the war. One of Mommy Meggie's Louis cousins, a member of parliament, married a Cuban wife.

Mommy Meggie would occasionally request a cattle to have some beef in our diet. Grandpa Ralph also had his workers deliver vegetable produce provisions to us, as always. Grandma Lucia, Mommy Meggie, and siblings, Aunt Jen, Aunt Jo, Uncle Tony, Grandaunt Amy, and Grandaunt Maggie, shared vegetable provisions, poultry, and meats, as is normal and customary practice. They also gave to our cousins Hillary and Valerie dear friends of Mommy Meggie on Windsor Farm who live in boundary with Grandaunt Amy. Their mothers are Irene and Philippa, the daughters of late Great-uncle Peter Charles and his widow our family oral historian Great-aunt Ethel. Great-uncle Peter was the late brother of Great-grandma Clara Charles. The childhood home of Daddy Harry's father and his paternal relatives is within close walking proximity to our Charles relatives. During the war, the children of Windsor Farm, on behalf of their parents, showed up knocking at our door with bags in hand asking for rations and staples such as sugar, rice, flour, more often than they usually did prior. Mommy Meggie fed the village.

There is no fishing in the ocean or rivers during the war. When at home on La Concepción Island, Daddy Harry usually spends his spare time fishing, and we all miss not having an abundance of seafood. Mommy Meggie also requested our workers to deliver the same in kind meats and poultry, fresh produce of ground vegetables and fruits to our dearly beloved Grandma Violet, Daddy Harry's mother, in the neighboring communityof Vincences whenever they could during brief ceasefires. They kindly obliged Mommy Meggie, as always. Our dedicated and devoted farmworkers would race back to their homes as the bombing raids were still in full swing with the frequent sounds of gunfire and other heavy artillery and the sights of very low flying helicopters loaded with armed soldiers smiling and waving to civilians on the ground. Each low flight and bomb explosion, we run down the stairs and under the dining table to crouch with our hands over the back of our heads until all is calm. Then we would emerge and return upstairs to our bedroom play area or the living room to listen to the radio and back downstairs again, repeating this survival technique countless times every day during the lockdown shelter in place, until the war was over.

On the morning of October 25th, the radio announcer had put on a song *"Every Breath You Take,"* by the music group 'The Police.' The repetition of that rift played without interruption for almost a full week and had a chilling effect on every household of being watched and having to look over our shoulders. There was no usual syncopation in music genre of the region such as by the Calypso King of the World – The Mighty Sparrow, Reggae especially Bob Marley songs such as One Love and War, and Latin Soca. Also American and British Popular Culture Hip Hop, all the greatest hits of the 70's and 80s, like Diana Ross and Tina Turner and Michael Jackson and Madonna, Euro Disco from The Beatles and ABBA and The Bee Gees and others. Rhythm and Blues call and response genre like Louis Armstrong and Count Basie, the acoustics and percussion in the improvision and scat of Cool Jazz like Duke Ellington. Especially the Motown Disco and other artists like The Jacksons and Lionel Richie and Stevie Wonder. And Country Music especially ladies like Patsy Cline and Loretta Lynn and Dolly

Parton and Reba McIntyre and gentlemen like Oxonian Kris Kristofferson, Kenney Rogers and his rendition with Dolly of *'Islands in the Stream,'* Willi Nelson's *'The Sunny Side of the Street'* are among our favorites, rising star Vincent Gill whom Mommy Meggie likes, Cher and Naomi and Wynonna Judd whom I love. There was no coverage of sports – especially West Indies Cricket.

Then, in what seemed like an eternity of curfew, one day, *'The Police'* record stopped playing. We all fell silent. We waited with great anticipation of what would come about. The voice of God speaking through an American senior military commanding officer stated something to the effect,

"This is the Military of the United States of America." Hope is alive!

The crescendo of the collective celebratory eruption from every household seemed as loud as the combined total of all the sounds of machine gunfire and bombing explosions from air, land, and sea, which we heard for almost a week prior; and might have registered on the Geological Richter Scale. Bursting with contentment, Mommy Meggie echoed the late Dr. Martin Luther King,

"Free at last! Free at last! Thank God Almighty, we are free at last!"

We children started screaming her sentiments as loud as we could. The US military officer requested everyone to remain indoors, for our safety, as the war was not yet over. Each day, the radio announcements gave us instructions regarding specific times we could move about to purchase goods.

During the war, all the clothes is being washed in the bathroom and hung inside the shower room on the ground floor of the cottage next to our English kitchen and dining room. Mommy Meggie was not in the habit of washing laundry, especially because she got a cold when she has to due to the absence of a maid on account of illness. Daddy Harry requested that she refrain from doing such chores, and he would do the laundry whenever the laundry maids were absent prior to working on board the cruise and during his vacation periods at home, when the ship is on dry dock. Mommy Meggie did not risk taking the clothes to the huge washing sinks in the shared garden with Grandpa Ralph's main house, where the maids took care of our laundry.

Luckily, she did not catch a cold having to do the wash under these circumstances. During the war, the maids came occasionally whenever the radio announcements granted permission during short ceasefire rules of armed conflict engagement to leave homes for necessary reasons for specific periods of time.

To conserve the cooking gas in the three cylinders, Mommy Meggie cooked only breakfast on the kitchen stove. She started cooking lunch and dinner on the barbeque grill on the patio outside the kitchen. The two pots got very darkened by the charcoal. She sacrificed those skillets that she's intending to take with us to our new seaside home nearing construction completion in the posh petite bourgeois Southeast Coast region here on La Concepción Island.

Star of the Sea

La Concepción

A Short Story

Part Three

The war was essentially over within a month, in late November 1983, around Thanksgiving in our United States of America. Aunt Laura's husband, was freed by the Military Forces of our United States of America. He's appointed Chief Magistrate Judge in St. George's. Mommy Meggie's two Louis' cousins, who were Members of Parliament are also freed by the American Military. Daddy Harry says we are lucky that the United States of America has a rational interest to act in La Concepción Island. Daddy Harry told us the offshore St. George's School of Medicine here on La Concepción Island made a good case for intervening. Also, our strategic location between Fidel Castro's Cuba and the Panama Canal gave our United States of America another good reason to intervene, asserting the Monroe Doctrine, Manifest Destiny.

Daddy Harry is of the perception that once the intervention mission is complete, La Concepción Island would experience subsequent years of rapid capitalist development due to the impending United States Dollar Diplomacy Foreign Policy. Much like the case of Puerto

Rico, during the transition of becoming an American Overseas Territory. Although La Concepción Island will endeavor to remain part of the British Commonwealth, with our dearest, beloved, greatest British Monarch of all time, Queen Elizabeth II, as our Head of State, then her Royal Heirs and theirs forevermore.

Daddy Harry is, alas, at home for Christmas with Mommy Meggie, me Charlotte, George, and Caroline the baby of our family. We are grateful and forever indebted to the United States of America and the brave American soldiers who planted the American flag on the soil of our La Concepción Island. Their sacrifice has brought about freedom, peace, and security in less than two months. Indeed, December 25th, 1983, is arguably the most 'ginormous' Christmas feast ever on La Concepción Island. Matched only by an encore to scale on the anniversary celebration of Christmas 1984 as a free nation state in the region, with a government elected by we the people of La Concepción, for we the people of La Concepción. Daddy Harry celebrated that Christmas holiday with us and vowed to retire from the cruise ship and come home to La Concepción permanently the following Christmas. Christmas Day is also special for being the birthday of our dearly beloved Grandma Lucia, therefore a double celebration. Aunt Camilla and Mommy Meggie makes the best Christmas cake with blended fruits of cheeries, currants, raisens, prunes, kitchen bouquet, cinnamon, nutmeg, clove, vanila extract, and loaded with sweet red wine. This cake is known in the region of these islands as 'Black Cake.' They also make homemade gingerbeer and sorrel drinks during the holiday season.

Daddy Harry concur, we all love and pray that God Bless and Save our greatest Queen, Her Majesty Elizabeth II.

God save our gracious Queen!
Long live our noble Queen!
God save the Queen!
Send her victorious,
Happy and glorious,
Long to reign over us:
God save the Queen!

Thy choicest gifts in store,
On her be pleased to pour;
Long may she reign:
May she defend our laws,
And ever give us cause,
To sing with heart and voice,
God save the Queen!

We must now also pray that God Bless America. Daddy Harry said, that in a very long time from now, we will sing God Bless and Save our Great King, to our King Charles III. He also insists that each of us need to learn the pledge of the United States of America. Daddy Harry had learned the pledge during his years working aboard the cruise ship. He recited.

"I pledge allegiance to the Flag,
Of the United States of America
And to the Republic for which it stands,
One Nation under God
Indivisible, with liberty and justice for all."

At Christmas, we have much more presents under our tree in our seaside Mediterranean architectural style residence with neoclassical elements, with wide wrap-around verandas with decorative balusters and private porches from the bedroom suite chambers, and grand interior staircase. There are three living rooms, three kitchens, six bedrooms, six bathrooms and two powder rooms, three laundry rooms, and garage. Mommy Meggie got all the home décor items on her long bucket list, signed, sealed, and delivered with love by Daddy Harry, who purchased all the items at his various ports of call. In our new home on the Southeast Coast, Mommy Meggie and Daddy Harry have a new pride and confidence about them seen in the air of Grandpa Ralph. We children, in good zest, make fun of Daddy Harry, asking him whether we ought to give him a new nickname,

"'Daddy Seahawk,' now that we're living at the seaside."

Like our cottage on Windsor Farm is a central gathering place, so too our seaside home in the Southeast is a convalescing central space for our relatives and friends, and visitors from overseas, especially Mommy Meggie's paternal brother Uncle Cecil, and her maternal cousin, teacher at St. Dominic's School, then headmaster, Uncle Bobby.

Here on the Southeast Coast, Greg, Carli, and I would take strolls from our home to spend our sunshine weekends and summers playing endlessly on the private beaches and in the coves along the seashore at Fort Jeudy. Mommy Meggie would accompany us on some occasions; sometimes, she would ring the dinner bell to call us up to the house from our playtime on the beach, where Carli and I collected shells to decorate the entire circumference perimeter of the koi pond that Daddy Harry created in the garden with Greg as his helper, and Mommy Meggie selected the pretty water lilies. We would spend endless hours resting under the shade umbrella of the great flamboyant trees, admiring their brilliance enveloped in the canopy branches that served as our hammocks loaded with the rich, beautiful radiance of their crimson flowers, eating the thick peach color flesh bounty of sea eggs we collect during low tides, which has become our readily available food snack source here at Fort

Jeudy, like golden apples and bananas and mangoes are in Windsor Farm. The Long Gars that Daddy Harry catches on his weekly fishing at the Fort Jeudy Point has replaced the easily available chickens in our diet that we kept in the garden coop at Windsor Farm. He occasionally catches Grouper and Snapper which he talks about at the dinner table until he catches another worthy of conversation.

World Famous Grand Anse Beach: Home to St. George's University School of Medicine Anatomy Department.

The sound of music I miss in the voices and instruments of our lovely Lett ladies – Elizabeth and Lillian and Cora, our good Gabriel sisters, Forsyth, Rush, Brizan, Honore, Charles, Louison, Greenidge, DeCoteau, Douglas, Leed, Patterson, Chateau, Thomas, Simon, Miles, Frazer, and all the families and community members at St. Dominics church where Carli and Greg were Christened and made their First Communion and where I chose to make my Confirmation, that resonates throughout Windsor Farm, Laura Farm and Pedmontemps. I now hear at the beaches in Fort Jeudy, in the waves gently rolling on the calm water towards the shore and breaking in that beautiful form upon the sand, much like the pyroclastic flow that gave birth to her, long before she was discovered by Europeans, lives up to the saying by Bob Marley, that one good thing about music, when it hits, you feel no pain. La Concepcion citizens are in solidarity in our commitment to lasting peace and reconciliation.

Mommy Meggie and the three of us children, would take trips nearby, within ten minutes' drive, to the three-kilometer long, stunning world-famous powder white sand Grand Anse Beach enticing crystal-clear turquoise waters. Located near Aunt Camilla and our cousins Beatrice and Astrid in their newly built grand home with wide sea views, wrap-around verandas, three living rooms, three kitchens, five bedrooms, four bathrooms, two laundry rooms, and motor court. They, too, relocated to the Southeast Coast after the war and are our regular visitors at our home overlooking Fort Jeudy, and likewise, we are theirs at their home in Grand Anse. We also spend time on the beaches in adjacent Morne Rouge, and in other posh Southeast Coastal communities like Lance Aux Epines, and True Blue, the location of St. George's University's main campus, the Anatomy campus is on Grand Anse Beach.

Our new seaside community seems very familiar for three reasons: the view of the Southeast Coast when we lived at Windsor Farm has been etched in our early childhood memories, also we occasionally visited our relative Ms. Norris in Westerhall, she was a teacher at St. Dominics

School, prior to migrating to the USA with her two daughters Veronica and Keisha, after the first coup; and several of our neighbors here attended St. Dominic's Catholic Church when we lived at Windsor Farm. One is Mommy Meggie's paternal sister, second daughter of Grandpa Ralph, Aunt Rosalynn and her husband, their son Teodore whom we fondly nick named Teddy, and their daughter Charlene. Aunt Rosalynn's husband is a Member of Parliament. He's also the younger brother of the Chief Magistrate – the husband of my paternal aunt, Laura. Similarly, Daddy Harry's eldest sister, Aunt Sophie, and her husband are the godparents of my paternal cousin William, the son of Aunt Laura and her husband. While Aunt Laura and her husband are the godparents of Aunt Sophie and her husband's eldest daughter, Tatiana. Daddy Harry's mommy Violet was the widow of Grandma Lucia's relative, the father of Aunt Sophie. These familial examples, illustrates the nature of connections between and among families in small states of this region. Cherlene is one of Carli's favorite cousins. William and Teodore are among my very favorite male cousins. Aunt Rosalynn's elder maternal half-sister Matilda has four daughters, three much older; Eleanor a Physician is Mommy Meggie's doctor, Antoinette, Ananastasia, and the youngest Kristen, is my age, and good friends with Carli and I.

Two of the siblings of Sr. Lecabel at St. Joseph's Convent, who attend church at St. Dominic's are also our neighbors, Constantine and his wife Teresa and their son Devon and their daughter Danielle, and Ruth and her husband Donnie. Their youngest sister Leah is the only sibling remaining at their Pedmontemps family home. Next door to Constantine, is Jacqueline and her husband Marshall with their two young children, son Matt and daughter Tara.

Another of our neighbors here from Pedmontemps, who are in the process of building their home in this community, are renting an apartment in our multi-story home, Blaire and Jerry with their little girl Gail and their baby girl Gisele also attended church at St. Dominic's when we lived at Windsor Farm. Our new neighbors, the Andersons and their five children, Jeremy, Colin, Anita, Jill, and Joshua. The Flemings and their three sons, Bradley, Brian, and Brent. The Mickelsons and their little girl Melia; and Mommy Meggie's friend Ms. Jennifer and her children Heidi, my friend, Wesley and Nicholas are friends of Greg, and baby Gavin who adores Carli, a short walk down the road, already living in this area and now likes coming to our home to take in the sea views, have warmly received us. Near Ms. Jennifer is an old man Mr Hagleigh who lives alone in a small cottage. Living across the street from Ms. Jennifer, are Mr. Dominic and is wife Mrs. Tracey Walters and their daughter, Lauren, and son, Ryan. Up from the Walters is a lovely senior childless couple, Mrs. and Mr. Aberdeen whose the brother of Aunt Matilda's husband. We get our eggs from their farm in Calivigny. Around the corner from the Flemings, is an interracial couple, the Afro Indian family – Indian Mr. Narine and African ancestry Mrs. Narine and their two mix-race children, Nari and Sharonda.

Our dearest, most dearly beloved, neighbor of all, a is couple a decade the senior to Mommy Meggie and Daddy Harry, our newly adopted surrogate Aunt and Uncle, generous, and kind St. Joseph's Convent alumna, Aunt Charlotte and her British husband, Uncle Phillip Spencer. Their home is built on a plat they purchased from Mommy Meggie and Daddy Harry. They had a gorgeous beachfront house, however after their only dearly beloved son Richard passed away in London England without any heirs, they desired to move up the hill at the top of the plateau, to be much closer to our family. Their home is elegant, a lovely two-story Mediterranean with Victorian elements with large bay and bow windows, including wide wrap-around verandas front and back and private porches from the bedroom chambers, two living rooms, two kitchens, five bedrooms, four bathrooms, a powder room, two laundry rooms, and garage. Mommy Meggie and Daddy Harry have given Greg his large private ensuite bedroom that he selected prior to the completion of the construction, also his very own plat of land between our home and Aunt Charlotte and Uncle Phil with the same wide panoramic sea views to build himself a beautiful three-story home that he has already designed for when he's married with children.

Carli and I are Mommy Meggie and Daddy Harry's heirs, as well as the Spencer's heirs, also Aunt Jennah and Aunt Johanna do not desire to have children. A feature of the matrifocal Anglophone Commonwealth in the islands of our Americas, wherein the only part of our developing world girls is advantage in their education and inheritance over boys. Whereas in nuclear families the family estate most often becomes the ancestral home via male heredity. Since Carli and I do not desire to have children, we will leave everything to Greg's children as he desires to have a family. The future grandchildren of Mommy Meggie and Daddy Harry. We will leave Grandma Lucia's and Aunt Jennah's and Aunt Johanna's homes and land to our cousins Melvin and Ivan. Their children will be the great-grandchildren of Grandma Lucia, the great great-grandchildren of Great Great Great-grandpa Albert Louis and Great Great Great-grandma Clara Louis.

Aunt Charlotte and Uncle Phil Spencer like watching the BBC News and their favorite 007 Movies. Mommy Meggie likes watching her favorite movie of Shirley Temple,

'The Blue Bird.' I like watching Headline News with brilliant Journalist Anchor Wolf Blitzer, as well as pioneering Lady Barbara Walters on 20/20, Meet the Press on Sundays, and 60 Minutes on Sunday evenings. Our entire family likes the new talk show and host, the beautiful, awesome, and amazing Oprah Winfrey! And we're a family of sports fans, we all love watching NFL, NBA, Major League Baseball, Soccer, the Olympics Track and Field also including the Winter Games for Figure Skating and Skiing and our Land of Reggae Bob Sled Team, and on Saturday mornings Wrestling and The Soul Train dancing.

The three giants of our world visited our region of the Americas after the US intervention. His Holiness Pope John Paul II, visited the land of the Hummingbird, signaling he's supporting the new direction of democracy in La Concepción. I wished I could visit and get an opportunity to touch his hands. I do hope that some day our Blessed Holy Roman Catholic Church will elect a Pope like His Holiness Pope John Paul II from among our Cardinals in our Latin

American region and also from among our Asian Cardinals. Similarly, our Head of State, Her Majesty Queen Elizabeth II, and US Vice President George H.W. Bush made State visits to La Concepción. I was one of the students in both their audiences. I hope in my life time to see an African American male President. And African American female President of our United States of America who is raised with Catholic values.

I also flew solo for the first time to visit my aunts in the Land of the Hummingbird in August 1985 where I had a marvelous time with all my family on that large island known as little America in the region, especially with Aunt Michelle, whom I miss immensely and she surprised us all with a visit soon thereafter. My heart is at home upon landing in my dearly beloved petite La Concepción. Now my aspiration extends beyond Governor General and Prime Minister. I have the audacity to think I can become a Cardinal, and perhaps even Pope.

Daddy Harry would disembark the cruise ship Victoria one final time at the port in our capital city, St. George's, on our beloved La Concepción Island in August 1985, during the renormalization period. After all the tanks have cleared the streets and the Peace Keeping Forces have departed La Concepción. Post Interim Government period, after elections supervised by the United States of America have taken place in mid 1984 and Sir Herbert Blaize is Prime Minister, with Sir Nicholas Brathwaite becoming Deputy Prime Minister. Daddy Harry's maternal cousin, the author of *'Grenada Island of Conflict,'* is a Cabinet Member and later interim Prime Minister. The newly elected Member of Parliament in 1984 to watch, is Grandma Lucia's paternal cousin, The Right Honorable Dr. Keith Mitchell who's destined to become the longest serving Prime Minister of La Concepcion. Uncle Einstein told me that the mother of Prime Minister Dr. Mitchell is a member of our Louison Family Tree. Another newly elected Member of Parliament in 1984 to watch, is the Human Rights Lawyer Mr. Tillman Thomas. His good works will certainly get him elected Prime Minister in the years ahead.

Daddy Harry's arrival in La Concepcion is at the start of the building boom. All deferred housing and private sector commercial projects that were considered economic risks during the communist era are now on the rise with urgency. Daddy Harry quickly jumped at the opportunity with his building construction and trucking business. La Concepcion is now entering a promising stage of prosperity.

We thank our Heavenly Father Almighty God and our Heavenlty Mother Blessed Virgin Mary for their blessings bestored upon us, our Stars of the Sea Earthly Fathers and Mothers, Daddy Harry and Mommy Meggie, Sisters of St. Joseph De Cluny, His Holiness Pope John Paul II, Her Majesty Queen Elizabeth II, President Reagan, Vice President Bush, the Congress of our United States of America, our USA Military and their families, the citizens of our USA, and the Allied Military Forces, for the sacrifice made on behalf of my dearest, dearly beloved family, and my fellow citizens of La Concepción Island.

All God's abiding love and richest abundant blessings of good health and happiness to our La Concepción, our

Vatican, our Buckingham Palace, our Canterbury, our United States of America and Americans, our United Kingdom and Britons, all our Countries, all our Nations, and to all our Peoples around our World. Indeed, all politics is global.

Star of the Sea, my beautiful sunray. In fame and in war, my small home. My guardian blessed mother, royal exotic queen, energy helper and stimulator. The Court has given you leave. Thou hath liberty!

About the Author

The University of Oxford-Educated Social Scientist, Charlotte Courtenay, a New Times Best Seller, the most influential Political Strategist of our 21st Century, achieving political victories in elections for new and incumbent candidates for US Presidents, both Chambers of Congress and State Governors, inlucencing the appointments of Cabinet Members and Supreme Court Justice Nominees, UK Prime Ministers, G20 and OECD Heads of State, Heads of Multi-National Organizations, such as the Head of the UN and G20 and EU and OECD Heads of State, and leaders in countries and organizations such as the World Bank and IMF and University Chancellors & Presidents at institutions in the USA & UK and other leaders in countries and organizations around our world, has gifted the first subtitle 'La Conception' in her '**Star of the Sea**' series. The brilliance of President Reagan and President Bush shines through in Charlotte Courtenay's storytelling through the eyes of a young girl Charlotte Louis, who lived the experience during the US Military Operation Urgent Fury, which liberated Grenada, the Spice Island of the Caribbean, as the Medieval discovery named La Concepción by Columbus, is known in modern history.

Milton Keynes UK
Ingram Content Group UK Ltd.
UKHW020640120124
435913UK00008B/27

9 781917 054485

Elevation (m)

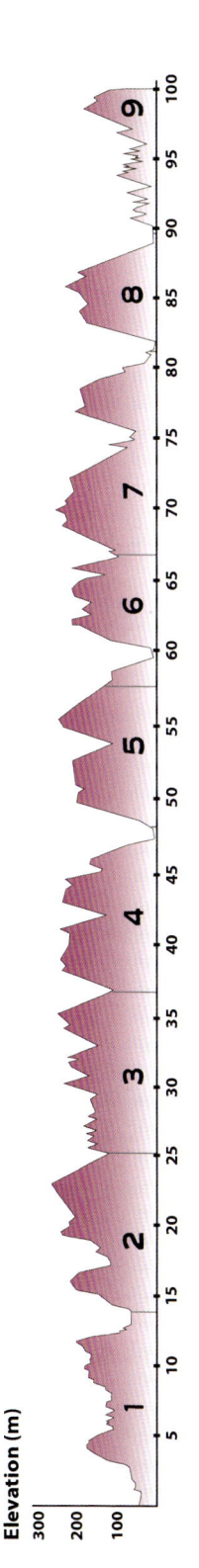

- 🛏 Accommodation: B&B, pub/inn, hostel and/or hotel
- ▲ Campsite
- 🍴 Food: pub, restaurant and/or café serving lunch and/or dinner
- 🛒 Shop or supermarket selling food or groceries
- 🚌 Bus services: may not be daily
- 🚆 Train services
- 🚰 Water Point: either a tap or pub that will top up water bottles

Note: It is not possible to list all of the locations with facilities in the diagram. Only key locations are shown. For facilities at other minor locations, check the table on pages 36 to 39 and the detailed facilities listings in the route descriptions.

Ask the Author

If you have any questions which are not answered by this book, then you can ask the author on our Facebook group, 'The South Downs Way'. The group's URL is www.facebook.com/groups/SouthDownsWay

About the Author

Andrew McCluggage is an outdoor writer and photographer from Northern Ireland. After 20 years as a corporate lawyer, he decided to do something interesting and started writing walking guidebooks.

His first book was Walking in the Briançonnais, covering a beautiful part of the French Alps. Since then, he has written a variety of guidebooks for hiking and trekking.

Other Knife Edge Outdoor Guidebooks written by Andrew include:

- **Trekking the Hadrian's Wall Path**
- **Northern Ireland: The Unmissable Walks**
- **The Mourne Mountains**
- **Tour du Mont Blanc**
- **Trekking the Dolomites AV1**
- **Walker's Haute Route: Chamonix to Zermatt**
- **Trekking the Corsica GR20**
- **Walking Chamonix-Mont Blanc**
- **Walking Brittany**
- **Tour of the Écrins National Park (GR54)**

Views of the Weald from near Firle Beacon (Stage 8b/8c)

KNIFE EDGE
Outdoor Guidebooks

Key for Route Maps

- **S/F** Start/Finish of Stage
- **1** Waypoint
- **Accommodation**
- **Campsite**
- **Water Point**
- **Train Station**

0 — 1km

Publisher: Knife Edge Outdoor Limited (NI648568)
12 Torrent Business Centre, Donaghmore, County Tyrone, BT70 3BF, UK
www.knifeedgeoutdoor.com

©Andrew McCluggage 2021
All photographs: ©Andrew McCluggage 2021
ISBN: 978-1-912933-06-8

First edition 2021

A catalogue record for this book is available from the British Library.

All rights reserved. No part of this publication may be reproduced in any form without the prior written consent of the publisher and copyright owner.

Map on inside cover: ©Knife Edge Outdoor Limited
Other maps: ©Crown Copyright and database rights 2021
OS 100063385

Front cover: Littleton Down (Stage 4b)
Title page: Climbing Old Winchester Hill (Stage 2a)
This page: The white cliffs of Beachy Head (Stage 9c)

All routes described in this guide have been recently walked by the author and both the author and publisher have made all reasonable efforts to ensure that all information is as accurate as possible. However, while a printed book remains constant for the life of an edition, things in the countryside often change. Trails are subject to forces outside our control. For example, landslides, tree-falls or other matters can result in damage to paths or route changes; waymarks and signposts may fade or be destroyed by wind, snow or the passage of time; or trails may not be maintained by the relevant authorities. If you notice any discrepancies between the contents of this guide and the facts on the ground, then please let us know. Our contact details are listed at the back of this book.

Contents

Getting Help 1
Introduction 3
    How hard is the SDW? 4
    Direction and start/finish points 5
    Hiking shorter sections of the SDW 5
    Guided tours, self-guided tours or independent walking? 5
    When to go 6
    Using this book 8
Itinerary Planner 10
Suggested Itineraries: West to East 12
Suggested Itineraries: East to West 16
Accommodation 20
Camping 22
Accommodation Listings 24
Facilities 36
Food 40
Travel 41
    Travel to Southern England 41
    Travel to/from the primary trail-heads 41
    Returning to the start from the finish of the SDW 42
    Public transport along the SDW 43
    Secondary trail-heads 47
On the Trail 51
    Costs & budgeting 51
    Weather 51
    Maps 52
    Paths and waymarking 52
    Storing bags 53
    Baggage transfer 53
    Fuel for camping stoves 54
    Water 54
Equipment 56
    Recommended basic kit 57
    Additional gear for campers 59
Safety 61
General Information 62
Wildlife 63
Plants and Flowers 64
Geology 65
History of the South Downs 66
    South Downs National Park 67
Route Descriptions 69
Section 1: Winchester/Exton 70
    Stage 1a: Winchester/Chilcomb 74
    Stage 1b: Chilcomb/Holden Farm 76
    Stage 1c: Holden Farm/The Milbury's 78
    Stage 1d: The Milbury's/Exton 78
Section 2: Exton/Buriton-Petersfield exit 80
    Stage 2a: Exton/Meon Springs 84

Stage 2b: Meon Springs/The Sustainability Centre	84
Stage 2c: The Sustainability Centre/Buriton-Petersfield exit	86
Section 3: Buriton-Petersfield exit/Cocking exit	**88**
Stage 3a: Buriton-Petersfield exit/South Harting exit	92
Stage 3b: South Harting exit/Cocking exit	94
Section 4: Cocking exit/Houghton Bridge	**96**
Stage 4a: Cocking exit/Graffham exit	100
Stage 4b: Graffham exit/Bignor-Sutton exit	100
Stage 4c: Bignor-Sutton exit/Bury exit	104
Stage 4d: Bury exit/Houghton Bridge	104
Section 5: Houghton Bridge/Steyning exit	**106**
Stage 5a: Houghton Bridge/Storrington exit	110
Stage 5b: Storrington exit/Washington exit	110
Stage 5c: Washington exit/Steyning exit	112
Section 6: Steyning exit/Pyecombe	**114**
Stage 6a: Steyning exit/Upper Beeding exit	118
Stage 6b: Upper Beeding exit/Truleigh Hill	118
Stage 6c: Truleigh Hill/Saddlescombe Farm	120
Stage 6d: Saddlescombe Farm/Pyecombe	120
Section 7: Pyecombe/Rodmell exit	**122**
Stage 7a: Pyecombe/Jack & Jill exit	126
Stage 7b: Jack & Jill exit/Ditchling Beacon	126
Stage 7c: Ditchling Beacon/Housedean Farm	129
Stage 7d: Housedean Farm/Kingston exit	130
Stage 7e: Kingston exit/Rodmell exit	130
Section 8: Rodmell exit/Alfriston	**132**
Stage 8a: Rodmell exit/YHA South Downs	136
Stage 8b: YHA South Downs/Firle Beacon	136
Stage 8c: Firle Beacon/Bostal Hill	138
Stage 8d: Bostal Hill/Alfriston	138
Section 9: Alfriston/Meads	**140**
Stage 9a: Alfriston/Exceat	144
Stage 9b: Exceat/Belle Tout Lighthouse	144
Stage 9c: Belle Tout Lighthouse/Meads	148
Section v9: Alfriston/Meads (Inland Route)	**150**

Getting Help

Emergency services number: dial 999

Distress signal

The signal that you are in distress is 6 blasts on a whistle spaced over a minute, followed by a minute's silence. Then repeat. The acknowledgment that your signal has been received is 3 blasts of a whistle over a minute followed by a minute's silence. At night, flashes of a torch can also be used in the same sequences. **Always carry a torch and whistle.**

Signalling to a helicopter from the ground

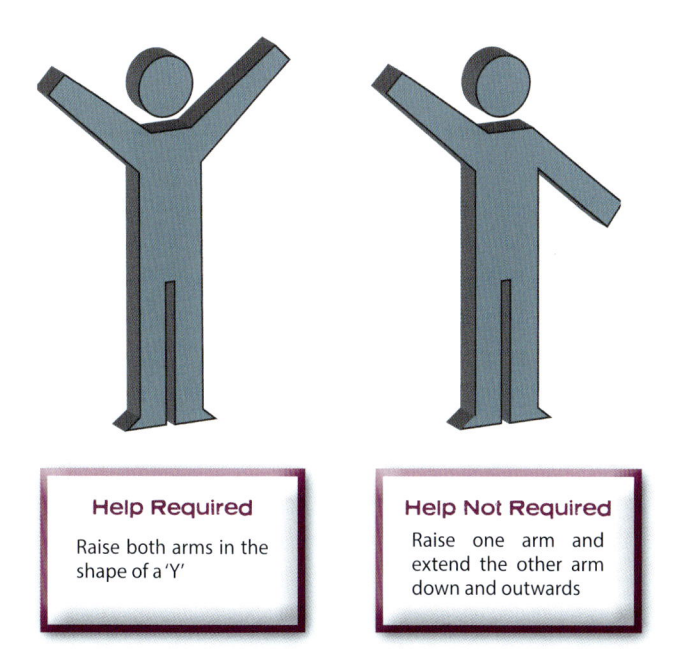

Help Required
Raise both arms in the shape of a 'Y'

Help Not Required
Raise one arm and extend the other arm down and outwards

WARNING

Hills, cliffs and mountains can be dangerous places and walking is a potentially dangerous activity. Many of the routes described in this guide cross exposed and potentially hazardous terrain. You walk entirely at your own risk. It is solely your responsibility to ensure that you and all members of your group have adequate experience, fitness and equipment. Neither the author nor the publisher accepts any responsibility or liability whatsoever for death, injury, loss, damage or inconvenience resulting from use of this book, participation in the activity of mountain walking or otherwise.

Some land may be privately owned so we cannot guarantee that there is a legal right of entry to the land. Occasionally, routes change as a result of land disputes.

The working windmill on Stage 7a/7b

Introduction

E-W trekkers on Stage 5c

When envisaging the South Downs, many people probably picture themselves strolling along the instantly recognisable white sea-cliffs of the Seven Sisters, under the cobalt skies of a bright summer's day, far above the shimmering sea. Others may see, in their mind's eye, one of the iconic viewpoints above the candy-striped lighthouse at Beachy Head, the scene of a million selfies. However, those 'in the know' probably have other delights in mind because there is much more to the South Downs ('SDs') than the famous chalk cliffs: in fact, the SDs are a huge range of chalk hills which stretch across the English counties of Hampshire and Sussex. Such aficionados might visualise the rolling hills and meadows, bedecked with wild-flowers, with far-reaching views over the valleys below; or perhaps the seemingly endless fields of golden corn, the long stalks rippling hypnotically under a warm breeze; or maybe even a beer garden on a balmy day in one of the quaint, picture-postcard, Hampshire or Sussex villages. If you find these sorts of things appealing, then the SDs are for you! And walking some, or all, of the South Downs Way ('SDW') is the perfect way to experience the best the region has to offer.

The SDW is utterly unique and it is one of England's official 'National Trails'. For most of its 100 miles, it follows the crest of the SDs between Winchester in the west and Eastbourne in the east, remaining close to the edge of the steep northern escarpment. The route really only leaves the crest five times and that is out of necessity: there are five rivers along the way which run south towards the sea (the Rivers Meon, Arun, Adur, Ouse and Cuckmere) and the SDW must cross the base of the valleys which those rivers have, over time, carved out of the chalk hills. From the northern escarpment, there are sublime views (to the N) of the 'Weald' which is an area of lower-lying countryside between the SDs and the North Downs.

The SDW trekker negotiates the gently undulating terrain on a meticulously waymarked series of chalk paths and tracks, following in the footsteps of traders from as long ago as the Bronze Age. Along the route, the trekker passes magnificent rolling hills with stunning views, striking chalk grassland with rare flowers and butterflies, awe-inspiring sea-cliffs, wonderful woodland filled with native trees, unspoilt villages and towns which ooze history, countless well-preserved Iron Age hill-forts and burial grounds (tumuli), and some of the most exquisite farmland that Britain has to offer. Such is the beauty and importance of this countryside that it is protected within the South Downs National Park (see page 67) and the SDW remains almost entirely within that park.

On the high downs, you are far away from the region's urban centres. Occasionally, you will cross a minor road or pass through a tiny village (with little more than a local pub) but otherwise, the experience is one of pure tranquillity. The SDW is perhaps the most relaxing way to enjoy rural Hampshire and Sussex.

The SDW is 100 miles (162km) in length with approximately 12,000ft (3,700m) of ascent and descent. If those statistics sound intimidating then do not worry: with the right preparation, planning and approach, the SDW is perfectly manageable for most people of reasonable fitness. Yes, it is a challenge but it is an achievable one. And that is where this book comes in! Most of what you need to know to plan, and prepare for, the SDW is here within these pages and the entire route is described in detail to guide you on the trek itself. Furthermore, unlike some other books, this one contains real Ordnance Survey maps: for each stage, there are 1:25,000 scale maps to go with the accurate and concise route descriptions. Because all the maps are set out within the guidebook itself, there is no need to fumble about with a guidebook in one hand and a map in the other.

We aim to ensure that you have the best chance possible of completing the trek. We place great importance on the correct preparation and we focus in detail on modern lightweight equipment (see 'Equipment'). We also believe that it is crucial to match your itinerary to your experience, fitness and ability. Accordingly, we have included here an extraordinary level of detail on itinerary planning: our unique itinerary planner has 18 different itineraries to choose from. For each itinerary, we have completed for you all the difficult calculations of time, distance and altitude gain/loss. This makes it easy for you to design a manageable itinerary that fits your specific needs. Once on the trail, you will be able to relax and fully enjoy one of the world's great treks.

How hard is the SDW?

Notwithstanding the challenges, it is estimated that thousands of hikers walk the full length of the SDW each year. It is therefore an achievable endeavour. However, each day you will need to walk a significant distance across undulating terrain so a reasonable level of fitness is required. That said, the SDW has much less climbing and descending than many other treks and it is considered to be one of the easiest multi-day hikes in the UK. In fact, there are only about 12,000ft (3,700m) of ascent and descent on the entire trek and these are relatively well spread out across the length of the route.

It is probably easier to hike W-E than E-W. One of the hardest sections of the trek is Section 9 which is the most easterly part of the route. If you are walking W-E then Section 9 is saved for last so it is easier to plan a balanced route starting with short slow days and increasing the difficulty as you go along. E-W hikers, on the other hand, must start with the relentless undulations of Section 9 without the opportunity to warm-up first on easier parts of the trail.

For the most part, the SDW uses clear paths and tracks which are simple to negotiate. There are also some short sections along minor roads. The route is well marked. Most people walk the SDW in eight to ten days. However, very fit and experienced hikers can finish it in six days or less and endurance runners often do it even faster. Others prefer to walk more slowly and take 11 or 12 days, soaking up all of the delights on offer, lingering over packed lunches whilst savouring the magnificent views, searching for the remains of Iron Age hill forts and enjoying the real ale in the country pubs along the way. There is plenty of accommodation on, or near, the trail so it is simple to plan daily distances to suit your requirements.

Direction and start/finish points

The SDW runs between Winchester in the W and Eastbourne in the E. You can hike it in either direction so this book describes both approaches in full. However, there are some sensible reasons for hiking W-E. Firstly, Section 9 at the E end of the trail (between Alfriston and Eastbourne) is arguably the most challenging part of the SDW: the route is long, the terrain undulates relentlessly and it usually has to be completed in one day as there is little accommodation along the way to break up the journey. Accordingly, it is preferable to walk Section 9 at the end of the trek when you are 'trail-hardened' rather than at the start of it when your legs will not yet have become accustomed to the rigours of daily walking.

Secondly, the cliffs at Beachy Head and the Seven Sisters on Stages 9b and 9c are highlights of the trek and for W-E hikers are an epic climax to a wonderful journey. E-W trekkers, on the other hand, will pass this key attraction on the first day (before they have found rhythm and fitness) and will be less able to relax and enjoy Section 9's scenic delights. Thirdly, there is wind direction to consider: the prevailing winds in the UK are from the SW or W. So if you walk W-E, there is a higher probability that the wind will be on your back: you expend less energy walking away from the wind.

However, some maintain that Winchester is a more pleasant town to finish at than Eastbourne and for that reason, they elect to hike E-W. In this book, we cater for both E-W and W-E trekkers: route descriptions and a variety of itineraries are given for each approach. The numbered waypoints on the real maps make the route simple to follow in either direction.

Hiking shorter sections of the SDW

Walking the SDW in one go is a wonderful experience but there are other ways to enjoy this incredible trail. If you do not wish to walk the entire route, it is possible to walk shorter sections of it. There are numerous escape/access points along the route where you could leave or join the trek using public transport or taxis: see 'Secondary trail-heads'. You could start at any of these places and walk a few sections. Or you could skip sections by leaving the route at one of these points.

Furthermore, a great many people prefer to hike the SDW in day-long sections using public transport to travel to/from the start and finish points: see 'Public Transport along the SDW'. Over the course of months or years, they will eventually complete the entire trek. Many others have no desire to walk the SDW in its entirety and simply want to experience a few of its highlights. The Itinerary Planner should help you to plan day-walks along the SDW. Often day-walkers hike in groups, leaving a car at each end of their route.

Guided tours, self-guided tours or independent walking?

A frequently asked question is whether to walk independently or with an organised group. The answer is a personal one, depending upon your own particular circumstances and requirements. For many, the decision to organise the trek themselves, and to walk independently, can be almost life-changing, opening the door for other challenges in the future. There is much satisfaction to be gained from planning and navigating a trek yourself and the sense of achievement on completion is to be savoured.

However, the independent trekker usually carries a full pack and is responsible for all daily decisions such as pacing, which way to go at junctions, when to stock up with food and water and choice of route in bad weather. For some, this will be too great a burden on top of the physical effort required simply to walk the route. For those walkers, a guided group is a great solution: the tour company typically organises food, accommodation and (if possible) transfer of luggage each night. And the guide makes all the decisions, enabling the walker to concentrate on the walking. There are a few tour companies operating guided trips on the SDW but you should check whether they cover the full official route or just some of the highlights.

Self-guided tours are much more popular and are a sensible middle-ground. The tour company books all the accommodation and provides all the advice and information required to complete the trek. However, you will walk the trail without a guide. Normally, your breakfast will be provided and you can request packed lunches. For evening meals, they will usually provide details of pubs and restaurants which are walking distance from your accommodation. Often they can transfer your baggage to your accommodation each night so you only need to carry a small day-pack on the trail.

There are also some businesses offering accommodation booking services only: they do not offer advice about the trek itself. In fact, these days there are so many self-guided tour companies and accommodation booking services that some of the accommodation along the SDW is block-booked months in advance. At peak times, this makes it harder for the independent trekker to secure first choice accommodation unless booked well in advance. As a result, many confident trekkers (who would be perfectly capable of walking independently) book a self-guided trip simply to avail of the accommodation booking service. By booking a self-guided tour or using an accommodation booking service, much of the hassle of planning the trek is alleviated, albeit at a price.

When to go

The climate in SE England is milder than in most other parts of the UK and the SDs are one of the sunniest places in the country. This means that you are comparatively more likely to enjoy some sunshine and comparatively less likely to suffer torrential rain. In theory, you could tackle the SDW at almost any time of year (weather permitting). Even in winter, there is rarely snow in sufficient quantities to prevent normal hiking. However, the main trekking season runs from Easter to October. Before Easter and after October, some accommodation will be closed.

Spring (March to May): this can be the most beautiful time of year for walking. Many wild-flowers are on show and the gorse will also be in full bloom with its vivid yellow flowers and coconut aroma. By May, new growth will be upon the deciduous plants and grass is at its greenest. The weather is often sunny and warm. Indeed, May can be the finest month in England and in recent years, the weather in May has tended to be more favourable than in July and August. Visibility in spring is generally excellent so views are wide-ranging. Of course, rain is a possibility at this time of year but it usually decreases as the season progresses. Early in spring, the number of walkers is lower (except at Easter), gradually increasing throughout the season.

Summer (June to August) this is the peak walking season and visitor numbers are at their greatest. The days are long and statistically, your chances of good weather are highest in this period. Often June is the best month and August is sometimes more unsettled. Temperatures are at their peak and there is sometimes haze. There are still plenty of flowers on show throughout the summer.

Autumn (September to November): September is still a busy month on the SDW but visitor numbers reduce, and some accommodation closes, as the season progresses. Autumn sometimes provides excellent walking conditions: the weather in September and October can be more settled, with less rain, than in summer. Temperatures are lower but still comfortable. Skies can be very clear giving excellent visibility and the quality of the low light is magnificent. The wide variety of deciduous plants in the UK means that the autumn colours are stunning. However, as the days get shorter, it is wise to start walking early. If something were to go wrong, you would have less daylight in which to seek help than in summer.

Winter (December to February): these are the coldest months and although it snows occasionally, heavy falls are not that common these days. A light sprinkling of snow can be a delight for a suitably-equipped walker although care should be taken. However, walking in deep snow is best left to those with the appropriate winter experience and the correct equipment. Even if there is no snow, watch out for ice which forms in places where water collects. Cold months often bring crisp, clear weather and the low sun makes the light very beautiful. A sunny day in winter can be one of the best of the year. Days are short so start early.

Season	Pros	Cons
Spring	Pleasant temperatures Frequent sunny skies Good visibility Gorse and wild-flowers Fewer visitors Butterflies & bluebells in May	Rainy spells are common in March and April Ground can be wet
Summer	Generally reliably fine weather Wild-flowers & butterflies	Sometimes hazy Visitor numbers highest
Autumn	Pleasant temperatures Frequent sunny skies Excellent visibility Fewer visitors Autumn colours	Shorter days Cooler evenings Rainy spells
Winter	Sometimes crisp clear skies Excellent visibility Fewer visitors	Shortest days Can be cold and icy Occasionally, there is snow

Using this book

This book is designed to be used by walkers of differing abilities. Many guidebooks for long-distance treks rigidly divide the route into a fixed number of long day stages, leaving it up to the walker to break down those stages to design daily routes which suit his/her abilities. This book, however, has been laid out differently to give the trekker flexibility: it divides the route into 32 shorter stages which you can combine to design daily routes that meet your own specific needs.

Each of the 32 stages covers the distance between one accommodation option and the subsequent one. Most accommodation options on the route are the start/finish point of a stage. You can choose how many of these stages you wish to walk each day. Each stage has its own walk description, route map and elevation profile.

The labelling of the stages uses a combination of numbers and letters. It is a simple system but requires a little bit of explanation. Firstly, we have divided the route into nine 'Sections' (numbered from 1 to 9 from W-E): each Section represents one day of our standard 9-day schedule. Within each Section, the route is broken down into stages: every stage is labelled with a number between 1 and 9, representing the relevant Section that the stage is part of. Every stage is also labelled (in order from W-E) with a letter. So, for example, the first stage in Section 4 would be 'Stage 4a', the next stage would be 'Stage 4b' and so on. Take a look at the detailed Itinerary Planner below and all should become clear.

The Itinerary Planner includes a range of tables outlining 18 suggested itineraries of 4, 5, 6, 7, 8, 9, 10, 11 and 12 days. We include itineraries for both E-W and W-E walkers. In each table, the maths have been done for you so there is no need for you to waste time (and mental strength!) working out daily distances, timings and height gain.

Of course, the suggested itineraries are only suggestions. You can shorten or lengthen your day in any number of ways to suit yourself: just decide how many stages you want to walk that day. It is up to you. As there is accommodation near the end of each stage, it is easy to design your own bespoke itinerary and adjust it on the ground as you go along.

For example, day 2 of the standard 9-day route involves walking Stages 2a, 2b and 2c. But you could decide to extend your day 2 by walking Stages 2a, 2b, 2c and 3a, all on the same day. Or you might be tired and decide to shorten your day by walking only Stages 2a and 2b. With some other guidebooks, you would have to work out how to split stages yourself, involving some complicated maths to plan distances and times going forward. This guide, however, does all the hard mental work for you.

In this book:

Timings indicate the approximate time required by a reasonably fit walker to complete a stage. They do not include stoppage time. Do not get frustrated if your own times do not match ours: everyone walks at different speeds. As you progress through the trek, you will soon learn how your own times compare with those given here and you will adjust your plans accordingly.

Walking distances are given in both miles and kilometres (km). One mile equates to approximately 1.6km.

Place names in brackets in the route descriptions indicate the direction to be followed on signposts. For example, "('Exton')" would mean that you follow a sign for Exton.

Ascent/descent numbers are the aggregate of all the altitude gain or loss (measured in feet and metres) on the uphill or downhill sections of a stage. As a rule of thumb, a fit walker climbs 1000 to 1300 feet (300 to 400m) in an hour. The ascent/descent data in the tables in the route descriptions is based on W-E itineraries: E-W walkers should simply swap the ascent and descent figures.

Elevation profiles are provided for each Section, indicating where the climbs and descents fall on the route. The profiles are based on W-E itineraries: E-W walkers should simply read them in reverse.

Spellings of place names are normally derived from the OS maps. However, there is sometimes disagreement over how places are spelt. Accordingly, you may notice different spellings elsewhere.

Real maps are included. These are extracts from 1:25,000 scale Explorer maps produced by Ordnance Survey, the mapping agency for GB. The maps are divided into 4cm grid squares: each square represents 1km x 1km. On the maps, we have marked the route of the trek, the start/finish points of stages, significant waypoints and WPs. Because there is accommodation near every start/finish point, we have not marked such accommodation specifically on the maps: however, any accommodation located mid-stage is clearly marked. On each map, N is at the top of the page.

The following abbreviations are used:

BCE	Before the Common Era (a secular alternative to 'BC')
CE	The Common Era (a secular alternative to 'AD')
GB	Great Britain
OR	Off-route
OS	Ordnance Survey
SDs	South Downs
SDNP	South Downs National Park
SDW	South Downs Way
WP	Water Point
WW2	World War 2
TL	Turn left
TR	Turn right
SH	Straight ahead
N, S, E and W, etc.	North, South, East and West, etc.
E-W	East to west; Eastbourne to Winchester
W-E	West to east; Winchester to Eastbourne

The northern escarpment overlooks the Weald

Itinerary Planner
West to East

Stage	Start	Time (hr)	Distance miles	Distance km	Ascent ft	Ascent m	Descent ft	Descent m
1a	Winchester	1:00	2.7	4.3	131	40	33	10
1b	Chilcomb	2:15	4.9	7.9	476	145	374	114
1c	Holden Farm Camping	0:45	1.5	2.4	197	60	33	10
1d	The Milbury's	1:30	3.9	6.3	164	50	492	150
2a	Exton	1:45	4.2	6.7	525	160	197	60
2b	Meon Springs	1:30	2.9	4.7	443	135	148	45
2c	Sustainability Centre	2:30	5.7	9.2	640	195	820	250
3a	Buriton/Petersfield exit	1:30	3.3	5.3	394	120	377	115
3b	South Harting exit	3:15	7.8	12.5	1116	340	1198	365
4a	Cocking	1:30	2.8	4.5	492	150	115	35
4b	Graffham exit	2:00	4.4	7.0	459	140	492	150
4c	Bignor/Sutton exit	1:30	3.7	5.9	98	30	820	250
4d	Bury exit	0:20	0.8	1.3	33	10	0	0
5a	Houghton Bridge	1:45	3.1	5.0	623	190	66	20
5b	Storrington exit	0:45	2.0	3.2	82	25	82	25
5c	Washington exit	2:00	4.2	6.8	459	140	640	195
6a	Steyning exit	1:00	2.8	4.5	0	0	525	160
6b	Upper Beeding exit	1:00	2.0	3.2	581	177	0	0
6c	Truleigh Hill	2:00	3.6	5.8	591	180	394	120
6d	Saddlescombe Farm	1:00	1.7	2.8	361	110	400	122
7a	Pyecombe	0:45	1.1	1.8	295	90	39	12
7b	Jack & Jill exit	0:45	1.5	2.4	312	95	49	15
7c	Ditchling Beacon	2:00	5.3	8.5	213	65	902	275
7d	Housedean Farm	1:15	2.4	3.8	541	165	98	30
7e	Kingston exit	1:30	3.7	6.0	66	20	656	200
8a	Rodmell exit	0:30	0.9	1.5	66	20	98	30
8b	YHA South Downs	1:45	3.8	6.1	722	220	148	45
8c	Firle Beacon	0:30	1.3	2.1	164	50	197	60
8d	Bostal Hill	0:45	1.9	3.0	131	40	722	220
9a	Alfriston	1:30	3.2	5.1	394	120	377	115
9b	Exceat	2:30	4.7	7.5	968	295	1181	360
9c	Belle Tout Lighthouse	1:45	3.2	5.1	607	185	525	160
Finish	Meads							

East to West

Stage	Start	Time (hr)	Distance miles	Distance km	Ascent ft	Ascent m	Descent ft	Descent m
9c	Meads	1:45	3.2	5.1	525	160	607	185
9b	Belle Tout Lighthouse	2:30	4.7	7.5	1181	360	968	295
9a	Exceat	1:30	3.2	5.1	377	115	394	120
8d	Alfriston	1:00	1.9	3.0	722	220	131	40
8c	Bostal Hill	0:30	1.3	2.1	197	60	164	50
8b	Firle Beacon	1:30	3.8	6.1	148	45	722	220
8a	YHA South Downs	0:30	0.9	1.5	98	30	66	20
7e	Rodmell exit	1:45	3.7	6.0	656	200	66	20
7d	Kingston exit	1:00	2.4	3.8	98	30	541	165
7c	Housedean Farm	2:30	5.3	8.5	902	275	213	65
7b	Ditchling Beacon	0:45	1.5	2.4	49	15	312	95
7a	Jack & Jill exit	0:45	1.1	1.8	39	12	295	90
6d	Pyecombe	1:00	1.7	2.8	400	122	361	110
6c	Saddlescombe Farm	2:00	3.6	5.8	394	120	591	180
6b	Truleigh Hill	0:45	2.0	3.2	0	0	581	177
6a	Upper Beeding exit	1:15	2.8	4.5	525	160	0	0
5c	Steyning exit	2:00	4.2	6.8	640	195	459	140
5b	Washington exit	0:45	2.0	3.2	82	25	82	25
5a	Storrington exit	1:45	3.1	5.0	66	20	623	190
4d	Houghton Bridge	0:20	0.8	1.3	0	0	33	10
4c	Bury exit	1:30	3.7	5.9	820	250	98	30
4b	Bignor/Sutton exit	2:00	4.4	7.0	492	150	459	140
4a	Graffham exit	1:15	2.8	4.5	115	35	492	150
3b	Cocking exit	3:15	7.8	12.5	1198	365	1116	340
3a	South Harting exit	1:30	3.3	5.3	377	115	394	120
2c	Buriton/Petersfield exit	2:30	5.7	9.2	820	250	640	195
2b	Sustainability Centre	1:15	2.9	4.7	148	45	443	135
2a	Meon Springs	1:45	4.2	6.7	197	60	525	160
1d	Exton	1:30	3.9	6.3	492	150	164	50
1c	The Milbury's	0:45	1.5	2.4	33	10	197	60
1b	Holden Farm Camping	2:15	4.9	7.9	374	114	476	145
1a	Chilcomb	1:00	2.7	4.3	33	10	131	40
Finish	Winchester							

Suggested Itineraries: West to East

12 Days (W-E)

Our most leisurely itinerary is perfect for those who want to relax and take their time. The final day is fairly long but it enables you to spend the previous night in Alfriston (a highlight of the SDW).

Day	Stages	Time (hr)	Distance miles	Distance km	Ascent ft	Ascent m	Descent ft	Descent m
1	1a, 1b	3:15	7.6	12.2	607	185	407	124
2	1c, 1d, 2a	4:00	9.6	15.4	886	270	722	220
3	2b, 2c	4:00	8.6	13.9	1083	330	968	295
4	3a, 3b	4:45	11.1	17.8	1509	460	1575	480
5	4a, 4b	3:30	7.1	11.5	951	290	607	185
6	4c, 4d, 5a	3:30	7.6	12.2	755	230	886	270
7	5b, 5c, 6a	3:45	9.0	14.5	541	165	1247	380
8	6b, 6c, 6d	4:00	7.3	11.8	1532	467	794	242
9	7a, 7b, 7c	3:30	7.9	12.7	820	250	991	302
10	7d, 7e, 8a	3:15	7.0	11.3	673	205	853	260
11	8b, 8c, 8d	3:00	7.0	11.2	1017	310	1066	325
12	9a, 9b, 9c	5:45	11.0	17.7	1969	600	2083	635

11 Days (W-E)

The last four days of the 10-day itinerary are spaced out into five days, making for a more relaxing second half of the trek. The final day is fairly long but it enables you to spend the previous night in Alfriston (a highlight of the SDW).

Day	Stages	Time (hr)	Distance miles	Distance km	Ascent ft	Ascent m	Descent ft	Descent m
1	1a, 1b, 1c	4:00	9.1	14.6	804	245	440	134
2	1d, 2a, 2b	4:45	11.0	17.7	1132	345	837	255
3	2c, 3a	4:00	9.0	14.5	1034	315	1198	365
4	3b, 4a	4:45	10.6	17.0	1608	490	1312	400
5	4b, 4c, 4d	3:45	8.8	14.2	591	180	1312	400
6	5a, 5b, 5c	4:30	9.3	15.0	1165	355	787	240
7	6a, 6b, 6c	4:00	8.4	13.5	1171	357	919	280
8	6d, 7a, 7b, 7c	4:30	9.6	15.5	1181	360	1391	424
9	7d, 7e, 8a	3:15	7.0	11.3	673	205	853	260
10	8b, 8c, 8d	3:00	7.0	11.2	1017	310	1066	325
11	9a, 9b, 9c	5:45	11.0	17.7	1969	600	2083	635

10 Days (W-E)

A more balanced itinerary than our standard 9-day plan. The route is more evenly divided up and the trek eases you in more gently. A few nightly stops are at less obvious locations but that is no bad thing.

Day	Stages	Time (hr)	Distance miles	Distance km	Ascent ft	Ascent m	Descent ft	Descent m
1	1a, 1b, 1c	4:00	9.1	14.6	804	245	440	134
2	1d, 2a, 2b	4:45	11.0	17.7	1132	345	837	255
3	2c, 3a	4:00	9.0	14.5	1034	315	1198	365
4	3b, 4a	4:45	10.6	17.0	1608	490	1312	400
5	4b, 4c, 4d	3:45	8.8	14.2	591	180	1312	400
6	5a, 5b, 5c	4:30	9.3	15.0	1165	355	787	240
7	6a, 6b, 6c, 6d, 7a	5:45	11.2	18.1	1828	557	1358	414
8	7b, 7c, 7d, 7e	5:30	12.9	20.7	1132	345	1706	520
9	8a, 8b, 8c, 8d	3:30	7.9	12.7	1083	330	1165	355
10	9a, 9b, 9c	5:45	11.0	17.7	1969	600	2083	635

9 Days (W-E)

This is our standard schedule which is popular with many walkers because the nightly stops are at some of the loveliest villages on the SDW (usually with a pub or two and a variety of places to stay). However, because the emphasis is on finding the best places to stay, the itinerary is not always evenly balanced: days 1 and 2 are longer than the subsequent four and day 7 is much longer than the final two days.

Day	Stages	Time (hr)	Distance miles	Distance km	Ascent ft	Ascent m	Descent ft	Descent m
1	1a, 1b, 1c, 1d	5:30	13.0	20.9	968	295	932	284
2	2a, 2b, 2c	5:45	12.8	20.6	1608	490	1165	355
3	3a, 3b	4:45	11.1	17.8	1509	460	1575	480
4	4a, 4b, 4c, 4d	5:15	11.6	18.7	1083	330	1427	435
5	5a, 5b, 5c	4:30	9.3	15.0	1165	355	787	240
6	6a, 6b, 6c, 6d	5:00	10.1	16.3	1532	467	1319	402
7	7a, 7b, 7c, 7d, 7e	6:15	14.0	22.5	1427	435	1745	532
8	8a, 8b, 8c, 8d	3:30	7.9	12.7	1083	330	1165	355
9	9a, 9b, 9c	5:45	11.0	17.7	1969	600	2083	635

Iron Age hill-fort on Old Winchester Hill (Stage 2a)

8 Days (W-E)

Days 5 to 8 of the 9-day itinerary are squeezed into three longer days.

Day	Stages	Time (hr)	Distance miles	Distance km	Ascent ft	Ascent m	Descent ft	Descent m
1	1a, 1b, 1c, 1d	5:30	13.0	20.9	968	295	932	284
2	2a, 2b, 2c	5:45	12.8	20.6	1608	490	1165	355
3	3a, 3b	4:45	11.1	17.8	1509	460	1575	480
4	4a, 4b, 4c, 4d	5:15	11.6	18.7	1083	330	1427	435
5	5a, 5b, 5c, 6a, 6b	6:30	14.1	22.7	1745	532	1312	400
6	6c, 6d, 7a, 7b, 7c	6:30	13.2	21.3	1772	540	1785	544
7	7d, 7e, 8a, 8b, 8c, 8d	6:15	14.0	22.5	1690	515	1919	585
8	9a, 9b, 9c	5:45	11.0	17.7	1969	600	2083	635

7 Days (W-E)

For fit hikers. Every day is long except for the final one which is deliberately shorter: this enables you to take your time along the cliffs of the Seven Sisters and to spend the night in Alfriston (both highlights of the SDW).

Day	Stages	Time (hr)	Distance miles	Distance km	Ascent ft	Ascent m	Descent ft	Descent m
1	1a, 1b, 1c, 1d	5:30	13.0	20.9	968	295	932	284
2	2a, 2b, 2c, 3a	7:15	16.1	25.9	2001	610	1542	470
3	3b, 4a, 4b	6:45	14.9	24.0	2067	630	1805	550
4	4c, 4d, 5a, 5b, 5c, 6a	7:15	16.6	26.7	1296	395	2133	650
5	6b, 6c, 6d, 7a, 7b, 7c	7:30	15.2	24.5	2352	717	1785	544
6	7d, 7e, 8a, 8b, 8c, 8d	6:15	14.0	22.5	1690	515	1919	585
7	9a, 9b, 9c	5:45	11.0	17.7	1969	600	2083	635

The SDW is extremely well marked (Stage v9)

6 Days (W-E)

For very fit and experienced hikers who like to move quickly. Every day is long.

Day	Stages	Time (hr)	Distance miles	Distance km	Ascent ft	Ascent m	Descent ft	Descent m
1	1a, 1b, 1c, 1d, 2a	7:15	17.1	27.6	1493	455	1129	344
2	2b, 2c, 3a, 3b	8:45	19.7	31.7	2592	790	2543	775
3	4a, 4b, 4c, 4d, 5a, 5b	7:45	16.7	26.9	1788	545	1575	480
4	5c, 6a, 6b, 6c, 6d	7:00	14.4	23.1	1992	607	1959	597
5	7a, 7b, 7c, 7d, 7e, 8a	6:45	14.9	24.0	1493	455	1844	562
6	8b, 8c, 8d, 9a, 9b, 9c	8:45	18.0	28.9	2986	910	3150	960

5 Days (W-E)

A tough itinerary for fit and experienced walkers and runners. The times are based on walking speeds (to enable accurate comparison with the other itineraries) so runners will need to adjust them accordingly.

Day	Stages	Time (hr)	Distance miles	Distance km	Ascent ft	Ascent m	Descent ft	Descent m
1	1a, 1b, 1c, 1d, 2a, 2b	8:45	20.0	32.2	1936	590	1276	389
2	2c, 3a, 3b, 4a	8:45	19.6	31.5	2641	805	2510	765
3	4b, 4c, 4d, 5a, 5b, 5c, 6a	9:15	20.9	33.7	1755	535	2625	800
4	6b, 6c, 6d, 7a, 7b, 7c, 7d, 7e	10:15	21.3	34.3	2959	902	2539	774
5	8a, 8b, 8c, 8d, 9a, 9b, 9c	9:15	18.9	30.4	3051	930	3248	990

4 Days (W-E)

A very demanding itinerary for experienced long-distance runners. The times are based on walking speeds (to enable accurate comparison with the other itineraries) so runners will need to adjust them accordingly.

Day	Stages	Time (hr)	Distance miles	Distance km	Ascent ft	Ascent m	Descent ft	Descent m
1	1a, 1b, 1c, 1d, 2a, 2b, 2c	11:15	25.7	41.4	2576	785	2097	639
2	3a, 3b, 4a, 4b, 4c, 4d, 5a	11:45	25.8	41.5	3215	980	3068	935
3	5b, 5c, 6a, 6b, 6c, 6d, 7a, 7b, 7c,	11:15	24.2	39.0	2894	882	3032	924
4	7d, 7e, 8a, 8b, 8c, 8d, 9a, 9b, 9c	12:00	25.0	40.2	3658	1115	4003	1220

Suggested Itineraries: East to West

12 Days (E-W)

Our most leisurely itinerary is perfect for those who want to relax and take their time. Day 1 is very short but it enables you to stay at the historic Belle Tout Lighthouse which has an exquisite location on the edge of the white cliffs.

Day	Stages	Time (hr)	Distance miles	Distance km	Ascent ft	Ascent m	Descent ft	Descent m
1	9c	1:45	3.2	5.1	525	160	607	185
2	9b, 9a	4:00	7.8	12.6	1558	475	1362	415
3	8d, 8c, 8b, 8a	3:30	7.9	12.7	1165	355	1083	330
4	7e, 7d, 7c	5:15	11.4	18.3	1657	505	820	250
5	7b, 7a, 6d, 6c	4:30	8.0	12.8	883	269	1558	475
6	6b, 6a, 5c	4:00	9.0	14.5	1165	355	1040	317
7	5b, 5a, 4d, 4c	4:15	9.6	15.4	968	295	837	255
8	4b, 4a	3:15	7.1	11.5	607	185	951	290
9	3b	3:15	7.8	12.5	1198	365	1116	340
10	3a, 2c	4:00	9.0	14.5	1198	365	1034	315
11	2b, 2a, 1d	4:30	11.0	17.7	837	255	1132	345
12	1c, 1b, 1a	4:00	9.1	14.6	440	134	804	245

11 Days (E-W)

Identical to the 12-day itinerary except that the first two days are combined into one day. It is a tough start to the trek but it enables you to spend the night in Alfriston (a highlight of the SDW).

Day	Stages	Time (hr)	Distance miles	Distance km	Ascent ft	Ascent m	Descent ft	Descent m
1	9c, 9b, 9a	5:45	11.0	17.7	2083	635	1969	600
2	8d, 8c, 8b, 8a	3:30	7.9	12.7	1165	355	1083	330
3	7e, 7d, 7c	5:15	11.4	18.3	1657	505	820	250
4	7b, 7a, 6d, 6c	4:30	8.0	12.8	883	269	1558	475
5	6b, 6a, 5c	4:00	9.0	14.5	1165	355	1040	317
6	5b, 5a, 4d, 4c	4:15	9.6	15.4	968	295	837	255
7	4b, 4a	3:15	7.1	11.5	607	185	951	290
8	3b	3:15	7.8	12.5	1198	365	1116	340
9	3a, 2c	4:00	9.0	14.5	1198	365	1034	315
10	2b, 2a, 1d	4:30	11.0	17.7	837	255	1132	345
11	1c, 1b, 1a	4:00	9.1	14.6	440	134	804	245

10 Days (E-W)

This is a more balanced itinerary than our standard 9-day plan because the route is more evenly divided up. A few nightly stops are at less obvious locations but that is no bad thing. The first stage is fairly hard but that cannot be avoided if you wish to spend the night at Alfriston (which is a highlight of the SDW).

Day	Stages	Time (hr)	Distance miles	Distance km	Ascent ft	Ascent m	Descent ft	Descent m
1	9c, 9b, 9a	5:45	11.0	17.7	2083	635	1969	600
2	8d, 8c, 8b, 8a	3:30	7.9	12.7	1165	355	1083	330
3	7e, 7d, 7c	5:15	11.4	18.3	1657	505	820	250
4	7b, 7a, 6d, 6c	4:30	8.0	12.8	883	269	1558	475
5	6b, 6a, 5c, 5b	4:45	11.0	17.7	1247	380	1122	342
6	5a, 4d, 4c, 4b	5:30	11.9	19.2	1378	420	1214	370
7	4a, 3b	4:30	10.6	17.0	1312	400	1608	490
8	3a, 2c	4:00	9.0	14.5	1198	365	1034	315
9	2b, 2a, 1d	4:30	11.0	17.7	837	255	1132	345
10	1c, 1b, 1a	4:00	9.1	14.6	440	134	804	245

9 Days (E-W)

This is our standard schedule which is popular with many walkers because the nightly stops are at some of the loveliest villages on the SDW (usually with a pub or two and a variety of places to stay). However, because the emphasis is on finding the best places to stay, the itinerary is not always evenly balanced: day 3, for example, is very long.

Day	Stages	Time (hr)	Distance miles	Distance km	Ascent ft	Ascent m	Descent ft	Descent m
1	9c, 9b, 9a	5:45	11.0	17.7	2083	635	1969	600
2	8d, 8c, 8b, 8a	3:30	7.9	12.7	1165	355	1083	330
3	7e, 7d, 7c, 7b, 7a	6:45	14.0	22.5	1745	532	1427	435
4	6d, 6c, 6b, 6a	5:00	10.1	16.3	1319	402	1532	467
5	5c, 5b, 5a	4:30	9.3	15.0	787	240	1165	355
6	4d, 4c, 4b, 4a	5:00	11.6	18.7	1427	435	1083	330
7	3b, 3a	4:45	11.1	17.8	1575	480	1509	460
8	2c, 2b, 2a	5:30	12.8	20.6	1165	355	1608	490
9	1d, 1c, 1b, 1a	5:30	13.0	20.9	932	284	968	295

8 Days (E-W)

Days 2 to 7 of the 9-day itinerary are squeezed into five days. Days 2, 4 and 6 are fairly long.

Day	Stages	Time (hr)	Distance miles	Distance km	Ascent ft	Ascent m	Descent ft	Descent m
1	9c, 9b, 9a	5:45	11.0	17.7	2083	635	1969	600
2	8d, 8c, 8b, 8a, 7e, 7d	6:15	14.0	22.5	1919	585	1690	515
3	7c, 7b, 7a, 6d	5:00	9.6	15.5	1391	424	1181	360
4	6c, 6b, 6a, 5c, 5b	6:45	14.6	23.5	1641	500	1713	522
5	5a, 4d, 4c, 4b	5:30	11.9	19.2	1378	420	1214	370
6	4a, 3b, 3a	6:00	13.9	22.3	1690	515	2001	610
7	2c, 2b, 2a	5:30	12.8	20.6	1165	355	1608	490
8	1d, 1c, 1b, 1a	5:30	13.0	20.9	932	284	968	295

7 Days (E-W)

For fit hikers. The first day is one of the shortest allowing you time to warm up before the more difficult stages ahead. This also enables you to take your time along the cliffs of the Seven Sisters and to spend the night in Alfriston (both highlights of the SDW).

Day	Stages	Time (hr)	Distance miles	Distance km	Ascent ft	Ascent m	Descent ft	Descent m
1	9c, 9b, 9a	5:45	11.0	17.7	2083	635	1969	600
2	8d, 8c, 8b, 8a, 7e, 7d	6:15	14.0	22.5	1919	585	1690	515
3	7c, 7b, 7a, 6d, 6c, 6b	7:45	15.2	24.5	1785	544	2352	717
4	6a, 5c, 5b, 5a, 4d, 4c	7:30	16.6	26.7	2133	650	1296	395
5	4b, 4a, 3b	6:30	14.9	24.0	1805	550	2067	630
6	3a, 2c, 2b, 2a	7:00	16.1	25.9	1542	470	2001	610
7	1d, 1c, 1b, 1a	5:30	13.0	20.9	932	284	968	295

The exquisite Cuckmere Valley (Stage 9b)

6 Days (E-W)

For very fit and experienced hikers who like to move quickly. Every day is long, however, the first day is comparatively shorter, allowing time to warm up before the harder stages.

Day	Stages	Time (hr)	Distance miles	Distance km	Ascent ft	Ascent m	Descent ft	Descent m
1	9c, 9b, 9a	5:45	11.0	17.7	2083	635	1969	600
2	8d, 8c, 8b, 8a, 7e, 7d, 7c	8:45	19.3	31.0	2822	860	1903	580
3	7b, 7a, 6d, 6c, 6b, 6a, 5c	8:30	17.0	27.3	2047	624	2599	792
4	5b, 5a, 4d, 4c, 4b, 4a	7:30	16.7	26.9	1575	480	1788	545
5	3b, 3a, 2c, 2b	8:30	19.7	31.7	2543	775	2592	790
6	2a, 1d, 1c, 1b, 1a	7:15	17.1	27.6	1129	344	1493	455

5 Days (E-W)

A tough itinerary for fit and experienced walkers and runners. The times are based on walking speeds (to enable accurate comparison with the other itineraries) so runners will need to adjust them accordingly.

Day	Stages	Time (hr)	Distance miles	Distance km	Ascent ft	Ascent m	Descent ft	Descent m
1	9c, 9b, 9a, 8d, 8c, 8b	8:45	18.0	28.9	3150	960	2986	910
2	8a, 7e, 7d, 7c, 7b, 7a, 6d	8:15	16.7	26.8	2244	684	1854	565
3	6c, 6b, 6a, 5c, 5b, 5a, 4d, 4c	10:15	22.2	35.7	2526	770	2467	752
4	4b, 4a, 3b, 3a, 2c	10:30	23.9	38.5	3002	915	3101	945
5	2b, 2a, 1d, 1c, 1b, 1a	8:30	20.0	32.2	1276	389	1936	590

4 Days (E-W)

A very demanding itinerary for experienced long-distance runners. The times are based on walking speeds (to enable accurate comparison with the other itineraries) so runners will need to adjust them accordingly.

Day	Stages	Time (hr)	Distance miles	Distance km	Ascent ft	Ascent m	Descent ft	Descent m
1	9c, 9b, 9a, 8d, 8c, 8b, 8a, 7e	11:00	22.6	36.4	3904	1190	3117	950
2	7d, 7c, 7b, 7a, 6d, 6c, 6b, 6a, 5c	12:00	24.6	39.6	3048	929	3353	1022
3	5b, 5a, 4d, 4c, 4b, 4a, 3b	10:45	24.5	39.4	2772	845	2904	885
4	3a, 2c, 2b, 2a, 1d, 1c, 1b, 1a	12:30	29.0	46.7	2474	754	2969	905

Accommodation

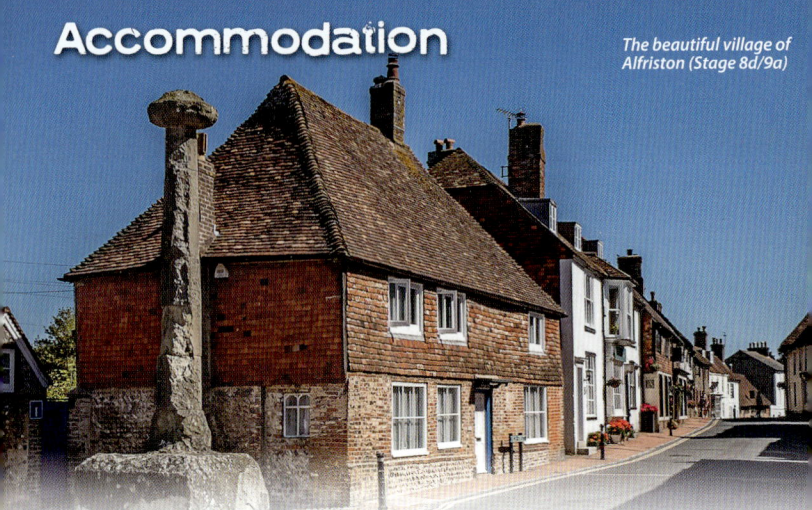

The beautiful village of Alfriston (Stage 8d/9a)

The SDW is a popular trek and there is a wide range of accommodation including 'bed and breakfasts', pubs, hotels, hostels and a few bunkhouses/camping barns. Detailed accommodation listings are provided on pages 24 to 34: there are so many places to stay in the SDs that it is not possible to list all of them. All contact details were correct at the date of press but be aware that this information frequently changes. Please let us know about any changes you notice. For camping, see page 22.

Although there is plenty of accommodation, relatively little of it actually lies on the SDW itself. Frequently, you will have to descend off the high ground of the northern escarpment to seek a bed in the villages just below. Bear in mind that the extra time and distance required to travel to accommodation away from the actual route of the SDW is excluded from the statistics for each stage in the Itinerary Planner: depending upon where you plan to stay, you will need to allow for this extra time and effort when planning. And do not forget that if you descend to the low ground in the evening, you will have to climb back up again the next morning.

These days, most people have their entire trip booked before they depart. The rise in the number of companies offering unguided trips means that an increasing number of SDW beds are block-booked months in advance. This makes it harder for the independent trekker to secure the best accommodation unless booked well in advance.

In July/August and during public holidays, the trail is very busy and forward booking is normally essential. You might get lucky and be able to cobble together a set of bookings at the last minute but you are unlikely to get 'first-choice' accommodation right next to the trail.

Even outside of July/August, it is wise to book ahead, particularly at weekends and on stages where there is only one place to stay. That said, in April, May, June, September and October, it is still perfectly possible for the independent trekker to secure last-minute bookings, particularly if you are flexible with dates and places and are prepared to stay in towns/villages a short distance OR. The accommodation right next to the SDW books up most quickly. As you move further away from the trail, bookings are often easier to secure. Some places will be willing to pick you up from the trail and leave you back the next morning: check when booking. Alternatively, there are many local taxi companies who will pick you up for a very reasonable price: see 'Public Transport along the SDW'.

In April (excluding Easter) and October, fewer people walk the route so there is less demand for accommodation. Before April, and from November onwards, some accommodation may be closed so check in advance. For more booking tips, see page 34.

Bed & Breakfasts (B&Bs): these form the back-bone of SDW accommodation. Traditionally, they were private homes which offered rooms and breakfast to visitors. Nowadays, however, you find many bigger and more professionally run properties. Bed and breakfast normally cost £35-70 per person sharing a double/twin room. Rates for solo travellers are usually higher because they pay a single occupancy rate. Normally, the ensuite bedrooms are basic but clean and comfortable. 'Full English' breakfast is the norm: a large helping of bacon, sausage, eggs, mushrooms and black pudding. Most do not provide evening meals but the owner should be able to recommend a local pub or restaurant. Most B&Bs have their own websites and many list their rooms on the generic travel booking sites such as expedia.com or booking.com.

Pubs & Inns: most villages have a pub and many of them offer bed and breakfast accommodation. This normally costs £35-70 per person sharing a double/twin room. Rates for solo travellers are usually higher because they pay a single occupancy rate. Evening meals are usually available and the standard of food these days is fairly high. Most of the pubs serve a selection of the excellent cask ales for which England is famous: for some, this is a highlight of the SDW. Most pubs have their own websites.

Hotels: the hotels on offer range from basic ones to more luxury properties. Prices vary widely. They all provide 'Full English' breakfast and most also offer evening meals. Most hotels have their own websites and many list their rooms on the generic travel booking sites such as expedia.com or booking.com.

Hostels: these offer beds in dormitories and sometimes private rooms. Generally, they will have shared bathrooms, self-catering kitchen facilities and communal areas. Continental breakfast (tea and toast) is sometimes available. Bedding is usually supplied. Like B&Bs, hostels are becoming more upmarket and prices rise along with the quality of the offering. A bed usually costs £20-30 per person. Groups of two or more may find B&Bs to be better value.

Bunkhouses & camping barns: these are dormitories at farms, country houses or hotels. Quality varies and often the accommodation is very basic: you will usually need to bring your own sleeping bag. Sometimes there will be showers and self-catering facilities. Prices are low. There are only a few bunkhouses/camping barns on the SDW.

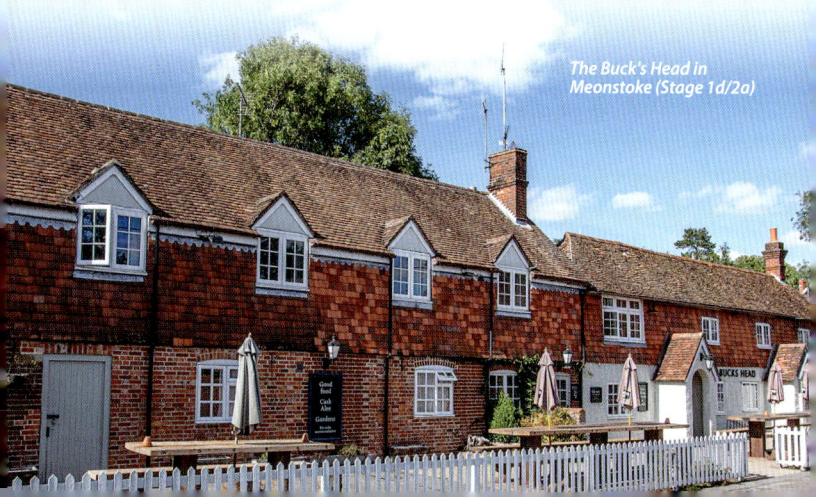

The Buck's Head in Meonstoke (Stage 1d/2a)

Camping

The campsite at Meon Springs (Stage 2a/2b)

Camping is the cheapest way to hike the SDW: a pitch each night costs £7-20 per person. It also usually offers more freedom because campsites rarely need to be booked far in advance (except during July/August and public holiday weekends) and you can often adjust your itinerary as you go. Wild camping is not permitted on the SDW so campers must stay in the privately-owned campsites along the route. There are campsites on most parts of the trail, however, there are none E of Alfriston. Furthermore, there are none on Section 3 except for Manor Farm at the E end of it. To help campers plan, a list of campsites is set out below: contact details and information on the facilities are set out in the full Accommodation Listings (see pages 24 to 34).

Normally campsites are clean and well-maintained. Frequently, they are part of a farm and can be some of the loveliest places to spend the night. Showers are normally provided but you may pay a little extra for this luxury. Even if you have booked in advance, it is always sensible to telephone at least a day or two before so the campsite knows when to expect you.

The obvious downside to camping is that you need to carry a lot more gear: tents, sleeping mats, sleeping bags and stoves all add weight to your pack, making the trek more difficult. In the 'Equipment' section, we provide advice on how to lighten your load. However, another solution is to use a baggage transfer service to transfer your heavy bags between campsites (see 'Baggage transfer').

Stage	Campsite
1b Morn Hill (1.4 miles OR)	Morn Hill Caravan Club Site
1b/1c	Holden Farm Camping
1d Kilmeston (1.4 miles OR)	College Down Farm
1d/2a Corhampton (1.3 miles OR)	Corhampton Lane Farm B&B
2a/2b	Meon Springs

Stage	Campsite
2b/2c East Meon (1.4 miles OR)	Meonside Camping
2b/2c	The Sustainability Centre
2c (0.8 miles OR)	Upper Parsonage Farm
3b/4a Cocking	Manor Farm
4a East Dean (1.6 miles OR)	Newhouse Farm Camping
4a/4b Graffham (2.5 miles OR)	Graffham Camping & Caravanning Site
Stage 4b (0.9 miles OR)	Gumber Camping Barn & Campsite
Stage 4b/4c Bignor (1.2 miles OR)	Bignor Farms Camping (at Bignor Roman Villa)
4d/5a Houghton Bridge	Foxleigh Barn
5b/5c (1 mile OR)	Swipes Farm
5b/5c Washington (1.6 miles OR)	Washington Park
5c/6a (0.7 miles OR)	White House Caravan Site
6b/6c	Truleigh Hill YHA
6c/6d Newtimber Hill	Saddlescombe Farm
6d/7a Pyecombe	Chantry Farm
7b (1.4 miles OR)	Southdown Way Caravan & Camping Park
7b (0.7 miles OR)	Ditchling Camp
7c Streat (1.3 miles OR)	Blackberry Wood
7c/7d	Housedean Farm Campsite
8a/8b Southease	YHA South Downs
8b/8c Firle (1.5 miles OR)	Firle Camp
8d/9a Alfriston	Alfriston Camping Park

Accommodation Listings

- 🛏 Dormitory/Bunkhouse
- 🔒 Private Room
- ⛺ Camping
- 🍷 Drinks
- 🍔 Lunch
- 🍴 Evening Meals
- 🥐 Breakfast
- 🛒 Food shop
- 📶 WiFi
- **OR** Off-route

Stage	Name	Facilities	Contact Details
1a Winchester	The Black Hole B&B	🔒 📶 🥐	01962 807 010 Reservations@theblackholebb.co.uk www.theblackholebb.co.uk
1a Winchester	Wolvesey View B&B	🔒 📶 🥐	07984 612614 johnh@wintonian.co.uk
1a Winchester	St John's Croft B&B	🔒 📶 🥐	07734 888 934/01962 859 976 dottyfraser@gmail.com www.st-johns-croft.co.uk
1a Winchester	Magdalen House B&B	🔒 📶 🥐	01962 869 634 liz@magdalen-house.co.uk www.magdalen-house.co.uk
1a Winchester	Cathedral Cottage B&B	🔒 📶 🥐	01962 878 975 christine@ cathedralcottagebandb.co.uk www.cathedralcottagebandb.co.uk
1a Winchester	The Westgate Pub	🔒 📶 🍷 🥐 🍔 🍴	01962 820 222 info@westgatewinchester.com www.westgatewinchester.com
1a Winchester	The Wykeham Arms	🔒 📶 🍷 🥐 🍔 🍴	01962 853 834 wykehamarms@fullers.co.uk www.wykehamarmswinchester.co.uk
1a Winchester	Mercure Winchester Wessex Hotel	🔒 📶 🍷 🥐 🍔 🍴	01962 861 611 H6619@accor.com www.all.accor.com
1a Winchester	Winchester Royal Hotel	🔒 📶 🍷 🥐 🍔 🍴	0330 102 7242 reception@winchesterroyalhotel.com www.winchesterroyalhotel.com

Stage	Name	Facilities	Contact Details
1a Winchester	Hotel du Vin	🔐 📶 🍸 🥧 🍔 🍴	0330 016 0390 theteam@hotelduvin.com www.hotelduvin.com
1a Winchester	The Old Vine	🔐 📶 🍸 🥧 🍔 🍴	01962 854 616 reservations@oldvinewinchester.com www.oldvinewinchester.com
1a Winchester	Travelodge Winchester	🔐 📶 🍸 🥧 🍔 🍴	08719 846 552 www.travelodge.co.uk
1a Winchester	Premier Inn Winchester Hotel	🔐 📶 🍸 🥧 🍔 🍴	0333 321 9308 www.premierinn.com
1a/1b Chilcomb	Complyns B&B	🔐 📶 🥧	01962 861 600/07890 447 982 stay@complyns.co.uk www.complyns.co.uk
1b Morn Hill (1.4 miles OR)	Morn Hill Caravan Club Site	⛺ 📶	01962 869 877 www.caravanclub.co.uk
1b Morn Hill (1.4 miles OR)	Holiday Inn Winchester	🔐 📶 🍸 🥧 🍔 🍴	01962 670 700 info@hiwinchester.co.uk www.ihg.com
1b Cheriton (1.5 miles OR)	The Brick House B&B	🔐 📶 🥧	07908 757 255/01962 771 334 mark@brickhousecheriton.co.uk www.brickhousecheriton.co.uk
1b/1c	Holden Farm Camping	⛺	07599 553 740 camping@holdenfarm.co.uk www.holdenfarm.co.uk
1c Shorley (1.5 miles OR)	Shorley Wood B&B	🔐 📶 🥧	01962 771 831 info@shorleywood.co.uk www.shorleywood.co.uk
1c/1d	The Milbury's	🔐 📶 🍸 🥧 🍔 🍴	01962 771 248 www.themilburyspub.synthasite.com
1d Kilmeston (1.4 miles OR)	Dean Farm B&B	🔐 📶 🥧	07786 921 208/07786 921 208 warrdeanfarm@gmail.com www.warrdeanfarm.co.uk
1d Kilmeston (1.4 miles OR)	College Down Farm	🔐 ⛺	01962 771 345 marjorie@collegedownfarm.co.uk www.collegedownfarm.co.uk
1d/2a Exton	Exton B&B Manor House	🔐 📶 🥧	01489 877 529 manorhouseexton@gmail.com www.extonbedandbreakfast.com
1d/2a Exton	Crossways B&B	🔐 📶 🥧	01489 878 545 crosswaysbb@hotmail.com www.crosswaysb.com

Stage	Name	Facilities	Contact Details
1d/2a Meonstoke (0.6 miles OR)	The Buck's Head	🔒 📶 🍷 🥐 🍔 🍴	01489 877 313 info@thebucksheadmeonstoke.co.uk www.thebucksheadmeonstoke.co.uk
1d/2a Corhampton (1.3 miles OR)	Corhampton Lane Farm B&B	🔒 ⛺ 📶 🥐 Pick-up from Exton	01489 878 755 info@corhamptonlanefarm.co.uk www.corhamptonlanefarm.co.uk
2a/2b	Meon Springs	⛺	01730 823 134 admin@meonsprings.com www.meonsprings.com
2b Coombe (0.4 miles OR)	The Bed in the Shed B&B	🔒 📶 🥐	01730 823 541/07760 178 099 cmathews@talk21.com www.southdownsbnb.com
2b East Meon (1 mile OR)	Ye Olde George Inn	🔒 📶 🍷 🥐 🍔 🍴	01730 823 481 info@yeoldegeorgeinn.net www.yeoldegeorgeinn.net
2b/2c East Meon (1.4 miles OR)	Meonside Camping	⛺ 🍷 🥐	meonsidecamping@outlook.com meonsidecamping.weebly.com
2b/2c East Meon (1.9 miles OR)	The Long House B&B	🔒 📶 🥐	01730 823 239/07889 640 353 mgreenwood@btinternet.com www.thelonghouseeastmeon.co.uk
2b/2c	The Sustainability Centre	🔒 ⛺ 📶 🥐 🍔	01730 823 549 accommodation@ sustainability-centre.org www.sustainability-centre.org
2c (0.8 miles OR)	Upper Parsonage Farm	🔒 ⛺ 📶 🥐	01730 823 490 info@upperparsonagefarm.co.uk www.upperparsonagefarm.co.uk
2c (1 mile OR)	The Hampshire Hog	🔒 📶 🍷 🥐 🍔 🍴	023 9259 1083 hampshirehog@fullers.co.uk www.thehampshirehog.com
2c/3a Buriton (0.5 mile OR)	The Village Inn	🔒 📶 🍷 🥐 🍔 🍴	01730 233 440 thevillageinnburiton@gmail.com www.villageinnburiton.co.uk
2c/3a Buriton (0.5 mile OR)	The Five Bells	🔒 📶 🍷 🥐 🍔 🍴	01730 263 584 www.fivebells-buriton.co.uk
2c/3a Nursted (1.8 miles OR)	Nursted Farm B&B	🔒 📶 🥐	01730 264 278 Elaine.Bray@btconnect.com www.nurstedfarm.co.uk
2c/3a Petersfield (2.8 miles OR)	The Causeway Guest House	🔒 📶 🥐	01730 262 924 www.petersfieldbedandbreakfast.co.uk

Stage	Name	Facilities	Contact Details
2c/3a Petersfield (2.8 miles OR)	The Old Drum	🔐 📶 🍷 ☕ 🍔	01730 300 208 info@theolddrum.com www.theolddrum.com
2c/3a Petersfield (2.8 miles OR)	Rushes Road B&B	🔐 📶 ☕	01730 261 638/07710 460 159 collinstudor@waitrose.com www.rushes-road.co.uk
2c/3a Petersfield (2.8 miles OR)	South Downs B&B	🔐 📶 ☕	01730 263 750 reservations@ southdownsbandb.co.uk www.southdownsbandb.co.uk
2c/3a Petersfield (2.8 miles OR)	The Good Intent Pub	🔐 📶 🍷 ☕ 🍔 🍴	01730 263 838 info@thefriendlyfox.co.uk www.good-intent-petersfield.co.uk
2c/3a Petersfield (2.8 miles OR)	1 The Spain B&B	🔐 📶 ☕	01730 263 261 www.1-the-spain-bb.business.site
3a (1.1 miles OR)	Copper Beeches B&B	🔐 ☕	01730 826 662/07976 234 030 www.copperbeeches.net
3a/3b South Harting (0.6 miles OR)	The White Hart	🔐 📶 🍷 ☕ 🍔 🍴	01730 825 124 info@the-whitehart.co.uk www.the-whitehart.co.uk
3a/3b South Harting (0.6 miles OR)	South Gardens Cottage	🔐 📶 ☕	01730 825 040 julia@randjholmes.plus.com
3a/3b South Harting (0.6 miles OR)	Shotgun Cottage	🔐 📶 ☕	01730 826 878 qejoy@icloud.com
3b/4a Cocking	Manor Farm	🔐 ⛺ 📶 ☕ 🛒	01730 814 156 info@manorfarmcocking.co.uk www.manorfarmcocking.co.uk
3b/4a Cocking (0.8 mile OR)	Moonlight Cottage B&B	🔐 📶 ☕	01730 813 336 moonlightcottage@gmail.com www.moonlightcottage.co.uk
3b/4a Cocking (0.8 mile OR)	The Blue Bell	🔐 📶 🍷 ☕ 🍔 🍴	01730 239 669 info@thebluebellatcocking.co.uk www.thebluebellatcocking.co.uk
3b/4a Cocking (0.8 mile OR)	Hyesett House B&B	🔐 ☕	07799 674 075 www.hyesetthousebb.co.uk
3b/4a Cocking (0.8 mile OR)	Downsfold B&B	🔐 📶 ☕	01730 814 376 b&b@downsfold.co.uk www.downsfold.co.uk

Stage	Name	Facilities	Contact Details
4a East Dean (1.6 miles OR)	Newhouse Farm Camping	▲	01243 811 685 nhfcamping@gmail.com
4a/4b Graffham (1.3 miles OR)	The Foresters Arms	🔒 📶 🍷 🥧 🍔 🍴	01798 867 386 info@forestersarms-pub.co.uk www.forestersarms-pub.co.uk
4a/4b Graffham (1.3 miles OR)	The White Horse	🔒 📶 🍷 🥧 🍔 🍴	01798 867 331 info@whitehorsegraffham.com www.whitehorsegraffham.com
4a/4b Graffham (1.3 miles OR)	Brook Barn B&B	🔒 📶 🥧	01798 867 356/07947 003 441 www.brookbarn-graffham.co.uk
4a/4b Graffham (2.5 miles OR)	Graffham Camping & Caravanning Site	▲ 📶	01798 867 476 campingandcaravanningclub.co.uk
Stage 4b/4c (0.9 miles OR)	Gumber Camping Barn & Campsite	🛏 ▲	01243 814 484 gumberbothy@nationaltrust.org.uk www.nationaltrust.org.uk
Stage 4b/4c Bignor (1.2 miles OR)	Bignor Farms Camping (at Bignor Roman Villa)	▲ 🍔 🛒 Groceries available to order	01798 869 259 enquiries@bignorromanvilla.co.uk www.bignorromanvilla.co.uk
Stage 4b/4c Bignor (1.2 miles OR)	Stane House B&B	🔒 📶 🥧	01798 869 454 stanehouse@gmail.com www.stanehouse.co.uk
Stage 4b/4c Sutton (1.7 miles OR)	The White Horse	🔒 📶 🍷 🥧 🍔 🍴	01798 869 191 info@whitehorseinn-sutton.co.uk www.whitehorseinn-sutton.co.uk
4c/4d Bury (1.1 miles OR)	Harkaway Guest House	🔒 📶 🥧	01798 831 843/07825 068113 carol@harkaway.org.uk www.harkaway.org.uk
4c/4d Houghton (0.3 miles OR)	South Downs Bunkhouse	🛏	01798 831 100/07710 630 219 kate@southdownsbunkhouse.co.uk www.southdownsbunkhouse.co.uk
4c/4d Houghton (0.3 miles OR)	Arun Valley B&B	🔒 📶 🥧	01798 831 142 kate@arunvalleybandb.co.uk www.arunvalleybandb.co.uk
4c/4d Houghton (0.3 miles OR)	A Barn	🔒 📶 🥧	01798 839 256/07947 108 825 info@southdownsstay.co.uk www.southdownsstay.co.uk
4d/5a Houghton Bridge	Foxleigh Barn	▲ 🔒	01798 839 113 pete@foxleighbarn.co.uk

Stage	Name	Facilities	Contact Details
4d/5a Amberley (0.4 miles OR)	The Black Horse	🔒 📶 🍷 ◐ 🍔 🍴	01798 831 183 manager@amberleyblackhorse.co.uk www.amberleyblackhorse.co.uk
4d/5a Amberley (0.4 miles OR)	The Sportsman	🔒 📶 🍷 ◐ 🍔 🍴	01798 831 787 www.thesportsmansussex.co.uk
4d/5a Amberley (0.4 miles OR)	Amberley Castle	🔒 📶 🍷 ◐ 🍔 🍴	01798 831 992 info@amberleycastle.co.uk www.amberleycastle.co.uk
4d/5a Amberley (0.4 miles OR)	Woodybanks Cottage B&B	🔒 📶 ◐	01798 831 295 enquiries@woodybanks.co.uk www.woodybanks.co.uk
4d/5a Amberley (0.4 miles OR)	Two Farm Cottages B&B	🔒 📶 ◐	01798 831 266 / 07464 970 620 enquiries@twofarmcottages.co.uk www.twofarmcottages.co.uk
5a/5b Storrington (1.3 miles OR)	The White Horse Hotel	🔒 📶 🍷 ◐ 🍔 🍴	01903 745 760 bookings@thewhitehorsehotel.uk www.whitehorsestorrington.co.uk www.oyorooms.com
5b/5c (1 mile OR)	Swipes Farm	▲	07808 141 752 pnewman1@hotmail.co.uk
5b/5c Washington (1.6 miles OR)	Washington Park	▲ 📶 ◐ 🍴	01903 892 869 washingtoncampsite@yahoo.co.uk www.washcamp.com
5b/5c Washington (1.6 miles OR)	Holt House B&B	🔒 📶 ◐	01903 893 542/07796 936 444 annesimmonds_holthouse@ yahoo.co.uk
5c/6a (0.7 miles OR)	White House Caravan Site	▲	01903 813 737
5c/6a Steyning (1.2 miles OR)	Chequer Inn	🔒 📶 🍷 ◐ 🍔 🍴	01903 814 437 www.chequerinn.co.uk
5c/6a Steyning (1.2 miles OR)	Springwells Country House B&B	🔒 📶 ◐	01903 812 446 contact@springwells.co.uk www.springwells.co.uk
6a/6b Bramber (1-1.5 mile OR)	Old Tollgate Hotel	🔒 📶 🍷 ◐ 🍔 🍴	01903 879 494 info@oldtollgatehotel.com www.oldtollgatehotel.com
6a/6b Bramber (1-1.5 mile OR)	Castle Inn Hotel	🔒 📶 🍷 ◐ 🍔 🍴	01903 812 102 www.castleinnhotel.co.uk

Stage	Name	Facilities	Contact Details
6a/6b Upper Beeding (1-1.5 mile OR)	The Rising Sun	🔑 📶 🍺 🥧 🍔 🍴	01903 814 424 info@risingsunupperbeeding.co.uk www.risingsunupperbeeding.co.uk
6a/6b Upper Beeding (1-1.5 mile OR)	Downs View B&B	🔑 📶 🥧	01903 816 125 downsview@upperbeeding.com www.upperbeeding.com
6b/6c	Truleigh Hill YHA	🔑 🛏 📶 ⛺ 🛒 🍺 🥧 🍔 🍴	0345 371 9047 truleigh@yha.org.uk www.yha.org.uk
6c Poynings (1 mile OR)	South Downs Way B&B	🔑 📶 🥧	01273 857 220 mike@southdownswaybandb.co.uk www.southdownswaybandb.co.uk
6c/6d Newtimber Hill	Saddlescombe Farm	⛺ 🍔 🍺	01273 857712 saddlescombefarmcampsite@nationaltrust.org.uk www.nationaltrust.org.uk
6d/7a Pyecombe	Duck Lodge B&B	🔑 📶 🥧	07966 292 601 www.duck-lodge.com
6d/7a Pyecombe	Tallai B&B	🔑 📶 🥧	01273 845 848 grahamsmudge@talk21.com www.pyecombebb.co.uk
6d/7a Pyecombe	Waydown Shepherds Huts	🔑	07885 360 369 andrew@waydownshepherdshuts.co.uk www.waydownshepherdshuts.co.uk
6d/7a Pyecombe	Chantry Farm	⛺ 🔑	07540 350 384 info@chantryfarm.org www.chantryfarm.org
7a/7b Clayton (1 mile OR)	Jack & Jill Inn	🔑 📶 🍺 🥧 🍔 🍴	01273 843 595 availability@thejackandjillinn.co.uk www.thejackandjillinn.co.uk
7b (1.4 miles OR)	Southdown Way Caravan & Camping Park	⛺	01273 841 877 site@southdown-caravancamping.org.uk www.southdown-caravancamping.org.uk
7b (0.7 miles OR)	Ditchling Camp	⛺	07733 103 309 www.yampcamp.co.uk
7b/7c (1 mile OR)	Tovey Lodge	🔑 📶 🥧	01273 256 156/07711 446 625 info@toveylodge.co.uk www.toveylodge.co.uk

Stage	Name	Facilities	Contact Details
7b/7c Ditchling (1.8 miles OR)	The Bull	🔒 📶 🍺 🥧 🍔 🍴	01273 843 147 info@thebullditchling.com www.thebullditchling.com
7b/7c Ditchling (1.8 miles OR)	The White Horse Inn	🔒 📶 🍺 🥧 🍔 🍴	01273 842 006 whitehorseditchling@outlook.com www.whitehorseditchling.com
7b/7c Ditchling (1.8 miles OR)	Jointure Studios	🔒 📶 🥧	01273 841 244 thejointurestudios@gmail.com www.jointurestudiosbandb.co.uk
7c Streat (1.3 miles OR)	Blackberry Wood	⛺ 🔒	01273 890 035 www.blackberrywood.com
7c Lewes (3.4 miles OR)	White Hart Hotel	🔒 📶 🍺 🥧 🍔 🍴	01273 476 694 info@whitehartlewes.com www.whitehartlewes.com
7c Lewes (3.4 miles OR)	The Dorset	🔒 📶 🍺 🥧 🍔 🍴	01273 474 823 thedorsetlewes@outlook.com www.thedorsetlewes.co.uk
7c Lewes (3.4 miles OR)	The King's Head	🔒 📶 🍺 🥧 🍔 🍴	01273 474 628 info@kingsheadlewes.co.uk www.kingsheadlewes.co.uk
7c Lewes (3.4 miles OR)	Murrell's B&B	🔒 📶 🥧	01273 487 728 murrells@bedandbreakfastlewes.co.uk www.bedandbreakfastlewes.co.uk
7c Lewes (3.4 miles OR)	Dubois B&B	🔒 📶 🥧	01273 479 865/07919 607 591 www.duboisbedandbreakfast.co.uk
7c Lewes (3.4 miles OR)	Montys	🔒 📶	01273 476 750/07866 818 505 info@montysaccommodation.co.uk www.montysaccommodation.co.uk
7c Lewes (3.4 miles OR)	Premier Inn Lewes Town Centre Hotel	🔒 📶 🍺 🥧 🍴	0333 234 6628 www.premierinn.com
7c/7d	Housedean Farm Campsite	⛺ 🔒	07919 668 816 camping@housedean.co.uk www.housedean.co.uk
7d (0.5 miles OR)	The Newmarket Inn	🔒 📶 🥧 🍺 🍔 🍴	01273 470 021 newmarketinn@relaxinnz.co.uk
7d/7e Kingston-near-Lewes (0.7 miles OR)	Nightingales B&B	🔒 📶 🥧	01273 475 673 nightingalesbandb@gmail.com
7e/8a Rodmell (0.5 miles OR)	The Loft at Deep Thatch Cottage	🔒 📶 🥧	01273 470 297 deepthatchcottage@gmail.com www.airbnb.co.uk/rooms/19307822

Stage	Name	Facilities	Contact Details
7e/8a Rodmell (0.5 miles OR)	Sunnyside Cottages B&B	🔒 🍽	01273 476 876 www.lewesbandb.co.uk
7e/8a Rodmell (0.5 miles OR)	No.1 Rodmell House	🔒 📶 🍽	01273 479 620/07570 715 053 lornaamelia@gmail.com
7e/8a Rodmell (0.5 miles OR)	No.2 Rodmell House	🔒 📶 🍽	01273 809 613 vickymappin@hotmail.com
8a/8b Southease	YHA South Downs	🔒 🛏 📶 ⛺ 🍷 🍽 🍔 🍴	0345 371 9574 southdowns@yha.org.uk www.yha.org.uk
8b Beddingham (1.8 miles OR)	Blue Door Barns	🔒 📶 🍽	01273 858 893/07788 446 621 contact@bluedoorbarns.com www.bluedoorbarns.com
8b/8c Firle (1.4 miles OR)	The Ram Inn	🔒 📶 🍽 🍷 🍔 🍴	01273 858 222 www.raminn.co.uk
8b/8c Firle (1.5 miles OR)	Firle Camp	⛺	07733 103 309 info@firlecamp.co.uk www.yampcamp.co.uk
8c (0.8 miles OR)	Tilton House	🔒 📶 🍽	01323 811 570 info@tiltonhouse.co.uk www.tiltonhouse.co.uk
8c (0.6 miles OR)	Bo-Peep Farmhouse B&B	🔒 📶 🍽	01323 871 299 bopeepfarmhouse@gmail.com www.bopeepfarmhouse.co.uk
8c/8d Alciston (1 mile OR)	The Rose Cottage	🔒 📶 🍽	01323 870 377 www.therosecottagealciston.co.uk
8d/9a Alfriston	Deans Place Hotel	🔒 📶 🍽 🍷 🍔 🍴	01323 870 248 mail@deansplacehotel.co.uk www.deansplacehotel.co.uk
8d/9a Alfriston	Wingrove House	🔒 📶 🍽 🍷 🍔 🍴	01323 870 276 info@wingrovehousealfriston.com www.wingrovehousealfriston.com
8d/9a Alfriston	Ye Olde Smugglers Inne	🔒 📶 🍽 🍷 🍔 🍴	01323 870 241 www.smugglersalfriston.co.uk
8d/9a Alfriston	The George Inn	🔒 📶 🍽 🍷 🍔 🍴	01323 870 319 office@thegeorgealfriston.com www.thegeorge-alfriston.com

Stage	Name	Facilities	Contact Details
8d/9a Alfriston	The Star	🔒 📶 🥐 🍷 🍔 🍴	Closed at the date of press. Due to re-open in June 2021 www.thepolizzicollection.com
8d/9a Alfriston	Chestnuts B&B	🔒 📶 🥐 🍷 🍔	01323 870 959 info@chestnutsalfriston.co.uk www.chestnutsalfriston.co.uk
8d/9a Alfriston	Riverdale House	🔒 📶 🥐	01323 871 038 info@riverdalehouse.co.uk www.riverdalehouse.co.uk
8d/9a Alfriston	Alfriston Camping Park	▲	07920 879 098/07591 880 129 www.alfristoncamping.com
8d/9a Alfriston	Alfriston Woodland Cabins	🔒	07748 987 691 info@alfristoncabins.co.uk www.alfristoncabins.co.uk
9a/9b Exceat	Saltmarsh Farmhouse	🔒 📶 🥐 🍷 🍔	01323 870 218 info@saltmarshfarmhouse.co.uk www.saltmarshfarmhouse.co.uk
9b/9c	Belle Tout Lighthouse	🔒 📶 🥐	01323 423 185 info@belletout.co.uk www.belletout.co.uk
9c Meads	The Pilot Inn	🔒 📶 🥐 🍷 🍔 🍴	01323 723 440 thepilotinneastbourne@hotmail.co.uk www.pilot-inn.co.uk
9c Meads	Beachy Rise	🔒 📶 🥐	01323 639 171 info@beachyrise.com www.beachyrise.com
v9 Wilmington (0.8 miles OR)	Crossways Hotel	🔒 📶 🥐 🍷 🍔 🍴	Closed down at date of press. It is uncertain if it will re-open.
v9 Jevington	The Paddocks B&B	🔒 📶 🥐	01323 482 499 www.thepaddockstables.co.uk
Eastbourne	The Cherry Tree Guest House	🔒 📶 🥐	01323 722 406 melanie@cherrytree-eastbourne.co.uk www.cherrytree-eastbourne.co.uk
Eastbourne	The Grand Hotel	🔒 📶 🥐 🍷 🍔 🍴	01323 412 345 enquiries@grandeastbourne.com www.grandeastbourne.com
Eastbourne	Best Western Lansdowne Hotel	🔒 📶 🥐 🍷 🍔 🍴	01323 725 174 reception@lansdowne-hotel.co.uk www.bw-lansdownehotel.co.uk
Eastbourne	Citrus Hotel	🔒 📶 🥐 🍷	01323 722 676 enquiry@citrushoteleastbourne.co.uk www.citrushoteleastbourne.co.uk
Eastbourne	The Mowbray	🔒 📶 🥐	01323 720 012 www.themowbray.com

Stage	Name	Facilities	Contact Details
Eastbourne	Brayscroft House	🔒 📶 🥐	01323 647 005
Eastbourne	Southcroft Guest House	🔒 📶 🥐	01323 729 071 www.southcrofthotel.co.uk
Eastbourne	Premier Inn Eastbourne Town Centre Hotel	🔒 📶 🥐 🍷 🍔 🍴	0333 321 9323 www.premierinn.com
Eastbourne	Da Vinci Hotel	🔒 📶 🥐	01323 727 173 contact@davinci.uk.com www.davinci.uk.com
Eastbourne	YHA Eastbourne	🔒 🛏 📶	0345 371 9316 eastbourne@yha.org.uk www.yha.org.uk

Booking Tips

▶ The SDW becomes more popular each year. To ensure that you secure your accommodation of choice, book as early as you can. Many trekkers start booking in autumn (just after the current summer season has ended) for the following season.

▶ Try to book 'hot-spots' first: generally, these are places where there are only a few accommodation options. Once you have secured the accommodation which books up most quickly, you can normally slot in the rest of your accommodation more easily. If you leave hot-spots until last then you might have to unwind and rebook other reservations if any hot-spots that you desire are unavailable.

▶ Start mid-week. A large number of trekkers start the trail at the weekend. Those who start mid-week are often 'out of sync' with the bulk of the trekkers and may therefore find accommodation more easily.

▶ Weekends are normally busier (even in low season).

▶ If you cannot get accommodation along the SDW itself, try looking for beds in towns/villages a few miles away.

▶ Those who hike alone, or in pairs, will find it easiest to find beds. For larger groups, it is more difficult.

▶ If you cannot secure the accommodation that you need then contact one of the unguided tour companies or accommodation booking services. They block-book accommodation months in advance and may have spaces.

▶ Occasionally, the last-minute booker can get lucky: tour companies which pre-book in blocks will release unsold beds a few weeks or months before the relevant dates. If you call a few weeks before your trip, you may be lucky enough to bag some beds which have just been released.

Enjoying views of the Weald near Firle Beacon (Stage 8b)

Facilities

Stage	Place	Dormitory Beds	Private Rooms	Camping	Meals/Drinks	Food Shop	Transport
1a	Winchester		🛏		🍽🍷	🛒	🚌🚍
1a/1b	Chilcomb		🛏				
1b (1.4 miles OR)	Morn Hill		🛏	▲	🍽🍷		🚍
1b (1.5 miles OR)	Cheriton		🛏		🍽🍷		
1b/1c	Holden Farm Camping			▲			
1c (1.5 miles OR)	Shorley		🛏				
1c/1d	The Milbury's		🛏		🍽🍷		
1d (1.4 miles OR)	Kilmeston		🛏	▲			
1d/2a	Exton/Meonstoke (OR)/Corhampton (OR)		🛏	▲	🍽🍷	🛒	🚍
2a/2b	Meon Springs			▲			
2b (0.4 miles OR)	Coombe		🛏				
2b/2c (1-1.9 miles OR)	East Meon		🛏	▲	🍽🍷	🛒	🚍

Stage	Place	Dormitory Beds	Private Rooms	Camping	Meals/Drinks	Food Shop	Transport
2b/2c	The Sustainability Centre			◀			
2c/3a (0.5 miles OR)	Buriton		🛏		🍴🍷		🚌
2c/3a (2.8 miles OR)	Petersfield		🛏		🍴🍷	🛒	🚆 🚌
2c/3a (1.8 miles OR)	Nursted		🛏				
3a/3b (0.6 miles OR)	South Harting exit		🛏		🍴🍷	🛒	🚌
3b/4a	Cocking (0.8 mile OR)/Manor Farm		🛏	◀	🍴🍷	🛒	🚌
4a (1.6 miles OR)	East Dean			◀	🍴🍷	🛒	
4a/4b (1.3 miles OR)	Graffham		🛏	◀			🚌
4b (0.9 miles OR)	Gumber	⌐		◀			
4b/4c (1.2 miles OR)	Bignor		🛏		🍴🍷	🛒	🚌
4b/4c (1.7 miles OR)	Sutton	⌐	🛏		🍴🍷		🚌
4c/4d (0.3 miles OR)	Houghton		🛏				🚌
4c/4d (1.1 miles OR)	Bury		🛏		🍷		🚌

Stage	Place	Dormitory Beds	Private Rooms	Camping	Meals/Drinks	Food Shop	Transport
4d/5a	Houghton Bridge				▶		🚂
4d/5a (0.4 miles OR)	Amberley		🔑	◀	▶	🛒	
5a/5b (1.3 miles OR)	Storrington		🔑		▶	🛒	🚌
5b/5c (0.6-1.6 miles OR)	Washington		🔑	◀	▶		🚌
5c/6a (0.7-1.2 miles OR)	Steyning		🔑	◀	▶	🛒	🚌
6a/6b (1-1.5 mile OR)	Upper Beeding/Bramber		🔑		▶	🛒	🚌
6b/6c	Truleigh Hill	🛏	🔑	◀	▶	🛒	
6c (1 mile OR)	Poynings		🔑		▶		
6c/6d	Saddlescombe Farm			◀	▶		
6d/7a	Pyecombe		🔑	◀	▶	🛒	🚌
7a/7b (1 mile OR)	Clayton		🔑		▶		🚌
7b/7c (1.8 miles OR)	Ditchling/Ditchling Beacon			◀	▶		🚌
7c (1.3 miles OR)	Streat		🔑	◀	▶		

38

Stage	Place	Dormitory Beds	Private Rooms	Camping	Meals/Drinks	Food Shop	Transport
7c (3.4 miles OR)	Lewes		🛏		🍽	🛒	🚌 🚍
7c/7d	Housedean Farm			▲			🚍
7d/7e (0.7 miles OR)	Kingston-near-Lewes		🛏		🍽		🚍
7e/8a (0.5 miles OR)	Rodmell		🛏		🍽		🚍
8a/8b	Southease	🛌	🛏	▲	🍽		🚌 🚍
8b/8c (1-1.4 miles OR)	Firle		🛏	▲	🍽		🚍
8c/8d (0.6-1 miles OR)	Bostal Hill/Alciston		🛏	▲			
8d/9a/v9	Alfriston		🛏		🍽	🛒	🚍
9a/9b	Exceat		🛏		🍽		🚍
9b/9c	Belle Tout Lighthouse						
9c/v9	Meads		🛏		🍽	🛒	🚍
	Eastbourne	🛌			🍽	🛒	🚌 🚍

39

Food

Our favourite Sussex beer: Long Blonde from the Long Man Brewery

For most trekkers, breakfast will be provided as part of the overnight package at B&Bs, pubs or hotels: normally a 'Full English' breakfast which is a large helping of bacon, sausage, eggs, mushrooms and black pudding.

For lunch, most accommodation providers can prepare a packed lunch for you: be sure to request this the night before. Alternatively, you could stop for lunch at a pub or café along the route. If your accommodation does not offer evening meals then the staff will usually be able to recommend a pub or restaurant within walking distance.

Most villages have a pub/inn, serving food and excellent beer. In fact, for many trekkers the 'pub grub' and real ale are highlights of the SDW: in recent years, traditional English beer has been enjoying a major revival spurred on by the craft beer revolution. The local beer available on the SDW is some of England's finest as there are some famous Sussex breweries nearby: Harveys of Lewes is probably the most well-known of the breweries but our favourite beer is the Long Blonde ale made by the Long Man Brewery in Litlington (which is along the route of Stage 9a).

There are many grocery shops that serve the SDW where you can buy self-catering supplies: a few of these are in towns and villages which the trail actually passes through. However, other shops are a short distance OR. All of the shops are listed in the route descriptions. Often the shops are small with a limited range of products but, as long as you are not too fussy, you should find plenty to eat. However, if you are more particular, or you have specific nutritional requirements, you may wish to stock up on supplies in Winchester or Eastbourne before setting out on the trek.

However, remember that food is heavy so unless you are travelling very quickly, you may not be able to start the trek with all the food that you will require for the full distance. It is much better to accept at the outset that you can only carry a few days' food than to exhaust yourself in the early stages of the trek by carrying too much. Many campers carry only a small amount of food which they supplement with meals at pubs and cafés along the way. It is sensible to carry dried food (such as pasta and rice): water is food's heaviest component. Pre-packed freeze-dried meals for backpackers are an excellent choice because they are light and are prepared simply by adding boiling water.

Travel

Steyning Bowl (Stage 5c/6a)

Travel to Southern England

By air: there are numerous airports in the UK and, in normal times, there are plenty of domestic and international flights available. At the date of press, however, many services were not operating due to COVID-19 and it was not clear if, or when, they would resume. Southampton has probably the most convenient airport for the SDW as Winchester (the W trail-head) is only 10min away from the airport by train: the trains leave regularly throughout the day (www.southwesternrailway.com). There are flights to Southampton from a variety of cities in the UK and mainland Europe.

London Gatwick Airport is also a good option. It has numerous domestic and international flights. There are regular trains from the airport to both Winchester (1.75hr; www.southwesternrailway.com; www.southernrailway.com) and Eastbourne (1hr; www.southernrailway.com).

London Luton Airport also has international/domestic flights and there are trains to Eastbourne (2.5hr; www.thameslinkrailway.com; www.southernrailway.com). Other airports to consider are London Heathrow, London Stansted and London City.

By ferry: there are numerous ferries to GB from the island of Ireland and mainland Europe. The most useful services for the SDW are those from France to Portsmouth (www.brittany-ferries.co.uk). There are trains from Portsmouth Harbour to Winchester (1hr) and Eastbourne (2.25hr): see www.southwesternrailway.com.

Travel to/from the primary trail-heads

Those walking W-E will first need to get to Winchester. Those walking E-W will first need to get to Eastbourne.

By train: both Winchester and Eastbourne are well-connected to the rest of GB by rail although, depending upon your departure point, you may have to change a few times. For train travel from nearby airports to Winchester or Eastbourne, see 'Travel to Southern England'. To check train times and buy tickets, see www.thetrainline.com.

By bus: there are numerous buses from around GB to London. From London, there are buses to Winchester and Brighton. There are direct trains from Brighton to Eastbourne (40min; www.southernrailway.com). For bus timetables, see www.nationalexpress.com. Long-distance buses within the UK often take longer than trains.

Primary Trail-head	Transport to secondary trail-heads & airports (Places in red have train stations)
Winchester	▶ Stagecoach bus 67 to/from **Cheriton** (Stage 1b; 1.5 miles OR), **East Meon** (Stage 2b/2c; 1 mile OR) and **Petersfield** (Stage 2c/3a; 2.8 miles OR) ▶ Trains to/from **Eastbourne** (Stage 9c), **Lewes** (Stage 7c; 3.4 miles OR) and **Southease** (Stage 8a) as well as **Southampton**, **London** and **Gatwick Airport**
Eastbourne	▶ **Compass 125/Cuckmere Buses 25** to/from **Lewes** (Stage 7c; 3.4 miles OR), **Firle** (Stage 8b/8c; 1.4 miles OR), **Alfriston** (Stage 8d/9a) and **Wilmington** (Stage v9; 0.8 miles OR) ▶ Brighton & Hove bus 12/12A/12X to/from **Brighton** and **Exceat** (Stage 9a/9b) ▶ Brighton & Hove bus 13X to/from **Brighton**, **Exceat** (Stage 9a/9b), **Birling Gap** (Stage 9b) and **Beachy Head** (Stage 9c) ▶ Cuckmere Buses 41 to/from **Jevington** (Stage v9) ▶ Stagecoach 3 to/from **Meads** (Stage 9c) ▶ Trains to/from **Winchester** (Stage 1a), **Lewes** (Stage 7c; 3.4 miles OR) and **Southease** (Stage 8a), as well as **Brighton**, **Gatwick Airport**, **London** and **Southampton**

By car: you could park your car in Eastbourne or Winchester and use public transport to return to it at the end of the trek (see 'Public Transport along the SDW'). You can book reasonably priced parking at www.yourparkingspace.co.uk.

By taxi: there are plenty of taxi services in both Winchester and Eastbourne including those listed below.

Winchester Taxi Operators:

▶ Winchester Taxis (Winchester): www.winchester-taxis.co.uk; 02380 553 631

▶ Wessex Cars (Winchester): www.wessexcars.com; 01962 877 749

▶ Wintax (Winchester): www.wintaxcars.com; 01962 250 250

Eastbourne Taxi Operators:

▶ 720 Taxis (Eastbourne): www.720taxis.com; 01323 720 720

▶ Call-a-cab (Eastbourne): www.746746.co.uk; 01323 746 746

▶ Sussex Cars (Eastbourne): www.726726.co.uk; 01323 726 726

Returning to the start from the finish of the SDW

If you have left a car or luggage at your start point, you can use one of the train services to return to it at the end of the trek. From Eastbourne, there are trains to Winchester and vice versa but you may have to change a few times. To check train times and buy tickets, see www.thetrainline.com.

Public transport along the SDW

There are numerous bus and train services that are useful to the SDW walker. Some stop at places along the SDW itself but more often they serve towns and villages which are a short distance OR: frequently, these are the same places that offer SDW accommodation. In this book, we refer to these places as 'secondary trail-heads' and there is a list of them on pages 47 to 50, together with details of the relevant transport options: these services can be useful if you need to abandon the trek for any reason or if you wish to skip a stage or two. They can also assist if you are only intending to walk part of the SDW: see 'Hiking shorter sections of the SDW'.

Train: other than the train stations at the primary trail-heads (Winchester and Eastbourne), the only stations actually located on the SDW itself are at Houghton Bridge/ Amberley (Stage 4d/5a) and Southease (Stage 8a). However, there are also stations at some towns which are a short distance away from the trail. From stations, there is normally easy access to London and Gatwick Airport and in fact, it is possible to travel to almost any other part of the UK (although, depending upon your destination, you might have to change a few times). For further details on the places that have train stations, see 'Secondary trail-heads': towns with stations are highlighted in red. The SDW Transport Map on page 44 should also help. For tickets and timetables, see www.thetrainline.com.

Buses: the key services operating close to the SDW are set out below. There are too many bus services operating in the region to list them all.

Bus Service (W-E)	Key Information (Places in red have train stations)
Stagecoach 67	Buses between Winchester and Petersfield (Stage 2c/3a; 2.8 miles OR) via Cheriton (Stage 1b; 1.5 miles OR) and East Meon (Stage 2b; 1 mile OR). Monday to Saturday
Xelabus X17	Buses between Eastleigh and Petersfield (Stage 2c/3a; 2.8 miles OR) via Corhampton (Stage 1d/2a; 1 mile OR) and East Meon (Stage 2b; 1 mile OR). Wednesdays only
Stagecoach 37	Buses between Havant and Petersfield (Stage 2c/3a; 2.8 miles OR) via Clanfield (Stage 2c; 1 miles OR). Monday to Saturday
Wheel Drive 94	Buses between Buriton (Stage 2c/3a; 0.5 mile OR) and Petersfield (Stage 2c/3a; 2.8 miles OR)
Stagecoach 54	Buses between Chichester and Petersfield (Stage 2c/3a; 2.8 miles OR) via South Harting (Stage 3a/3b; 0.6 miles OR). Monday to Saturday
Stagecoach 91	Buses between Midhurst and Petersfield (Stage 2c/3a; 2.8 miles OR) via South Harting (Stage 3a/3b; 0.6 miles OR). Monday to Saturday
Stagecoach 60	Daily buses between Midhurst and Chichester via Cocking (Stage 3b/4a; 1 mile OR)
Compass 99	Buses between Chichester and Petworth. If booked in advance, the bus will stop at Graffham (Stage 4a/4b; 1.3 miles OR), Sutton (Stage 4b/4c; 1.7 miles OR) or Bignor (Stage 4b/4c; 1.2 miles OR). Monday to Saturday
Compass 71	Buses between Chichester and Storrington (Stage 5a/5b; 1.3 miles OR) via Houghton (Stage 4c/4d; 0.3 miles OR) and Bury (Stage 4c/4d; 1.1 miles OR). Wednesdays only

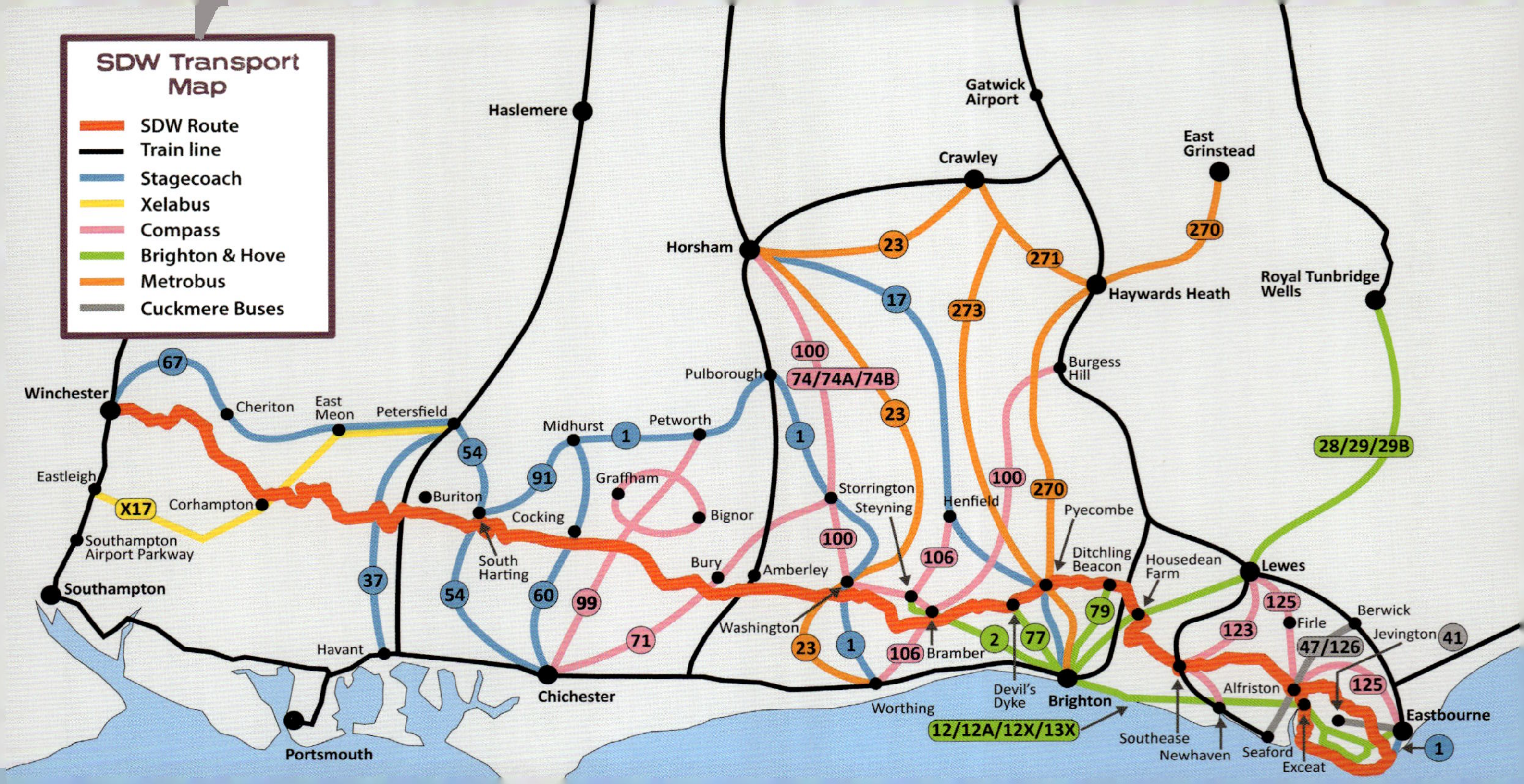
SDW Transport Map
SDW Route
Train line
Stagecoach
Xelabus
Compass
Brighton & Hove
Metrobus
Cuckmere Buses
Haslemere
Gatwick Airport
Crawley
East Grinstead
Horsham
Haywards Heath
Royal Tunbridge Wells
Winchester
Cheriton
East Meon
Petersfield
Midhurst
Petworth
Pulborough
Burgess Hill
Eastleigh
Corhampton
Buriton
Cocking
Graffham
Bignor
Storrington
Steyning
Henfield
Pyecombe
Southampton Airport Parkway
South Harting
Bury
Amberley
Ditchling Beacon
Housedean Farm
Lewes
Southampton
Havant
Chichester
Washington
Bramber
Worthing
Devil's Dyke
Brighton
Southease
Newhaven
Seaford
Exceat
Alfriston
Firle
Berwick
Jevington
Eastbourne
Portsmouth
67
X17
54
37
91
60
99
71
1
100
74/74A/74B
23
17
273
271
270
106
2
77
79
28/29/29B
12/12A/12X/13X
125
123
47/126
41

Bus Service (W-E)	Key Information (Places in red have train stations)
Compass 74/74A/74B	Buses from **Storrington** (Stage 5a/5b; 1.3 miles OR) to **Horsham Train Station**. Mondays to Fridays
Compass 100	Buses between **Horsham** and **Burgess Hill** via **Storrington** (Stage 5a/5b; 1.3 miles OR), **Washington** (Stage 5b/5c; 0.6 miles OR), **Steyning** (Stage 5c/6a; 1.2 miles OR), **Bramber** (Stage 6a/6b; 1-1.5 miles OR) and **Upper Beeding** (Stage 6a/6b; 1-1.5 miles OR). Monday to Saturday
Stagecoach 1	Daily buses between **Midhurst** and **Worthing** via **Pulborough**, **Washington** (Stage 5b/5c; 0.6 miles OR) and **Storrington** (Stage 5a/5b; 1.3 miles OR)
Metrobus 23	Daily buses between **Crawley** and **Worthing** via **Horsham Train Station**, and **Washington** (Stage 5b/5c; 0.6 miles OR)
Brighton & Hove 2	Buses between **Rottingdean** and **Steyning** (Stage 5c/6a; 1.2 miles OR) via **Brighton**, **Bramber** (Stage 6a/6b; 1-1.5 miles OR) and **Upper Beeding** (Stage 6a/6b; 1-1.5 miles OR). Monday to Saturday
Compass 106	Buses between **Henfield** and **Worthing** via **Steyning** (Stage 5c/6a; 1.2 miles OR), **Bramber** (Stage 6a/6b; 1-1.5 miles OR) and **Upper Beeding** (Stage 6a/6b; 1-1.5 miles OR)
Brighton & Hove 77	Daily buses between **Devils Dyke** (Stage 6c; 0.2 miles OR) and **Brighton**
Metrobus 270	Daily buses between **East Grinstead** and **Brighton**, via **Haywards Heath**, **Pyecombe** (Stage 6d/7a) and **Clayton** (Stage 7a/7b; 1 mile OR)
Metrobus 271/273	Buses between **Crawley** and **Brighton**, via **Pyecombe** (Stage 6d/7a) and **Clayton** (Stage 7a/7b; 1 mile OR). 271 (daily); 273 (Monday to Saturday)
Stagecoach 17	Buses between **Horsham Train Station** and **Brighton**, via **Pyecombe** (Stage 6d/7a). Monday to Saturday
Brighton & Hove 79	Daily buses between **Ditchling Beacon** (Stage 7b/7c) and **Brighton**. Saturday, Sunday and public holidays
Brighton & Hove 28/29/29B	Buses between **Brighton** and **Royal Tunbridge Wells** via **Lewes** (Stage 7c; 3.4 miles OR) and **Housedean Farm** (Stage 7c/7d). Monday to Saturday
Compass 123	Buses between **Lewes** (Stage 7c; 3.4 miles OR) and **Newhaven** via **Rodmell** (Stage 7e/8a; 0.5 miles OR), **Southease** (Stage 8a/8b) and **Kingston-near-Lewes** (Stage 7d/7e; 0.7 miles OR)
Compass 125/ Cuckmere Buses 25	Buses between **Lewes** (Stage 7c; 3.4 miles OR) and **Eastbourne** via **Firle** (Stage 8b/8c; 1.4 miles OR), **Alfriston** (Stage 8d/9a) and **Wilmington** (Stage v9; 0.8 miles OR). Fridays and Saturdays
Cuckmere Buses 126	Buses between **Seaford** and **Berwick** via **Alfriston** (Stage 8d/9a). Tuesday, Thursday & Saturday
Cuckmere Buses No. 47: Cuckmere Valley Ramblerbus	An hourly circular service from **Berwick** to **Alfriston** (Stage 8d/9a), **Seaford**, **Exceat** (Stage 9a/9b), **Litlington** (Stage 9a) and **Wilmington** (Stage v9; 0.8 miles OR)
Brighton & Hove 12/12A/12X	Buses between **Brighton** and **Eastbourne** via **Exceat** (Stage 9a/9b). Monday to Saturday

Bus Service (W-E)	Key Information (Places in red have train stations)
Brighton & Hove 13X	Buses between **Brighton** and **Eastbourne** via **Exceat** (Stage 9a/9b), Birling Gap (Stage 9b) and Beachy Head (Stage 9c). Saturday, Sunday and public holidays
Cuckmere Buses 41	Buses between **Eastbourne** and **Jevington** (Stage v9). Thursday
Stagecoach 3	Daily buses from Meads (Stage 9c) to **Eastbourne** town centre

Further information about bus travel:

Stagecoach: www.stagecoachbus.com

Xelabus: www.xelabus.info

Compass Travel: www.compass-travel.co.uk

Brighton & Hove: www.buses.co.uk

Metrobus: www.metrobus.co.uk

Cuckmere Buses: www.cuckmerebuses.org.uk

Wheel Drive: 01730 892 052

By taxi

There are countless taxi businesses operating from towns and villages close to the SDW. They can pick you up from the SDW, drive you to nearby accommodation and leave you back to the SDW the next morning. Some of them operate surprisingly far from their hubs. There are too many taxi businesses to list here but some of the useful services include:

- Winchester taxi services: see 'Travel to/from the primary trail-heads'
- Gravers Taxis (Petersfield): www.petersfieldtaxis.co.uk; 01730 303 030
- A2B Taxis (Petersfield): www.a2btaxispetersfield.co.uk; 01730 233 299
- Midhurst Taxi Service (Midhurst): www.midhurstcars.co.uk; 01730 821 044/07789 710 424
- MJ cars (Petworth, Pulborough & Storrington): www.mj-cars.co.uk; 07595 067 163 (Petworth)/01798 874 321 (Pulborough)/01903 745 414 (Storrington)
- RH20 Cars (Pulborough): serves Houghton Bridge/Amberley; www.rh20taxis.co.uk; 01798 669 437/07511 500 265
- Castle Cars (Arundel): serves Houghton Bridge/Amberley; www.castlecarsltd.co.uk; 01903 884 444
- Crosslink (Storrington): 01903 740 365
- Steyning Airport Transfers (Steyning): www.steyning.airport-transfers.info; 01903 258 584
- Russell Private Hire (Steyning): www.russellpickupprivatehire-steyning.co.uk; 07506 271 877
- Steyning Village Taxis (Steyning): www.steyningvillagetaxis.co.uk; 07928 479 922
- Brighton & Hove Radio Taxis (Brighton): www.brightontaxis.com; 01273 204 060
- City Cabs (Brighton): www.205205.com; 01273 205 205
- Beacon Taxis (Seaford): serve Alfriston; 01323 898 888

- iCarz (Seaford): serve Alfriston; www.icarzuk.com; 01323 802 025
- Lewes Town Taxis (Lewes): www.lewestowntaxis.co.uk; 01273 474 747
- Lewes Country cars (Lewes): www.lewescountycars.co.uk; 01273 474 444
- GM Taxis (Lewes): www.gmtaxislewes.co.uk; 01273 473 737
- Eastbourne taxi services: see 'Travel to/from the primary trail-heads'

Secondary trail-heads

Stage/Place (W-E)	Transport Options (Towns in red have train stations)
1b Cheriton (1.5 miles OR)	▶ Stagecoach bus 67 to/from **Winchester**, **East Meon** (Stage 2b; 1 mile OR) and **Petersfield** (Stage 2c/3a; 2.8 miles OR)
1d/2a Corhampton (1 miles OR)	▶ Xelabus X17 to/from **Eastleigh**, **East Meon** (Stage 2b; 1 mile OR) and **Petersfield** (Stage 2c/3a; 2.8 miles OR)
2b East Meon (1 mile OR)	▶ Stagecoach bus 67 to/from **Winchester**, **Cheriton** (Stage 1b; 1.5 miles OR) and **Petersfield** (Stage 2c/3a; 2.8 miles OR) ▶ Xelabus X17 to/from **Eastleigh**, **Corhampton** (Stage 1d/2a; 1 mile OR) and **Petersfield** (Stage 2c/3a; 2.8 miles OR)
2c Clanfield (1 mile OR)	▶ Stagecoach bus 37 to/from **Havant** and **Petersfield** (Stage 2c/3a; 2.8 miles OR)
2c/3a Buriton (0.5 mile OR)	▶ Wheel Drive No. 94 between **Buriton** (Stage 2c/3a; 0.5 mile OR) and **Petersfield** (Stage 2c/3a; 2.8 miles OR)
2c/3a Petersfield (2.8 miles OR)	▶ Stagecoach bus 67 to/from **Winchester**, **Cheriton** (Stage 1b; 1.5 miles OR) and **East Meon** (Stage 2b; 1 mile OR) ▶ Stagecoach bus 54 to/from **Chichester** and **South Harting** (Stage 3a/3b; 0.6 miles OR) ▶ Stagecoach bus 91 to/from **Midhurst** and **South Harting** (Stage 3a/3b; 0.6 miles OR) ▶ Stagecoach bus 37 to/from **Havant** and **Clanfield** (Stage 2c; 1 mile OR) ▶ Xelabus X17 to/from **Eastleigh**, **Corhampton** (Stage 1d/2a; 1 mile OR) and **East Meon** (Stage 2b; 1 mile OR) ▶ Wheel Drive No. 94 between **Buriton** (Stage 2c/3a; 0.5 mile OR) and **Petersfield** ▶ Trains to/from **London**, **Portsmouth** and **Southampton**. You could also travel to **Winchester** or **Eastbourne** with a few changes
3a/3b South Harting (0.6 miles OR)	▶ Stagecoach bus 54 to/from **Chichester** and **Petersfield** (Stage 2c/3a; 2.8 miles OR) ▶ Stagecoach bus 91 to/from **Midhurst** and **Petersfield** (Stage 2c/3a; 2.8 miles OR)

Stage/Place (W-E)	Transport Options (Towns in red have train stations)
3b/4a Cocking (0.8 mile OR)	▶ Stagecoach bus 60 to/from **Midhurst** and **Chichester**
4a/4b Graffham (1.3 miles OR)	▶ Compass bus 99 to/from **Chichester** and **Petworth.** Advance booking essential
Stage 4b/4c Bignor (1.2 miles OR)	▶ Compass bus 99 to/from **Chichester** and **Petworth.** Advance booking essential
Stage 4b/4c Sutton (1.7 miles OR)	▶ Compass bus 99 to/from **Chichester** and **Petworth.** Advance booking essential
4c/4d Bury (1.1 miles OR)	▶ Compass bus 71 to/from **Chichester**, **Houghton** (Stage 4c/4d; 0.3 miles OR), and **Storrington** (Stage 5a/5b; 1.3 miles OR)
4c/4d Houghton (0.3 miles OR)	▶ Compass bus 71 to/from **Chichester**, **Bury** (Stage 4c/4d; 1.1 miles OR) and **Storrington** (Stage 5a/5b; 1.3 miles OR)
4d/5a Houghton Bridge/Amberley	▶ Trains to/from **Gatwick Airport**, **London**, **Chichester**, **Portsmouth** and **Southampton**. You could also travel to **Winchester** or **Eastbourne** with a few changes
5a/5b Storrington (1.3 miles OR)	▶ Compass bus 74/74A/74B to/from **Horsham Train Station**. From **Horsham** there are trains to **Gatwick Airport**, **London** and **Southampton** ▶ Compass bus 100 to/from **Horsham Train Station**, **Washington** (Stage 5b/5c; 0.8 miles OR), **Steyning** (Stage 5c/6a; 1.2 miles OR), **Bramber** (Stage 6a/6b; 1-1.5 miles OR), **Upper Beeding** (Stage 6a/6b; 1-1.5 miles OR) and **Burgess Hill** ▶ Compass bus 71 to/from **Chichester**, **Houghton** (Stage 4c/4d; 0.3 miles OR), and **Bury** (Stage 4c/4d; 1.1 miles OR) ▶ Stagecoach bus 1 to/from **Midhurst**, **Pulborough**, **Washington** (Stage 5b/5c; 0.8 miles OR) and **Worthing**
5b/5c Washington (0.8 miles OR)	▶ Stagecoach bus 1 to/from **Midhurst**, **Pulborough**, **Storrington** (Stage 5a/5b; 1.3 miles OR) and **Worthing** ▶ Compass bus 100 to/from **Horsham Train Station**, **Storrington** (Stage 5a/5b; 1.3 miles OR), **Steyning** (Stage 5c/6a; 1.2 miles OR), **Bramber** (Stage 6a/6b; 1-1.5 miles OR), **Upper Beeding** (Stage 6a/6b; 1-1.5 miles OR) and **Burgess Hill** ▶ Metrobus 23 to/from **Crawley**, **Horsham** and **Worthing**
5c/6a Steyning (1.2 miles OR)	▶ Compass bus 100 to/from **Horsham Train Station**, **Washington** (Stage 5b/5c; 0.8 miles OR), **Storrington** (Stage 5a/5b; 1.3 miles OR), **Bramber** (Stage 6a/6b; 1-1.5 miles OR), **Upper Beeding** (Stage 6a/6b; 1-1.5 miles OR) and **Burgess Hill** ▶ Compass bus 106 to/from **Henfield**, **Worthing**, **Bramber** (Stage 6a/6b; 1-1.5 miles OR) and **Upper Beeding** (Stage 6a/6b; 1-1.5 miles OR) ▶ Brighton & Hove bus 2 to/from **Brighton**, **Bramber** (Stage 6a/6b; 1-1.5 miles OR) and **Upper Beeding** (Stage 6a/6b; 1-1.5 miles OR)

Stage/Place (W-E)	Transport Options (Towns in red have train stations)
6a/6b Bramber/Upper Beeding (1-1.5 mile OR)	▶ Compass bus 100 to/from **Horsham Train Station**, **Washington** (Stage 5b/5c; 0.8 miles OR), **Storrington** (Stage 5a/5b; 1.3 miles OR), **Steyning** (Stage 5c/6a; 1.2 miles OR) and **Burgess Hill** ▶ Compass bus 106 to/from **Henfield**, **Worthing**, and **Steyning** (Stage 5c/6a; 1.2 miles OR) ▶ Brighton & Hove bus 2 to/from **Brighton** and **Steyning** (Stage 5c/6a; 1.2 miles OR)
Stage 6c Devil's Dyke (0.2 miles OR)	▶ Brighton & Hove bus 77 to/from **Brighton**
6d/7a Pyecombe	▶ Metrobus 270/271/273 to/from **East Grinstead**, **Crawley**, **Haywards Heath**, **Brighton** and **Clayton** (Stage 7a/7b; 1 mile OR) ▶ Stagecoach bus 17 to/from **Brighton** and **Horsham Train Station**
7a/7b Clayton (1 mile OR)	▶ Metrobus 270/271/273 to/from **East Grinstead**, **Crawley**, **Brighton**, **Haywards Heath**, and **Pyecombe** (Stage 6d/7a)
7b/7c Ditchling Beacon	▶ Brighton & Hove bus 79 to/from **Brighton**
7c Lewes (3.4 miles OR)	▶ Brighton & Hove bus 28/29/29B to/from **Brighton**, **Royal Tunbridge Wells** and **Housedean Farm** (Stage 7c/7d) ▶ Compass 125/Cuckmere Buses 25 to/from **Eastbourne**, **Firle** (Stage 8b/8c; 1.4 miles OR), **Alfriston** (Stage 8d/9a) and **Wilmington** (Stage v9; 0.8 miles OR) ▶ Compass bus 123 to/from **Southease** (Stage 8a/8b), **Rodmell** (Stage 7e/8a; 0.5 miles OR), **Kingston-near-Lewes** (Stage 7d/7e; 0.7 miles OR) and **Newhaven** ▶ Trains to/from **Southease** (Stage 8a/8b), **Brighton**, **Eastbourne**, **Gatwick Airport**, **London** and **Portsmouth**. You could also travel to **Winchester** and **Southampton** with a few changes
7c/7d Housedean Farm	▶ Brighton & Hove bus 28/29/29B to/from **Brighton**, **Royal Tunbridge Wells** and **Lewes** (Stage 7c; 3.4 miles OR)
7d/7e Kingston-near-Lewes (0.7 miles OR)	▶ Compass bus 123 to/from **Lewes** (Stage 7c; 3.4 miles OR), **Rodmell** (Stage 7e/8a; 0.5 miles OR), **Southease** (Stage 8a/8b) and **Newhaven**
7e/8a Rodmell (0.5 miles OR)	▶ Compass bus 123 to/from **Lewes** (Stage 7c; 3.4 miles OR), **Southease** (Stage 8a/8b), **Kingston-near-Lewes** (Stage 7d/7e; 0.7 miles OR) and **Newhaven**
8a/8b Southease	▶ Compass bus 123 to/from **Lewes** (Stage 7c; 3.4 miles OR), **Rodmell** (Stage 7e/8a; 0.5 miles OR), **Kingston-near-Lewes** (Stage 7d/7e; 0.7 miles OR) and **Newhaven** ▶ Trains to/from **Lewes** (Stage 7c; 3.4 miles OR), **Brighton**, **Eastbourne**, **Gatwick Airport**, **London** and **Portsmouth**. You could also travel to **Winchester** and **Southampton** with a few changes

Stage/Place (W-E)	Transport Options (Towns in red have train stations)
8b/8c Firle (1.4 miles OR)	▶ **Compass 125/Cuckmere Buses 25** to/from **Lewes** (Stage 7c; 3.4 miles OR), **Eastbourne**, **Alfriston** (Stage 8d/9a) and **Wilmington** (Stage v9; 0.8 miles OR)
8d/9a Alfriston	▶ **Compass 125/Cuckmere Buses 25** to/from **Lewes** (Stage 7c; 3.4 miles OR), **Eastbourne**, **Firle** (Stage 8b/8c; 1.4 miles OR) and **Wilmington** (Stage v9; 0.8 miles OR) ▶ **Cuckmere Buses 126** to/from **Seaford** and **Berwick** ▶ **Cuckmere Buses 47** to/from **Berwick**, **Seaford**, **Exceat** (Stage 9a/9b), **Litlington** (Stage 9a) and **Wilmington** (Stage v9; 0.8 miles OR)
v9 Wilmington (0.8 miles OR)	▶ **Compass 125/Cuckmere Buses 25** to/from **Lewes** (Stage 7c; 3.4 miles OR), **Eastbourne**, **Firle** (Stage 8b/8c; 1.4 miles OR) and **Alfriston** (Stage 8d/9a) ▶ **Cuckmere Buses 47** to/from **Berwick**, **Alfriston** (Stage 8d/9a), **Seaford**, **Exceat** (Stage 9a/9b) and **Litlington** (Stage 9a)
v9 Jevington	▶ **Cuckmere Buses 41** to/from **Eastbourne** town centre
9a/9b Exceat	▶ **Cuckmere Buses 47** to/from **Berwick**, **Alfriston** (Stage 8d/9a), **Seaford**, **Litlington** (Stage 9a) and **Wilmington** (Stage v9; 0.8 miles OR) ▶ Brighton & Hove bus 12/12A/12X to/from **Brighton** and **Eastbourne** ▶ Brighton & Hove bus 13X to/from **Brighton**, **Eastbourne**, **Birling Gap** (Stage 9b) and **Beachy Head** (Stage 9c)
Stage 9b Birling Gap	▶ Brighton & Hove bus 13X to/from **Brighton**, **Eastbourne**, **Exceat** (Stage 9a/9b) and **Beachy Head** (Stage 9c)
Stage 9c Beachy Head	▶ Brighton & Hove bus 13X to/from **Brighton**, **Eastbourne**, **Exceat** (Stage 9a/9b) and **Birling Gap** (Stage 9b)
9c Meads	▶ Stagecoach bus 3 to/from **Eastbourne** town centre

The famous Victorian pier in Eastbourne

On the Trail

Clear marking on Section v9

Costs & budgeting

As vacations go, long-distance trekking in the UK is relatively inexpensive. The walking itself is free as no permits are required. The main components of daily expenditure are food and accommodation/camping: approximate costs are set out below.

	Approximate Cost (subject to change)
Room in pub/inn	£35-70 per person sharing a double/twin room
B&B	£35-70 per person sharing a double/twin room
Bed in hostel	£20-30 per person
Bed in bunkhouse	£10-20 per person
Camping	£7-20 per person
Meal in pub/inn	£12-20
Packed lunch	£6-10
Beer (1 pint)	£4-6

Weather

England has famously green countryside and this beautiful greenery requires plenty of water. The water is of course supplied by rain and GB's location near the Atlantic Ocean ensures that there is plenty of it: the island bears the brunt of many Atlantic fronts as they make their way eastwards. That said, SE England has possibly the mildest climate in the UK and therefore receives less rain, and more sunshine, than most other parts of the country. It is not uncommon to spend a week or so on the SDW without experiencing wet weather. Nevertheless, you should still be prepared for rain, even in summer.

In summer, the sun in the SDs can be very hot: temperatures can reach 30°C or more. The heat saps your energy and often there is little shade. Such conditions can reduce the distance that you can cover each day. De-hydration and sunstroke are possibilities and you must carry more water than normal. The SDs can also be windy and in such conditions, you should exercise caution on the higher and more exposed parts of the SDW: in particular, take care on the high sea-cliffs on Section 9.

The SDW runs for 100 miles across SE England and, at any given time, the weather on one part of the trail can be completely different from the weather on another section: for example, it could be raining in Winchester and sunny in Eastbourne or vice versa.

Always get a weather forecast before setting out. Many internet sites provide forecasts, with a varying degree of reliability. The UK Met Office (www.metoffice.gov.uk) is one of the most reliable as it provides regularly updated localised forecasts for different places along the SDW. It also provides, free of charge, an excellent smart-phone app that gives local forecasts.

Maps

In this book, we have included real maps for the entire SDW. Each stage has 1:25,000 scale maps produced by Ordnance Survey, GB's mapping agency. We believe that these are the finest, and most detailed, maps available. They are perfect for navigating the SDW. However, if you would also like sheet maps, there are a number of options:

- **OS Explorer 1:25,000**: the maps that are printed in this book are based on OS Explorer sheets. Six sheets are required to cover the entire SDW: sheets OL32 (Winchester), OL3 (Meon Valley), OL8 (Chichester), OL10 (Arundel & Pulborough), OL11 (Brighton & Hove) and OL25 (Eastbourne & Beachy Head).

- **OS Landranger 1:50,000**: four sheets are required to cover the entire SDW - 185 (Winchester & Basingstoke), 197 (Chichester & the South Downs), 198 (Brighton & Lewes) and 199 (Eastbourne & Hastings).

- **Harveys South Downs Way XT40**: this single sheet 1:40,000 waterproof strip map covers the entire trek.

However, perhaps the best overall solution is to combine the real maps provided in this book with OS's excellent smart-phone app: it provides 1:25,000 maps for the whole of GB and uses GPS to show your location and direction on the map. As the app's maps are the same as those provided in this book, they can be used together seamlessly. In the past, people often uploaded a series of GPS waypoints to their devices. However, because the OS app is so effective (showing both the SDW route and your actual location), in our opinion, there is now little point in bothering with GPS waypoint uploads. One month's subscription to the app is only £3.99 so it is ideal for SDW walkers.

Paths and waymarking

The SDW normally follows clear paths and tracks. Often the surface is comprised of chalk and/or flint and is hard underfoot in dry summer conditions. When it rains on the hard chalk, paths can be slippery. In early spring and late autumn, or after sustained periods of rain, some paths can be muddy. There are also some short sections along minor roads and the SDW frequently crosses roads and farm tracks: be sure to take care at crossings, looking both ways for traffic.

Much of the countryside is farmland so there are numerous gates along the route. Like many routes in rural England, the SDW has plenty of twists and turns as it negotiates rights-of-way through farmland and villages. Consequently, the route has been extremely well marked and navigation is usually straightforward: almost every junction has a sign or a white acorn (which is the generic symbol for England's National Trails). You will quickly get into a rhythm, looking for the next waymark every time you pass one. In the route descriptions, we do not highlight every junction because the waymarking is so good: generally, we only mention junctions if they are particularly significant or if there are no waymarks. Bear in mind though that waymarking is at the mercy of the environment: for example, signs and waymarks are occasionally obscured by vegetation or destroyed by falling trees.

The terrain undulates regularly but gradients are rarely very steep. Furthermore, there are few long climbs or descents on the SDW except for the handful of occasions when the route drops into valleys (to cross rivers) and climbs back up the other side.

Storing bags

Often walkers from the UK travel to the SDW carrying only the gear that they will actually take on the trek. However, trekkers from further afield, and those who want to spend some time elsewhere after the trek, will probably have additional baggage which they need to store while trekking. Normally, a hotel that you have stayed at near the start of the trek will let you store bags until your return: check when booking. At the end of the trek, it is straightforward to get back to the start by train: see 'Returning to the start from the finish of the SDW'. As an alternative, consider a baggage transfer service which delivers your bags to your accommodation each night: see below.

A typical waymark

Baggage transfer

Businesses offering baggage transfer services can transport your bags to your accommodation each night so that you only need to carry a small day-pack on the trail. This spares you from the burden of having to carry a heavy backpack and enables you to pack more clean clothes and some luxuries. Most of the companies offering unguided tours can organise baggage transfers. However, at the date of press, we could only find one business offering a baggage transfer service along the entire SDW without a requirement to book an unguided tour:

▶ **South Downs Discovery**: www.southdownsdiscovery.com;
  info@southdownsdiscovery.com; 01962 867 728/07934 880 917;
  £23 per transfer for a 20kg bag with discounts for more than one bag.

Another company, **Sherpa Van**, previously offered baggage transfers, however, when we contacted them at the time of writing, they informed us that they had ceased operating on the SDW and it was unclear if their services would be resuming. Further information: www.sherpavan.com; info@sherpavan.com; 01748 826 917.

Occasionally, taxi companies will transport bags to your next destination. However, each business normally only operates within a certain radius of their base so will not cover the entire SDW: for example, Gravers Taxis (www.petersfieldtaxis.co.uk; 01730 303 030) will only provide a service to/from Exton, Buriton, South Harting, Cocking and Petersfield. This means that to cover the whole route, you would need to endure the frustrating and time-consuming task of organising a series of baggage transfers with different taxi companies. For a list of taxi companies, see 'Public transport along the SDW': they may be able to assist, depending upon your specific requirements.

Fuel for camping stoves

Airlines will not permit you to transport fuel so campers who are flying to Southern England will need to source it upon arrival, before setting out on the trek. There are outdoor shops in Winchester, Eastbourne and Lewes: methylated spirits and standard screw-in gas canisters are normally available but it is wise to call in advance to check. Canisters are also usually available in branches of Halfords: you can order online for collection in-shop.

- **Winchester**: Mountain Warehouse (01962 866 332); Halfords (01962 849 411)
- **Lewes**: The Outdoor Shop (01273 487 840; info@outdoorshoplewes.co.uk); Mountain Warehouse (01273 472 623)
- **Eastbourne**: Blacks (01323 401 041); Millets (01323 409 340); Wildtrak (0191 261 4191); Halfords (01323 500 555)

If you need petrol or diesel for a multi-fuel stove, there are service stations at the primary trail-heads (Winchester and Eastbourne) and along the SDW at Pyecombe (Stage 6d/7a). There are also service stations OR at Petersfield, Midhurst, Storrington and Lewes.

Water

Drinking water will be one of your primary considerations each day. Even in England, the sun can be hot: dehydration and sunstroke are always possibilities. Finding water while on the trail can be tricky. You pass relatively few lakes and rivers and anyway, drinking from them is not advisable: farmers in rural England often use pesticides and fertilisers and traces of them may find their way into the watercourses.

Fortunately, there are water points ('WPs') along the trail where you can top up your bottles: a list of official WPs is available at www.nationaltrail.co.uk but there are other non-official WPs which are not included on this list. Some of the WPs are taps located at the side of the trail. In other instances, official WPs are pubs which will provide you with water but only during opening hours. In fact, the staff at most pubs and cafés (whether or not they are official WPs) will be happy to fill your water bottles for free if you buy some food or a drink: licensed premises in England (those that are authorised to serve alcohol) are required by law to provide "free potable water" to their customers upon request. Campsites will also have water taps: if you ask nicely when passing, they may allow you to fill up. Between November and March, taps at WPs are sometimes drained and turned off to prevent them freezing.

We have set out below a list of WPs along the SDW: this includes official WPs as well as non-official ones that we have found. The WPs are also shown on the route maps. Furthermore, in the introduction to each section, we list the places where refreshments are available, as well as any WPs, along the route. It is good practice to fill up in the morning at your accommodation, starting the day with at least 1.5 litres. However, water is heavy so you will not want to carry more than you need: plan carefully so that you know where your next WP will be. Furthermore, always check your water levels when you pass a WP.

A typical WP

Stage	WP Location Black: on official WP list Red: not on official WP list	Details
1a/1b	Chilcomb	Tap beside the route
1b/1c	Holden Farm	Tap
1c/1d	The Milbury's	Pub
1d	Lomer Farm	Tap beside the route
1d/2a	The Shoe Inn, Exton	Pub
2a/2b	Meon Springs	Tap beside the route
2b/2c	The Sustainability Centre	Tap beside the Beech Café
2c	Queen Elizabeth Country Park	Tap beside the café
3b/4a	Manor Farm (near Cocking)	Tap beside the route
4d	Houghton Bridge	Tap beside the sewage works NE of the River Arun crossing
5b/5c (0.6 miles OR)	Franklin Arms, Washington	Pub
5c	Parkfield Farm (near Washington)	Tap beside the route about 100m W of the A24
6a/6b	Upper Beeding exit	Tap beside the route: just E of the River Adur crossing
6b/6c	Truleigh Hill	Tap at the YHA Hostel
6c	Devils Dyke Pub	Pub
6c/6d	Saddlescombe Farm	Tap
7c/7d	Housedean Farm	Tap beside the route
8a	Southease church	Tap on the churchyard wall
8d/9a	Alfriston	Various pubs
9a	The Plough & Harrow, Litlington	Pub
9a/9b	Exceat	Tap at the toilet block of the Seven Sisters Country Park visitor centre
9b	Birling Gap	Tap at the National Trust visitor centre
9c	Beachy Head Pub	Pub
v9	St. Andrew's Church, Jevington	Tap at the churchyard entrance
v9	The Eight Bells, Jevington	Pub

Equipment

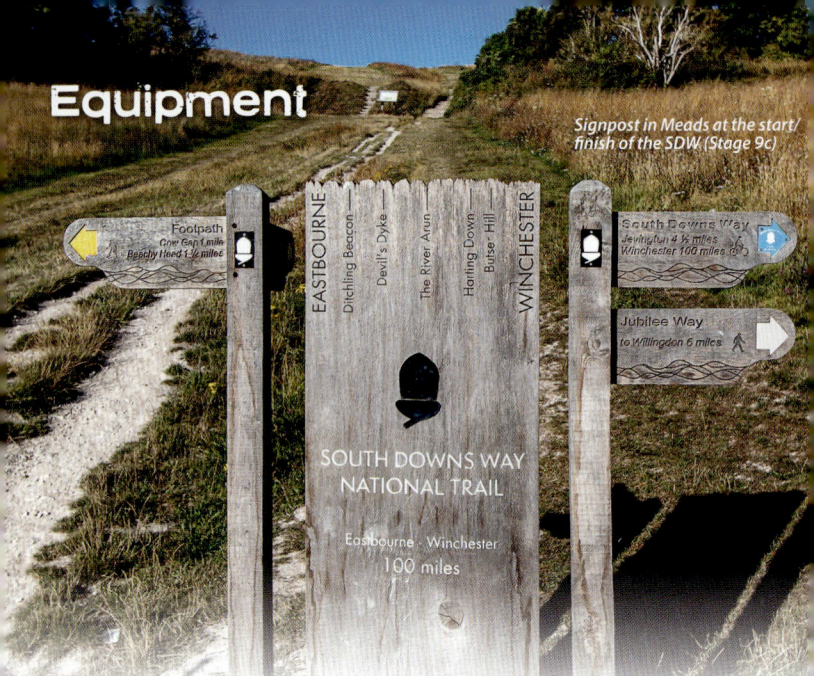

Signpost in Meads at the start/finish of the SDW (Stage 9c)

The long-distance trekker has no influence over challenges like weather and terrain but can control the contents of a pack carried on the trail. Some trekkers carry only a light day-pack, paying for a baggage transfer service to transport the bulk of their gear to their nightly accommodation: see 'Baggage transfer'. Many others, however, elect to carry all their own gear and it is fair to say that a lot of those people set off carrying equipment which is unnecessary or simply too heavy: this can result in injury and/or exhaustion, leading to abandonment. If you are intending to carry your own gear, then you should give equipment choice careful consideration: it will be crucial to your enjoyment of the trek and the likelihood of success.

When undertaking any long-distance route, you should be properly equipped for the worst terrain and the worst weather conditions which you could encounter. On the SDW, a key consideration is rain: you might not get any in practice but you should expect it when planning. In late spring, summer and early autumn, you should carry clothing to combat cold, heat, sun and rain. Even in England, the sun can be strong and getting cold and wet in the hills is unpleasant and can be dangerous.

However, the dilemma is that you should also consider weight and avoid carrying anything unnecessary. The heavier your pack, the harder the trek will be. A trekker's base weight is the weight of his/her pack, excluding food and water. If you are not carrying your own camping gear and cooking equipment, it is perfectly possible to get by with a base weight of 5-6kg (13lb) or less. If you intend to carry camping equipment then, by investing in some modern lightweight gear, you could start the trek with a base weight of 8-9kg (17lb) or less. Many people are quick to tell you that the lighter the gear, the greater the price but that is not always the case. While it is true that lightweight gear can be expensive, there are also some excellent lightweight products which are great value. Tents, sleeping bags and backpacks are the three heaviest items that you will carry so they offer the biggest opportunities for weight-saving. But do not ignore the smaller items either as the weight can quickly add up. So, if you can afford it, it is sensible to invest some money in gear before you go. The lighter your gear, the more you will enjoy the trek and the better your chance of success. Be ruthless as every ounce counts.

Recommended basic kit

Layering of clothing is the key to warmth. Do not wear cotton: it does not dry quickly and gets cold. Modern walking clothes are light so make sure that you have a spare set to change into if you get wet.

Boots/Shoes	Good quality, properly fitting and worn in. Robust soles (such as Vibram) are advisable to cope with the hard chalk/flint ground. For the SDW, trail-running shoes are perfectly adequate but many prefer boots with ankle support. Shoes/boots with a waterproof membrane (such as Gore-Tex) are a good idea.
Socks	2 pairs of good quality, quick-drying walking socks: wash one, wear one. Wash them regularly, helping to avoid blisters. As a luxury, it is nice to have a third pair to wear in the evenings.
Waterproof jacket and trousers	A waterproof and breathable rain jacket is essential although it might never leave your pack. Many also carry waterproof trousers.
Base layers	2 T-shirts and underpants of man-made fabrics or merino wool, which wick moisture away from your body: wash one, wear one. As a luxury, it is nice to have a third set to wear in the evenings.
Fleeces	2 fleeces. Man-made fabrics.
Shorts/ Trousers	2 pairs of shorts or walking trousers. Convertible trousers are practical as you can remove the legs on warm days. One pair of shorts and one pair of trousers is also a good combination in summer.
Warm hat	Always carry a warm hat. Even in summer it can be cold particularly on windy days.
Gloves	Early or late season trekkers may wish to bring gloves.
Down jacket	Advisable in spring, autumn and winter when low temperatures are more likely, especially in the evening and early morning.
Camp shoes	It is nice to have shoes to wear in the evenings. Flip-flops or Crocs are a common choice as they are light. However, if you have comfortable hiking boots/shoes then you might consider not bringing camp shoes to save weight.
Waterproof pack liner	Most backpacks are not very waterproof. An internal liner will keep your gear dry if it rains. Many trekkers use external pack covers but we do not find them to be very useful: they flap in the wind and in heavy rain, water still finds its way into the pack around the straps (so you need an internal liner anyway).
Whistle	For emergencies. Many rucksacks have one incorporated into the sternum strap.
Head-light with spare batteries	You will need a flashlight if you are camping. And it is good practice to carry one for emergencies: it can assist if you get caught out late and enable you to signal to rescuers.

Basic first-aid kit	Including plasters, a bandage, antiseptic wipes and painkillers. Blister plasters, moleskin padding or tape (such as Leukotape) can be useful to prevent or combat blisters. A tick removal tool or card is also recommended.
Map and compass	For maps see above. A GPS unit or a smart-phone app can be a useful addition but they are no substitute for a map and compass: after all, batteries can run out and electronics can fail.
Knife	Such as a Swiss Army knife. You are going to need to cut that cheese!
Sunglasses, sun hat, sunscreen and lip salve	Even in England, the sun can be strong so do not set out without these items.
Walking poles	These transfer weight from your legs onto your arms, keeping you fresher. They also save your knees (particularly on descents) and can reduce the likelihood of falling or twisting an ankle.
Phone and charger	A smart-phone is a very useful tool on a trek. It can be used for emergencies. Furthermore, apps for weather, mapping and hotel booking are invaluable. It can also replace your camera to save weight.
Towel	If you are staying at campsites or bunkhouses, you will need a towel: lightweight trekking towels are a sensible choice.
Toiletries	Campers will need to bring soap/shower gel: a small hotel-size bottle should be enough to last the trek, saving a lot of weight. Toothbrush and toothpaste: an almost empty tube will save weight. For those who shave, shaving oil is a lightweight alternative to a can of foam/gel. Leave that make-up behind!
Ziplock plastic bag	A lightweight way of keeping money, passport and credit cards dry.
Ear plugs	Useful if staying in dormitories: you will thank us if someone snores!
Emergency food	Carry some emergency food over and above your planned daily ration. Energy bars, nuts and dried fruit are all good.
Water	See 'Water' above. Hydration packs with tubes enable drinking on the move.
Toilet paper and trowel	Bring a backpacking trowel in case nature calls on the trail: bury toilet waste and carry out used toilet paper. Leave no trace.
Backpack	The weight of a backpack itself is often overlooked but it is one of the heaviest items that you will carry. The difference in the weights of various packs can be surprisingly large. 35-40 litres should be sufficient if you are not carrying camping gear. 45-60 litres should be adequate for campers. If you need a pack bigger than these then you are most likely carrying too much. Look for well-padded shoulder straps and waist band. Much of the weight of the pack should sit on your hips rather than your shoulders.

Additional gear for campers

Tent: this is one of the heaviest things that you will carry so it provides a big opportunity for weight saving. Some 2-person tents weigh more than 3kg while others weigh less than 0.6kg. The heaviest ones are normally built for extreme winter conditions and are overkill for the SDW. The lightest ones are quite fragile but this is not normally an issue on the SDW where campsites are often grassy. Although a few premium brands charge a lot for their products and there are some very expensive tents at the lightest end of the scale, these days there are plenty of lightweight tents available at a reasonable price. Tents weighing 1 to 1.5kg often strike a good balance between price, longevity and weight. Consider money spent here as an investment in your well-being and enjoyment of one of the world's great trails. Believe us when we say that a few kgs can be the difference between success and failure.

Your tent should be waterproof to ensure that you stay dry during rainy nights. If you are going to use a very light tent then a footprint can be a good idea to protect its base: 'footprint' is a trendy, modern word for what used to be known as a groundsheet. Sometimes you can buy footprints specific to your tent model but we prefer to use a sheet of Tyvek which can be cut to size: Tyvek is extremely tough and is cheaper, and normally lighter, than most branded footprints.

Tent Pegs: : tent weights provided by manufacturers normally exclude the weight of the pegs. The pegs actually provided with tents tend to be quite heavy and many trekkers buy replacement ones which are lighter. Six heavy pegs can weigh as much as 240g while 6 light pegs can weigh as little as 6g. There are many different types available these days and it is important to match the peg with the type of ground they will be used in. The ground on the SDW is soft and normally grassy so it is usually easy to get pegs into it. Accordingly, they do not need to be too strong.

Sleeping bag: each bag has a 'comfort rating': This is the lowest temperature at which the standard woman should enjoy a comfortable night's sleep. There is also a 'lower comfort limit' which is for men. That may sound simple but it is not. Although all reputable sleeping bag manufacturers use the same independent standard, the bags are not tested in the same place so there is a lack of consistency amongst ratings. Also, the ratings are designed with an average man and woman in mind but every person is different: some people get colder than others. The ratings should therefore be used as a guide only and it is wise to choose a bag with a comfort rating which is a few degrees lower than the night temperatures that you will encounter. In June, July and August a bag rated between 5 and 10°C is normally sufficient, depending on whether you 'sleep hot' or 'sleep cold'. In early and late season, you may want something warmer. However, you do not want to bring a bag that is much too warm as that would add unnecessary weight to your pack.

Unfortunately, with sleeping bags, price tends to be inversely proportional to weight. This is largely because the lightest bags are filled with goose/duck down which is expensive. Synthetic bags are also available but they are much heavier so down is the better choice for the SDW. The disadvantage of down bags is that they can lose their warmth if they get wet but that is less likely if you have a good tent and pack liner. Our advice is first to decide what comfort rating you will require. Then choose the lightest bag (with that rating) which you can afford.

Sleeping mat: this makes it comfortable for you to sleep on the hard ground and insulates you from the ground's cold surface. There are three types: air, self-inflating and closed-cell foam. The advantages and disadvantages of each are set out below. For the SDW, weight is normally more of an issue than warmth so we prefer air mats.

Sleeping Mat Type	Pros	Cons
Air mats: need to be blown up	Lightest Very comfortable Most compact when packed Thicker: good for side sleepers	Most expensive Hard work to inflate Can be punctured Less warm than self-inflating
Self-inflating mats: a combination of air and closed-cell foam. The mat partially inflates itself when the valve is opened	Warmest Very comfortable Quite compact More durable than air mats Firmness is adjustable by adding air	Heavier More expensive than closed-cell foam Can be punctured
Closed-cell foam mats	Light Least expensive Most durable Cannot be punctured	Not compact: needs to be strapped to the outside of your pack Least warm Least comfortable

Pillow: some use rolled-up clothing but we prefer inflatable trekking pillows which only weigh around 50g.

Stove: you should choose a stove that uses a type of fuel which is available on the SDW. Airlines do not permit you to carry fuel on planes so, if you are flying to Southern England, you will need to source fuel on arrival. Although methylated spirits are sometimes stocked in outdoor shops, these days gas is more widely available (see 'On the Trail'). Most gas stoves are designed to fit generic screw-on canisters (not Campinggaz) which are readily available in the UK. Canisters for Campinggaz stoves (which are popular in France) are much harder to find so are not a good choice for the SDW. Multi-fuel stoves that burn petrol and/or diesel are useful though: there are service stations in Winchester, Pyecombe (Stage 6d/7a) and Eastbourne.

Hundreds of different stoves are available, some more complicated than others. Often the lightest ones are the most simple and often the most simple ones are relatively inexpensive. If, like most campers, you will eat dried food such as pasta and rice then your stove will need to do little more than boil water. A basic stove which mounts on top of a gas canister will therefore be adequate: such a stove should also be cheap and lightweight (less than 100g).

Pots: if, like most campers, you eat dried food such as pasta and rice then you will only need one pot which will do little more than boil water. To save weight, go for the smallest pot that you can get away with. For example, if you are travelling solo and planning to use freeze-dried backpacking meals then you would need nothing bigger than a 500-600ml pot. Titanium pots are usually the lightest but they are slightly more expensive. Get the lightest one that you can afford.

Fork/Spoon: we love Sporks! They have a spoon at one end and a fork at the other. They weigh a mere 9g and cost very little.

Safety

Views of Littleton Down (Stage 4b)

On a calm summer's day, the SDs are paradise. But a sudden weather shift or an injury can change things dramatically so treat the hills with respect and be conscious of your experience levels and physical capabilities. The following is a non-exhaustive list of recommendations:

- The fitter you are at the start of your trip, the more you will enjoy the hiking.
- Start early to avoid walking during the hottest part of the day and to allow surplus time in case something goes wrong.
- Do not stray from the waymarked paths so as to avoid getting lost and to help prevent erosion of the landscape.
- Before you set out each day, study the route and make plans based upon the abilities of the weakest member of your party.
- Get a weather forecast (daily if possible) and reassess your plans in light of it. Avoid exposed routes if the weather is uncertain.
- Never be too proud to turn back if you find the going too tough or if the weather deteriorates.
- Bring a map and compass and know how to use them.
- Carry surplus food and clothing for emergencies.
- Avoid exposed high ground in a thunderstorm. If you get caught out in one then drop your walking poles and stay away from trees, overhanging rocks, metal structures and caves. Generally accepted advice is to squat on your pack and keep as low as possible.
- In the event of an accident, move an injured person into a safe place and administer any necessary first-aid. Keep the victim warm. Establish your exact coordinates and, if possible, use your cell-phone to call for help. The emergency number is 999. If you have no signal then send someone for help.
- When cooking on a camping stove, place the stove on the ground. Do not use it on a picnic table. We have witnessed a walker knocking over his stove and spilling boiling water on his legs: this is a sure-fire way to end your trek.
- Hikers share much of the SDW with mountain-bikers. This is not normally an issue because the SDW has been designed as both a bridleway and footpath: most of the shared sections are wide enough to allow both types of users to co-exist. Nevertheless, exercise caution as a collision between a hiker and a mountain-bike could be serious.

General Information

Language: English is the main language.

Charging electronic devices: the UK uses a 3-pin plug. Visitors from outside the UK or Ireland will need an adapter. Some campsites, bunkhouses and camping barns facilitate the charging of electronic devices but this may not be possible at the more basic places. Some people carry their own portable charging devices.

Money: the UK uses Sterling (£). On the SDW itself, there are ATMs only in Winchester, Pyecombe (at the service station) and Eastbourne. It is therefore preferable to start the SDW carrying all the cash you will need for the trek. Off the main route, there are ATMs at Petersfield, Arundel, Storrington, Upper Beeding and Lewes. Credit cards are accepted almost everywhere.

Visas: citizens of the European Union, Australia, New Zealand, Canada or the US do not need a visa for short tourist trips to the UK.

Cell-phones: there is network in most places along the SDW. However, in the more remote parts, it can occasionally be difficult to get a signal. When network is available, it is likely to be a 3G/4G service enabling access to the internet from smart-phones. In the UK, work has started on a new 5G network.

International dialling codes: the country code for the UK is +44. If dialling from overseas, the 0 in UK area codes is omitted.

WiFi: nearly all hotels, pubs and B&Bs have WiFi (see Accommodation Listings). Some campsites and bunkhouses may not offer it.

Emergencies and rescue: rescue services are normally free and are provided by unpaid volunteers. The emergency number is 999: ask for 'mountain rescue'.

Insurance: depending upon your nationality, any required medical treatment in the UK may not be provided free of charge so it is wise to purchase travel insurance which covers hiking.

Ticks: as is often the case in Europe, ticks are present in England. They can carry Lyme disease or tick-borne encephalitis so check yourself regularly. Remove ticks with a specialist tick removal tool or card (making sure you get all of it out) and then disinfect the area.

Tourist Information: there are tourist information centres at **Winchester** (Stage 1a; 01962 840 500), **Petersfield** (OR from Stage 2c/3a; 01730 268 829), **Lewes** (OR from Stage 7c; 01273 483 448) and **Eastbourne** (Stage 9c; 01323 415 415). Information is also available from the **South Downs Visitor Centre** in Midhurst (01730 814 810; info@southdowns.gov.uk) and online at the following sources:

- www.nationaltrail.co.uk: information on all England's National Trails, including the SDW
- www.visitwinchester.co.uk: information for visitors to Winchester
- www.visitlewes.co.uk: information for visitors to Lewes
- www.visiteastbourne.com: information for visitors to Eastbourne
- www.southdowns.gov.uk: website for the SDNP
- visitsouthdowns.com: a non-profit organisation, promoting the SDNP
- www.nationaltrust.org.uk: this charity owns/manages many sites along the SDW

Wildlife

A cow near Chanctonbury Hill (Stage 5c)

Much of the fauna in the SDs is similar to that in other parts of the UK. There are roe deer, foxes, badgers, rabbits, grey squirrels, hedgehogs, mice, shrews, voles, stoats, weasels and bats. There are also hares which are often confused with rabbits but in fact they are quite easy to tell apart: hares have distinctive pointy faces and longer ears (with black tips). It is of interest to the SDW trekker that, as well as cultivating large parts of the SDs, the Romans probably introduced rabbits to Britain. There are snakes too: adders (which are venomous) and grass snakes (which are not venomous). The clear chalk streams and rivers in the SDs are famous for their trout and also support rare species such as otter and water vole: unfortunately, populations of the latter have been devastated by American mink, an invasive species.

However, it is the colourful butterflies which are most likely to catch your eye along the SDW: during spring and summer they are seemingly everywhere. The chalk grassland of the SDs supports a wide variety of wild-flowers upon which butterflies thrive, including rare chalk specialists such as the Adonis Blue (with its bright blue wings, fringed with white), the Chalkhill Blue (with its pale blue colouring) and the orange-brown Duke of Burgundy.

Many of the birds are also similar to those in other parts of the UK. However, there are also rare species of farmland birds such as corn bunting, skylark, yellowhammer, lapwing and grey partridge. There are woodpeckers and owls too. Easier to spot though are the birds of prey such as buzzards, kestrels, red kites (recognisable by their forked tails) and sparrowhawks: they soar or hover above the Downs, searching for prey. The river valleys along the SDW support a wide variety of wading birds: Cuckmere Haven (Stage 9b), for example, has avocet, lapwing, snipe, oystercatcher and curlew, to name a few. On the coastal sections of the route (near Eastbourne), there are a variety of sea-birds including fulmars and kittiwakes.

Plants and Flowers

Wild-flowers alongside the path (Stage 7c)

The chalk rock and mild climate of the SDs has created a number of habitats that support rare plants and wild-flowers. In particular, the chalk grassland is unique, supporting more species of plant than anywhere else in GB: supposedly there are up to 40 species in a square metre. The clovers, herbs and wild-flowers form a thick springy carpet which is soft underfoot. Unfortunately, only a small fraction of the old chalk grassland survives today, mainly on slopes which are too steep to plough: Old Winchester Hill (Stage 2a) and Harting Down (Stage 3b) are good examples. Chalk grassland flowers include the yellow horseshoe vetch (which is the food of the Adonis Blue butterfly), cowslip, violets and orchids. However, one of the most distinctive wild-flowers is the round-headed rampion, the 'Pride of Sussex', which occurs in greater quantities than anywhere else.

23% of the SDNP is woodland and half of that is more than 400 years old. In fact, the SDs have more ancient woodland than any other national park in GB. Much of this is found on the slopes of the northern escarpment which was frequently too steep to plough. Common trees are beech, ash, oak and hazel, however, there are also some of the largest yew woodlands in GB. There are sweet chestnut trees too which were introduced to Britain by the Romans. Because the soils of the woods have been undisturbed for centuries, bluebells have spread in vast quantities and this is a sight to behold in April/May.

There are also areas of heathland in the SDs where yellow gorse and purple heather are widespread: anyone who walks through a section of bright gorse in spring will be struck by the mouth-watering coconut aroma.

Those walking the SDW in late summer and early autumn will find blackberries seemingly everywhere. Purple sloe berries (which grow on blackthorn) are common too: they look like giant blueberries but they do not taste like them! In fact, sloe berries are only really palatable when added to gin.

Geology

Chalk paths are a defining feature of the SDW

On the pale paths and tracks of the SDW, it quickly becomes apparent to the hiker that the SDs are predominantly made of chalk. Chalk is a sedimentary rock: a variety of limestone comprised mainly of calcium carbonate. It is usually white or light grey in colour. Chalk soils are often thin which means that vegetation is mostly grass. Chalk tends to form gentle hills inland and steep cliffs at the coast. Chalk escarpments are often gently sloping on one side and steep on the other: the northern escarpment of the SDs is a case in point.

During the Cretaceous period (75-95 million years ago), Southern England lay under a shallow tropical sea which covered much of NW Europe: the seabed was made of layers of greensands and gault clay which had formed millions of years earlier. Marine algae, or other tiny organisms living in the sea, died and accumulated on the bottom as 'ooze' consisting mainly of calcium carbonate. Over more than 20 million years, this ooze gradually built up, layer by layer, to form the chalk hills that you see today. Then, about 75 million years ago, during the Alpine Orogeny (the immense geological process that formed the Alpine chain of mountains), the layers were forced up and folded into a dome. Erosion cleared softer rocks across the middle of the dome leaving what is now the Weald with the SDs and the North Downs on either side of it. During the last ice age, the valleys were formed by erosion and weathering.

As is common in deposits of chalk, the rock of the SDs incorporates bands of flint. The flint is of excellent quality and has been used by mankind for various purposes over the centuries. In the Neolithic period, it was used to make axes, knives and other tools. More recently, the walls of buildings were made from flint stone: the farm buildings of Saddlescombe Farm (Stage 6c/6d) are a good example.

The chalk of the SDs plays an important role in the supply of water in SE England. Chalk soils are thin and fast draining, allowing water to pass quickly to the chalk rock below: there are no marshes or areas of standing water. The chalk stores the water like a sponge creating a massive underground reservoir. Natural springs feed water from this reservoir into rivers and streams.

Another feature of chalk is that it is soft and friable and this makes it prone to erosion. The white sea-cliffs of the Seven Sisters (Stage 9b), for example, are constantly battered by wind and waves and large chunks closest to the edge regularly fall into the sea. In fact, it is this constant erosion of the outer surface that enables the cliffs to remain such a startlingly bright shade of white.

History of the South Downs

Sheep grazing on Beddingham Hill (Stage 8b)

The term 'down' was derived from an old English word meaning 'hill'. Nowadays it is commonly used in England to describe a range of rolling hills.

The SDs have been occupied by humans for at least 5,000 years and many of the walking paths in the region have been in use for hundreds, if not thousands, of years. Originally, much of the SDs would have been covered with trees. During the Neolithic period, groups of people formed settlements and cleared woodland to facilitate the planting of crops and grazing of livestock: the dry chalk hills offered favourable living conditions compared to the damp lowlands below. These agricultural settlements grew in number and size during the Bronze Age and the clearing of trees continued. During the Iron Age, communities expanded and hill-forts were constructed to house and defend larger communities. You will pass many hill-forts on the SDW (such as those at Chanctonbury Ring and Old Winchester Hill), as well as ancient burial grounds ('tumuli').

The SDs had great significance during the Roman period of occupation (55 BCE to 407 CE): a lot of food was required to feed the vast Roman army and an ever-increasing population of Roman citizens. The mild climate of the SDs meant that it was an important 'bread-basket' for the Empire. To enable systematic exploitation of the land for agriculture, they built villas and roads: the SDW actually runs along the line of some of these roads and you can visit Bignor Roman Villa which is a short distance from the route of Stage 4b/4c. During Roman times, there would have been a thriving economy in the region based on agriculture and trade. In fact, some believe that woodland clearances were practically completed by 100 CE and that the levels of agricultural production at that time were not surpassed until the 20th century.

In medieval times, the villages of the SDs grew and the system of 'sheep-corn' farming developed. Farmers allowed sheep to graze open grassland during the day but during the night, they moved them to the corn fields: sheep droppings were excellent fertiliser so under this clever system, farmers used the sheep to transfer nutrients from the grass of the grazing land to the corn-fields. Each night, the sheep would have been moved to a different patch of the corn-fields and a village's entire stock of sheep would have been pooled for this purpose. On the SDW, you will pass many 'dew ponds' which were created by the farmers to water the sheep. Sheep-corn farming was perfect for the thin, quickly-draining chalk soil (which needed regular fertilisation). It was so efficient that it continued to be practised until 1940 when efforts to dramatically increase food production during WW2 saw large swathes of old chalk grassland ploughed up (for the first time in a thousand years) and turned into arable land. That fundamentally changed the landscape of the SDs in a way that would never be reversed. It is estimated that, since WW2, the UK has lost 80% of its chalk grassland and now only 4% of the SDNP is old chalk grassland.

Throughout history, the SDs have often been recognised for their defensive attributes. For example, in Tudor times, a network of beacons spanned the length of England's S coast: the beacons were barrels of flammable pitch on wooden posts and would have been lit to transmit (along the coast) warnings of attack from the sea. Many of the hills in the SDs were part of this system including Ditchling Beacon (Stage 7b/7c).

During WW2, the SDs also had strategic importance: the height of the Downs and their relative proximity to mainland Europe, meant that they would have served as a vital defensive buffer in the event of an attack from the S. Many airfields were built nearby and the S coast was heavily fortified with gun emplacements and anti-tank defences. Large swathes of the SDs were requisitioned by the War Department to garrison and train troops for the Normandy landings in 1944. Tracks were surfaced to facilitate the movement of tanks and many villages were badly damaged during training exercises: they needed to be re-built after the war.

After WW2, food shortages meant that the government encouraged intensive farming on the SDs and even more chalk grassland was ploughed-up. At that time, knowledge of archaeological sites was limited and sadly, many hill-forts and burial grounds were destroyed in the process. In the post-war years, interest in hiking as a pastime increased and in 1963, the SDW was approved as a National Trail. It officially opened in 1972 but originally, it only ran between Eastbourne and Buriton: it was later extended westwards to Winchester. There is a specific team at the South Downs National Park Authority which maintains the SDW.

South Downs National Park

The SDNP was officially created in 2010 and is the newest of the UK's 15 National Parks. It comprises 1600 km^2 of the SDs and the Weald (the area of lower-lying countryside between the high escarpments of the SDs and the North Downs). The park protects a number of rare habitats including the beautiful chalk grassland that you will enjoy on the SDW and lowland heath. Within the SDNP there are approximately 2,000 miles of paths and tracks for walkers. The SDW is almost entirely within the park.

The absence of light pollution in the park makes it one of the darkest places at night in the UK: campers often enjoy spectacular night skies. In 2016, the SDNP was confirmed as an 'International Dark Sky Reserve', one of only 16 in the world.

A chalk boulder near Firle Beacon (Stage 8b/8c)

*Belle Tout Lighthouse
(Stage 9c)*

Route Descriptions

1 Winchester/Exton

The cathedral city of Winchester is an excellent place to start or finish the SDW. It was the capital of England until the Norman conquest in the 11th century. The streets are packed with history and modern life has not managed to dim their charm and character. The current layout of the streets dates back to the 9th century when King Alfred the Great changed the city's plan to improve its defences under the threat of Viking attack. The most significant building is the cathedral which was originally built in 1079 and is the longest Gothic cathedral in Europe. However, there are plenty of other interesting sites including Winchester Castle which was founded by William the Conqueror in 1067. The magnificent Great Hall (which was built in the 13th century) is all that is left of the castle and on display inside is King Arthur's famous Round Table: Winchester is thought to have been the site of Camelot. You could easily spend a day taking in Winchester's sights and enjoying a pint or a meal at one of the excellent pubs and restaurants.

The SDW officially starts/finishes across the road from the City Mill, a restored water mill on the River Itchen: there has been a mill here for more than 1,000 years but the current structure was built in 1743 (although some of the structural timbers are much older). However, on the assumption that most trekkers will want to visit Winchester Cathedral, we prefer to start/finish the trek there: the route described here travels between the

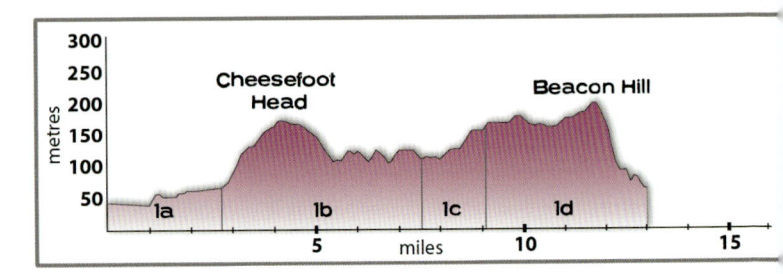

The approach to Cheesefoot Head (Stage 1b)

cathedral and the City Mill along the city's main shopping street, providing W-E hikers with an opportunity to stock-up at a supermarket on the way.

From the City Mill, W-E hikers briefly follow the River Itchen and then head E towards the SDs: you soon leave the city behind and enter a rural paradise of rolling arable farmland, wild flowers and butterflies. This section is perhaps most beautiful in mid-summer with a gentle breeze rippling through the vast corn-fields. E of the village of Chilcomb, the route passes over Cheesefoot Head (with its slopes of old chalk grassland) and the stunning Beacon Hill (where there is a Bronze Age tumulus). There are two Beacon Hills on the SDW: the other one is passed on Stage 3b.

Exton and Meonstoke, typical Hampshire villages, are beautiful places to spend the night. There are a couple of pubs and an excellent village shop where you can stock up on supplies.

The route is well marked and navigation is straightforward. There are two climbs but they are not too difficult: for W-E hikers, the climb to Cheesefoot Head is the steeper one but for E-W hikers, Beacon Hill is more demanding.

		Time	Distance	Ascent W-E	Descent W-E
Stage 1a	Winchester/ Chilcomb	1:00	2.7miles 4.3km	131ft 40m	33ft 10m
Stage 1b	Chilcomb/ Holden Farm	2:15	4.9miles 7.9km	476ft 145m	374ft 114m
Stage 1c	Holden Farm/ The Milbury's	0:45	1.5miles 2.4km	197ft 60m	33ft 10m
Stage 1d	The Milbury's/Exton	1:30	3.9miles 6.3km	164ft 50m	492ft 150m

Supplies/Water:

Winchester (Stage 1a) – supermarkets, shops & ATMs

Chilcomb (Stage 1a/1b) – WP (tap)

Holden Farm (Stage 1b/1c) – WP (tap)

The Milbury's pub (Stage 1c/1d) – WP

Lomer Farm (Stage 1d) – WP (tap)

Exton (Stage 1d/2a) – WP at the Shoe Inn

Meonstoke Post Office & Village Shop (Stage 1d/2a; 0.4 miles OR) – snacks, sandwiches, groceries & drinks

Refreshments/Food:

Winchester (Stage 1a) – pubs, restaurants and cafés

Morn Hill (Stage 1b; 1.4 miles OR) – the Holiday Inn

Cheriton (Stage 1b; 1.5 miles OR) – the Flower Pots Inn & Brewery

The Milbury's pub (Stage 1c/1d)

Exton (Stage 1d/2a) - the Shoe Inn

Meonstoke (Stage 1d/2a; 0.6 miles OR) – the Bucks Head

Accommodation:

Winchester (Stage 1a)
Chilcomb (Stage 1a/1b)
Morn Hill (Stage 1b; 1.4 miles OR)
Cheriton (Stage 1b; 1.5 miles OR)
Holden Farm (Stage 1b/1c)
Shorley (Stage 1c; 1.5 miles OR)
The Milbury's pub (Stage 1c/1d)
Kilmeston (Stage 1d; 1.4 miles OR)
Exton (Stage 1d/2a)
Meonstoke (Stage 1d/2a; 0.6 miles OR)
Corhampton (Stage 1d/2a; 1.3 miles OR)

Escape/Access:

Winchester (Stage 1a)
Cheriton (Stage 1b; 1.5 miles OR)
Corhampton (Stage 1d/2a; 1.3 miles OR)

Chalk grassland near Beacon Hill (Stage 1d)

King Alfred the Great

Alfred was King of the West Saxons (871-886 CE) and Anglo-Saxons (886-899). He defended his kingdom against the Vikings and became the dominant king in England, laying the foundations for a single kingdom of England. Winchester was his capital and many of its old streets were first established during his reign. He was an educated man and promoted learning. He also developed England's legal system and military structure. He is the only king of England to have been given the name 'the Great'. The statue of him in Winchester was erected in 1901.

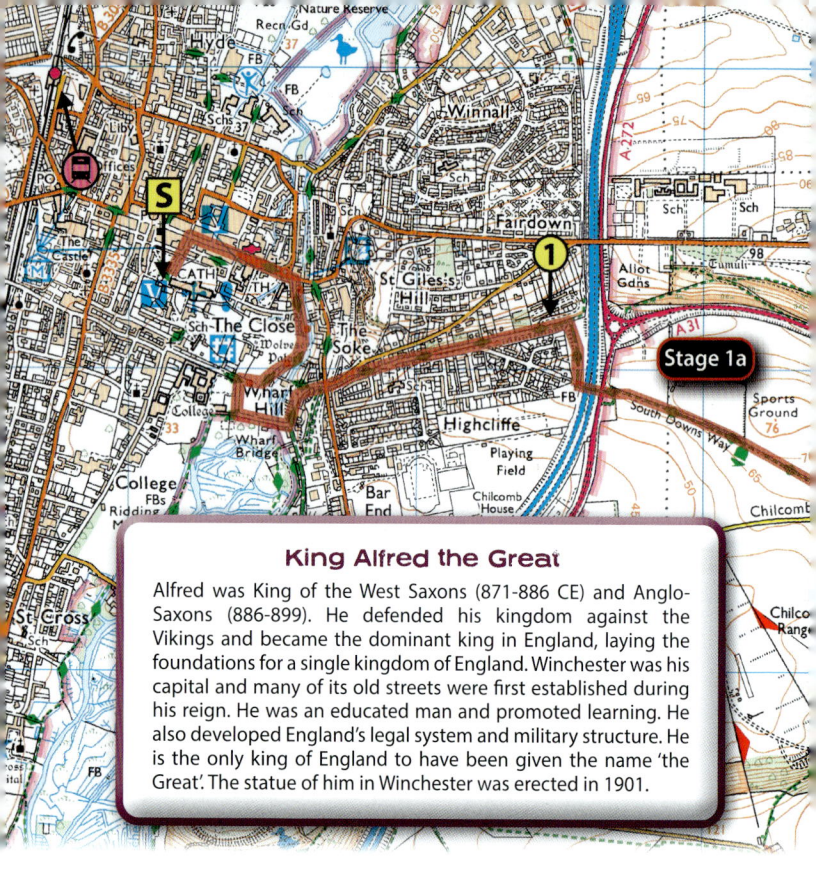

W-E

To reach the start from **Winchester station**, head E downhill, following signs for the city centre. At a junction, keep SH onto **City Road**. A few minutes later, TR onto **Jewry Street**. 5min later, TL onto **High Street** (the main shopping street where there are supermarkets). **Winchester Cathedral** is a short distance S of High Street.

Stage 1a: Winchester to Chilcomb

S From the front of the cathedral, head N. A few minutes later, TR along High Street. At a junction beside a statue of **King Alfred** (see box), keep SH. Shortly afterwards, TR at the **Old City Mill** onto a path beside the **River Itchen**: this is the official start of the SDW. Shortly afterwards, TR at a fork, heading away from the river. After the site of **Wolvesey Castle**, TL on **College Walk**: there are now blue SDW signs to guide you out of Winchester. Soon, TL onto **Wharf Hill**. At a junction, keep SH onto **East Hill**. Shortly afterwards, TR at a fork onto **Petersfield Road**.

1 0:35: Keep SH on a path. Shortly afterwards, TR at a junction. Soon, cross a bridge over the M3 motorway. Just afterwards, TL at a junction: almost immediately, emerge into open farmland.

2 0:55: Keep SH across a road junction ('St Andrew's Church').

F 1:00: Shortly afterwards, arrive at a junction in the village of **Chilcomb**.

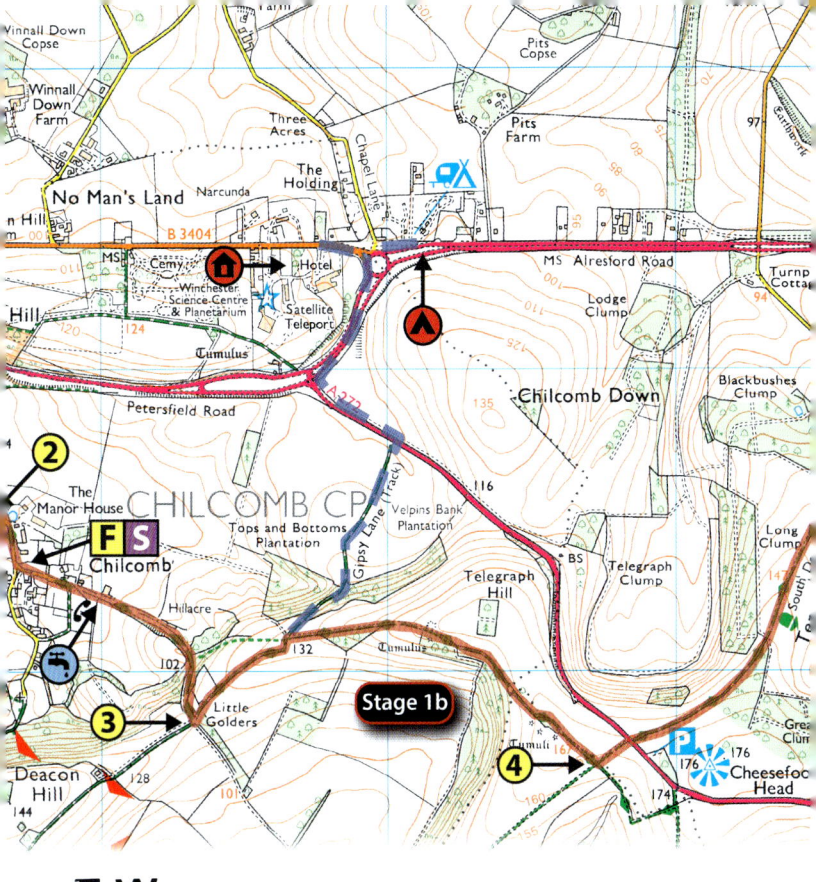

E-W

Stage 1a: Chilcomb to Winchester

F From the junction in **Chilcomb**, head initially N on a small road.

2 0:05: Shortly afterwards, keep SH at a road junction. Immediately afterwards, TR on a path. After a while, cross a bridge over the M3 motorway. Immediately afterwards, TR on a path. A few minutes later, TL at a junction.

1 0:25: Shortly afterwards, keep SH onto **Petersfield Road**. Keep SH onto **East Hill**. A few minutes later, keep SH across a junction onto **Wharf Hill**. Soon TR onto **College Walk**. At the entrance to **Wolvesey Castle**, TR on a path. When you reach the **River Itchen**, head N alongside it. At the **Old City Mill**, TL onto a road: this is the official finish of the SDW. At a junction beside a statue of **King Alfred** (see box), keep SH. Eventually, TL onto **Market Street**.

S 1:00: When the street bends right, keep SH on a path to arrive at **Winchester Cathedral**. Congratulations, you have completed the SDW.

Cheesefoot Head

Cheesefoot Head is also known as Matterley Bowl because of its shape which was created by melt-water during the last ice age. The banks of the bowl are one of the last remaining areas of old chalk grassland. The bowl was used as a natural amphitheatre during WW2: in June 1944, prior to the Normandy landings, General Eisenhower addressed 100,000 allied troops from it.

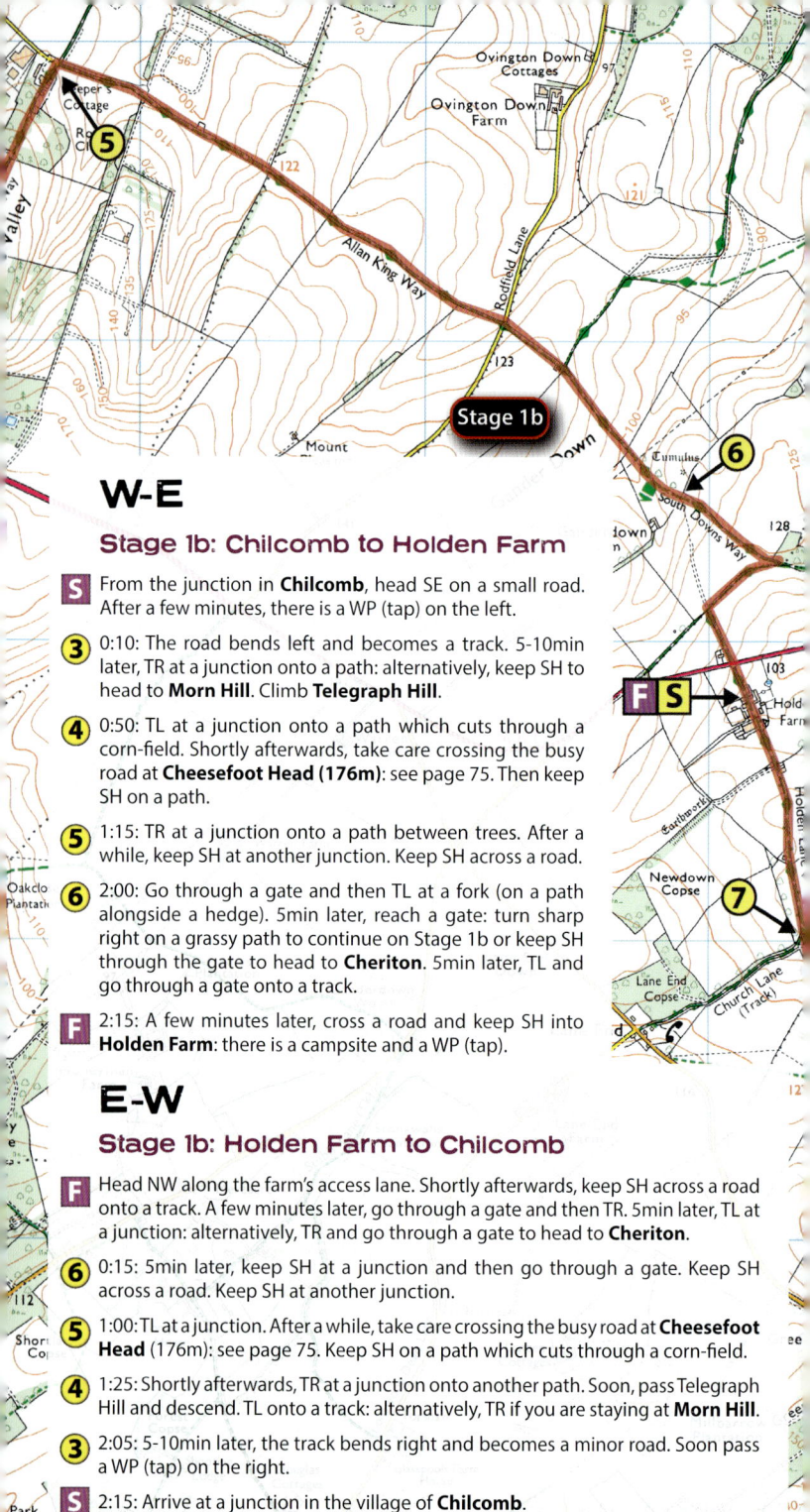

W-E

Stage 1b: Chilcomb to Holden Farm

S From the junction in **Chilcomb**, head SE on a small road. After a few minutes, there is a WP (tap) on the left.

3 0:10: The road bends left and becomes a track. 5-10min later, TR at a junction onto a path: alternatively, keep SH to head to **Morn Hill**. Climb **Telegraph Hill**.

4 0:50: TL at a junction onto a path which cuts through a corn-field. Shortly afterwards, take care crossing the busy road at **Cheesefoot Head (176m)**: see page 75. Then keep SH on a path.

5 1:15: TR at a junction onto a path between trees. After a while, keep SH at another junction. Keep SH across a road.

6 2:00: Go through a gate and then TL at a fork (on a path alongside a hedge). 5min later, reach a gate: turn sharp right on a grassy path to continue on Stage 1b or keep SH through the gate to head to **Cheriton**. 5min later, TL and go through a gate onto a track.

F 2:15: A few minutes later, cross a road and keep SH into **Holden Farm**: there is a campsite and a WP (tap).

E-W

Stage 1b: Holden Farm to Chilcomb

F Head NW along the farm's access lane. Shortly afterwards, keep SH across a road onto a track. A few minutes later, go through a gate and then TR. 5min later, TL at a junction: alternatively, TR and go through a gate to head to **Cheriton**.

6 0:15: 5min later, keep SH at a junction and then go through a gate. Keep SH across a road. Keep SH at another junction.

5 1:00: TL at a junction. After a while, take care crossing the busy road at **Cheesefoot Head** (176m): see page 75. Keep SH on a path which cuts through a corn-field.

4 1:25: Shortly afterwards, TR at a junction onto another path. Soon, pass Telegraph Hill and descend. TL onto a track: alternatively, TR if you are staying at **Morn Hill**.

3 2:05: 5-10min later, the track bends right and becomes a minor road. Soon pass a WP (tap) on the right.

S 2:15: Arrive at a junction in the village of **Chilcomb**.

Stage 1c

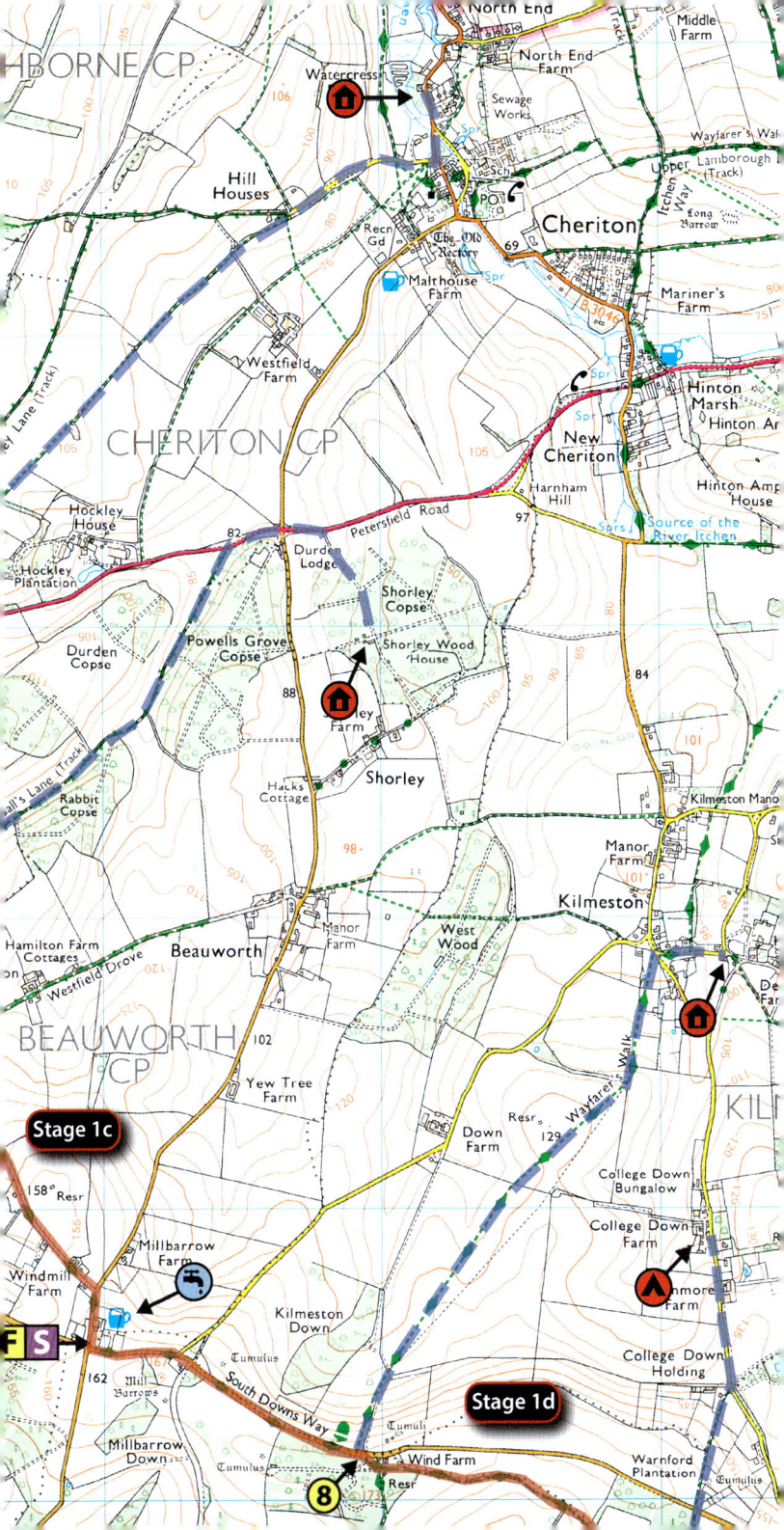

Stage 1d

W-E

Stage 1c: Holden Farm to the Milbury's

S Head SE through the farmyard and then continue on a track.

7 0:20: Keep SH on a lane: alternatively, TL to head to **Shorley**. 20min later, TR on a road.

F 0:45: Shortly afterwards, reach **the Milbury's** (a pub with accommodation and restaurant).

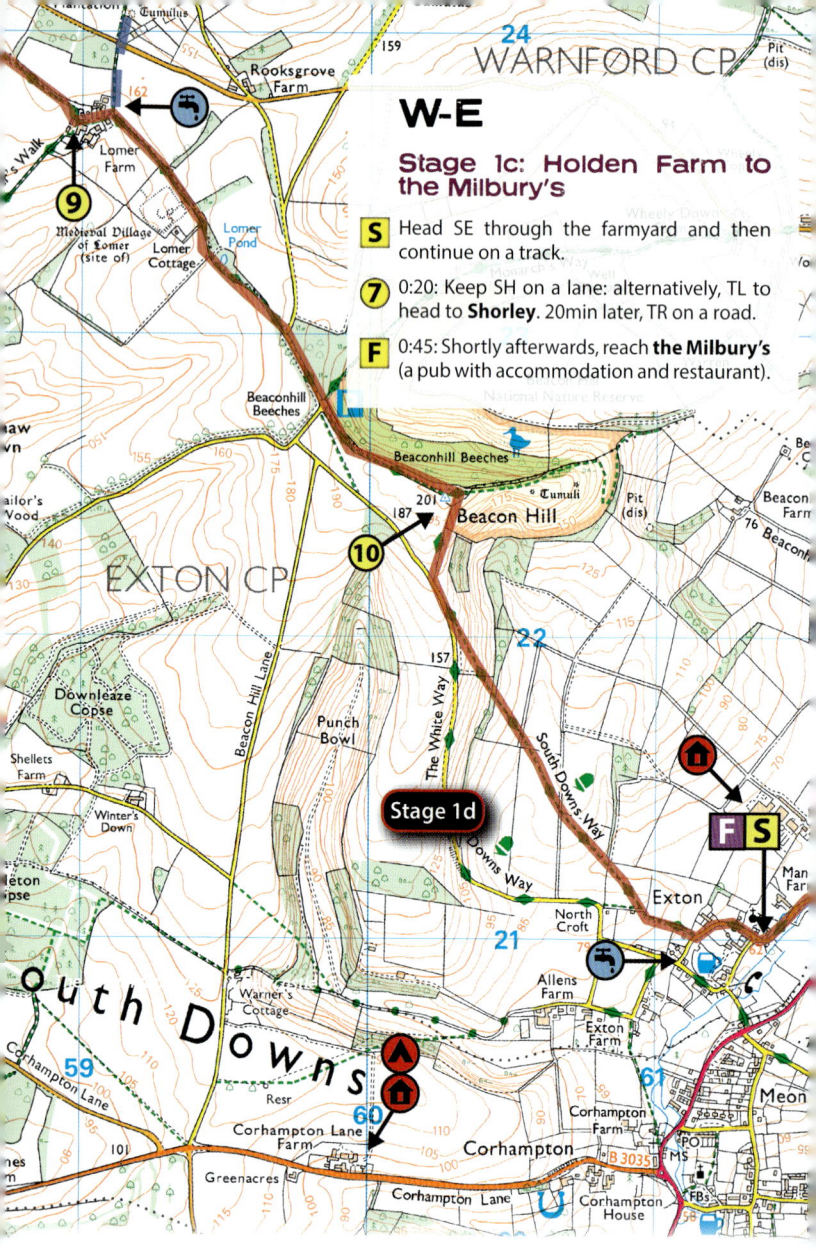

W-E

Stage 1d: The Milbury's to Exton

S From the pub, head E on a road. 5min later, bear left and continue on a path running parallel to the road.

8 0:15: TR and cross the road: alternatively, TL on a path to head to **Kilmeston**. Then bear left, go through a gate and continue on a track. Shortly afterwards, TL at a junction.

9 0:35: TL at **Lomer Farm**. Shortly afterwards, reach a junction where there is a WP (tap): TR onto a track to continue on Stage 1d or TL on a path to head to College Down Farm or Kilmeston. 15min later, keep SH on a minor road. 5min later, keep SH through a parking area, go through a gate and continue on a path.

(10) 1:05: Shortly after the trig point on **Beacon Hill (201m)**, TR on a grassy path. Go through a gate and descend. Soon, TL down a minor road. Shortly afterwards, TL, go through a gate and descend on a path which heads across fields: cross a series of gates and stiles.

F 1:30: TL onto a minor road. Shortly afterwards, arrive at a junction in the village of **Exton**: TR to head to the **Shoe Inn**, **Meonstoke** and **Corhampton**.

E-W

Stage 1d: Exton to the Milbury's

F From the junction in **Exton**, head NW on a minor road, passing a church. Shortly afterwards, TR and climb on a path which heads across fields: cross a series of gates and stiles. Eventually, go through a gate and TR up a minor road. Shortly afterwards, TR and climb on a path.

(10) 0:30: TL at the trig point on **Beacon Hill (201m)**. Soon, go through a gate and keep SH through a parking area. Then head NW on a road. 5min later, keep SH on a track.

(9) 1:00: 15min later, reach a junction where there is a WP (tap): TL into **Lomer Farm** to continue on Stage 1d or TR on a path to head to College Down Farm or Kilmeston. Shortly, TR on a track.

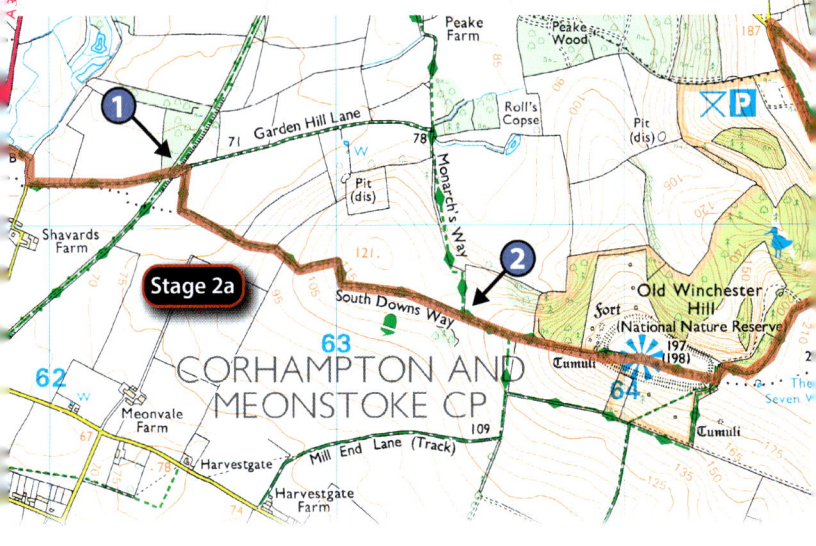

(8) 1:15: Go through a gate. Shortly afterwards, cross a road and then TL on a path running parallel to it: alternatively, TR on a path to head to **Kilmeston**.

S 1:30: Arrive at **the Milbury's** (a pub with accommodation and restaurant).

Stage 1c: The Milbury's to Holden Farm

F From the pub, head N on a road. Shortly afterwards, TL on a lane.

(7) 0:25: Keep SH at a junction onto a track. Alternatively, TR to head to **Shorley**.

S 0:45: Arrive at **Holden Farm**: there is a campsite and a WP (tap).

2 Exton/ Buriton-Petersfield exit

This section is an excellent showcase for the wonderful scenery of the SDW. Many different types of natural habitat are on display including beautiful farmland and the natural woodland of Queen Elizabeth Country Park. However, it is the old chalk grassland that steals the show and here you will find two of the finest examples of it: Old Winchester Hill and Butser Hill, both of which are home to rare species of flowers and butterflies. The views from both hills are exquisite and Old Winchester Hill also has the added interest of an Iron Age hill-fort and Bronze Age burial mounds. In WW2, the British Army used the hill to test mortars.

Except at Exton and the Sustainability Centre, there is no accommodation on the trail itself: you are forced to travel OR slightly to find a resting place. However, Buriton (an attractive village at the foot of the escarpment) is

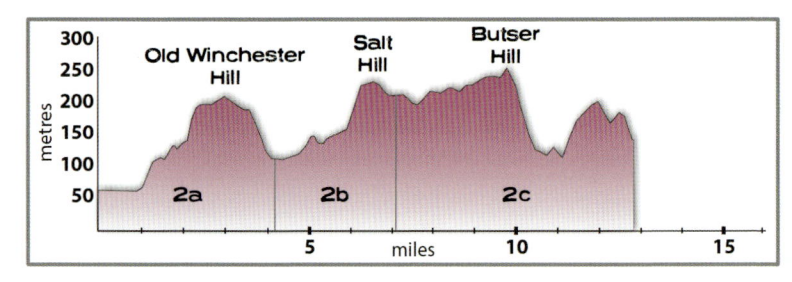

The hill-fort & chalk grassland on Old Winchester Hill (Stage 2a)

only 0.5 miles away and is a lovely place to stay. There are other options in Petersfield, a larger market town with plenty of shops and restaurants. However, Petersfield is not quite as charming as Buriton and is further away from the trail. Exton and Meonstoke, typical Hampshire villages, are also good places to spend the night: there are a couple of pubs and an excellent village shop where you can stock up on supplies.

The route is generally well marked and navigation is straightforward. However, follow waymarks carefully at the complicated series of junctions at Waypoint No.1. Take care on the climb/descent of Old Winchester Hill: it is very steep.

		Time	Distance	Ascent W-E	Descent W-E
Stage 2a	Exton/ Meon Springs	1:45	4.2miles 6.7km	525ft 160m	197ft 60m
Stage 2b	Meon Springs/ Sustainability Centre	1:30(W-E) 1:15(E-W)	2.9miles 4.7km	443ft 135m	148ft 45m
Stage 2c	Sustainability Centre/Buriton-Petersfield exit	2:30	5.7miles 9.2km	640ft 195m	820ft 250m

Supplies/Water:

Exton (Stage 1d/2a) – WP at the Shoe Inn

Meonstoke Post Office & Village Shop (Stage 1d/2a; 0.4 miles OR)

Meon Springs (Stage 2a/2b) – WP (tap)

East Meon (Stage 2b/2c; 1 mile OR) – East Meon Stores (groceries & sandwiches)

Beech Café at the Sustainability Centre (Stage 2b/2c) – WP (tap)

Queen Elizabeth Country Park (Stage 2c) - WP (tap) beside the café

Petersfield (Stage 2c/3a; 2.8 miles OR) – supermarkets, shops, pharmacy & ATMs

Refreshments/Food:

Exton (Stage 1d/2a) - the Shoe Inn

Meonstoke (Stage 1d/2a; 0.6 miles OR) – the Bucks Head

East Meon (Stage 2b/2c; 1 mile OR) – Ye Olde George Inn

Beech Café at the Sustainability Centre (Stage 2b/2c)

Queen Elizabeth Country Park (Stage 2c) - café

The Hampshire Hog (Stage 2c; 1 mile OR from Queen Elizabeth Country Park)

Buriton (Stage 2c/3a; 0.5 mile OR) – the Village Inn & the Five Bells pub

Petersfield (Stage 2c/3a; 2.8 miles OR) – pubs, restaurants & cafés

The magnificent farmland on Section 2

Accommodation:

Exton (Stage 1d/2a)
Meonstoke (Stage 1d/2a; 0.6 miles OR)
Corhampton (Stage 1d/2a; 1.3 miles OR)
Meon Springs (Stage 2a/2b)
Coombe (Stage 2b; 0.4 miles OR)
East Meon (Stage 2b/2c; 1-1.9 miles OR)
The Sustainability Centre (Stage 2b/2c)
Upper Parsonage Farm (Stage 2c; 0.8 miles OR)
The Hampshire Hog (Stage 2c; 1 mile OR from Queen Elizabeth Country Park)
Buriton (Stage 2c/3a; 0.5 mile OR)
Nursted (Stage 2c/3a; 1.8 miles OR)
Petersfield (Stage 2c/3a; 2.8 miles OR)

Escape/Access:

East Meon (Stage 2b/2c; 1-1.9 miles OR)
Clanfield (Stage 2c; 1 mile OR)
Buriton (Stage 2c/3a; 0.5 mile OR)
Petersfield (Stage 2c/3a; 2.8 miles OR)

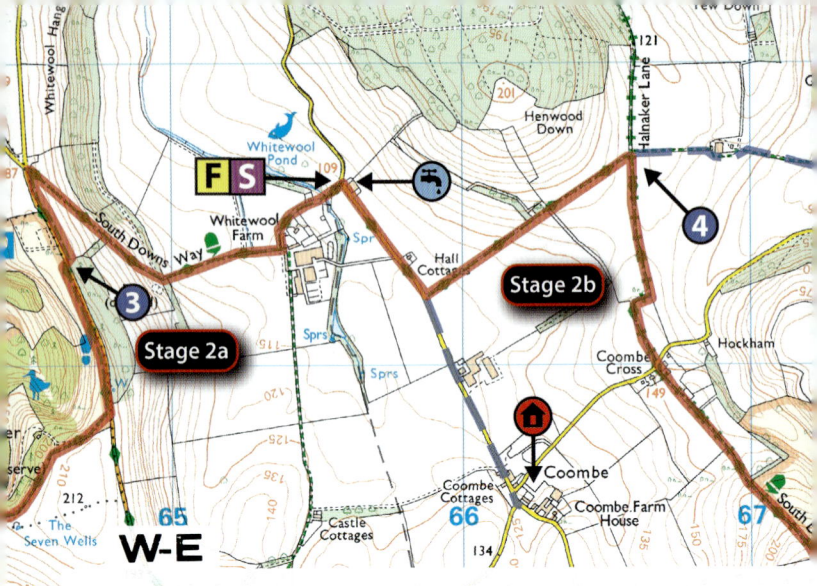

Stage 2a: Exton to Meon Springs

S From the junction in **Exton**, head NE on a minor road. After 10min, bear diagonally left across the A32 and pick up a path. 5min later, TL at a junction.

1 0:20: TL onto a broad path. Shortly afterwards, turn sharp right onto another path. Shortly after that, TR across a small footbridge.

2 0:50: From a junction, head E on a path to the left of a hedgerow: ignore the waymarked path to the right of the hedgerow. Climb steeply until you reach the summit of **Old Winchester Hill (197m)**. Head E along the summit. Soon, TL at a junction. Shortly afterwards, the path bends right and goes through a gate.

3 1:20: TR, cross a minor road and continue on a path. 5min later, turn sharp right, go through a gate and descend on a path cutting diagonally across the slope.

F 1:45: Immediately before the buildings of **Whitewool Farm**, TL on a lane. Soon cross a bridge and reach **Meon Springs** car park.

Stage 2b: Meon Springs to the Sustainability Centre

S From **Meon Springs** car park, head SE on a tarmac lane. 5min later, TL on a concrete track: alternatively, keep SH to head to **Coombe**. When the track ends, keep SH on a path.

4 0:30: TR at a crossroads onto a broad path: alternatively, keep SH to head to **East Meon**. 15min later, keep SH across a minor road, continuing on a track. Climb **Salt Hill (234m)** and then descend. TL onto a road: shortly, there is a path on the right of it.

F 1:30: Shortly afterwards, arrive at the **Sustainability Centre**.

E-W

Stage 2b: the Sustainability Centre to Meon Springs

F From the **Sustainability Centre**, head W on the path alongside the road. Shortly afterwards, TR on a track and climb **Salt Hill (234m)**: then descend the other side of it. Keep SH across a road onto a broad path.

4 0:55: 15min later, TL at a crossroads onto a path: alternatively, TR to head to **East Meon**. When the path ends, keep SH downhill on a concrete track. TR onto a tarmac lane: alternatively, TL to head to **Coombe**.

S 1:15: Arrive at **Meon Springs** car park.

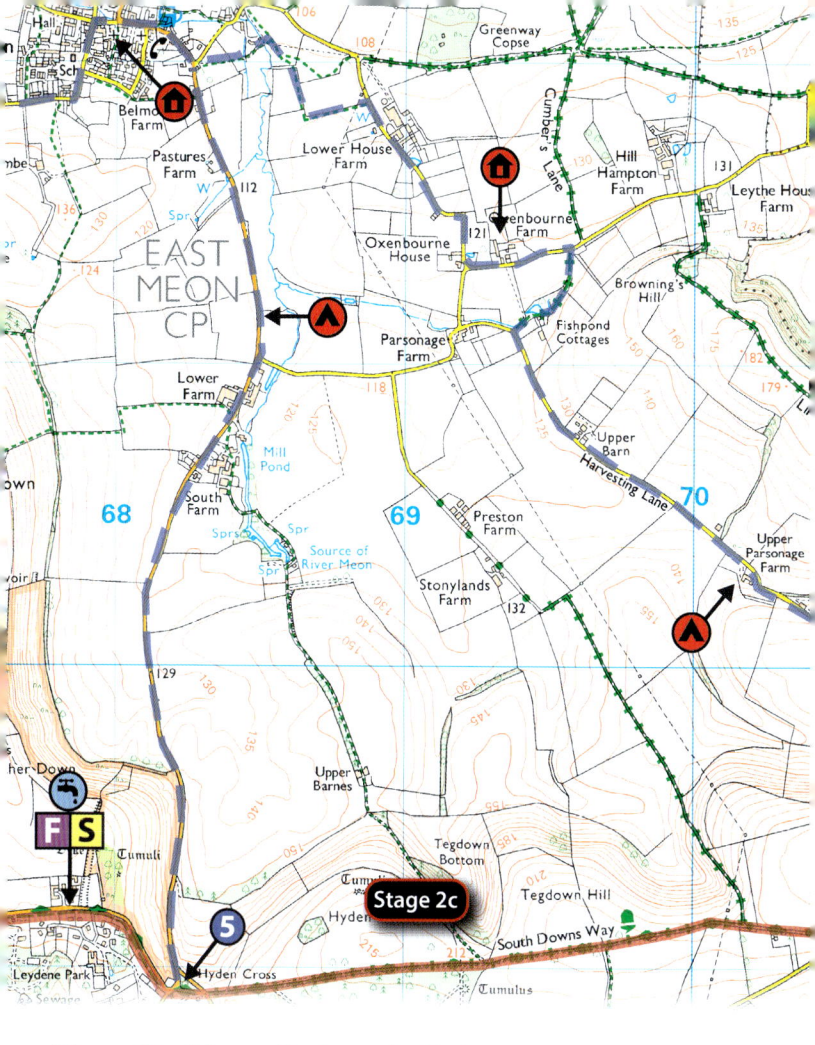

Stage 2a: Meon Springs to Exton

F From the car park, head SW. Pass through **Whitewool Farm**. Then TR and head W on a path. Soon bear right and climb up across the slope: at the top, go through a gate and then turn sharp left.

3 0:30: 5min later, TR, cross a minor road and continue on a path. Soon the path bends right away from the road. Eventually, go through a gate. At a junction, TR and head W along the top of **Old Winchester Hill**. From the trig point on the summit (197m), continue W and descend steeply.

2 1:00: At a junction, keep SH, heading W.

1 1:25: Cross a small footbridge. Just afterwards, TL on a path. Then follow waymarks carefully through a complicated series of junctions. 5-10min later, TR at a junction. When you reach the A32, bear diagonally left across it onto a minor road.

S 1:45: 10min later, arrive at a junction in the village of **Exton**: TL to head to the **Shoe Inn**, **Meonstoke** and **Corhampton**. Alternatively, keep SH for Stage 1d.

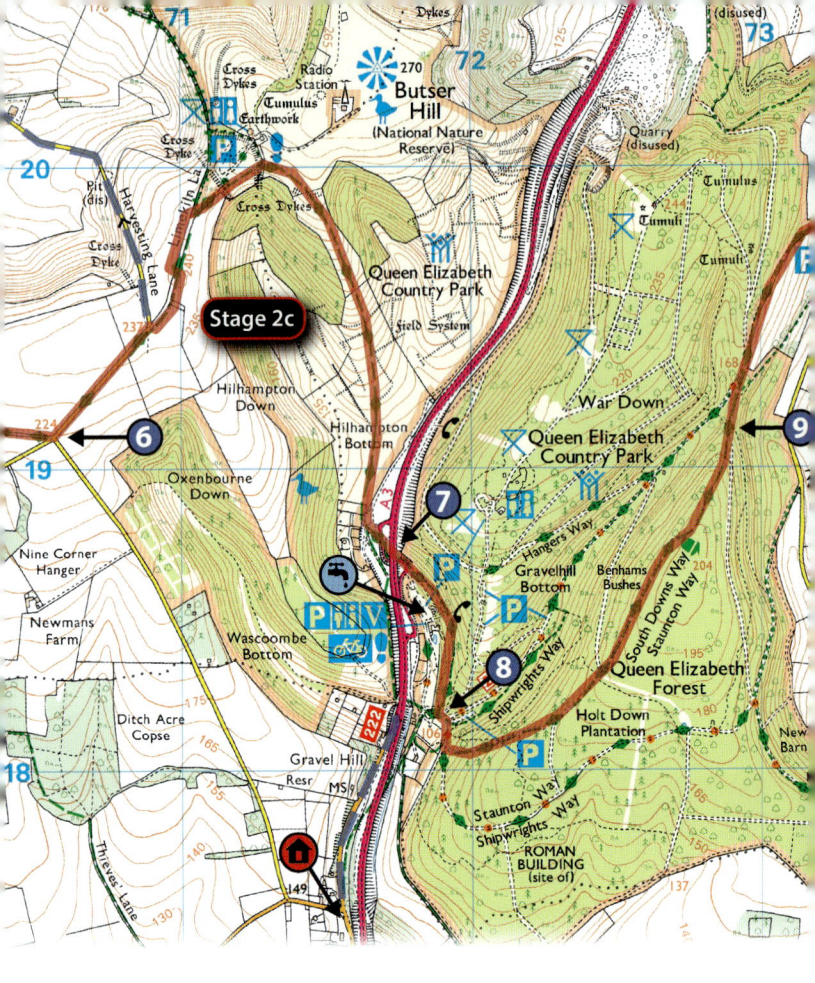

W-E

Stage 2c: the Sustainability Centre to Buriton-Petersfield exit

S From the **Sustainability Centre**, continue E on the path alongside the road. Soon the path drifts right into woods.

5 0:10: Keep SH on a road: alternatively, TL to head to **Meonside Camping** (which can also be accessed from East Meon). Shortly afterwards, keep SH across another road, continuing on a track.

6 0:45: TL at a road junction. 5min later, keep SH at a junction (where the SDW continues on a path on the right side of the road): alternatively, TL on Harvesting Lane to head to **Upper Parsonage Farm**. After a while, the path crosses over to the other side of the road. Just before Butser Hill car park, cross the road again. Soon go through a gate. Afterwards, the SDW skirts the SW slopes of **Butser Hill** (another important chalk grassland site) and then descends: however, most walkers will want to make the short diversion NE to the trig point (270m) at the summit which is the highest point on the SDs escarpment. At the bottom of the slope, go through a gate. Then keep SH at a few junctions. Just afterwards, cross a road and then TR on a path beside it.

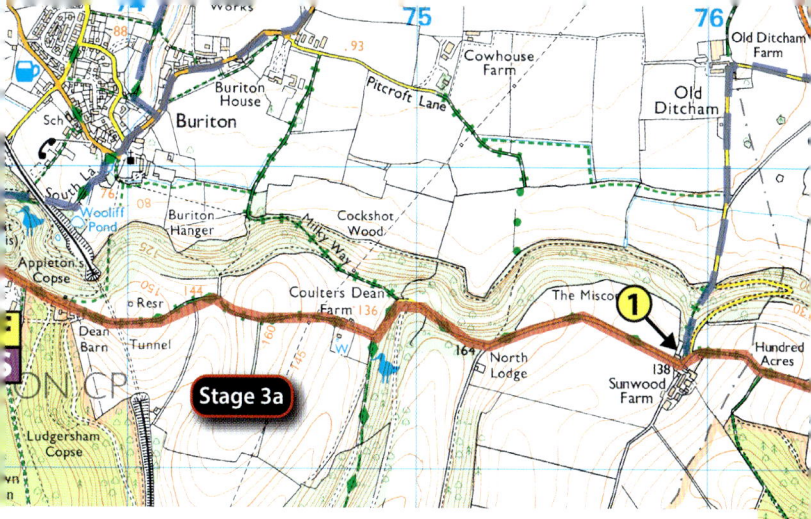

(7) 1:35: Shortly afterwards, pass under the A3 dual-carriageway. Soon TL on a path and climb through the forest of **Queen Elizabeth Country Park**: follow waymarks at any junctions.

(8) 1:45: Cross a forest road, keep SH and climb on a track: alternatively, TR and head S on a path to go to the **Hampshire Hog** pub. Soon, TL at a junction, climbing on a path through trees.

(9) 2:15: TL onto a track. 5min later, keep right at a fork.

F 2:30: Just after a car park, keep SH across a road junction. Just afterwards, TL on a path to head to **Buriton** (0.5 miles) or **Petersfield** (2.8 miles): alternatively, keep SH (heading SE) on a lane to start Stage 3a.

E-W

Stage 2c: Buriton-Petersfield exit to the Sustainability Centre

F From the road junction, head NW through a car park. Then climb NW on a track. After a while, TL at a fork.

(9) 0:20: Shortly afterwards, TR onto a path through **Queen Elizabeth Forest**. When you emerge from the trees at a track, TR and descend.

(8) 0:45: Cross a forest road and continue N through the forest (follow waymarks at any junctions): alternatively, TL and head S on a path to go to the **Hampshire Hog** pub.

(7) 0:55: TR on a road. Shortly afterwards, pass under the A3 dual-carriageway. Soon, cross the road and pick up a path. Go through a gate and then climb a hill. Near the top, the SDW skirts the SW slopes of **Butser Hill** (another important chalk grassland site): however, most walkers will want to make the short diversion NE to the trig point (270m) at the summit which is the highest point on the SDs escarpment. Go through a gate. Soon afterwards, cross a road: then TL and head SW on a path alongside it. After a while, the path crosses over to the other side of the road. Keep SH at a road junction: alternatively, TR on Harvesting Lane to head to **Upper Parsonage Farm**. When the path disappears, continue down the road.

(6) 1:50: TR onto a track.

(5) 2:15: Keep SH across a road. Shortly afterwards, keep SH at a road junction and climb on a path: alternatively, TR to head to **Meonside Camping** (which can also be accessed from East Meon).

S 2:30: Arrive at the **Sustainability Centre**.

3 Buriton-Petersfield exit/ Cocking exit

The SDW between Buriton and South Harting crosses lower-lying woodland and arable farmland. Although you do not climb any large hills, there are nevertheless excellent views of the Weald each time you emerge from the trees. E of South Harting, however, it is an entirely different story because you hike the wild high downs where you are rewarded with some magnificent open stretches of chalk grassland and wonderful native woodland. The highlight is probably Harting Downs where the white chalk paths cut across sublime flower-filled meadows still grazed by sheep. Take your time and savour the lovely views. Cocking Down is beautiful too: be sure to look out for the huge chalk stone placed beside the trail by the artist, Andy Goldsworthy (see page 94 and the image above).

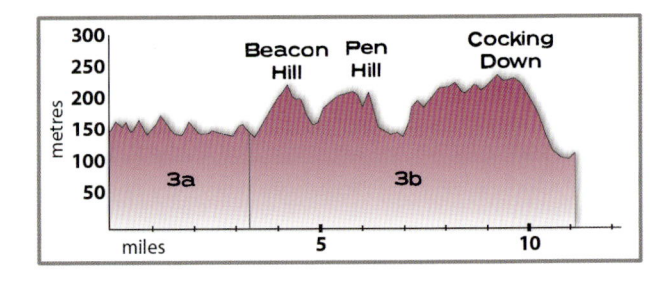

The chalk boulder on Stage 3b, placed by Andy Goldsworthy

Cocking is only 0.8 miles from the SDW and is a pleasant place to stay. However, we prefer to overnight at Manor Farm which is right on the trail near Cocking. Further W, there is the beautiful village of South Harting which has an excellent pub: it is a popular place to stay so book well in advance. Then there is Buriton (an attractive village at the foot of the escarpment) which is only 0.5 miles OR and is a lovely overnight stop. There are further options in Petersfield, a larger market town with plenty of shops and restaurants. However, Petersfield is not quite as charming as Buriton and is further away from the trail.

The route is well marked and navigation is straightforward. Take care if you are taking the Beacon Hill short-cut which is steep. There are two Beacon Hills on the SDW: the other one is crossed on Stage 1d

		Time	Distance	Ascent W-E	Descent W-E
Stage 3a	Buriton-Petersfield exit/South Harting exit	1:30	3.3miles 5.3km	394ft 120m	377ft 115m
Stage 3b	South Harting exit/ Cocking exit	3:15	7.8miles 12.5km	1116ft 340m	1198ft 365m

Supplies/Water:

Petersfield (Stage 2c/3a; 2.8 miles OR) – supermarkets, shops, pharmacy & ATMs

South Harting (Stage 3a/3b; 0.6 miles OR) – village shop (groceries, drinks & sandwiches)

Manor Farm (Stage 3b/4a) - WP (tap) & Richline Farm Shop

Cocking (Stage 3b/4a; 0.8 mile OR) – Cocking Stores & Post Office (closed at the date of press and may not re-open)

Refreshments/Food:

Buriton (Stage 2c/3a; 0.5 mile OR) – the Village Inn & the Five Bells pub

Petersfield (Stage 2c/3a; 2.8 miles OR) – pubs, restaurants & cafés

South Harting (Stage 3a/3b; 0.6 miles OR) – the White Hart

Manor Farm (Stage 3b/4a) - Richline Farm Shop

Cocking (Stage 3b/4a; 0.8 mile OR) – the Bluebell Inn

Accommodation:

Buriton (Stage 2c/3a; 0.5 mile OR)
Nursted (Stage 2c/3a; 1.8 miles OR)
Petersfield (Stage 2c/3a; 2.8 miles OR)
Copper Beeches B&B (Stage 3a; 1.1 miles OR)
South Harting (Stage 3a/3b; 0.6 miles OR)
Manor Farm (Stage 3b/4a)
Cocking (Stage 3b/4a; 0.8 mile OR)

Escape/Access:

Buriton (Stage 2c/3a; 0.5 mile OR)
Petersfield (Stage 2c/3a; 2.8 miles OR)
South Harting (Stage 3a/3b; 0.6 miles OR)
Cocking (Stage 3b/4a; 0.8 mile OR)

Cocking Down (Stage 3b)

W-E

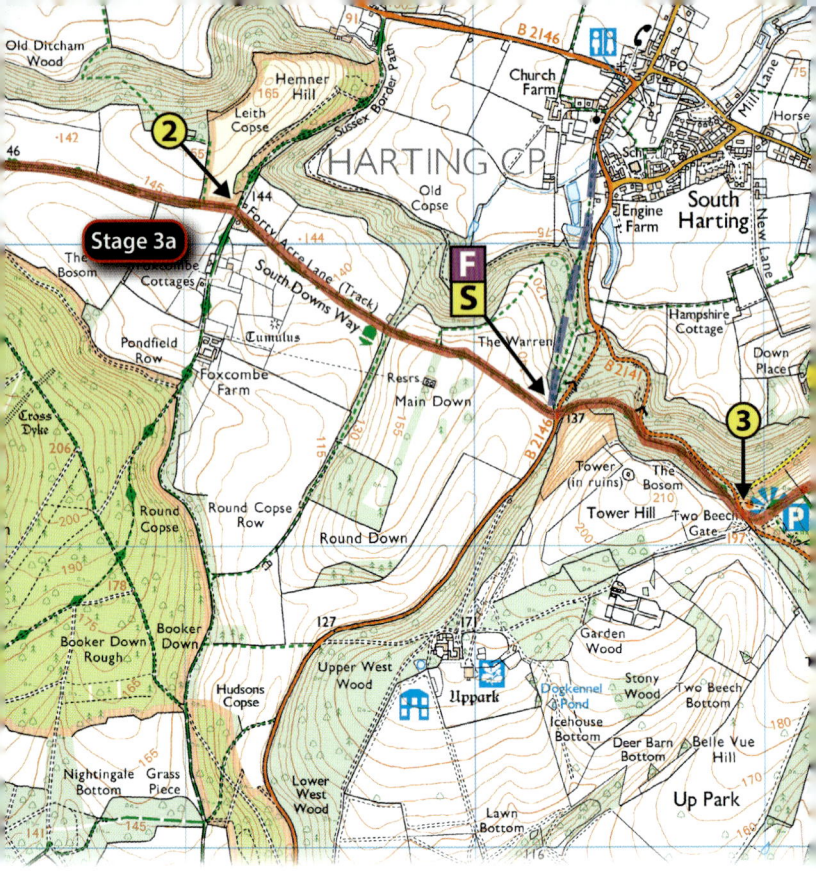

Stage 3a: Buriton-Petersfield exit to South Harting exit

S From the road junction, head SE on a lane. Soon keep SH on a track. After a while, the track becomes a lane: soon notice the magnificent copper beech trees alongside it.

① 0:45: Just after the road bends left at a house, TR on a track and climb E: alternatively, head N on another path to head to **Copper Beeches B&B**. A few minutes later, TL at a junction and descend.

② 1:10: Keep SH at a junction, crossing a lane.

F 1:30: Reach a parking area near the B2146. TL on a path (yellow waymark) for the **South Harting Detour** (see box): alternatively, cross the road to start Stage 3b.

Harting Downs

Harting Downs, which is cared for by the National Trust, is one of the largest remaining areas of ancient chalk grassland. In spring, the wild-flowers and butterflies are magnificent. It is also a popular place to spot birds of prey such as buzzards and red kites. Sheep are still grazed on the land to help to preserve it. Nearby, there are significant areas of woodland.

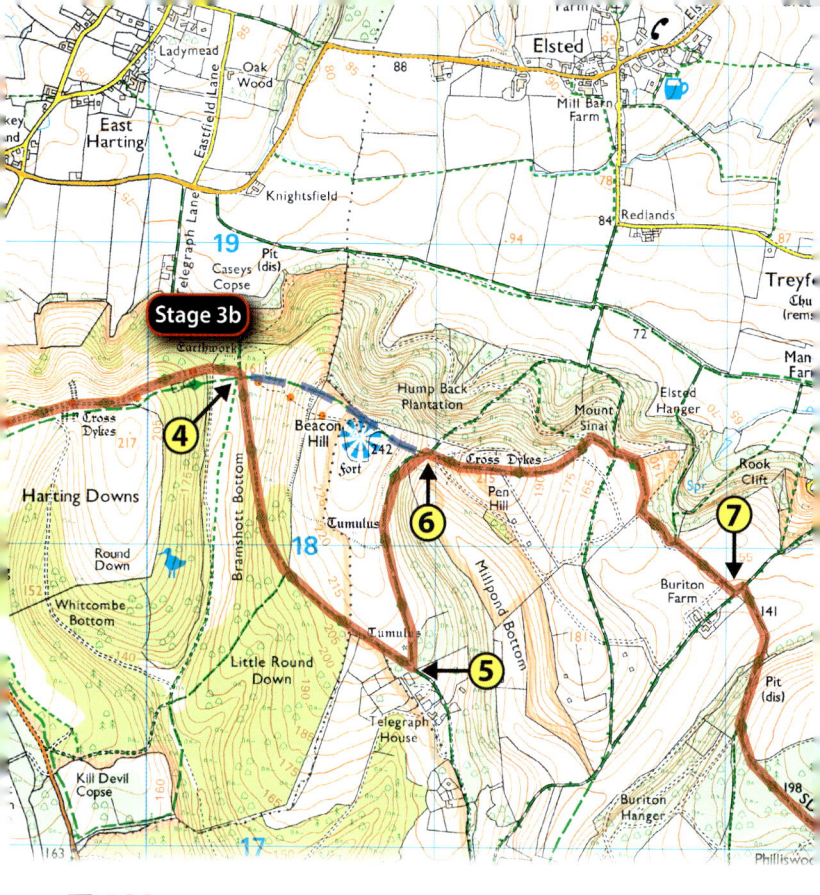

E-W

Stage 3a: South Harting exit to Buriton-Petersfield exit

F From the parking area, head NW.

2 0:20: Keep SH at a junction, crossing a lane. 15min later, keep SH at a junction and descend.

1 0:45: A few minutes later, TL on a lane: alternatively, head N on another path to head to **Copper Beeches B&B**. Shortly afterwards, the lane bends right at a house and soon climbs: notice the magnificent copper beech trees alongside the lane. After a while, the lane becomes a track.

S 1:30: Arrive at a road junction. TR on a path to head to **Buriton** (0.5 miles) or **Petersfield** (2.8 miles): alternatively, keep SH and head NW through a car park to start Stage 2c.

South Harting Detour (0.6 miles)

From the parking area near the B2146, descend N on a path (yellow waymark) to head to South Harting. At any junctions, keep heading downhill. Keep SH past some ponds and a play-park. Finally, keep SH on a road to enter South Harting. Re-trace your steps the next morning to return to the SDW.

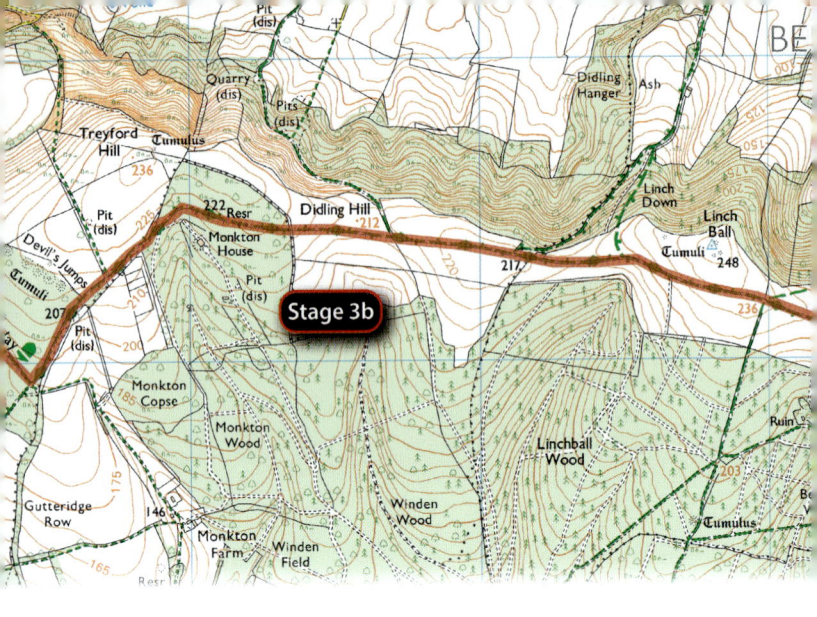

Stage 3b: South Harting exit to Cocking exit

S From the parking area, cross the road and climb on a bridleway.

3 0:15: Cross a road and pick up a path. Head across **Harting Downs** (see page 92).

4 0:40: Arrive at a saddle: for the official route of the SDW (which skirts Beacon Hill but unfortunately, does not visit the summit), TR and head SSE on a grassy path, climbing gently towards a prominent tree. Alternatively, keep SH at the saddle for an excellent, but steep, short-cut which passes over the top of **Beacon Hill (242m)**: you will re-join the SDW at Waypoint No.6.

5 1:00: Turn sharp left at a junction.

6 1:20: Keep SH across a saddle: this is where the Beacon Hill short-cut re-joins the main SDW. Climb **Pen Hill (215m)** and then descend. 5min later, TR at a junction.

7 1:40: TL at a junction. Shortly afterwards, TR. 15min later, pass a **memorial** to a German airman who was shot down in WW2. Shortly afterwards, TL at a junction. 5min later, there is a short detour on the left to the **Devil's Jumps** (Bronze Age burial mounds). Eventually, descend across **Cocking Down**.

8 3:00: Pass a prominent boulder on the right (see box). 10min later, pass through a farmyard. Shortly afterwards, cross the A286 and keep SH on a tarmac lane.

F 3:15: 5min later, arrive at **Manor Farm**. TL just after the farm buildings to head to **Cocking**: alternatively, keep SH (E) on the lane to start Stage 4a. At Manor Farm, there is B&B accommodation, a campsite and **Richline Farm Shop** (which sells ice cream, drinks and snacks, as well as meat from the farm).

Andy Goldsworthy's Chalk Stones Trail

Andy Goldsworthy is a British artist who makes sculptures from natural materials. In 2002 he laid out 14 giant chalk boulders in the countryside around Cocking Down. Initially, it was estimated that they would only last a few years but, given their current rate of weathering, they could survive for decades. One of the boulders is located at Waypoint No.8. You can visit all of the boulders on a 5-mile trail between West Dean and Bepton.

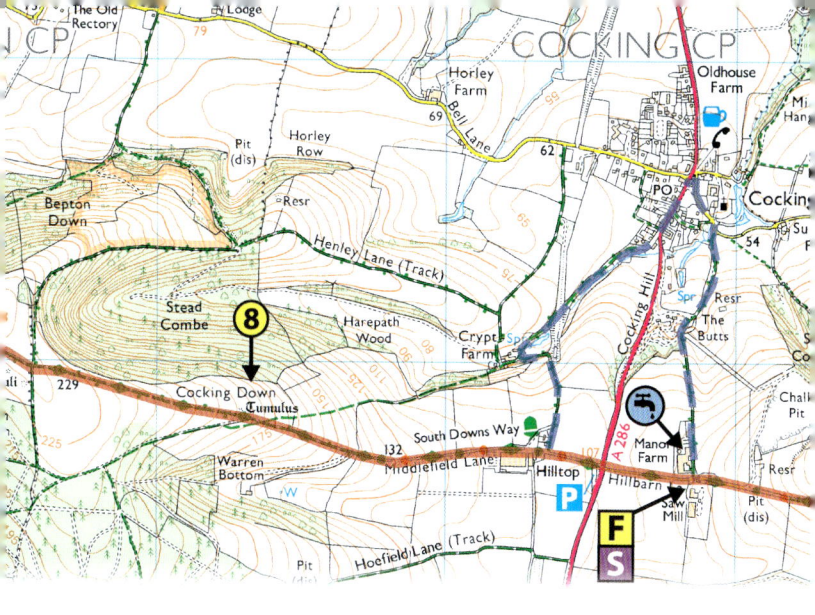

Stage 3b: Cocking exit to South Harting exit

F From **Manor Farm**, head W on a lane. 5min later, cross the A286 and keep SH on a tarmac lane. Shortly afterwards, pass through a farmyard and start to climb **Cocking Down**.

8 0:20: Pass a prominent boulder on the left (see box). 1hr later, the path bends left to head SW. 5min later, there is a short detour on the right to the **Devil's Jumps** (Bronze Age burial mounds). 5min after that, TR at a junction. Shortly afterwards, pass a **memorial** to a German airman who was shot down in WW2.

7 1:40: TL at a junction. Shortly afterwards, TR. 5-10min later, TL at a junction and climb. Cross **Pen Hill (215m)** and then descend.

6 2:05: Reach a saddle: for the official route of the SDW (which skirts Beacon Hill but unfortunately, does not visit the summit), bear left on a path heading S. Alternatively, keep SH at the saddle for an excellent, but steep, short-cut which passes over the top of **Beacon Hill (242m)**: you will re-join the SDW at Waypoint No.4.

5 2:25: Turn sharp right at a junction.

4 2:45: TL at a saddle: this is where the Beacon Hill short-cut re-joins the SDW. Head across **Harting Downs** (see page 92).

3 3:05: Cross a road and descend on a bridleway.

S 3:15: Cross the B2146 to arrive at a parking area. TR on a path (yellow waymark) for the **South Harting Detour** (see page 93): alternatively, head NW to start Stage 3a.

The slopes of Pen Hill (Stage 3b)

95

4 Cocking exit/ Houghton Bridge

Although there is little chalk grassland to view, the farmland on this section is nothing short of spectacular: a magnificent patchwork of yellow and green with huge fields of wheat and barley shimmering in the breeze. On a bright summer's day, the journey across Littleton Down is sublime, particularly for W-E trekkers. The route across Bignor Hill and the descent into the Arun Valley are also wonderful.

There is history on offer too with many Bronze Age burial mounds to spot on Heyshott and Graffham Downs. However, it is the Roman history which really resonates: you will walk, for a while, on old Roman roads and Bignor Roman Villa (1.2 miles OR), with its incredible mosaics, is exceptional.

The area around Houghton Bridge and Amberley is one of the loveliest places on the whole trek to spend the night. There are plenty of places to stay and eat. For campers, Foxleigh Barn at Houghton Bridge is a real treat: although the beautiful campsite spans a couple of acres, only a handful of tents are allowed so it is a tranquil experience. The facilities are excellent and the owners are incredibly helpful. Bignor Farms Camping is

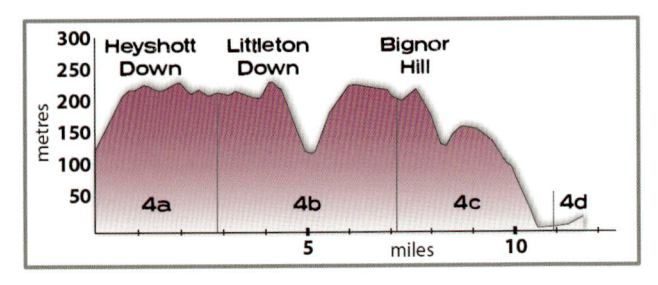

One of the many chalk paths on the SDW

also a superb experience: the small campsite is located at Bignor Roman Villa itself and they will provide groceries and a portable BBQ if booked in advance.

Amberley, Houghton Bridge and Houghton are quite spread out so, if you are staying in this area, make sure that you are clear about which one you need to go to. Amberley is 1 mile N of Houghton Bridge and is actually accessed on foot from the W end of Stage 5a. Houghton Bridge is 0.5 miles NE of Houghton. Confusingly, Amberley Train Station is actually at Houghton Bridge.

The route is well marked and navigation is straightforward. The ascent/descent between Bignor Hill and Houghton Bridge is one of the longest on the SDW.

		Time	Distance	Ascent W-E	Descent W-E
Stage 4a	Cocking exit/ Graffham exit	1:30(W-E) 1:15(E-W)	2.8miles 4.5km	492ft 150m	115ft 35m
Stage 4b	Graffham exit/ Bignor-Sutton exit	2:00	4.4miles 7.0km	459ft 140m	492ft 150m
Stage 4c	Bignor-Sutton exit/ Bury exit	1:30	3.7miles 5.9km	98ft 30m	820ft 250m
Stage 4d	Bury exit/ Houghton Bridge	0:20	0.8miles 1.3km	33ft 10m	0ft 0m

Supplies/Water:

Manor Farm (Stage 3b/4a) - WP (tap) & Richline Farm Shop

Cocking (Stage 3b/4a; 0.8 mile OR) – Cocking Stores & Post Office (closed at the date of press and may not re-open)

Graffham (Stage 4a/4b; 1.3 miles OR) – village shop (groceries, snacks & sandwiches)

Bignor (Stage 4b/4c; 1.2 miles OR) – groceries available to order in advance if staying at Bignor Farm Camping

Houghton Bridge (Stage 4d) – WP (tap) beside the sewage works NE of the River Arun crossing

Amberley (Stage 4d/5a; 0.4 miles OR) – village store (groceries)

Refreshments/Food:

Manor Farm (Stage 3b/4a) – Richline Farm Shop

Cocking (Stage 3b/4a; 0.8 mile OR) – the Bluebell Inn

Heyshott (Stage 4a; 1 mile OR) – the Unicorn Inn

Graffham (Stage 4a/4b; 1.3 miles OR) – café at village shop & the White Horse pub

Bignor (Stage 4b/4c; 1.2 miles OR) – café at Bignor Roman Villa

Sutton (Stage 4b/4c; 1.7 miles OR) – the White Horse Inn

Bury (Stage 4c/4d; 1.1 miles OR) – the Squire & Horse Inn

Houghton Bridge (Stage 4d/5a) – the Bridge Inn, Riverside Café & Amberley Museum café

Amberley (Stage 4d/5a; 0.4 miles OR) – the Sportsman Inn, the Black Horse, Amberley Village Tearoom & Amberley Castle restaurant

Accommodation:

Manor Farm (Stage 3b/4a)

Cocking (Stage 3b/4a; 0.8 miles OR)

Newhouse Farm Camping, East Dean (Stage 4a; 1.6 miles OR)

Graffham (Stage 4a/4b; 1.3-2.5 miles OR)

Gumber Camping Barn & Campsite (Stage 4b; 0.9 miles OR)

Bignor (Stage 4b/4c; 1.2 miles OR)

Sutton (Stage 4b/4c; 1.7 miles OR)

Bury (Stage 4c/4d; 1.1 miles OR)

Houghton (Stage 4c/4d; 0.3 miles OR)

Houghton Bridge (Stage 4d/5a)

Amberley (Stage 4d/5a; 0.4 miles OR)

Escape/Access:

Cocking (Stage 3b/4a; 0.8 mile OR)

Graffham (Stage 4a/4b; 1.3-2.5 miles OR)

Bignor (Stage 4b/4c; 1.2 miles OR)

Sutton (Stage 4b/4c; 1.7 miles OR)

Bury (Stage 4c/4d; 1.1 miles OR)

Houghton (Stage 4c/4d; 0.3 miles OR)

Houghton Bridge (Stage 4d/5a)

Amberley (Stage 4d/5a; 0.4 miles OR)

Littleton Down (Stage 4b)

W-E

Stage 4a: Cocking exit to Graffham exit

S From **Manor Farm**, head E on a lane. Climb onto **Heyshott Down**.

1 0:50: TL at a fork. Shortly afterwards, notice the burial mounds of the **Heyshott Down Round Barrow Cemetery** on the left. 5-10min after the fork, a path on the right heads S to **East Dean** and **Newhouse Farm Camping**.

F 1:30: Arrive at a junction. TL to head to **Graffham** or keep SH to start Stage 4b. If you miss the junction, there is another route to Graffham 5-10min further E.

Stage 4b: Graffham exit to Bignor/Sutton exit

S From the junction, continue E across **Graffham Down**. 5-10min later, keep SH across a complicated junction: the first path on the left heads to **Graffham** if you missed the previous exit.

2 0:40: Go through a gate. Immediately afterwards, keep SH on a path through the middle of an arable field on **Littleton Down**. Soon descend through the field: the views are exquisite. After a while, go through a gate into another field. At the bottom of that field, keep SH, descending on a track. A few minutes later, bear diagonally right across the A285 and climb a track on the other side: stay on the main track, ignoring offshoots.

3 1:50: Arrive at a junction: TR to head to **Gumber Camping Barn & Campsite** or keep SH to continue on Stage 4b. You are now on **Stane Street**, an old Roman road. Shortly after passing through a gate, TL at a fork. A few minutes later, TR at a junction.

F 2:00: Arrive at a car park where there is a signpost in Latin. Keep SH through the car park onto a track to start Stage 4c. Alternatively, head NE on the car park access road to head to **Bignor** (1.2 miles OR) or the excellent **Bignor Roman Villa** (see page 102). **Sutton** is 0.5 miles NW of Bignor.

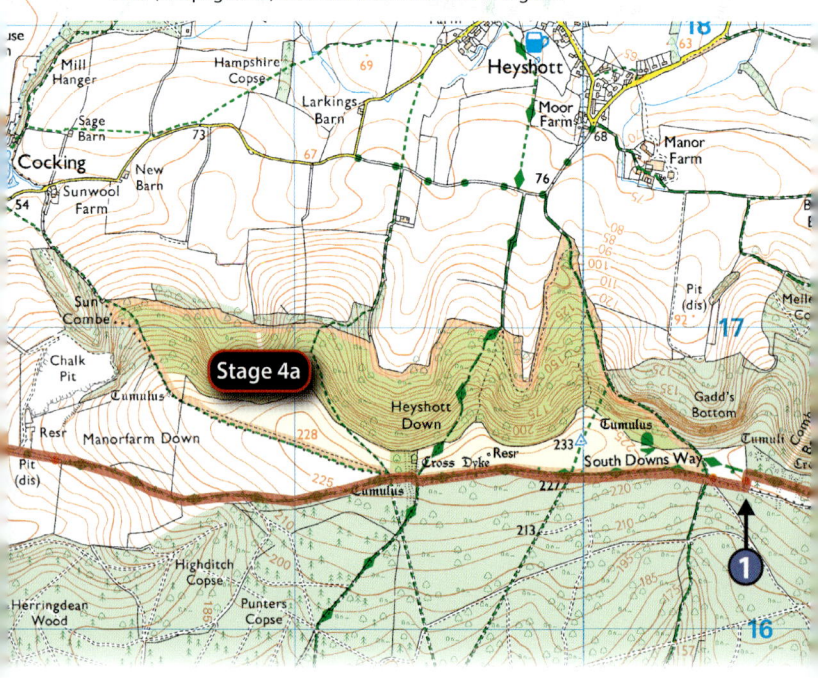

E-W

Stage 4b: Bignor/Sutton exit to Graffham exit

F From the car park, head W. A few minutes later, TL at a junction.

3 0:10: From a junction, head W across open ground: alternatively, TL (SW) to head to **Gumber Camping Barn & Campsite**. Soon descend across **Sutton Down**: stay on the main track, ignoring offshoots. Bear diagonally right across the A285 and climb a track on the other side. Soon climb through a field. After a while, go through a gate and climb through the middle of an arable field on **Littleton Down**: the views are exquisite.

2 1:20: Go through a gate and head NW on a path. 30min later, keep SH across a complicated junction: alternatively, head NW on a path to go to **Graffham**.

S 2:00: Arrive at a junction. Keep SH to start Stage 4a: alternatively, TR (NE) if you are staying at **Graffham**.

Stage 4a: Graffham exit to Cocking exit

F From the junction, continue W. 20min later, a path on the left heads S to **East Dean** and **Newhouse Farm Camping**. Afterwards, notice the burial mounds of the **Heyshott Down Round Barrow Cemetery** on the right.

1 0:30: The path bends left. Shortly, afterwards TR and continue W. Cross **Heyshott Down** and then descend.

S 1:15: Arrive at **Manor Farm**. TR at the farm buildings to head to **Cocking**: alternatively, keep SH (W) on the lane to start Stage 3b. At Manor Farm, there is B&B accommodation, a campsite and **Richline Farm Shop** (which sells ice cream, drinks and snacks, as well as meat from the farm).

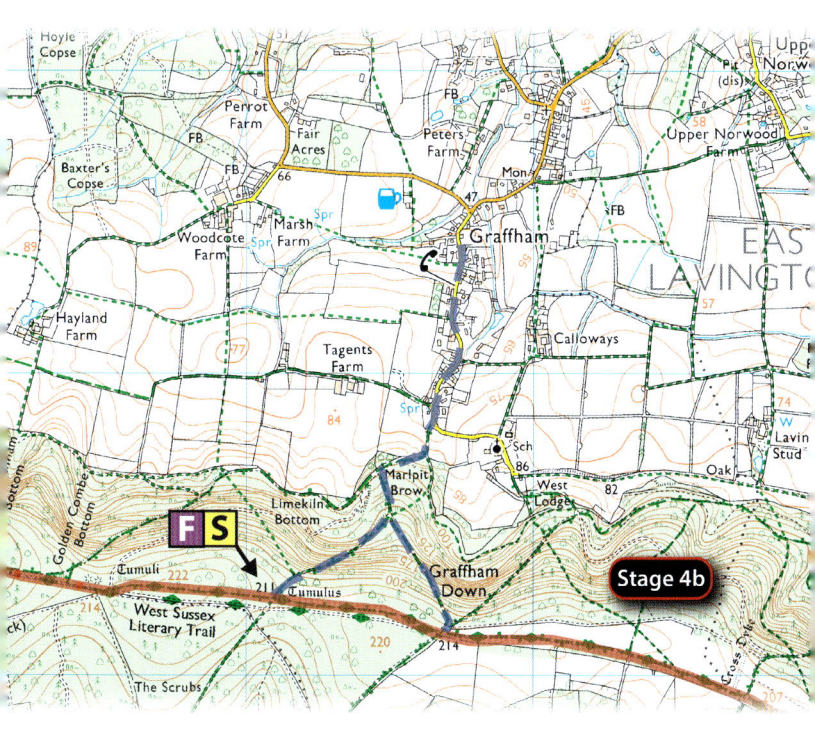

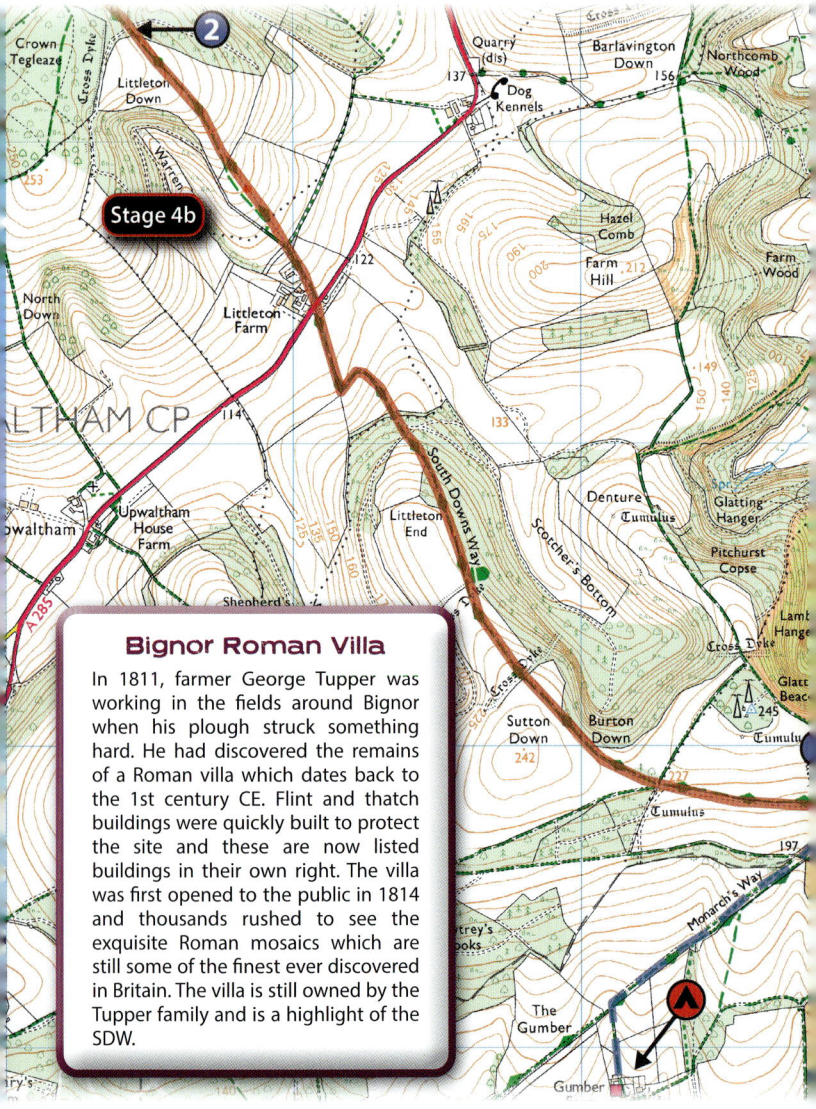

Manor Farm (Stage 3b/4a)

Bignor Roman Villa

In 1811, farmer George Tupper was working in the fields around Bignor when his plough struck something hard. He had discovered the remains of a Roman villa which dates back to the 1st century CE. Flint and thatch buildings were quickly built to protect the site and these are now listed buildings in their own right. The villa was first opened to the public in 1814 and thousands rushed to see the exquisite Roman mosaics which are still some of the finest ever discovered in Britain. The villa is still owned by the Tupper family and is a highlight of the SDW.

Graffham Down (Stage 4b)

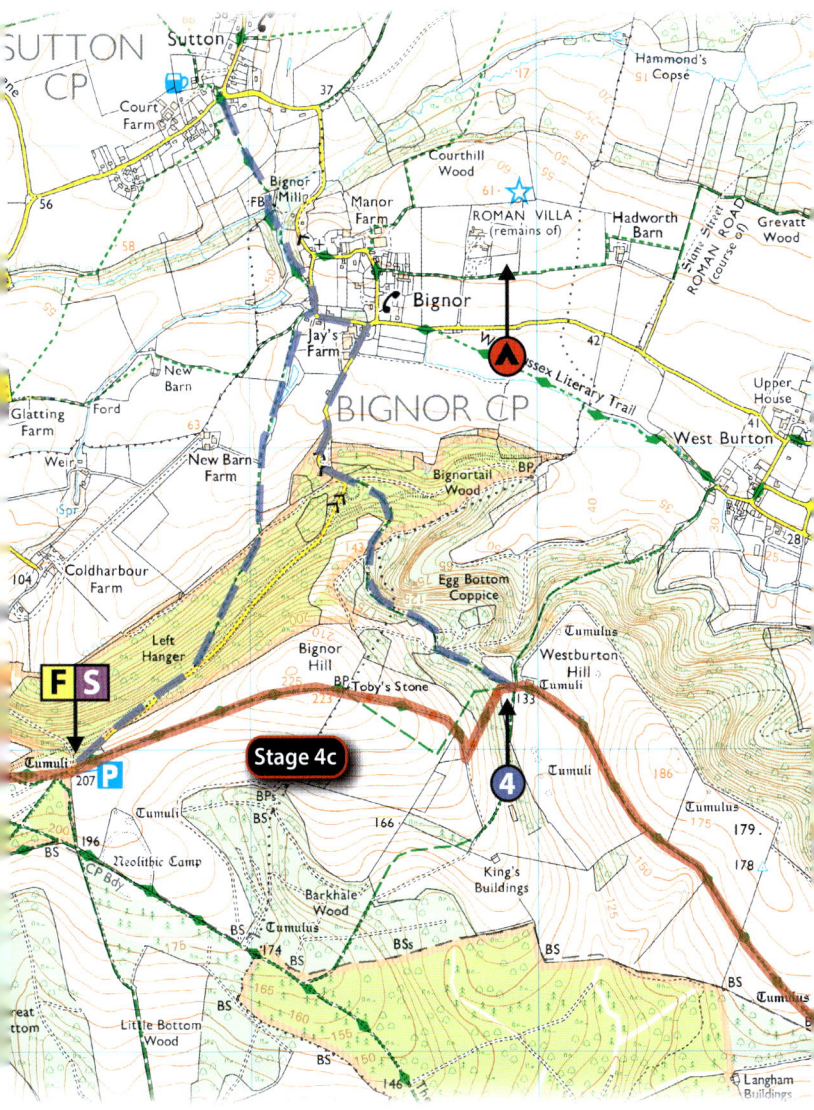

103

W-E

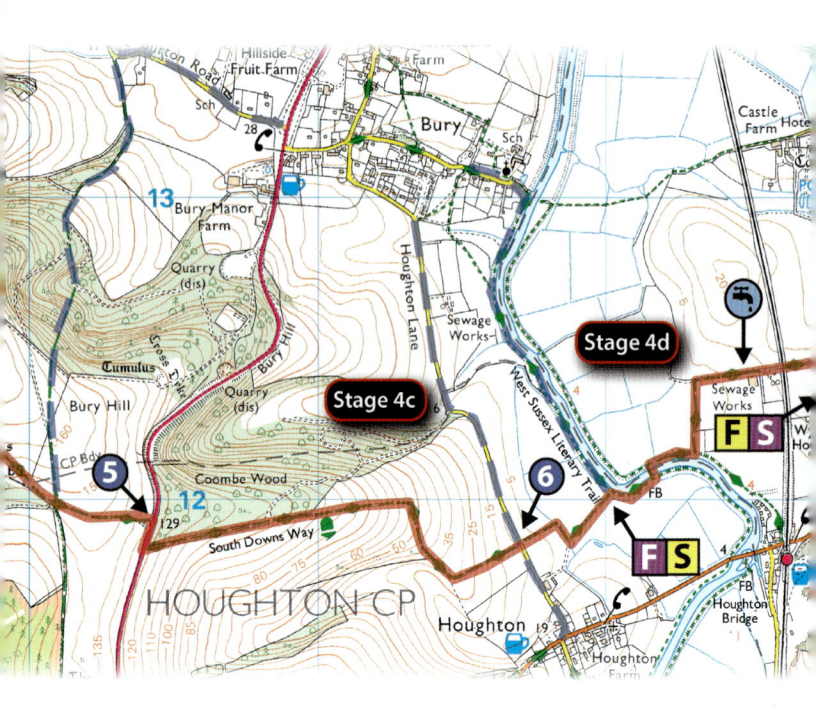

Stage 4c: Bignor/Sutton exit to Bury exit

S From the car park, climb E on a track through hayfields to the top of **Bignor Hill (225m)**: the views are magnificent.

4 0:30: After a steep descent, TR at a junction. Shortly afterwards, TR on a track: it soon narrows to a path and starts to climb SE. 20min later, a path on the left heads to **Bury**: however, there is a more scenic route to Bury from the E end of Stage 4c.

5 1:00: TR onto a footpath alongside the A29. Shortly afterwards, take care crossing the busy road and descend on a track.

6 1:25: Keep SH across a lane and continue on a path: alternatively, TR to head to **Houghton**. Shortly afterwards, go through a gate and TR.

F 1:30: Arrive at a junction beside the **River Arun**. TR to start Stage 4d. Alternatively, TL to head to **Bury**.

Stage 4d: Bury exit to Houghton Bridge

S From the junction beside the **River Arun**, head E. Shortly afterwards, TL and cross a bridge. Immediately afterwards, TR on a path. Soon TL, away from the river. A few minutes later, there is a WP (tap) on the right.

F 0:20: TR on a path alongside a road. Shortly afterwards, arrive at **Foxleigh Barn** near **Houghton Bridge**.

Heyshott Down (Stage 4a)

E-W

Stage 4d: Houghton Bridge to Bury exit

F From **Foxleigh Barn**, head N on a path beside the busy B2139. Shortly afterwards, TL on a path heading W. A few minutes later, there is a WP (tap) on the left. Soon TL, towards the **River Arun**. At the river, TR. Shortly afterwards, TL and cross a bridge. Immediately afterwards, TR on a path.

S 0:20: A few minutes later, arrive at a junction. TL to start Stage 4c. Alternatively, keep SH along the riverbank to head to **Bury**.

Stage 4c: Bury exit to Bignor/Sutton exit

F From the junction beside the **River Arun**, head SW. A few minutes later, TL and go through a gate.

6 0:05: Shortly afterwards, keep SH across a lane and climb on a track: alternatively, TL to head to **Houghton**.

5 0:30: Take care crossing the busy A29 and TR onto a footpath alongside it. Shortly afterwards, TL and climb on a path. After a while, descend.

4 1:00: Reach a junction: head W to continue on Stage 4c or head NW for **Bignor**/ **Bignor Roman Villa**. Shortly afterwards, TL and climb SW. After 5-10min, turn sharply right at a junction, still climbing. Head W over **Bignor Hill** on a track.

S 1:30: Arrive at a car park where there is a signpost in Latin. Keep SH through the car park to start Stage 4b. Alternatively, turn sharp right and head NE on the car park access road to head to **Bignor** (1.2 miles OR) or the excellent **Bignor Roman Villa** (see page 102).

Houghton Bridge/ Steyning exit

A beautiful journey spent almost entirely on the high crest of the northern escarpment. On the trail itself, there are no settlements of any kind so the experience is a tranquil one. There is more of the magnificent farmland that you will by now be accustomed to. The outlook over the Weald to the N is gorgeous but there are sea views too: W-E trekkers get closer to the sea as they proceed E.

E of Washington, the route crosses some wonderful open grassland where you will find the mysterious Chanctonbury Ring (see page 108), a lovely copse of beech trees on top of a hill which is one of the most famous landmarks in the SDs. Nearby, look out for a fine example of a dew pond, built by sheep-corn farmers back in the day to water their sheep.

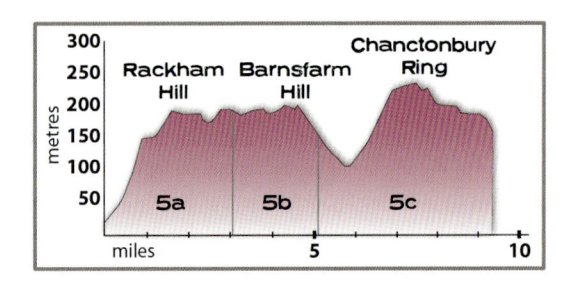

Chanctonbury Ring (Stage 5c)

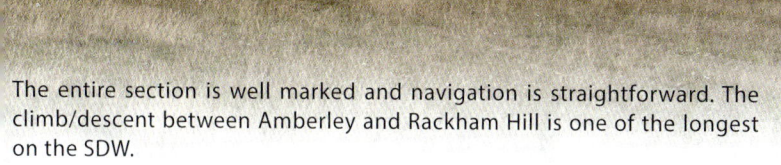

The entire section is well marked and navigation is straightforward. The climb/descent between Amberley and Rackham Hill is one of the longest on the SDW.

For accommodation, unless you are staying in Houghton Bridge/ Houghton/Amberley at the W end of this section, you will need to descend off the escarpment to one of the lowland towns/villages: Storrington, Washington or Steyning. Steyning is probably the nicest of these three places. Washington is pleasant but has no services other than a pub, a campsite and a B&B. However, Storrington and Steyning both have more to offer: shops where you can resupply and places to eat and sleep.

		Time	Distance	Ascent W-E	Descent W-E
Stage 5a	Houghton Bridge/ Storrington exit	1:45	3.1 miles 5.0km	623ft 190m	66ft 20m
Stage 5b	Storrington exit/ Washington exit	0:45	2.0 miles 3.2km	82ft 25m	82ft 25m
Stage 5c	Washington exit/ Steyning exit	2:00	4.2 miles 6.8km	459ft 140m	640ft 195m

Supplies/Water:

Amberley (Stage 4d/5a; 0.4 miles OR) – village store (groceries)

Storrington (Stage 5a/5b; 1.3 miles OR) – supermarket, shops, pharmacy & ATMs

Parkfield Farm (Stage 5c near Washington): tap beside the route about 100m W of the A24

Washington (Stage 5b/5c; 0.6 miles OR) – WP at the Franklin Arms

Steyning (Stage 5c/6a; 1.2 miles OR) – supermarket, shops, pharmacy & ATMs

Refreshments/Food:

Houghton Bridge (Stage 4d/5a) – the Bridge Inn, Riverside Café & Amberley Museum café

Amberley (Stage 4d/5a; 0.4 miles OR) – the Sportsman Inn, the Black Horse, Amberley Village Tearoom & Amberley Castle restaurant

Storrington (Stage 5a/5b; 1.3 miles OR) – tearooms, pubs & restaurants

Washington (Stage 5b/5c; 0.6-1.6 miles OR) – the Frankland Arms & hot food van at Washington Park campsite

Steyning (Stage 5c/6a; 1.2 miles OR) - tearooms, pubs & restaurants

The view from the Steyning exit (Stage 5c/6a)

Chanctonbury Ring

Chanctonbury Ring, one of the SD's most prominent landmarks, is a sizeable copse of beech trees near Chanctonbury Hill. It was originally planted in 1760, by Charles Goring of Wiston, on the site of an Iron Age hill-fort and a Roman Temple. During WW2, an anti-aircraft gun was placed at the site. Many of the trees were destroyed in the infamous hurricane of 1987 which swept across Southern England. However, replanting has ensured that the Ring has retained its character.

There is certainly something evocative and mysterious about the copse and perhaps this explains its place in local folklore. Some claim that the hill on which the Ring is situated was created by the Devil and that you can summon him by running backwards around it seven times in an anti-clockwise direction! The author, Robert Macfarlane, spent a night at the Ring and recounts his rather chilling experience in his book 'The Old Ways': he was woken up in the middle of the night by a series of high-pitched human screams. Who knows whether or not the screams were the result of human high jinks but apparently, few people are courageous enough to camp here!

Accommodation:

Houghton Bridge (Stage 4d/5a)

Amberley (Stage 4d/5a; 0.4 miles OR)

High Titten Campsite (Stage 4d/5a): closed at the date of press but may re-open under new ownership

Storrington (Stage 5a/5b; 1.3 miles OR)

Swipes Farm Campsite (Stage 5b/5c; 1 mile OR)

Washington (Stage 5b/5c; 0.6-1.6 miles OR)

White House Caravan Site (Stage 5c/6a; 0.7 miles OR)

Steyning (Stage 5c/6a; 1.2 miles OR)

Escape/Access:

Houghton Bridge (Stage 4d/5a)

Storrington (Stage 5a/5b; 1.3 miles OR)

Washington (Stage 5b/5c; 0.6 miles OR)

Steyning (Stage 5c/6a; 1.2 miles OR)

W-E

Stage 5a: Houghton Bridge to Storrington exit

S Take a path which runs S from Foxleigh Barn's entrance. Soon, TL up a minor road. A few minutes later, pass **High Titten Campsite** (closed: see above) on the right.

1 0:15: Arrive at a junction. TR to continue on Stage 5a: alternatively, TL to head to **Amberley**. Shortly afterwards, TL and climb on a path. The route crosses **Rackham Hill (193m)** and then descends gently to a car park. Afterwards, continue SE on the waymarked path, climbing again.

F 1:45: 5-10min later, reach a junction. TL to head to **Storrington** or keep SH to start Stage 5b.

Stage 5b: Storrington exit to Washington exit

S From the **Storrington** junction, head E.

F 0:45: Arrive at a junction. TL for the **Washington Detour for W-E hikers** (see box) or keep SH to start Stage 5c.

Washington Detour for W-E hikers (official SDW variant; 1.6 miles)

From the junction, head N on a path. Soon start to descend. 20min later, keep SH across a junction (waymark difficult to spot). Shortly afterwards, TR onto a lane: alternatively, keep SH to head to **Swipes Farm** campsite. A few minutes later, TL at a junction. Soon, cross a bridge over the A24. Shortly afterwards, enter **Washington**. When you reach a T-junction, TL (N) for the **Frankland Arms** and **Washington Park** campsite.

W-E hikers can return to the SDW by heading S from the T-junction. Shortly afterwards, cross the road and pick up a path heading SE. Climb and after 10min, reach the SDW at Waypoint No.2.

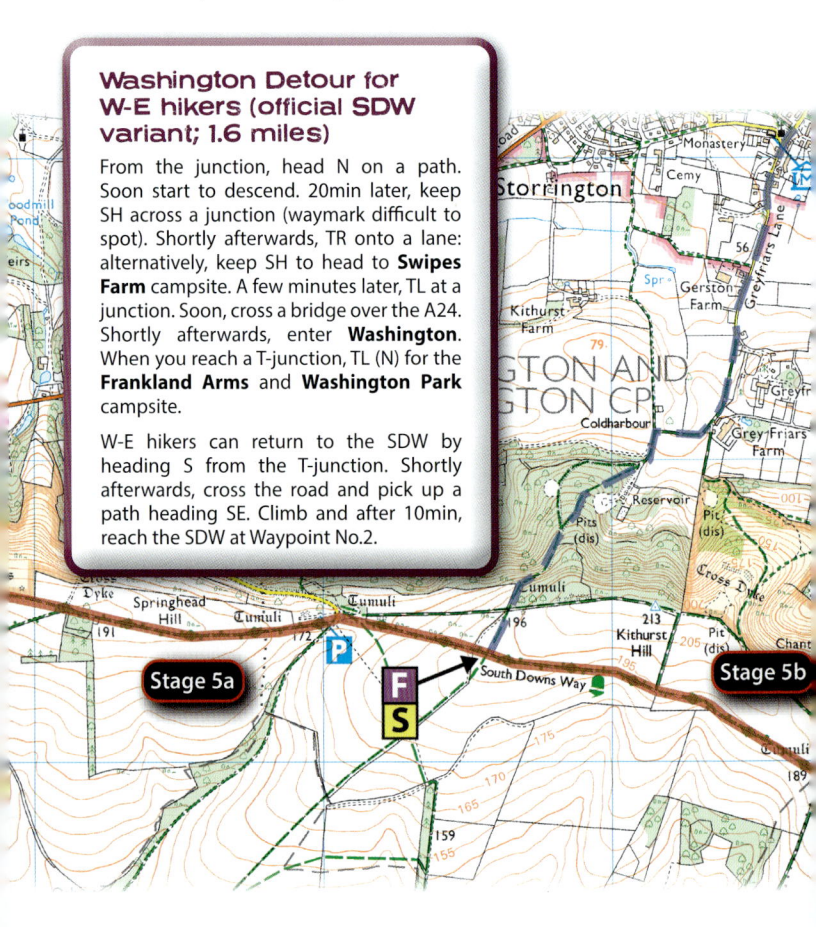

E-W

Stage 5b: Washington exit to Storrington exit

F From the junction, head W.

S 0:45: Arrive at a junction. TR to head to **Storrington** or keep SH to start Stage 5a.

Stage 5a: Storrington exit to Houghton Bridge

F From the **Storrington** junction, head W and descend. 5-10min later, keep SH at a car park and continue W, now climbing. Pass over **Rackham Hill (193m)** and then descend.

(1) 1:30: Arrive at a junction. TL to continue to **Houghton Bridge** on Stage 5a: alternatively, TR to head to **Amberley**. A few minutes later, pass **High Titten Campsite** (closed: see above) on the left. TR on a path beside the B2139.

S 1:45: Shortly afterwards, arrive at **Foxleigh Barn** near **Houghton Bridge**.

Washington Detour E-W hikers (0.6 miles)

From Waypoint No.2, descend S on a path. 5-10min later, TR onto a road. Shortly afterwards, ignore a road on the left (this is the path to return to the SDW). A few minutes later, reach the **Frankland Arms**. Continue N for **Washington Park** campsite.

E-W hikers can return to the SDW by heading NW on the road ignored previously (see above). A few minutes later, TR at a junction. A few minutes after that, TL at a junction and climb: alternatively, TR for **Swipes Farm** campsite. 25-30min later, TR onto the SDW.

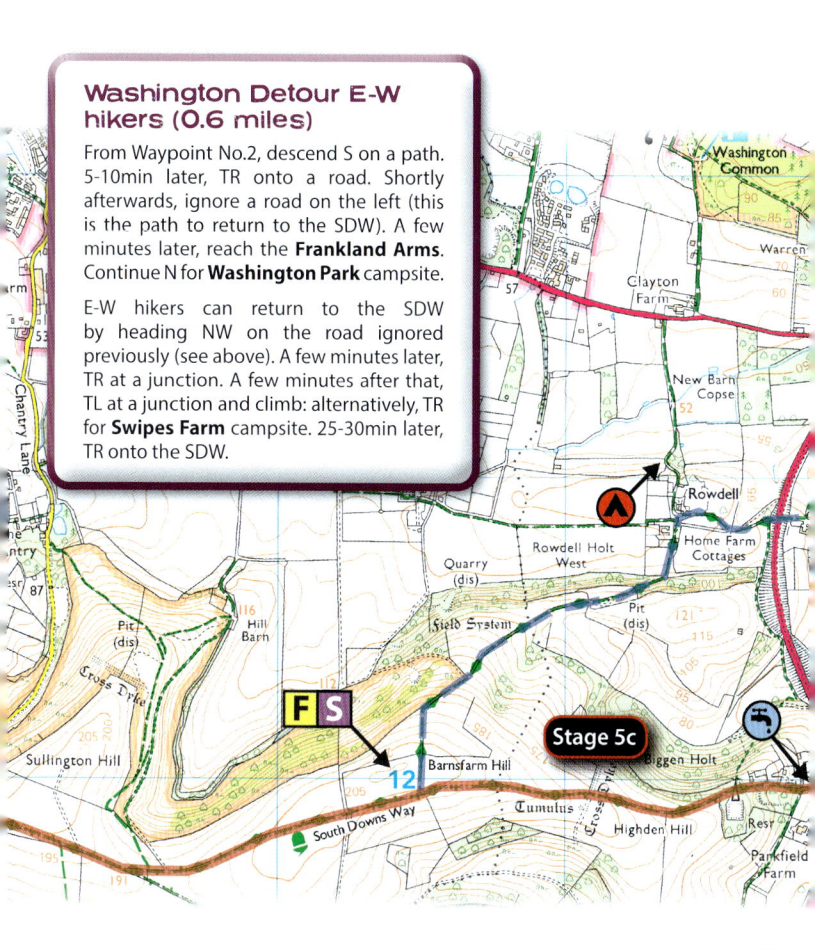

W-E

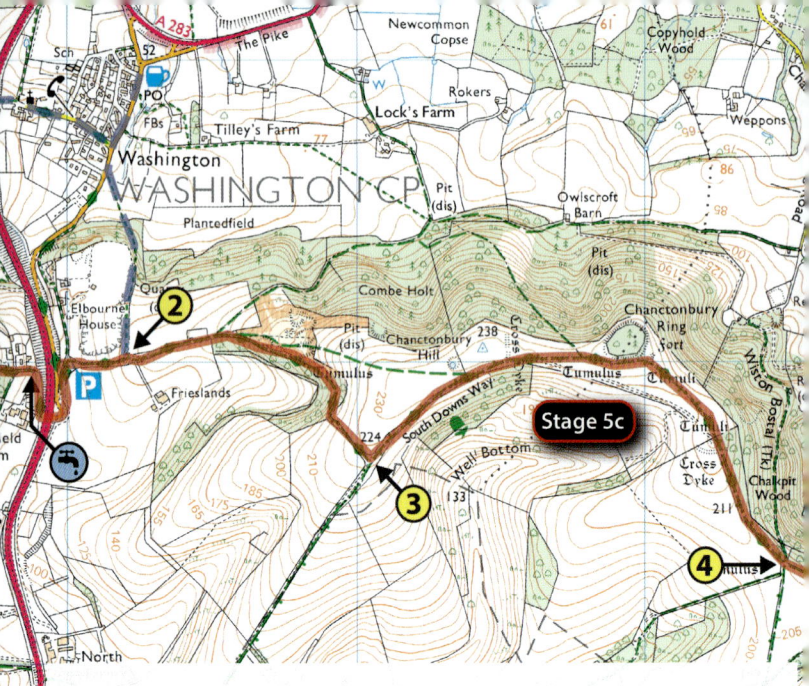

Stage 5c: Washington exit to Steyning exit

S From the junction, continue E. 20min later, cross the A24: a short distance W of the A24, there is a WP (tap) beside the path.

2 0:25: Pass a path on the left which descends to **Washington** (0.6 miles). Just afterwards, TL at a fork.

3 0:45: TL at a junction. 5-10min later, pass a **dew pond** on the left (see page 66). Shortly afterwards, cross **Chanctonbury Hill (238m)**. 10min later, pass **Chanctonbury Ring** (see page 108).

4 1:15: 10min later, keep SH at a junction.

F 2:00: Arrive at a junction (where there is a **memorial**). To head to **Steyning**, turn sharp left and head NE on a path: alternatively, keep SH (heading S) to start Stage 6a.

E-W

Stage 5c: Steyning exit to Washington exit

F From the junction (where there is a memorial), head NW.

4 0:45: Keep SH at a junction. 10min later, pass **Chanctonbury Ring** (see page 108). 5-10min later, cross **Chanctonbury Hill (238m)**. Shortly afterwards, pass a dew pond on the right (see page 66).

3 1:15: 5-10min later, TR at a junction. Stay on the main path, ignoring offshoots.

2 1:35: Pass a path on the right which descends to **Washington** (see **Washington Detour for E-W hikers** on page 111). 5min later, cross the A24. The SDW now heads briefly N and then bends left to the W. There is a WP (tap) beside the path.

S 2:00: Arrive at a junction: this is where the **Washington Detour for E-W hikers** returns to the SDW. Keep SH to start Stage 5b.

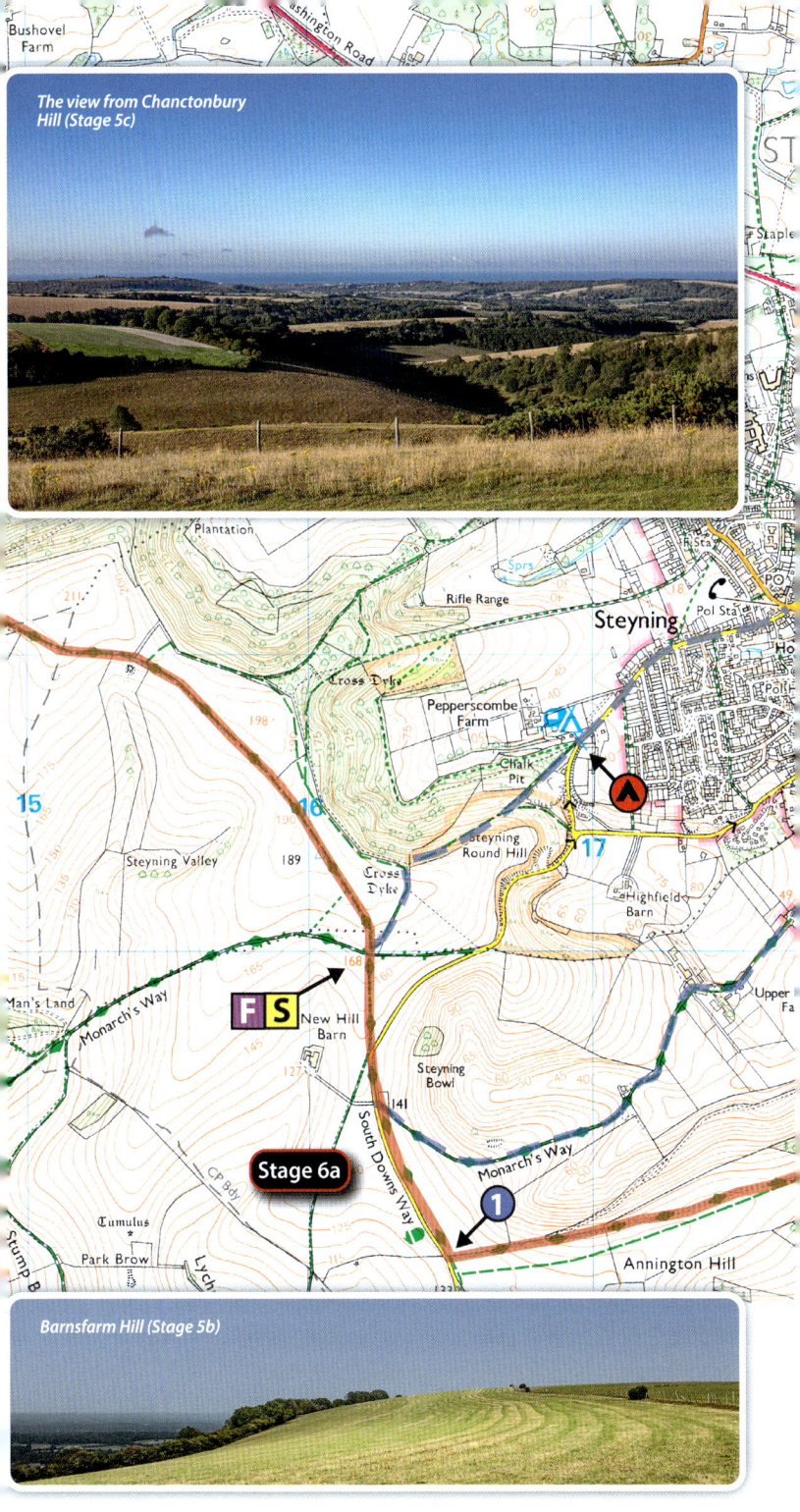

The view from Chanctonbury Hill (Stage 5c)

Barnsfarm Hill (Stage 5b)

113

6 Steyning exit/Pyecombe

A magnificent walk along a wind-swept part of the northern escarpment. Trees here are few and far between except for the occasional solitary outlier, bent and shaped by the strong winds. Consequently, the views of the Weald are largely unimpeded.

The best-known landmark along the way is the Devil's Dyke, a mile long dry valley formed more than 10,000 years ago in the last ice age: in fact, it is the longest, deepest and widest dry valley in the UK and is cared for by the National Trust. You can still see the contours of the walls of an Iron Age hill-fort above the dyke and the slopes are covered with wild-flowers in spring and summer. The beauty and uniqueness of the Devil's Dyke make it a popular place. More tranquil, but equally as scenic, are Steyning Bowl (Stage 6a) and the magnificent countryside E of Truleigh Hill (Stage 6c).

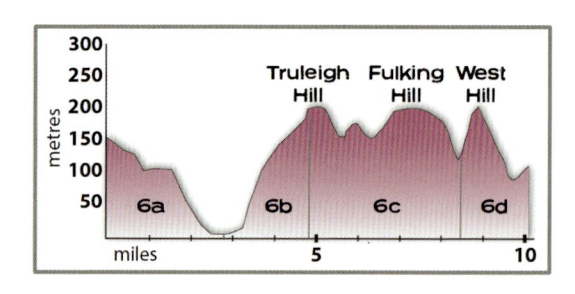

Arable fields above Steyning Bowl (Stage 6a)

There are plenty of places to stay including the YHA at Truleigh Hill and Saddlescombe Farm, both of which are right on the trail. Saddlescombe Farm, with its beautiful campsite, is a traditional sheep-corn farm complete with buildings made from flint. However, if you require something more comfortable, there are a few B&Bs at Pyecombe or you can travel a short distance OR: the villages of Steyning, Bramber and Upper Beeding have accommodation, pubs, restaurants and shops for resupply. The M&S supermarket close to Pyecombe is one of the best shops on the entire trek.

The section is well marked and navigation is straightforward. The climb/descent between the River Adur and Truleigh Hill is one of the longest on the SDW.

		Time	Distance	Ascent (W-E)	Descent (W-E)
Stage 6a	Steyning exit/Upper Beeding exit	1:00(W-E) 1:15(E-W)	2.8miles 4.5km	0ft 0m	525ft 160m
Stage 6b	Upper Beeding exit/ Truleigh Hill	1:00(W-E) 0:45(E-W)	2.0miles 3.2km	581ft 177m	0ft 0m
Stage 6c	Truleigh Hill/ Saddlescombe Farm	2:00	3.6miles 5.8km	591ft 180m	394ft 120m
Stage 6d	Saddlescombe Farm/Pyecombe	1:00	1.7miles 2.8km	361ft 110m	400ft 122m

Supplies/Water:

Steyning (Stage 5c/6a; 1.2 miles OR) – supermarket, shops, pharmacy & ATMs

Upper Beeding (Stage 6a/6b; 1-1.5 mile OR) – grocery shop & pharmacy

Upper Beeding exit (Stage 6b) – WP (tap) just E of the River Adur crossing

Truleigh Hill YHA (Stage 6b/6c) – WP (tap) & shop

Devil's Dyke (Stage 6c; 0.2 miles OR) – WP at the Devil's Dyke pub

Saddlescombe Farm (Stage 6c/6d) – WP (tap)

Pyecombe (Stage 6d/7a) – M&S Simply Food supermarket (at petrol station S of village)

Refreshments/Food:

Steyning (Stage 5c/6a; 1.2 miles OR) - tearooms, pubs & restaurants

Bramber (Stage 6a/6b; 1-1.5 mile OR) – restaurants

Upper Beeding (Stage 6a/6b; 1-1.5 mile OR) – pubs

Truleigh Hill YHA (Stage 6b/6c) – café

Fulking (Stage 6c; 0.4 miles OR) – the Shepherd & Dog pub

Devil's Dyke (Stage 6c; 0.2 miles OR) – the Devil's Dyke pub

Poynings (Stage 6c; 1 mile OR) – the Royal Oak pub

Saddlescombe Farm (Stage 6c/6d) – Wildflour Café

Pyecombe (Stage 6d/7a) – Wild Bean Café (at petrol station S of village) & the Plough pub

A windswept tree on Section 6

Accommodation:

White House Caravan Site (Stage 5c/6a; 0.7 miles OR)
Steyning (Stage 5c/6a; 1.2 miles OR)
Bramber (Stage 6a/6b; 1-1.5 mile OR)
Upper Beeding (Stage 6a/6b; 1-1.5 mile OR)
Truleigh Hill YHA (Stage 6b/6c)
Poynings (Stage 6c; 1 mile OR)
Saddlescombe Farm (Stage 6c/6d)
Pyecombe (Stage 6d/7a)

Escape/Access:

Steyning (Stage 5c/6a; 1.2 miles OR)
Bramber (Stage 6a/6b; 1-1.5 mile OR)
Upper Beeding (Stage 6a/6b; 1-1.5 mile OR)
Devil's Dyke (Stage 6c; 0.2 miles OR)
Pyecombe (Stage 6d/7a)

W-E

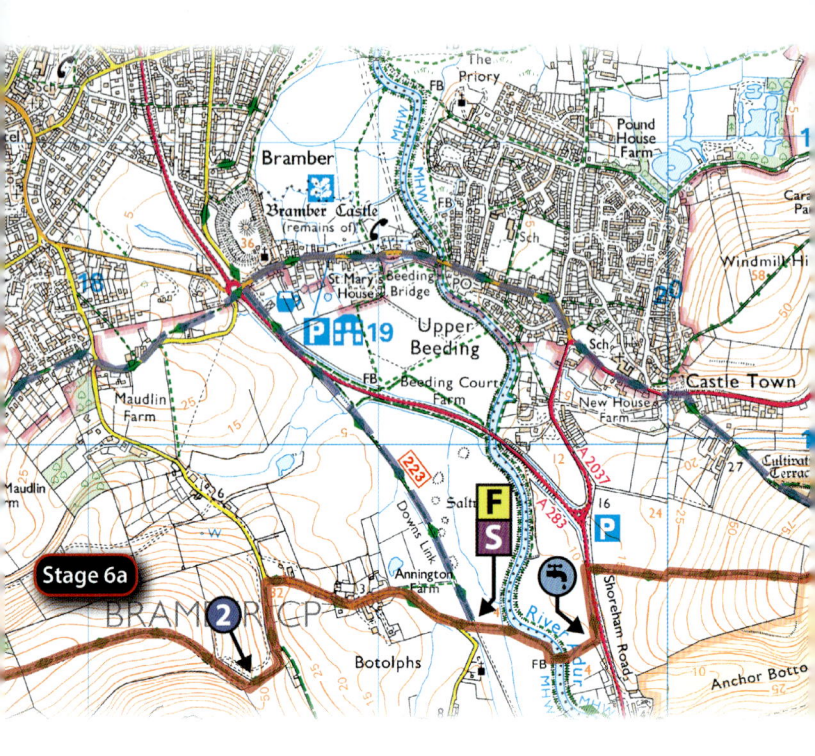

Stage 6a: Steyning exit to Upper Beeding exit

S From the junction at the **Steyning** exit, head S on a track. 5min later, TL, cross a minor road and pick up a path running S alongside it. A few minutes later, keep SH at a junction, go through a gate and continue along the edge of a hayfield: alternatively, you could TL at the junction to descend to **Bramber**, however, most prefer to access Bramber using the Downs Link from the end point of Stage 6a.

1 0:15: TL at a junction.

2 0:40: Go through a gate and descend on a path between trees. 5min later, TR onto a road. Soon, bear left onto a path which runs alongside the road. A few minutes later, TL onto a broad path.

F 1:00: Shortly afterwards, reach a junction: TL to head to **Bramber** (1 mile) or **Upper Beeding** (1.5 miles) on the Downs Link or keep SH to start Stage 6b.

Stage 6b: Upper Beeding exit to Truleigh Hill

S From the junction at the **Upper Beeding** exit, head E. A few minutes later, TR onto a path alongside the **River Adur**. A few minutes after that, TL and cross the river on a bridge. Then keep SH on a path. Shortly afterwards, reach a WP (tap) on the right: TL. At a bus stop, TR, cross a road and continue on a track (which soon climbs steeply).

3 0:35: Go through a gate and TR up a minor road. Keep SH on a track when the road ends.

F 1:00: Shortly afterwards, arrive at **Truleigh Hill YHA**.

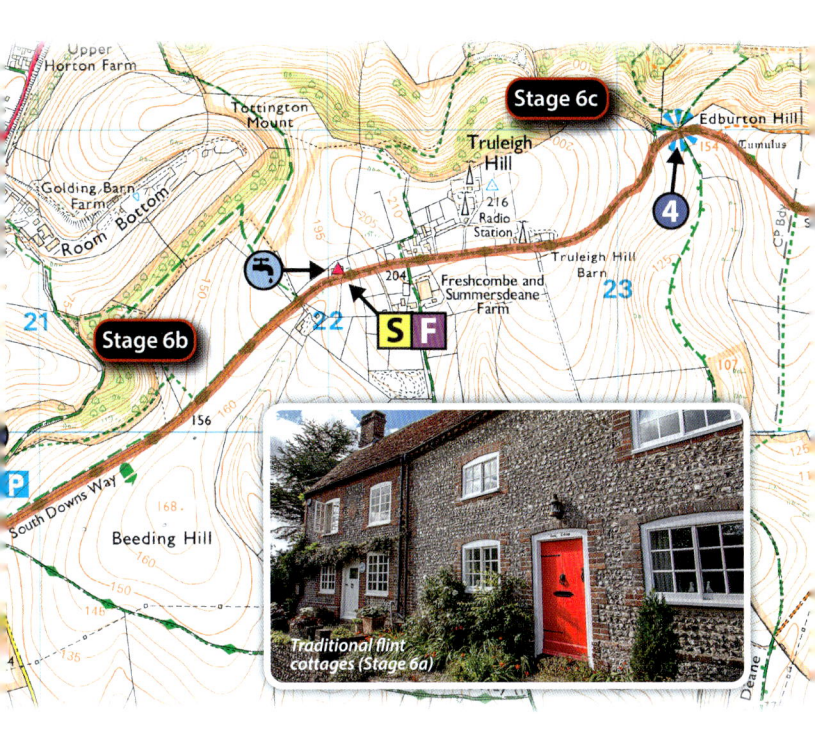

E-W

Stage 6b: Truleigh Hill to Upper Beeding exit

F From **Truleigh Hill YHA**, head SW, downhill on a track. Soon keep SH on a minor road.

3 0:20: From a junction, descend SW on a path: alternatively, descend NW on a track to head to **Upper Beeding** (1 mile) or **Bramber** (1.5 miles). When you reach a road, cross over and TL on an old road. A few minutes later, TR on a path: there is a WP (tap) on the left. Cross the **River Adur** on a bridge and then TR on a path. A few minutes later, TL.

S 0:45: Shortly afterwards, reach a junction: TR to head to **Bramber** (1 mile) or **Upper Beeding** (1.5 miles) on the Downs Link or keep SH to start Stage 6a.

Stage 6a: Upper Beeding exit to Steyning exit

F From the junction at the **Upper Beeding** exit, head W. Shortly afterwards, TR onto a path which runs alongside a road. Soon continue W along the road itself. 5min later, climb on a path.

2 0:20: 5min later, go through a gate.

1 0:55: TR at a junction and continue along the edge of a hayfield. 10min later, go through a gate and keep SH at a junction: alternatively, you could TR at the junction and descend from here to **Bramber**, however, most prefer to access Bramber from the start point of Stage 6a using the Downs Link. A few minutes later, cross a minor road and climb N on a track.

S 1:15: Arrive at a junction (where there is a memorial). To head to **Steyning**, TR and head NE on a path: alternatively, keep SH (heading N) to start Stage 5c.

W-E

Stage 6c: Truleigh Hill to Saddlescombe Farm

S From the YHA, head uphill (E) on a track. Soon start to descend.

4 0:25: Go through a gate and climb on a track.

5 1:10: Go through a gate. Just afterwards, TR at a fork: alternatively, TL for the **Devil's Dyke pub**. 5min later, cross a road: take care as there are blind corners in both directions. 5min later, if you wish to go to **Poynings** (1 mile OR), TL on a path descending into the dyke: otherwise keep SH to continue on Stage 6c. There are excellent views of the **Devil's Dyke** down to the left.

6 1:45: TL at a fork near a car park and descend.

F 2:00: Cross a road and continue on a path. Shortly afterwards, arrive at **Saddlescombe Farm**.

Stage 6d: Saddlescombe Farm to Pyecombe

S Head uphill from the café at **Saddlescombe Farm**. Shortly afterwards, the track bears to the right. A few minutes later, keep SH through a gate. Just afterwards, keep SH at a fork, climbing through trees. When you emerge from the trees, climb up the side of a field.

7 0:50: TL on a road. A few minutes later, cross the A23 on a bridge. Shortly afterwards, TR and climb on a lane.

F 1:00: A few minutes later, arrive at a road junction in **Pyecombe**.

The descent from Truleigh Hill (Stage 6c)

E-W

Stage 6d: Pyecombe to Saddlescombe Farm

F From the road junction in **Pyecombe**, descend W on **Church Hill**. Soon, TL onto a road and cross the A23 on a bridge. Shortly, afterwards, TL onto a road.

7 0:10: A few minutes later, TR and climb on a path. Head over **West Hill (211m)** and descend. TR at a junction. Just afterwards, keep SH through a gate.

S 1:00: Follow a track downwards and soon reach the café at **Saddlescombe Farm**.

Stage 6c: Saddlescombe Farm to Truleigh Hill

F From the café at **Saddlescombe Farm**, follow a path SW to a road: cross over and climb on a path.

6 0:20: Keep SH past a car park. 10min later, if you wish to go to **Poynings**, TR on a path descending into the Devil's Dyke: otherwise keep SH to continue on Stage 6c. There are excellent views of the **Devil's Dyke** down to the right. 5min later, keep SH across a road: alternatively, TR for the **Devil's Dyke pub**. Take care on the road as there are blind corners in both directions.

5 0:55: Go through a gate and continue W. Soon descend.

4 1:35: Go through a gate and climb on a track.

S 2:00: Arrive at **Truleigh Hill YHA**.

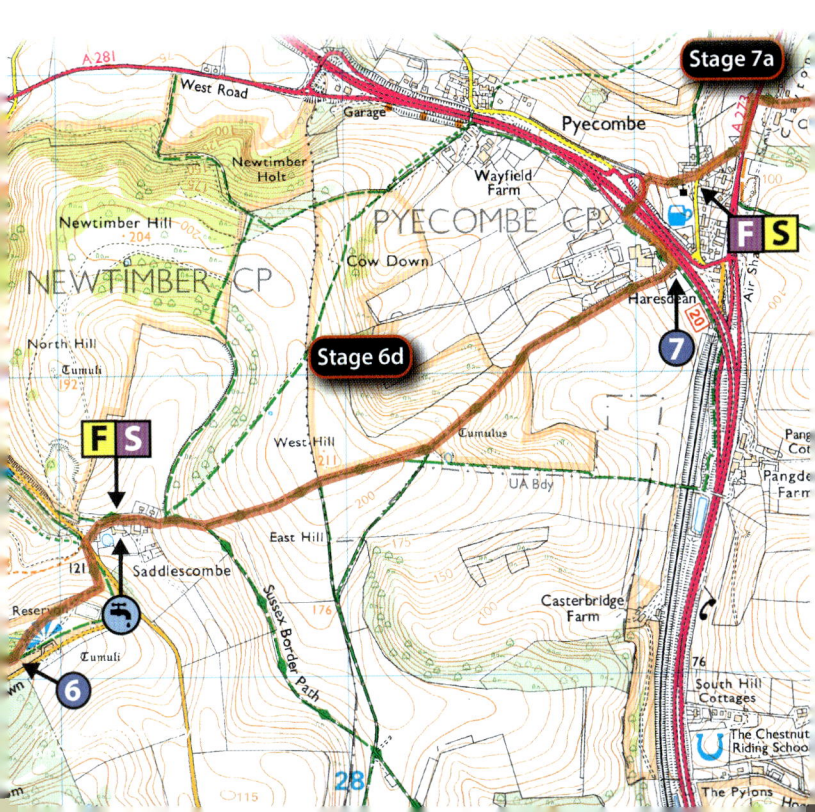

7 Pyecombe/Rodmell exit

The views on this open section of the SDW are wonderful: big skies and 360° panoramas are the order of the day. For much of the walk, you remain on the upper crest of the northern escarpment and a lovely mixture of wild grassland and sweeping arable fields keeps you company along the way. You also pass two historic windmills above Clayton (see page 127) which are only a few minutes OR. This is a walk to savour.

The high point is Ditchling Beacon which, at 248m, is the second highest place in the SDNP and offers excellent views out over the Weald. It is covered with some fine chalk grassland which is home to magnificent flowers and butterflies, including the rare Chalkhill Blue. The hill has historical interest too: it was the site of an Iron Age hill-fort and was one of a chain of beacons set up across Southern England many centuries ago

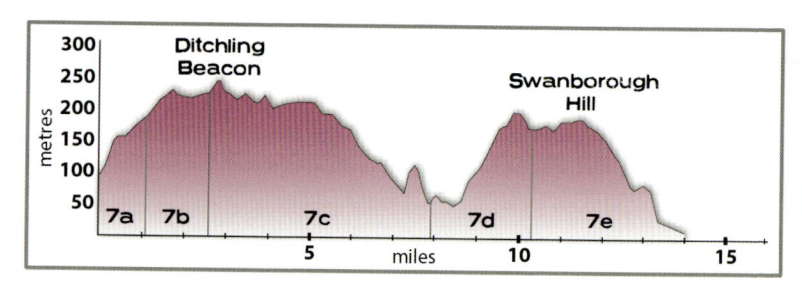

Beautiful scenes on Stage 7c

to warn of impending invasion from across the English Channel. Ditchling Beacon was actually used to warn Queen Elizabeth I of the approaching Spanish Armada in 1588: the fleet was spotted off the Lizard in Cornwall where the first beacon was lit and it is thought that it would have only taken 30min for the warning to have been received in London.

The section is well marked and navigation is straightforward.

		Time	Distance	Ascent (W-E)	Descent (W-E)
Stage 7a	Pyecombe/ Jack & Jill exit	0:45	1.1miles 1.8km	295ft 90m	39ft 12m
Stage 7b	Jack & Jill exit/ Ditchling Beacon	0:45	1.5miles 2.4km	312ft 95m	49ft 15m
Stage 7c	Ditchling Beacon/ Housedean Farm	2:00(W-E) 2:30(E-W)	5.3miles 8.5km	213ft 65m	902ft 275m
Stage 7d	Housedean Farm/ Kingston exit	1:15(W-E) 1:00(E-W)	2.4miles 3.8km	541ft 165m	98ft 30m
Stage 7e	Kingston exit/ Rodmell exit	1:30(W-E) 1:45(E-W)	3.7miles 6.0km	66ft 20m	656ft 200m

This working 19th century windmill is known as 'Jill' (Stage 7a/7b)

Supplies/Water:

Pyecombe (Stage 6d/7a) – M&S Simply Food supermarket (at petrol station S of village)

Ditchling (Stage 7b/7c; 1.8 miles OR) – newsagent (limited supplies), post office (limited supplies) & pharmacy

Lewes (Stage 7c; 3.4 miles OR) – supermarket, shops (including outdoor shops), pharmacy and ATMs

Housedean Farm (Stage 7c/7d) - WP (tap)

Service Station beside the Newmarket Inn (Stage 7d; 0.4 miles OR)

Refreshments/Food:

Pyecombe (Stage 6d/7a) – Wild Bean Café (at petrol station S of village) & the Plough pub

Clayton (Stage 7a/7b; 1 mile OR) - Jack & Jill Inn

Ditchling (Stage 7b/7c; 1.8 miles OR) – the Bull pub & the White Horse Inn

Lewes (Stage 7c; 3.4 miles OR) – pubs, restaurants and cafés

Newmarket Inn (Stage 7d; 0.4 miles OR)

Kingston-near-Lewes (Stage 7d/7e; 0.7 miles OR) – the Juggs pub

Rodmell (Stage 7e/8a; 0.5 miles OR) – the Abergavenny Arms

Accommodation:

Pyecombe (Stage 6d/7a)

Clayton (Stage 7a/7b; 1 mile OR)

Southdown Way Caravan & Camping Park (Stage 7b; 1.4 miles OR)

Ditchling Camp (Stage 7b; 0.7 miles OR)

Ditchling (Stage 7b/7c; 1.8 miles OR)

Streat (Stage 7c; 1.3 miles OR)

Lewes (Stage 7c; 3.4 miles OR)

Housedean Farm Campsite (Stage 7c/7d)

Newmarket Inn (Stage 7d; 0.4 miles OR)

Kingston-near-Lewes (Stage 7d/7e; 0.7 miles OR)

Rodmell (Stage 7e/8a; 0.5 miles OR)

Escape/Access:

Pyecombe (Stage 6d/7a)

Clayton (Stage 7a/7b; 1 mile OR)

Ditchling Beacon (Stage 7b/7c)

Lewes (Stage 7c; 3.4 miles OR)

Housedean Farm Campsite (Stage 7c/7d)

Kingston-near-Lewes (Stage 7d/7e; 0.7 miles OR)

Rodmell (Stage 7e/8a; 0.5 miles OR)

W-E

Stage 7a: Pyecombe to Jack & Jill exit

S From the road junction in **Pyecombe**, head NE down **School Lane**. Shortly afterwards, pass **Duck Lodge B&B** on the right. At the A273, TL on a path. A few minutes later, TR and cross the road. Then climb a lane into **Pyecombe Golf Club**: keep SH through the car park and climb on a track through the golf course.

1 0:35: TL at a junction.

F 0:45: Arrive at a junction. TR to start Stage 7b or keep SH (NW) to head to **Clayton** (1 mile) or the **Jack and Jill windmills** (see Windmill/Clayton Detour).

Stage 7b: Jack & Jill exit to Ditchling Beacon

S From the junction, head gently uphill (SE) on a track.

2 0:15: Keep SH at a junction: alternatively, TL to head to **Ditchling Camp** or **Southdown Way Caravan & Camping Park**.

3 0:20: Keep SH at a junction: alternatively, TL to head to **Ditchling** (1.8 miles). Soon climb over **Ditchling Beacon**.

F 0:45: Shortly afterwards, pass a parking area and reach a minor road. To start Stage 7c, cross the road and continue E along the crest of the ridge. Alternatively, TL on the road to head to **Ditchling**: soon pick up a path to the right of the road.

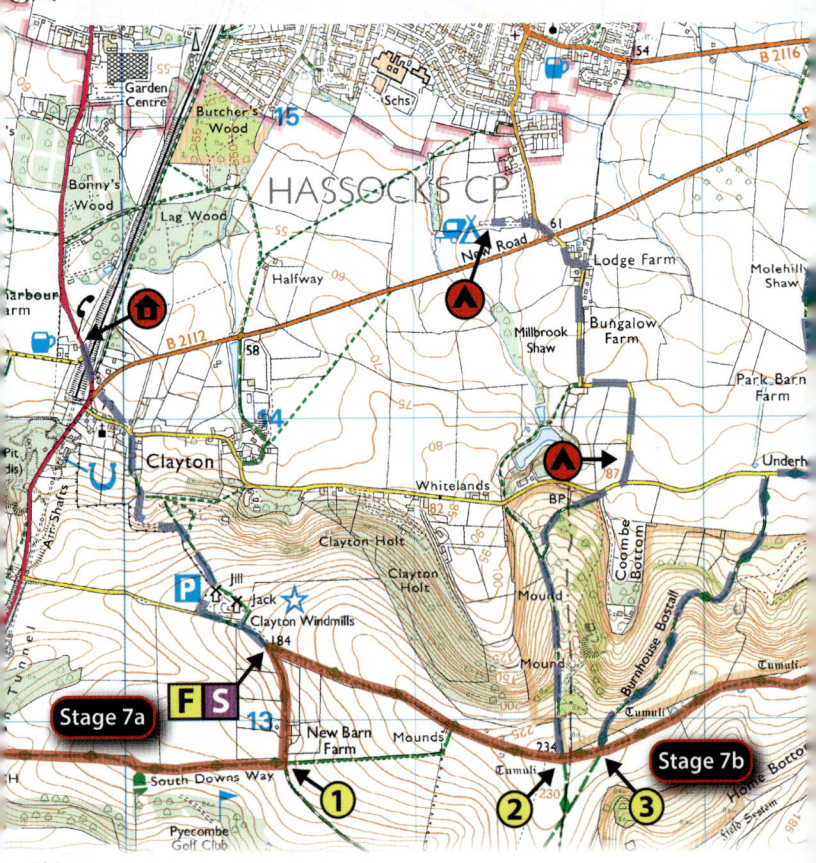

E-W

Stage 7b: Ditchling Beacon to Jack & Jill exit

F Cross the road and continue W along the crest of the ridge. Climb over **Ditchling Beacon** and then descend.

3 0:25: Keep SH at a junction: alternatively, TR to head to **Ditchling** (1.8 miles).

2 0:30: Keep SH at a junction: alternatively, TR to head to **Ditchling Camp** or **Southdown Way Caravan & Camping Park**.

S 0:45: Arrive at a junction. TL to start Stage 7a or keep SH (NW) to head to **Clayton** (1 mile) or the **Jack and Jill windmills** (see Windmill/Clayton Detour).

Stage 7a: Jack & Jill exit to Pyecombe

F From the junction, descend S.

1 0:10: TR at a junction and descend through **Pyecombe Golf Club**. Keep SH through the golf club car park. Then cross the A273 and TL on a path. A few minutes later, TR and climb SW up **School Lane** into Pyecombe. Soon pass **Duck Lodge B&B** on the left.

S 0:45: Shortly afterwards, arrive at a road junction in **Pyecombe**.

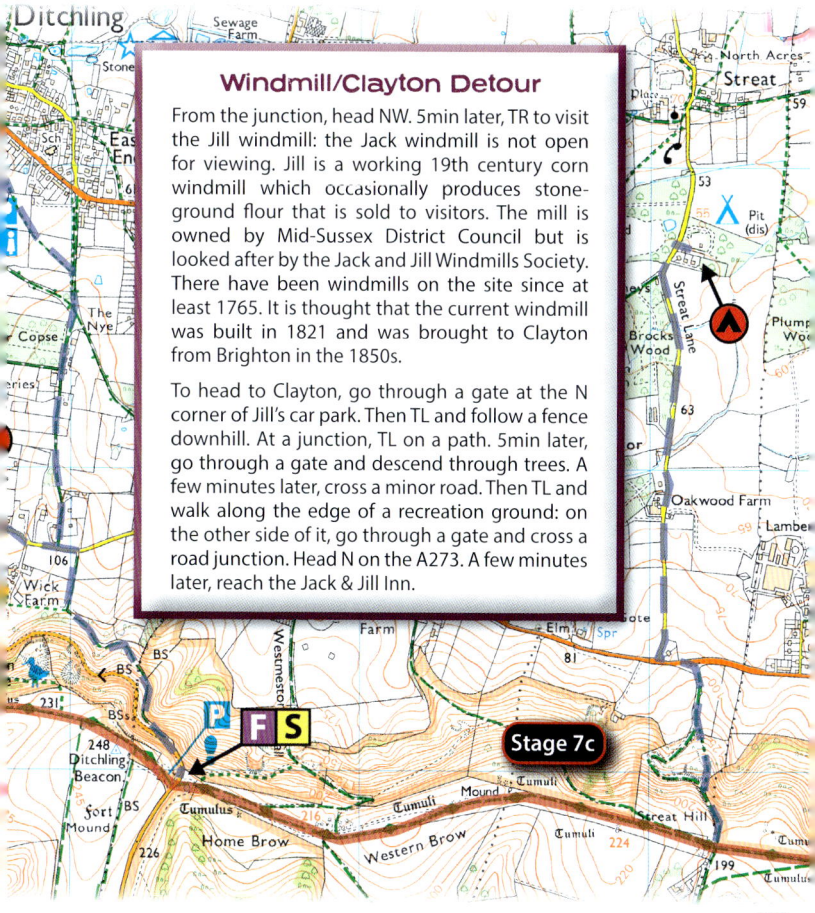

Windmill/Clayton Detour

From the junction, head NW. 5min later, TR to visit the Jill windmill: the Jack windmill is not open for viewing. Jill is a working 19th century corn windmill which occasionally produces stone-ground flour that is sold to visitors. The mill is owned by Mid-Sussex District Council but is looked after by the Jack and Jill Windmills Society. There have been windmills on the site since at least 1765. It is thought that the current windmill was built in 1821 and was brought to Clayton from Brighton in the 1850s.

To head to Clayton, go through a gate at the N corner of Jill's car park. Then TL and follow a fence downhill. At a junction, TL on a path. 5min later, go through a gate and descend through trees. A few minutes later, cross a minor road. Then TL and walk along the edge of a recreation ground: on the other side of it, go through a gate and cross a road junction. Head N on the A273. A few minutes later, reach the Jack & Jill Inn.

Stage 7c

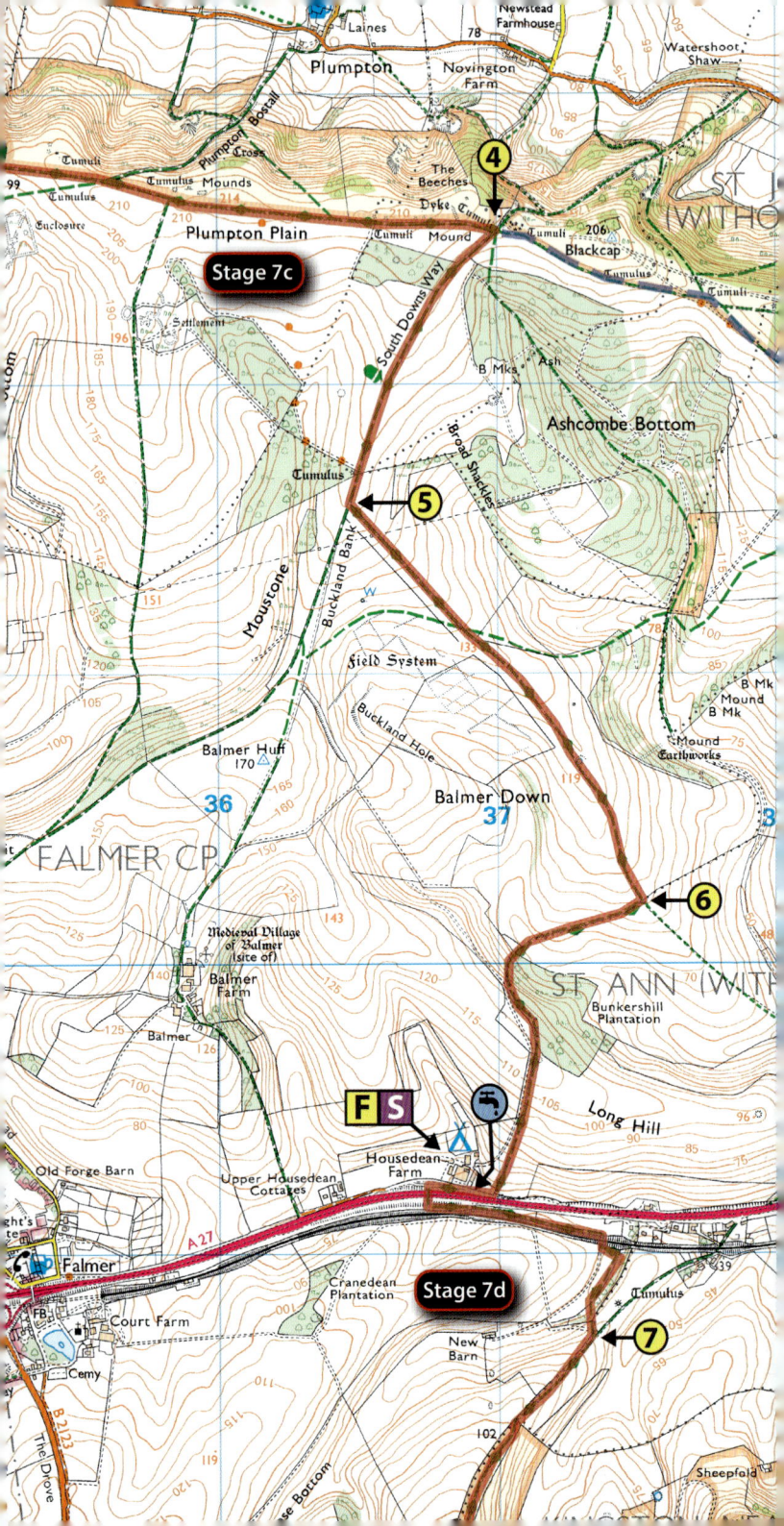

Stage 7d

W-E

Stage 7c: Ditchling Beacon to Housedean Farm

S Cross the road and continue E along the crest of the ridge. 30min later, keep SH at a junction: alternatively, TL to head to **Streat**.

4 1:00: TR just before the National Trust property of Blackcap: alternatively, keep SH to head to **Lewes** (3.4 miles). It is worth making a short detour to the summit of **Blackcap (206m)** which has fabulous views.

5 1:15: TL onto a track running along the side of a field.

6 1:40: TR at a junction.

F 2:00: Go through a gate. Then TR onto a path alongside the A27. Shortly afterwards, there is a WP (tap) on the right. Just afterwards, arrive at **Housedean Farm**.

E-W

Stage 7c: Housedean Farm to Ditchling Beacon

F From **Housedean Farm**, head E on a footpath alongside the A27. Soon TL, go through a gate and climb.

6 0:25: TL at a junction.

5 1:05: TR at a junction.

4 1:25: Arrive at a junction at the National Trust property of Blackcap. TL to continue on Stage 7c or TR to head to **Lewes** (3.4 miles). It is worth making a short detour to the summit of **Blackcap (206m)** which has fabulous views. 30min later, keep SH at a junction: alternatively, TR to head to **Streat**.

S 2:30: Reach a minor road near a parking area. To start Stage 7b, cross the road and continue W along the crest of the ridge. Alternatively, TR on the road to head to **Ditchling**: soon pick up a path to the right of the road.

The descent to Housedean Farm (Stage 7c)

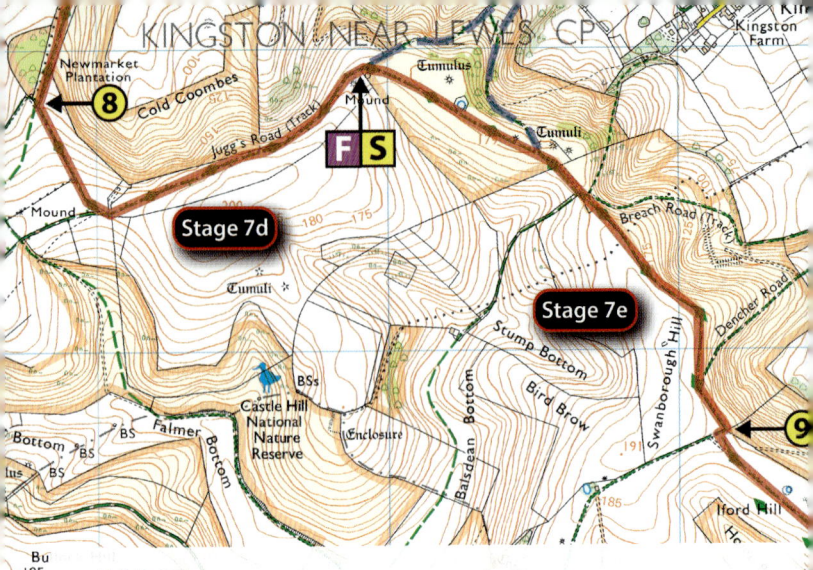

W-E

Stage 7d: Housedean Farm to Kingston exit

S From Housedean Farm, continue W along the footpath. Shortly afterwards, TL at a fork, climbing on a lane. Shortly after that, TL, crossing a bridge over the A27. A few minutes later, keep SH through a gate, leaving the lane. Soon start to climb.

7 0:20: TR at a junction: alternatively, TL to head to the **Newmarket Inn** or the nearby **service station**.

8 0:40: TL at a junction, still climbing. 5min later, keep SH through a gate into another field.

F 1:15: Arrive at a junction: bear right across open ground to start Stage 7e or keep SH to head to **Kingston-near-Lewes** (0.7 miles).

Stage 7e: Kingston exit to Rodmell exit

S From the junction, head SE across open ground (waymarks on posts).

9 0:30: TR and go through a gate, climbing briefly on a track. Shortly afterwards, TL onto a concrete lane. 20min later, keep SH across a lane and go through a gate. Then continue on a path along the side of a field. 5-10min later, pass a signpost marking the **Greenwich Meridian** (0° longitude).

10 1:10: Arrive at a tarmac lane. Go through a gate and keep SH to continue on Stage 7e: alternatively, TL to head to **Rodmell** (0.5 miles). Descend a steep slope: TL at the bottom of it. Shortly afterwards, TL on a track.

F 1:30: Arrive at a junction. TR to start Stage 8a or TL to head to **Rodmell** (0.5 miles).

E-W

Stage 7e: Rodmell exit to Kingston exit

F From the junction, head SW on a track. 15min later, TR. Shortly afterwards, TR and climb steeply.

10 0:25: Go through a gate and arrive at a tarmac lane. Keep SH to continue on Stage 7e: alternatively, TR to head to **Rodmell** (0.5 miles). Soon pass a signpost marking the **Greenwich Meridian** (0° longitude). 10min later, go through a gate and keep SH across a lane. 25-30min later, TR and descend briefly on a track.

Signpost marking the Greenwich Meridian (Stage 7e)

9 1:15: Shortly afterwards, go through a gate and continue NW. 20min later, reach a junction: keep SH to continue on Stage 7e or TR to head to **Kingston-near-Lewes** (0.7 miles).

S 1:45: Arrive at another junction. TL and head SW to start Stage 7d or TR to head to **Kingston-near-Lewes** (0.7 miles).

Stage 7d: Kingston exit to Housedean Farm

F From the junction, head SW. 20min later, the route bends right: descend NW.

8 0:25: TR at a junction and continue descending.

7 0:40: TL at a junction: alternatively, keep SH to head to the **Newmarket Inn** or the nearby **service station**. Soon the route bends left and heads W. 10min later, TR and cross a bridge over the A27: just afterwards, TR.

S 1:00: Shortly afterwards, arrive at **Housedean Farm**: there is a WP (tap) on a wall near the entrance.

131

8 Rodmell exit/Alfriston

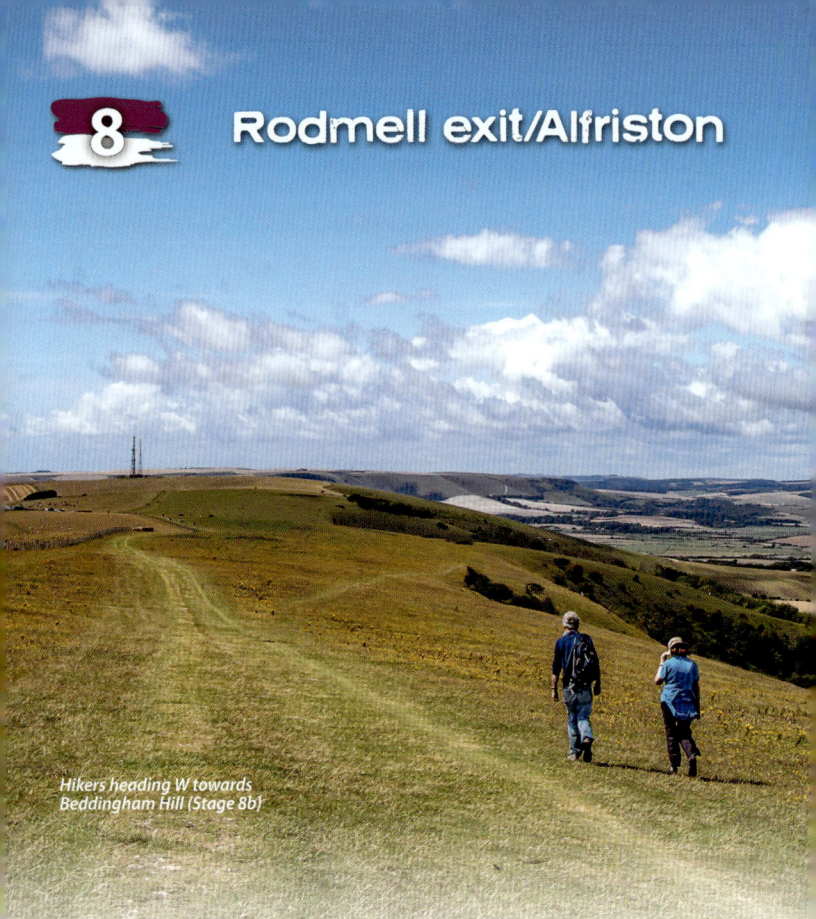

Hikers heading W towards Beddingham Hill (Stage 8b)

This section travels the high ground between the River Ouse and the River Cuckmere: on the flat open grassland in-between, there is little to impede the incredible views. Of course, this means that the Weald is on full display but you will also be close enough to the sea for its blue waters to draw the eye. Pray for good weather as this is a highlight of the SDW.

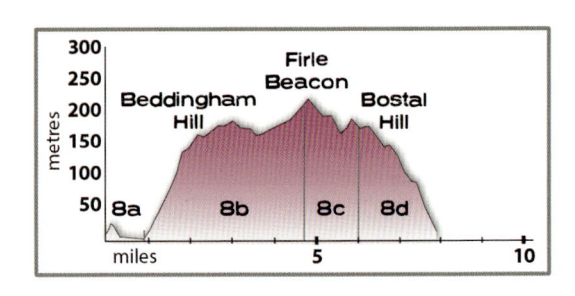

The picturesque village of Alfriston, at the E end of the route, is arguably the loveliest place to stay on the entire trek. Accordingly, a great many trekkers aim to overnight there and, although there are quite a few accommodation options, it is advisable to book well in advance. At the W end of the section, YHA South Downs is a great place to stay. There is also nearby Rodmell which has a pub and some B&Bs.

The section is well marked and navigation is straightforward. W-E hikers will have a long climb out of the Ouse valley and a long descent into the Cuckmere valley: obviously, E-W hikers do it the other way around and that is no easier. There are no WPs between Southease and Alfriston so be sure to fill up your bottles before starting the climb.

		Time	Distance	Ascent (W-E)	Descent (W-E)
Stage 8a	Rodmell exit/ YHA South Downs	0:30	0.9miles 1.5km	66ft 20m	98ft 30m
Stage 8b	YHA South Downs/ Firle Beacon	1:45(W-E) 1:30(E-W)	3.8miles 6.1km	722ft 220m	148ft 45m
Stage 8c	Firle Beacon/ Bostal Hill	0:30	1.3miles 2.1km	164ft 50m	197ft 60m
Stage 8d	Bostal Hill/Alfriston	0:45(W-E) 1:00(E-W)	1.9miles 3.0km	131ft 40m	722ft 220m

Supplies/Water:

Southease (Stage 8a) - WP (tap) on the wall at St Peter's Church

Firle (Stage 8b/8c; 1-1.4 miles OR) – Firle Stores (snacks & drinks)

Alfriston (Stage 8d/9a) – village store (snacks, sandwiches & drinks)

Refreshments/Food:

Rodmell (Stage 7e/8a; 0.5 miles OR) – the Abergavenny Arms

YHA South Downs at Southease (Stage 8a/8b) – café

Firle (Stage 8b/8c; 1-1.4 miles OR) – the Ram Inn

Alfriston (Stage 8d/9a) - tearooms, pubs & restaurants

Firle Beacon (Stage 8b/8c)

Accommodation:

Rodmell (Stage 7e/8a; 0.5 miles OR)
YHA South Downs at Southease (Stage 8a/8b)
Beddingham (Stage 8b; 1.8 miles OR)
Firle (Stage 8b/8c; 0.8-1.4 miles OR)
Tilton House (Stage 8c; 0.8 miles OR)
Bo-Peep Farmhouse B&B (Stage 8c; 0.6 miles OR)
Alciston (Stage 8c/8d; 1 mile OR)
Alfriston (Stage 8d/9a)

Escape/Access:

Rodmell (Stage 7e/8a; 0.5 miles OR)
Southease (Stage 8a)
Firle (Stage 8b/8c; 1-1.4 miles OR)
Alfriston (Stage 8d/9a)

Climbing E towards Beddingham Hill (Stage 8b)

W-E

Stage 8a: Rodmell exit to YHA South Downs

S From the junction, head S on a path. Climb briefly and keep SH across a road junction: shortly, descend E on a minor road. A few minutes later, pass **St Peter's Church** (see box) at **Southease** where there is a WP (tap) on the churchyard wall.

1 0:20: Cross a bridge over the **River Ouse**. At **Southease train station**, take care crossing the tracks (footbridge or level crossing).

F 0:30: Arrive at **YHA South Downs**.

Stage 8b: YHA South Downs to Firle Beacon

S From **YHA South Downs**, head S. Shortly afterwards, TL at a junction, climbing on a path. Cross a bridge over the A26 and continue climbing.

2 0:20: TL at a fork. 20-25min later, pass a trig point.

3 1:00: Keep SH at a junction: alternatively, TL if you are staying at **Beddingham**. 5min later, pass to the N of the radio masts on **Beddingham Hill (189m)**.

4 1:20: Keep SH into a car park. TL on a path at the E side of the car park: alternatively, TL on a minor road to head N to **Firle**. 20min later, another path on the left also heads to **Firle**.

F 1:45: Arrive at the trig point on **Firle Beacon (217m)**.

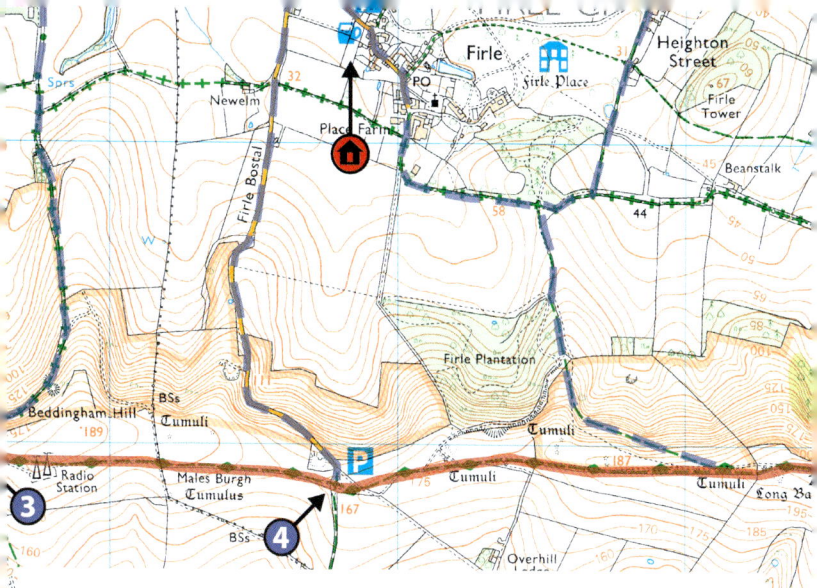

E-W

Stage 8b: Firle Beacon to YHA South Downs

F From **Firle Beacon**, head W. 5min later, reach a junction: keep SH (W) to continue on Stage 8b or TR to head to **Firle**.

4 0:25: From a car park, head W: alternatively, TR on a minor road to head N to **Firle**. 15min later, pass to the N of the radio masts on **Beddingham Hill (189m)**.

3 0:45: Keep SH at a junction: alternatively, TR if you are staying at **Beddingham**. 15min later, pass a trig point.

2 1:15: TR at a junction and continue descending. Cross a bridge over the A26 and descend on a path.

S 1:30: Arrive at **YHA South Downs**.

Stage 8a: YHA South Downs to Rodmell exit

F From **YHA South Downs**, head W. Shortly afterwards, at **Southease train station**, take care crossing the tracks (footbridge or level crossing).

1 0:15: Cross a bridge over the **River Ouse**. 10min later, climb NW past **St Peter's Church** (see box) at **Southease** where there is a WP (tap) on the churchyard wall. TR onto a road. Shortly afterwards, cross the road and TL onto a path which descends.

S 0:30: A few minutes later, arrive at a junction. TL to start Stage 7e or keep SH (N) to head to **Rodmell**.

St Peter's Church, Southease

Southease (including the site of the church) was granted to Benedictine monks in 966 CE. The nave of the church probably dates from the 11th century, however, the unusual round tower was built in the 12th century.

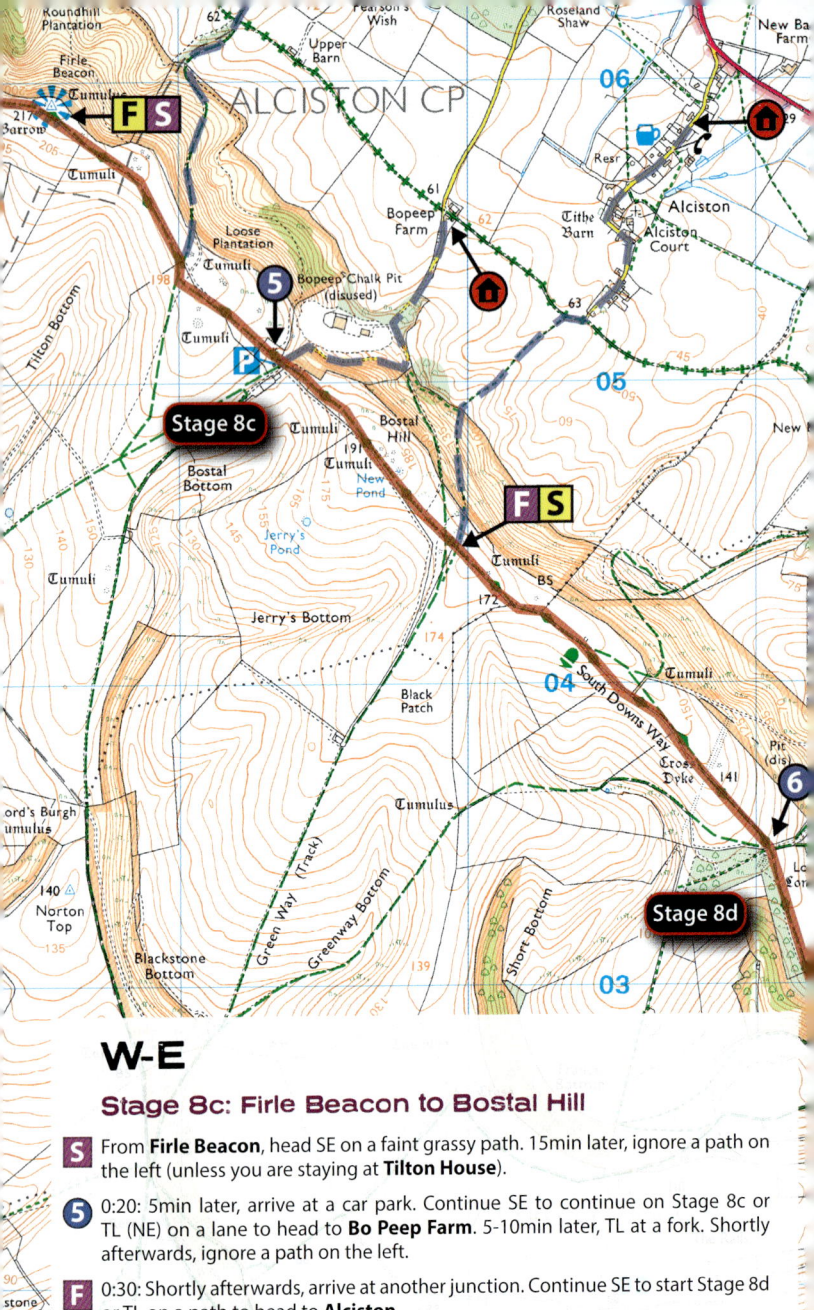

W-E

Stage 8c: Firle Beacon to Bostal Hill

S From **Firle Beacon**, head SE on a faint grassy path. 15min later, ignore a path on the left (unless you are staying at **Tilton House**).

5 0:20: 5min later, arrive at a car park. Continue SE to continue on Stage 8c or TL (NE) on a lane to head to **Bo Peep Farm**. 5-10min later, TL at a fork. Shortly afterwards, ignore a path on the left.

F 0:30: Shortly afterwards, arrive at another junction. Continue SE to start Stage 8d or TL on a path to head to **Alciston**.

Stage 8d: Bostal Hill to Alfriston

S From the junction, continue SE.

6 0:25: Go through a gate and keep SH at a junction.

7 0:40: Keep SH on a road (**Kings Ride**), still descending.

F 0:45: Arrive in the village of **Alfriston**.

E-W

Stage 8d: Alfriston to Bostal Hill

F From **Alfriston**, head W on **Star Lane**. Soon keep SH onto **Kings Ride** and climb.

7 0:10: Keep SH on a path.

6 0:30: Keep SH at a junction, climbing NW.

S 1:00: Arrive at a junction. Continue NW to start Stage 8c or TR on a path to head to **Alciston**.

Stage 8c: Bostal Hill to Firle Beacon

F From the junction, continue NW. Shortly afterwards, ignore a path on the right.

5 0:10: From a car park, head NW to continue on Stage 8c or TR (NE) on a lane to head to **Bo Peep Farm**. 5min later, ignore a path on the right (unless you are staying at **Tilton House**).

S 0:30: Arrive at the trig point on **Firle Beacon (217m)**.

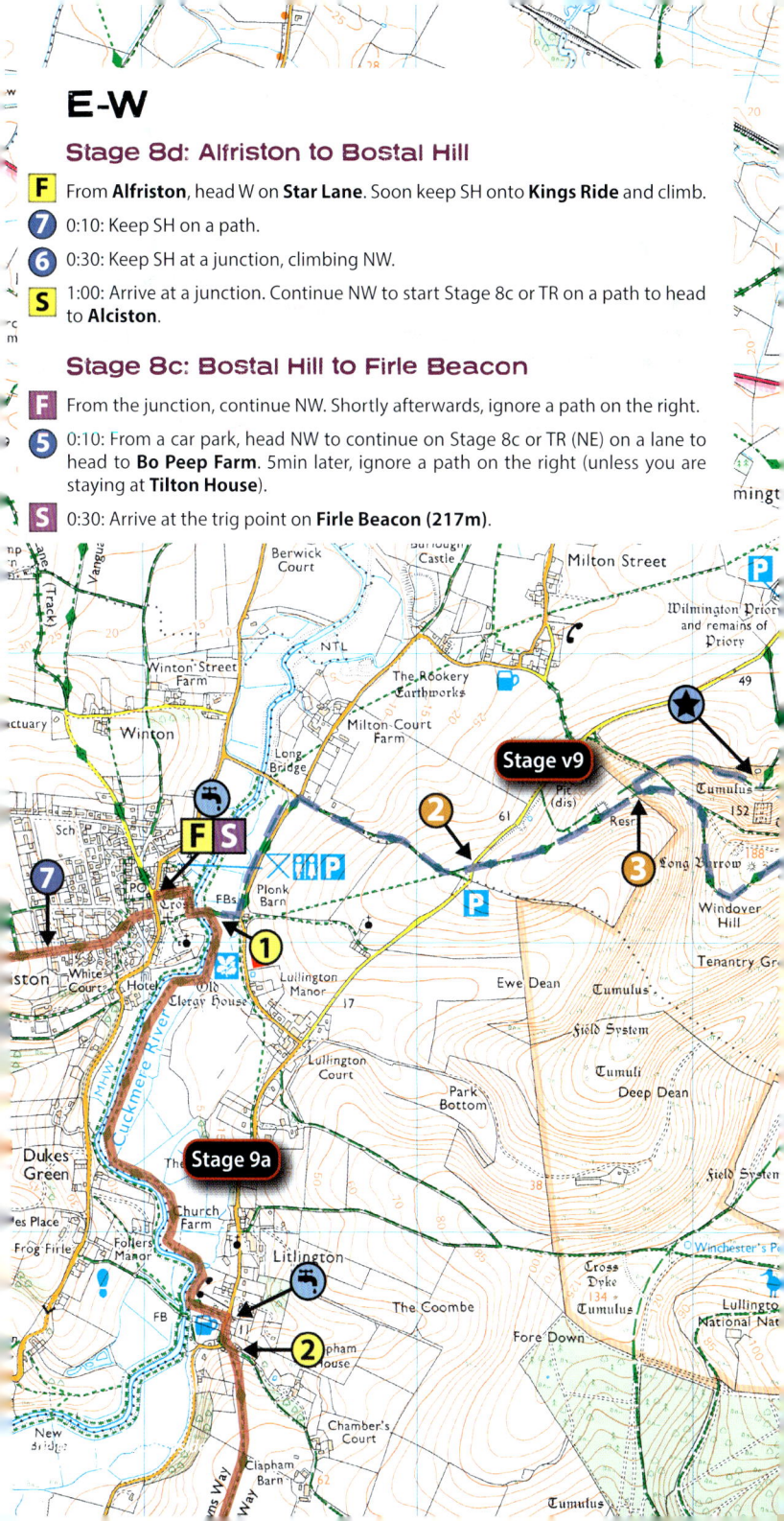

9 Alfriston/Meads

Because Britain is an island, it has no shortage of coastal scenery and on this section, you will view some of the best of it. Over the ages, the white cliffs of SE England have delighted those arriving by sea and the SDW is fortunate enough to possess perhaps the best white cliffs of all. For six glorious miles, the route negotiates the undulations of these wonderfully grassy cliff-tops, never far from the edge, high above the deep blue waters of the English Channel. For many, this stage is the overall highlight of the SDW and for W-E hikers, it provides an epic climax to the trek.

There are two main sections of cliffs here which are separated by Birling Gap (where the route drops almost to sea level). The Seven Sisters (W of Birling Gap) comprise perhaps the most famous stretch: a strikingly white section of chalk cliffs with a series of hills. As the name suggests, originally there were seven hills but in fact, an eighth hill has been created by erosion. The hills are called (W-E) Haven Brow, Short Brow, Rough Brow, Brass Point, Flagstaff Brow, Flat Hill, Baily's Hill and Went Hill. It is thought that the Seven Sisters were named by sailors who used them to navigate on their return to England.

E of Birling Gap, the cliffs are incredible too and they make an excellent vantage point from which to view the Seven Sisters lined up in a row far to the W. You will also pass the iconic candy-striped lighthouse at Beachy Head (see page 147).

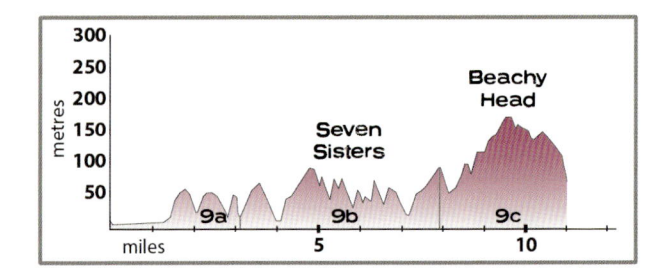

Beachy Head Lighthouse (Stage 9c)

The scenery is so beautiful that it is easy to overlook certain dangers. The cliffs are white because they are made of chalk which is soft and friable. The cliffs retain their bright white shade because they are constant victims of erosion: waves, wind, rain and ice continuously weather the cliff faces and, as the rock crumbles and falls into the sea, fresh bright white chalk is exposed. This erosion is unpredictable and, at any time, large sections of the cliffs could break away and tumble into the sea far below. It is a sobering fact that, on average, the cliffs recede by about 70cm a year. Make sure that you do not stray too close to the edges.

There is very little accommodation mid-route so most trekkers complete this section in one day. The picturesque village of Alfriston, at the W end of the route, is arguably the loveliest place to stay on the entire trek. Accordingly, a great many trekkers aim to overnight there and, although there are quite a few accommodation options, it is advisable to book well in advance. The seaside town of Eastbourne, with its famous Victorian pier, is a good place to end the trek: there are plenty of places to stay and eat. For E-W hikers, Eastbourne also has plenty of shops and supermarkets where you can stock up on supplies before starting the trek.

Navigation on the coastal section is straightforward as you simply follow the line of the cliffs. Inland, however, there are many twists and turns so follow the signs and waymarks closely. The constantly undulating terrain of the cliffs is quite tiring.

		Time	Distance	Ascent W-E	Descent W-E
Stage 9a	Alfriston/Exceat	1:30	3.2miles 5.1km	394ft 120m	377ft 115m
Stage 9b	Exceat/Belle Tout Lighthouse	2:30	4.7miles 7.5km	968ft 295m	1181ft 360m
Stage 9c	Belle Tout Lighthouse/Meads	1:45	3.2miles 5.1km	607ft 185m	525ft 160m

Supplies/Water:

Alfriston (Stage 8d/9a) – village store (snacks, sandwiches & drinks)

Litlington (Stage 9a) – WP (Plough & Harrow pub)

Exceat (Stage 9a/9b) – WP (tap) at the toilet block of the Seven Sisters Country Park visitor centre

Birling Gap (Stage 9b) – WP (tap) at the National Trust visitor centre

Beachy Head pub (Stage 9c) - WP

Meads (Stage 9c) – supermarkets, pharmacy & ATM

Eastbourne – shops, supermarkets, pharmacies & ATMs

Looking E along the Seven Sisters (Stage 9b)

Refreshments/Food:

Alfriston (Stage 8d/9a) - tearooms, pubs & restaurants

Litlington (Stage 9a) – the Plough & Harrow pub

Exceat (Stage 9a/9b) – Seven Sisters Country Park visitor centre (snacks & drinks) & the Cuckmere Inn (0.4 miles OR from Exceat; head SW along the A259)

Birling Gap (Stage 9b) – café (drinks and snacks)

Beachy Head (Stage 9c) - the Beachy Head pub

Meads (Stage 9c) – the Pilot Inn, the Ship pub & the Kiosk café

Eastbourne - pubs, restaurants & cafés

Accommodation:

Alfriston (Stage 8d/9a)
Exceat (Stage 9a/9b)
Belle Tout Lighthouse (Stage 9b/9c)
Meads (Stage 9c)
Eastbourne

Escape/Access:

Alfriston (Stage 8d/9a)
Exceat (Stage 9a/9b)
Birling Gap (Stage 9b)
Beachy Head (Stage 9c)
Meads (Stage 9c)
Eastbourne

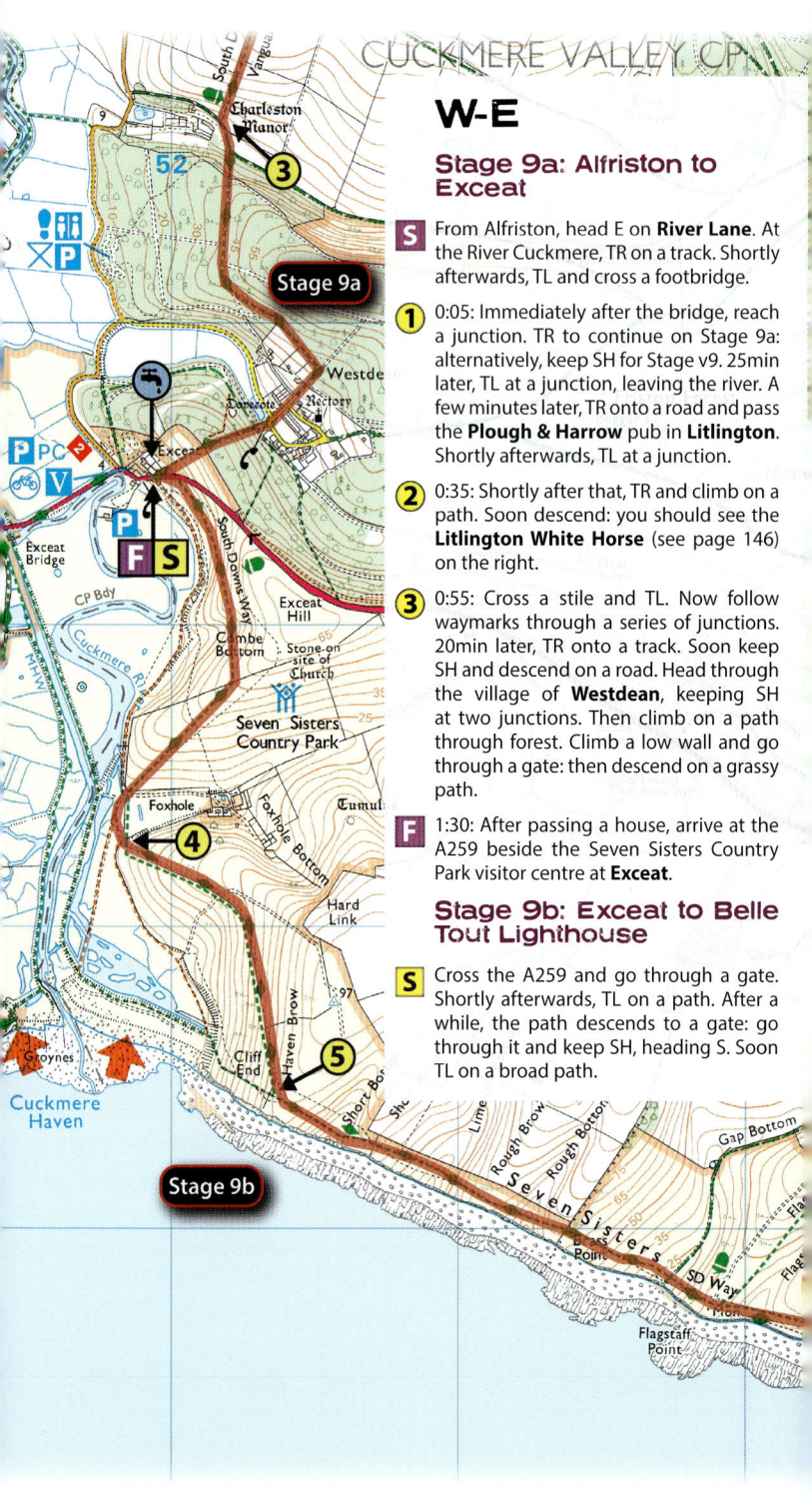

W-E

Stage 9a: Alfriston to Exceat

S From Alfriston, head E on **River Lane**. At the River Cuckmere, TR on a track. Shortly afterwards, TL and cross a footbridge.

1 0:05: Immediately after the bridge, reach a junction. TR to continue on Stage 9a: alternatively, keep SH for Stage v9. 25min later, TL at a junction, leaving the river. A few minutes later, TR onto a road and pass the **Plough & Harrow** pub in **Litlington**. Shortly afterwards, TL at a junction.

2 0:35: Shortly after that, TR and climb on a path. Soon descend: you should see the **Litlington White Horse** (see page 146) on the right.

3 0:55: Cross a stile and TL. Now follow waymarks through a series of junctions. 20min later, TR onto a track. Soon keep SH and descend on a road. Head through the village of **Westdean**, keeping SH at two junctions. Then climb on a path through forest. Climb a low wall and go through a gate: then descend on a grassy path.

F 1:30: After passing a house, arrive at the A259 beside the Seven Sisters Country Park visitor centre at **Exceat**.

Stage 9b: Exceat to Belle Tout Lighthouse

S Cross the A259 and go through a gate. Shortly afterwards, TL on a path. After a while, the path descends to a gate: go through it and keep SH, heading S. Soon TL on a broad path.

④ 0:25: Shortly afterwards, go through a gate and climb on a grassy path. Soon the views of **Cuckmere Haven** are magnificent.

⑤ 0:50: TL on a path which heads along the cliffs of the **Seven Sisters**. Much later, as you approach Birling Gap, TR on a track. Shortly afterwards, go through a gate.

⑥ 2:05: A few minutes later, head through the car park at **Birling Gap**. At the far side of it, pick up a path which climbs onto the cliffs again: do not forget to look behind you as there are wonderful views of the **Seven Sisters** to the NW.

F 2:30: Arrive at **Belle Tout Lighthouse** (see page 147).

E-W

Stage 9b: Belle Tout Lighthouse to Exceat

F The path skirts around the N side of the lighthouse and heads W towards the cliffs again: the white cliffs of the **Seven Sisters** are visible to the NW.

⑥ 0:20: Head through the car park at **Birling Gap**. At the far side of it, climb steps and TL on a track. A few minutes later, go through a gate. Shortly afterwards, TL onto a path which now heads over the **Seven Sisters**.

⑤ 1:45: Bear right on a broad, grassy path. The views of **Cuckmere Haven** are magnificent.

④ 2:05: Go through a gate onto a broad path. Shortly afterwards, TR onto another path. Shortly afterwards, cross a track. Soon go through a gate and head uphill on a grassy path.

S 2:30: TR onto a path. Immediately afterwards, go through a gate and reach the A259 beside the Seven Sisters Country Park visitor centre at **Exceat**.

Stage 9a: Exceat to Alfriston

F Cross the A259. Then climb past a house to find a grassy path heading uphill. After a short climb, go through a gate and climb a low wall. Then descend on a path through forest. Keep SH at two junctions to arrive at the village of **Westdean**. Climb on a road briefly: at a bend, keep SH on a track. A few minutes later, TL at a junction. Now follow waymarks through a series of junctions.

③ 0:35: TR, cross a stile and then climb on a path at the edge of a field. On the left, you should see the **Litlington White Horse** (see page 146). Soon descend again.

② 0:55: TL down a road at the village of **Litlington**. Shortly afterwards, TR at a junction. Shortly after that, pass the **Plough & Harrow** pub. Just afterwards, TL along a lane. A few minutes later, TR at a junction.

① 1:25: TL and cross a footbridge over the **River Cuckmere**: alternatively, TR to start Stage v9. Shortly afterwards, TR on a track.

S 1:30: A few minutes later, arrive in the village of **Alfriston**.

145

*The River Cuckmere
(Stage 9b)*

The Litlington White Horse

Unlike the Uffington White Horse in Oxfordshire which was made 3,000 years ago (during the Bronze Age), the Litlington White Horse is a much more modern creation. The original horse on the site was made in 1836 by some local men, perhaps to commemorate Queen Victoria's coronation. The current horse, however, was cut in a single night in 1924 and has been maintained by locals ever since. In WW2, it was covered to stop the Luftwaffe using it for navigation.

Belle Tout & Beachy Head Lighthouses

Belle Tout Lighthouse operated between 1834 and 1899. It had 30 oil lamps which could be seen up to 23 miles away. It was abandoned because fog often obscured the light and erosion of the cliffs threatened to destroy it. A replacement lighthouse was built at Beachy Head: it was made from granite and was completed in 1902. It is 33m high and its light is visible 16 nautical miles away. It was electrified in 1920 and had a full-time keeper until 1983 when it became fully automated. The lighthouse is operated by Trinity House, a charity dedicated to keeping seafarers safe.

After Belle Tout lighthouse was decommissioned, it became a private residence. However, its condition deteriorated and it was re-built in the 1950s. In 1999, the lighthouse had to be re-located after a large section of the nearby cliffs collapsed. Incredibly, the 850-ton building was raised on hydraulic jacks and moved 55 feet inland onto new foundations.

W-E

Stage 9c: Belle Tout Lighthouse to Meads

S The path skirts around the N side of the lighthouse and heads E along the cliffs again. Soon there are great views of the Beachy Head Lighthouse (see page 147). About an hour later, reach the remains of an old signal station. A few minutes after that, pass the **Beachy Head pub**. 5min later, pass a RAF war memorial.

7 1:30: TR at a junction and descend NE. At any junctions, keep SH (still descending NE).

F 1:45: Arrive at a sign (beside the Kiosk café) which marks the finish of the SDW at the village of **Meads**. Congratulations!

From **Meads**, the most enjoyable way to reach **Eastbourne Station** is to follow the seafront walkway NE all the way into Eastbourne. Just before the famous pier, TL onto **Terminus Road**: follow it until you reach the station. This journey is 1.9 miles and takes about 45min.

For a slightly more direct route (1.5 miles), from the sign at the finish of the SDW, walk NE on **Duke's Drive**. Shortly afterwards, TL and head N on **Holywell Road**. Keep SH onto **Meads Street**. TR onto **Meads Road**: stay on it until you reach the centre of Eastbourne. TL on **Grove Road**. A few minutes later, arrive at the station.

E-W

The SDW begins from a right-angle bend in **Duke's Drive** at the S corner of the village of **Meads**: there is a prominent sign marking the start of the trek (beside the Kiosk café). From **Eastbourne station**, the most enjoyable way to reach the start is to walk E along **Terminus Road** until you reach the seafront. Then, follow a walkway SW all the way to **Meads**. This journey is 1.9 miles and takes about 45min.

For a slightly more direct route (1.5 miles), from the train station, head S down **Grove Road**. TR onto **Meads Road**. 25min from the station, TL onto **Meads Street**: head S until you reach **Duke's Drive**. Then TR and shortly afterwards, reach the start point.

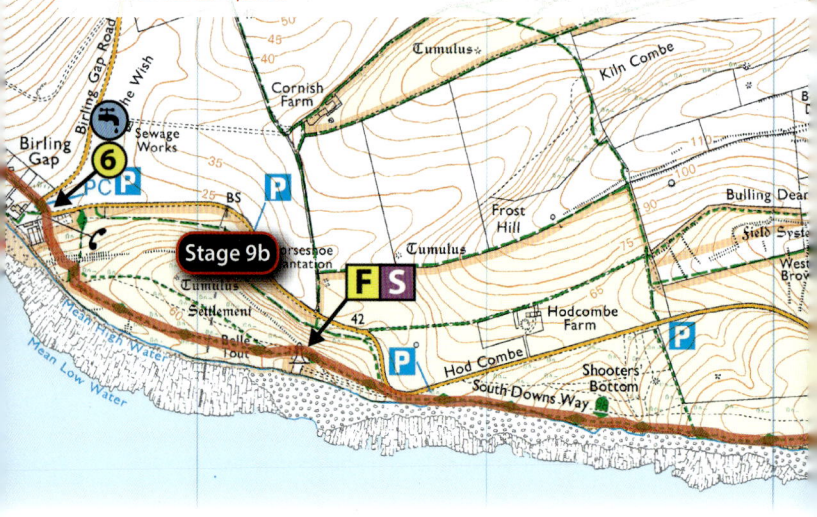

Stage 9c: Meads to Belle Tout Lighthouse

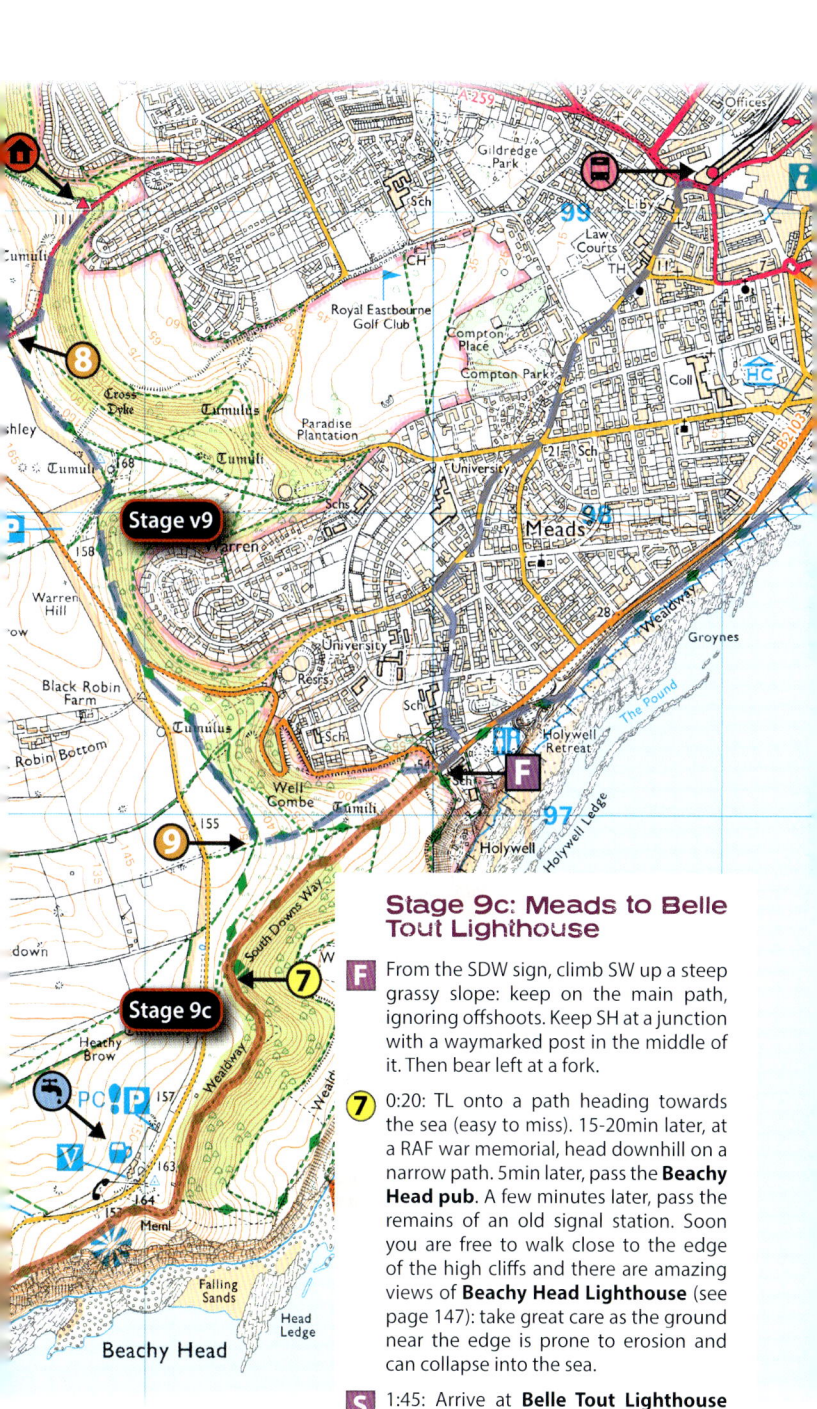

F From the SDW sign, climb SW up a steep grassy slope: keep on the main path, ignoring offshoots. Keep SH at a junction with a waymarked post in the middle of it. Then bear left at a fork.

7 0:20: TL onto a path heading towards the sea (easy to miss). 15-20min later, at a RAF war memorial, head downhill on a narrow path. 5min later, pass the **Beachy Head pub**. A few minutes later, pass the remains of an old signal station. Soon you are free to walk close to the edge of the high cliffs and there are amazing views of **Beachy Head Lighthouse** (see page 147): take great care as the ground near the edge is prone to erosion and can collapse into the sea.

S 1:45: Arrive at **Belle Tout Lighthouse** (see page 147).

Alfriston/Meads (Inland Route) v9

This official SDW variant has been designed for mountain-bikers as a more practical route between Meads and Alfriston than the undulating cliff-tops of the Seven Sisters. However, it is also a wonderful hiking route and offers some of the finest scenery on the SDW: the views are consistently wide-ranging. Furthermore, it has the Long Man of Wilmington as a drawcard (see page 152): the famous 70m high chalk drawing is etched into the slopes of Windover Hill, a short distance OR. The fascinating detour to view the Long Man takes only 20min.

However, not even the lure of the Long Man can persuade many SDW hikers to miss out on the white cliffs of Stages 9b and 9c. Consequently, there are far fewer walkers on Section v9 and it is a more tranquil experience than the honey-pots of Beachy Head and the Seven Sisters. Such is the beauty of Section v9 that we think that it is a great shame to miss out on it. Fortunately, there is a way to extend your trek by half a day so that

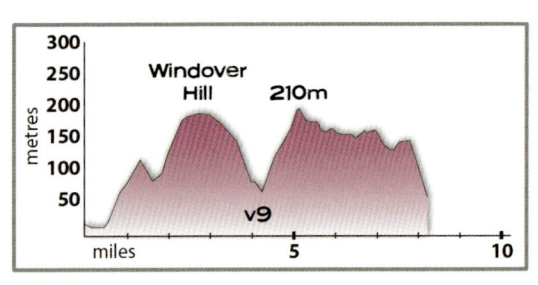

Few SDW hikers experience the scenic delights of Section v9

you can hike both Sections 9 and v9: we cannot recommend this highly enough. W-E hikers simply walk Section 9 W-E from Alfriston to Meads, stay overnight in Meads/Eastbourne and then walk Section v9 (E-W) back to Alfriston the following day. Afterwards, it is simple to take a taxi from Alfriston to the nearby train station at Berwick: there are services to London and Gatwick Airport. E-W trekkers could start the SDW from Alfriston: train to Berwick and taxi to Alfriston. They would then walk Section v9 W-E, stay overnight in Meads/Eastbourne and walk Section 9 E-W the following day.

The section is well marked with SDW waymarks and navigation is straightforward. However, W-E hikers should take care at the River Cuckmere bridge junction at Waypoint No.1 where there is no SDW waymark for the Section v9 route: take the path heading E (following a sign for 'Wilmington via the Long Man') and not the Section 9 path heading S (which has SDW markers).

		Time	Distance	Ascent (W-E)	Descent (W-E)
Stage 9c	Alfriston/Meads (Inland Route)	3:45	8.2miles 13.2km	1158ft 353m	1027ft 313m

Supplies/Water:

Alfriston – village store (snacks, sandwiches & drinks)

Jevington – WP (tap) at the entrance to St. Andrew's Church; WP at the Eight Bells pub

Meads – supermarkets, pharmacy & ATM

Eastbourne – shops, supermarkets, pharmacies & ATMs

Refreshments/Food:

Alfriston - tearooms, pubs & restaurants

Wilmington (0.8 miles OR) - Crossways Hotel (closed at date of press)

Jevington – the Eight Bells pub

Meads – the Pilot Inn, the Ship pub & the Kiosk café

Eastbourne - pubs, restaurants & cafés

The Long Man of Wilmington

From orange Waypoint No.3, head NE on a path (yellow waymark). Soon keep SH at a junction. 5-10min later, arrive at the base of the hill upon which the Long Man is carved.

To return to the SDW, re-trace your steps. At the first junction, you can either keep SH and return to Waypoint No.3 or TL and climb: with the latter option, you will meet the SDW further E. The entire detour takes about 20min.

At 70m high, the Long Man is Europe's largest representation of the human form. Mysteriously, nobody is sure when, or why, it was cut into the chalk slopes of Windover Hill near the village of Wilmington. Some believe that the figure is prehistoric but others reckon it was made by monks from Wilmington Priory somewhere between the 11th and 15th centuries. In 1873, it was marked out in yellow bricks to make it more visible. Local legend maintains that in the Victorian age, its manhood was prudishly removed but there is no supporting evidence of that. In WW2, it was painted green to prevent the Luftwaffe from using it for navigation. In 1969, the bricks were replaced with concrete blocks which are now painted white on a regular basis. In January 2021, during the Covid-19 pandemic, somebody painted a face-mask onto the Long Man: this was quickly removed!

Accommodation:

Alfriston
Wilmington (0.8 miles OR) - Crossways Hotel (closed at date of press)
Jevington
YHA Eastbourne (0.3 miles OR from Waypoint No.8)
Meads
Eastbourne

Escape/Access:

Alfriston
Wilmington (0.8 miles OR)
Jevington
Meads
Eastbourne

Wonderful sea views on Section v9

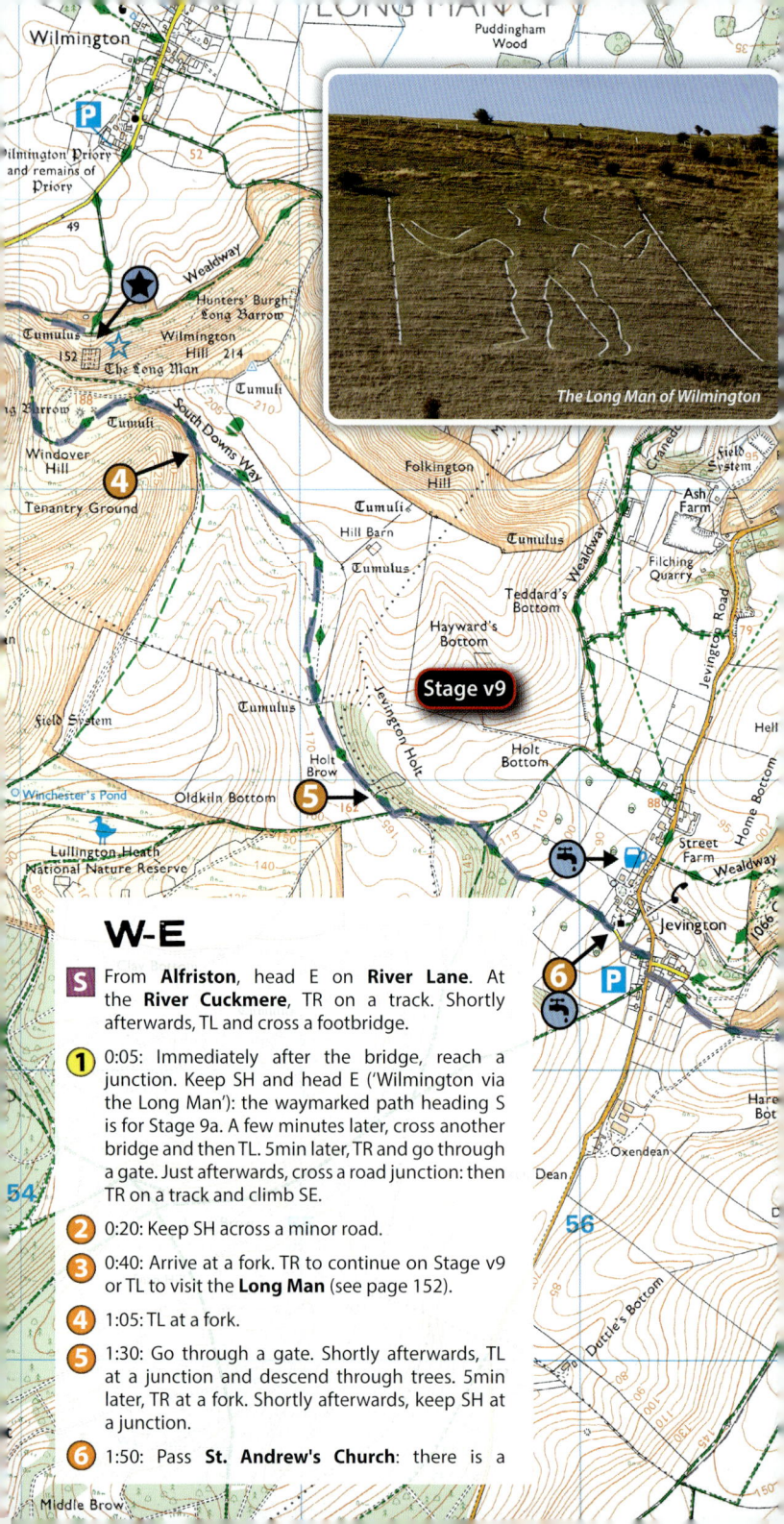

The Long Man of Wilmington

W-E

S From **Alfriston**, head E on **River Lane**. At the **River Cuckmere**, TR on a track. Shortly afterwards, TL and cross a footbridge.

1 0:05: Immediately after the bridge, reach a junction. Keep SH and head E ('Wilmington via the Long Man'): the waymarked path heading S is for Stage 9a. A few minutes later, cross another bridge and then TL. 5min later, TR and go through a gate. Just afterwards, cross a road junction: then TR on a track and climb SE.

2 0:20: Keep SH across a minor road.

3 0:40: Arrive at a fork. TR to continue on Stage v9 or TL to visit the **Long Man** (see page 152).

4 1:05: TL at a fork.

5 1:30: Go through a gate. Shortly afterwards, TL at a junction and descend through trees. 5min later, TR at a fork. Shortly afterwards, keep SH at a junction.

6 1:50: Pass **St. Andrew's Church**: there is a

WP (tap) at the churchyard entrance. Shortly afterwards, arrive at the road in **Jevington**: TL for the **Eight Bells pub** or, to continue on Stage v9, TR and walk down the road. Shortly afterwards, TL on a lane: soon start to climb.

7 2:30: Cross the top of an **unnamed hill (201m)**, keeping SH at a junction. Now Eastbourne is just to the E.

8 3:15: Approaching the A259, bear right at a fork. Shortly afterwards, cross the road and keep SH on a path: alternatively, TL and head NE along the road for **YHA Eastbourne** (5-10min). Shortly afterwards, when the path splits, stick to the wider branch. A few minutes later, TR at a fork: shortly afterwards reach a trig point with superb sea views. After a dew pond, TR on a broad path. Shortly afterwards, at a complicated junction, bear left on another broad path. Cross a road. Immediately afterwards, TL on a path.

9 3:40: TL on a path which descends towards the sea. A few minutes later, TL at a fork (no signposts).

F 3:45: Arrive at the kiosk café in **Meads**. Congratulations you have completed the SDW. For directions into **Eastbourne**, see page 148.

E-W

For directions to the start from **Eastbourne train station**, see page 148.

F From the sign marking the start of the SDW, TR and climb on a path ('SDW Jevington'). Soon the path bends left to head SW. At any junctions, continue SW.

9 0:15: TR at a junction, heading NW. Cross a road and continue N on a path. Bear right at a complicated junction. Shortly afterwards, TL and pass to the left of a dew pond. Shortly after that, reach a trig point with superb sea views. Shortly afterwards, keep SH at a junction.

8 0:40: Cross the A259 and keep SH on a path: alternatively, TR and head NE along the road for **YHA Eastbourne** (5-10min).

7 1:30: Cross the top of an unnamed hill (201m), keeping SH at a junction. Afterwards, descend. TR along a road in **Jevington**. Shortly afterwards, TL on a lane: alternatively, keep SH for the **Eight Bells pub**.

6 2:00: A few minutes later, pass **St. Andrew's Church**: there is a WP (tap) at the churchyard entrance. 15-20min later, keep SH at a junction. Shortly afterwards, TL at a junction and climb through trees.

5 2:25: TR at a junction. Shortly afterwards, go through a gate.

4 2:50: Keep SH at a junction.

3 3:10: Arrive at a junction: keep SH to continue Section v9 or TR for the **Long Man** (see page 152).

2 3:25: Keep SH across a minor road. 10min later, cross a road junction: then go through a gate and TL on a path. 5min later, TR and cross a bridge.

1 3:40: A few minutes later, reach a footbridge beside the **River Cuckmere**. Keep SH and cross the bridge to head to Alfriston or TL for Stage 9a. Shortly afterwards, TR on a track.

S 3:45: A few minutes later, arrive in the village of **Alfriston**.

KNIFE EDGE
Outdoor Guidebooks

We thought guidebooks were boring so we decided to change them. Mapping is better than 40 years ago. Graphics are better than 40 years ago. Photography is better than 40 years ago. So why have walking guidebooks remained the same?

Well our guidebooks are **different**:

- **We use Real Maps.** You know, the **1:25,000/1:50,000** scale maps that walkers actually use to navigate with. Not sketch maps that get you lost. Real maps make more work for us but we think it is worth it. You do not need to carry separate maps and you are less likely to get lost so we save you time!

- **Numbered Waypoints** on our Real Maps link to the walk descriptions, making routes easier to follow than traditional text-based guidebooks. No more wading through pages of boring words to find out where you are! You want to look at incredible scenery and not have your face stuck in a book all day. Right?

- **Colour, colour, colour.** Mountains and cliffs are **beautiful** so guidebooks should be too. We were fed up using guidebooks which were ugly and boring. When planning, we want to be **dazzled** with full-size colour pictures of the **magnificence** which awaits us! So our guidebooks fill every inch of the page with beauty: big, **spectacular** photos of mountains, etc. Oh yeah baby!

- **More practical size.** Long and slim. Long enough to have Real Maps and large pictures but slim enough to fit in a pocket.

Now all that sounds great to us but we want to know if you like what we have done. So hit us with your feedback: good or bad. We are not too proud to change.

Follow us for trekking advice, book updates, discount coupons, articles and other interesting hiking stuff.

www.knifeedgeoutdoor.com

info@knifeedgeoutdoor.com

@knifeedgeoutdoor

@knifeedgeout

@knifeedgeoutdoor

Facebook Groups

If you have any questions which are not answered in our books, then you can ask the author in one of our Facebook Groups. Updates to our books can be found in the topic sections of the groups.

The group for this book is '**The South Downs Way**'. The group's URL is **www.facebook.com/groups/SouthDownsWay**